PARIAH

BY
C.R. RICHARDS

Dedication

A special thanks to fellow author CRM for showing me HER Las Vegas. And as always, a heartfelt thank you to my Alpha Readers. Couldn't do this without you!

Chapter One

Family. It was a blessing to some and a soul-crushing inconvenience to others. Jin closed his eyes for a moment, willing the throbbing along his right rib cage to subside. Sticky blood soaked his shirt, binding the fabric to tender flesh. The bones in his family's closet were rattling again. Like a fool, he was dancing to their harsh beat. Old habits.

Jin steadied his body against the centuries-old window frame. Balancing on the ornate iron rod mounted four stories above the pavement, he was a black shadow against white stone. He remained perfectly still in the fading twilight of a Paris sky. Rue Saint-Dominique's ancient spine arched beneath him, a glittering highway for travelers in the evening rush. Normals, or humans as they preferred to be called, strolled obliviously hand in hand along the sidewalks below.

Two loud pings and spraying bits of stone brought Jin's focus back to the challenge at hand. Titanium quills were embedded deep into the building just inches from his head. Not a bad shot, but not good enough either. His intense eyes—not quite human—focused on the next section of window several feet above him. Nothing stood between him and the distant railing except empty air and a five-story drop.

Jin gave one last glance below then leapt into the nothingness. His flesh became tendrils of air drifting against the white stone.

Soon solid again, he was now suspended on the frame of the fifth-story window, a half-dreamed silhouette outlined by the cheery light of a single lamp in an empty parlor. Though to anyone watching it might have seemed as if he'd disappeared, that wasn't precisely true. Part elf, part air elemental, he had the ability to transform. Human science would attempt to define it as a kind of chemical sublimation, but Jin accepted it as magic, as his birthright. His body didn't transition from solids to gas. Rather, he became that sudden gust of wind snatching hats off heads and lifting skirts of the unprepared. All in harmless fun, of course.

Careful not to make any sudden movements, he examined the seemingly ancient lock with an expert eye. Sensors and advanced security systems on the lower floors had stymied a quick entrance. This floor, situated at the top of the building, warranted special security. Clan security. Jin knew what it guarded. The portal's magic called to him. Brushing a fingertip along the runes, he followed their lines etched into the metal of the device. Classic Seelie threshold protection spell. Jin had broken through plenty of those as a child.

A sparkling vision reflecting from the window surface drew his attention for a moment. He slowly turned his head to gaze out at the lights of Paris glistening over the rooftops. The Eiffel Tower stretched above, outshining every other structure within the city. Paris. It had survived the Black Death and endured the Nazi occupation. Could it withstand the war looming in the darkness? Could any of them?

The sharp tip of a metal quill sliced along Jin's jawline before shattering the window glass. He fell forward into the room, rolling over jagged shards into a crouch. Foolish move! Stopping to gawk at the sights had been one of many mistakes he'd made that evening. Allowing himself to be pulled into yet another Clan intrigue had been the first.

He carefully picked up a palm-sized piece of glass and threw it hard across the room. The lone lamp crashed to the floor. So much for a stealthy break-in or hiding in the darkness. A city like Paris was never completely asleep.

Fingers of artificial light stretched across the floor, chasing away much of the shadows. Those same fingers touched the building across the street. Jin detected a movement in a window on the top floor, so small he almost missed it. The sniper was watching. Half a room away, the safety of the portal waited, and Jin entered the apartment.

Decorated in elegant French Traditional, the parlor was perfectly arranged and perfectly fake. Jin guessed it had been at least a year since someone had actually set foot inside this facsimile of a human hotel. His shoulder bumped against the sharp corner of a table. The wood was real enough. Brushing irritably at the dust on his black jacket, Jin plucked up one of the many antique cigarette cases as it slid off a Louis XV cherry table. Peering into the distortion of the silver hammered surface, the uninvited guest blew off a thick layer of dust. Someone was neglecting his housekeeping.

Jin sniffed at the expensive cigarettes inside the case, then turned his nose away. He wasn't one to smoke tobacco or other weeds. Their odors lingering on the body were too easy to track. He didn't indulge in alcohol either. Jumping from place to place at the speeds he could produce demanded clarity of mind.

Jin did have his little vices though. He poured the cigarettes out of the valuable silver case and pocketed the treasure inside his jacket.

Movement again from his stalker across the street. The sniper had relocated to another window, trying for a better vantage point. He was certainly tenacious. They—four Vento Clan flunkies and this sniper—hadn't known Jin was coming to the Paris safe house this evening. Hiding in the recesses of an alley close by, they'd been waiting to ambush anyone who tried to enter. A faint thrill of apprehension rose in Jin's chest, confirming his suspicions. Trouble was coming this evening. Time to make a move.

He lifted a beautiful and very old silver tea pot from its service tray on the table. Throwing it hard against the curio cabinet to the right, he darted to his left at the same moment. Windows shattered, and a volley of quills flew into the parlor. A porcelain vase smashed as he passed by. The sniper hadn't been fooled for long.

Tumbling forward, Jin rolled to a stop in front of a hall door. Its ornate gold handle appeared real enough, but human hands would find a deadly surprise if they touched the surface. This door wasn't meant for just anyone. He ran his fingers through the wood facade and watched them disappear into the magic of the portal. Only one of Seelie blood could enter by way of a Pillar of Power. These were portals leading directly into the ancestral homes of the Clans. This one opened into the halls of the Girard Estate, third seat in the Clan pantheon.

Jin dived headfirst through the portal. Ancient power wrapped around him, bonding with the energy of his being. Otherworld welcomed him as a long-lost child. His power sprang forth, dissolving the glamour he wore in the Human Realm. He breathed out a deep sigh of relief and stretched his body as it truly existed. A whirlwind of air swirled around him for a moment, touching the ancient stone walls. Then he called back the tendrils of his air elemental form. Strands of green hair, so deep in hue they were almost black, drifted upon the gentle summer breeze coming through the open windows.

Pain from the cut at his side brought him back to reality. But his wound was a paper cut compare to what the guards on this side of the portal would do to him if he were caught. Then again, he detected no guards. No alarms either. That was odd.

Tucking his hair behind pointed elfin ears, Jin moved down the hall toward the living quarters. His gaze was irresistibly pulled to the view. Paris and the Human Realm were gone. Thick forest stretched along the ground beneath the manor house, replacing Rue Saint-Dominique and its modern lights. A flawless mountain range stood in the distance, taller than any manmade tower. Two moons shone in a midnight sky above them. Otherworld. This was Seelie paradise, or just about. This was home.

Brilliant planets of the infinite universe came sharply into focus as he looked up with his ""other"" sight. Energy swirled between celestial bodies, tying them and their living force together. Jin gripped the stone of the window frame. He'd never be allowed to join those bands of energy with the other Seelie.

He let his gaze fall to the dark boughs beneath him. Somewhere within the green trees below was a magical barrier to prevent him and those like him from entering Otherworld proper. The Clans had been banished from Otherworld millennia ago by the Seelie Court. His ancestors had backed the wrong side of a civil war. Some had thought the Seelie Court's anger would subside, but time proved they had a long memory. The Clans' punishment was eternal.

Each family had been given a thin strip of land on the edge of Otherworld and free reign in the Human Realm. It didn't sound like punishment for rebellion. He let the bitter smile come. An eternity spent nose pressed to the glass, knowing you will never enter true paradise was a special kind of hell.

Moving along the floor with an air elemental's stealth, Jin took in the quiet of the corridor. Elegant French décor lined the halls with satin splashes of white and gold. Parquet flooring drew his eye to a flow of intricate patterns toward the far end of the hall. The opulence was typical of Clan properties, yet none could compare to the beauty of the Girard Estate. Its central location and security made the

Girard home ideal to host diplomatic meetings and special occasions.

For Jin, its popularity added an extra element of danger. Rooms lining the fifth floor hall could right now be occupied by very powerful Clan members. Like Jin, these Seelie Descendants had been gifted at birth with special abilities. Most of them wouldn't appreciate his dropping by. They didn't have a sense of humor where he was concerned.

A piece of kite string dangled from the door at the end of the hall, the signal he'd been hoping to see. He picked the ancient lock and eased open the door. Bright eyes filled with surprise took him in, and a precious smile came to the girl's lips. Mai Ling, his baby sister and the youngest of his father's many children, hurried to her feet. She was careful not to rumple the little pink dress she wore. Tiny silk buds had been braided into her long, black hair, matching the embroidered yellow and red flowers flowing down the front of the garment.

"Jin!" She raced into his arms and giggled as he spun her around. "Where have you been?" The Cantonese passed her lips like delicate chimes in a gentle breeze. Mai Ling's Seelie gifts hadn't sprouted yet. Despite the pale green and blue of her skin, she still looked like a human child from Hong Kong, where the Zhao Pillar was located.

Jin tickled his sister's sides and kissed her cheek. "I've been hunting purple elephants in the deepest jungles of Africa. Did you miss me, my darling? It's only been two months."

"Four months! You nearly missed my sixth birthday." She folded her arms and eyed him with grown-up disapproval on her face.

He kept his own resentment and hurt carefully checked. It had, in fact, been four months and three days since he'd last seen her. She'd been staring after him from her bedroom window, little hand pressed against the glass in goodbye. His banishment from the family circle had punished more than a rebellious son. He wished his father could see the harm his unbendable resolve did to Mai Ling.

"Four months? Are you sure?" Jin shook his head and made a silly face until she giggled. "I'm a bad bunny!"

Holding her with one arm, Jin reached into his pocket and pulled out a little red gift box. Her eyes brightened as she hurriedly opened the present and pulled out a heart-shaped diamond pendant by its golden chain. She let it spin and watched the jewel glitter in the light.

"I want you to know you're the only young lady I've bought jewelry for."

"It's the prettiest thing I've ever seen. I'll wear it all the time." She lifted the gold chain over her head and let the pendant fall against the pink of her dress. Mai Ling then put her arms around his neck; she let her head rest on his shoulder. Jin waited, knowing whatever she was about to ask of him, he would move the heavens to give her.

"Jin, where were you really? Were you off on Clan business?"

"Where did you hear that?"

Mai Ling pulled up the fabric of Jin's right sleeve, exposing ribbons of emerald ink infused with magic that twisted to form an elaborate triangle on the inside of his wrist. It was a Clan tattoo, a two-inch badge denoting him as a Seelie Descendant and allowing him entry into their dark world. To the human eye, it appeared as a simple Celtic threefold spiral within a triangle. Seelie eyes could see more. Golden letters spelled "Past. Present. Future." The Trinity Badge reminded them of their gifts and their curse.

"Brother told Father you were playing thief and pilfering coins from trash bins." She ran her fingertip gently over his painted skin. "Were you?" Her innocent eyes waited for an answer and the ugly truth Jin never wanted her to know.

"Brother Qing was teasing you." The lie came easily. One part love and one part shame. Their father's oldest offspring, Qing, knew better than to speak of Clan business around Mai Ling. The ass. The time had come for another unpleasant conversation about discretion.

"But, Jin, Qing doesn't have a sense of humor. You say that all the time."

Jin laughed and hugged her close. "You are very clever, my darling. Now, what amusing activities do you have planned for your sixth birthday tomorrow?"

The door swung open with a boom. Several familiar black jackets and Frank Sinatra-wannabe haircuts rushed inside. Killing power vibrated around their bodies, hungry, ready to devour. Zhao Long, head of the most powerful family among the Clans, chose only the strongest and most ruthless of his men to protect the family. In their center was a younger, less impressive shadow. Zhao Qing, heir to their father's power and wealth, glared at his younger siblings.

"Hello, Qing, I believe my invitation to Mai Ling's birthday party has gone missing." Jin gently set Mai Ling on her feet and watched her walk to Qing as gracefully as any six-year-old ballerina.

"Why have you come, Pariah? Father hasn't summoned you, and I've no time for games." Jin's brother gave the signal to his guard and the killing energy in the room faded. "We have business tonight."

Qing ran a tense hand along his slicked-back short hair. Like their father, Qing maintained his human appearance even in Otherworld. While Zhao Long wore human glamour to subdue his great power. Qing used his to hide a power that paled in comparison. Though he tried to ape their father in every way, his unpleasant features made him look like an awkward version of his homely mother. A square jaw outlined by an unflattering anchor beard drew attention to Qing's suspicious dark eyes. Oppositely, Jin's features perfectly echoed those of his aristocratic English mother; she had been an amusing diversion. Qing's mother had been duty, with Qing a reminder their father found irritating.

"Nice to see you too, Brother. I cherish our times together." Jin pulled a mobile from the hidden pocket of his jacket. He handed it to his sibling. "I liberated this from one of the Vento Clan thugs staking out the safe house. Care to tell me why they were watching the building?"

The Vento Clan was the lowest pillar in the Clan pantheon. Their leader, Raul Vento, had aspirations to a higher ranking among the gods. He wasn't content to be fourth seat, the lowest man. Jin had seen Raul's brutality firsthand. No one—Normal or Clan folk—would be safe if Raul managed to topple the current order.

"Is this blood?" Qing wiped the mobile with his crisp linen handkerchief. He activated the phone's screen and frowned. "Five-million Euro each. Paris Pillar." He stopped reading and looked up at Jin. "It's from RG."

"RG could be Renee Girard. Father needs to be warned."

"Do you think this will put you back in his good graces? You're too late for grand gestures, Jin." Qing shook his head, rat eyes narrowing. "Father held his arms open, inviting you to be a permanent member of our Clan. You refused him."

"To join you as third drone on the left?" Jin looked at the security team. "No offense. I won't be anyone's hired killer."

"With your gifts, you would have been much more. But you lack the courage." Qing spat at Jin's feet. "Instead, you've chosen the path of mediocre thief. You're a shame to the family."

Jin turned his face away, hating the hurt he knew was mirrored there. Despite a childhood of careful training and brainwashing, his teachers couldn't turn him into what he hated most, a killer. The decision to walk another path had been an easy choice, but not everything had gone according to plan. The look of disapproval and disrespect on his father's face at their last meeting had been a crushing blow.

Mai Ling's innocent eyes stared at Jin from behind the chair. Everything he saw in them—disappointment, confusion, uncertainty—stabbed at his heart, opening up fresh wounds. He wanted to rush to her side and explain why her hero had fallen so far. Qing blocked his path. Jin was no longer a member of the family. He was a pariah, and it was Qing's duty as eldest brother to make certain Mai Ling remained untouched by such influences.

"The Zhao Clan has its own intelligence network. We do very well without your interference. Father has been troubled by Raul's recent disregard of Clan laws. Do you honestly think we would come all the way to Paris just for Mai Ling's birthday? Fool." Qing lifted his chin and gave Jin a derisive glare. "Father set this meeting with Monsieur Girard to stop Raul, perhaps cut short his leadership of the Vento Clan. You're jeopardizing our meeting and Father's safety. You shouldn't have come. If it were anyone else intruding, he would have ordered you killed. Why does Father indulge you more than the rest of his bastard children?"

"Because it irritates my mother. We all know how much she hates having the Wainwright name sullied," Jin said. Brick walls were more receptive than his brother. He let out a long breath, trying to remember why he'd bothered. "Calm yourself, Qing. Your fiefdom is safe. I'm still a free agent outside the Zhao Clan. I've no interest in taking it over."

"Perhaps you're waiting for your mother's invitation. That will never happen. She doesn't want you either." Qing let a vicious laugh echo in the uncomfortable silence. "You've gotten your wish. Now you walk alone. The balance is preserved."

Religiously maintained by the head of each Clan, balance of power among the Clans was their most precious rule. That didn't mean moments of indiscretion didn't occur. A few bottles of champagne shared between two rival Clan members, a bit of youthful adventure at a secluded beach house, and voilà, Jin was born. Sometimes a single moment could begin a chain reaction that would knock balance on its arse.

"We are interrupting perhaps?" A man dressed in an immaculate linen suit swept in from down the hall. The winter hue of his shirt matched the cold blue skin of his face. Renee Girard turned an affectionate smile toward the woman on his arm.

Mademoiselle Girard was a vision in expensive silk. Long, black hair fell across speckled scales as her body swayed under the enticing gown. She preferred to be called by her gift name, Viper, in the spirit of old traditions. Beautiful and deadly, she was a carefully wrapped package of seduction.

"Two of my sister's favorite toys in the same room. How entertaining." A sardonic smile flashed across Renee's face. "Are you here for some male bonding this evening or for some other reason perhaps?"

"My clever Renee, you do enjoy your teasing," Viper said. Her predator's eyes took in both brothers with a quick glance. "Jin's presence is completely innocent, no? I'm certain he has no aspirations to complicate the discussion this evening."

She gripped her brother's arm in a quick squeeze. Something passed between them as they shared a long look. When Renee turned his attention back toward the other occupants of the room, Jin caught the wild expression of a man on the verge of a great victory. It was no secret Renee coveted his father's power, but how much Viper wanted that power too might surprise others.

Renee pulled Viper into his body and wrapped an arm around her waist. His hand smoothed at his sister's side in a manner that didn't seem very brotherly; the caress was more that of an obsessed lover. Renee had always been unbalanced. He was the little boy who pulled the legs off insects, the teen who dismembered stray cats. The Clans viewed him as a high risk. His father, at their demand, had taken the precaution of naming another heir.

"My brother was just leaving," Qing said. He gave Jin a warning frown. "Clan gatherings aren't in his repertoire."

"I wouldn't dream of intruding. It sounds like something more akin to your tastes. Dull. Paris holds other amusements, as I'm sure our charming hostess can tell you. I could, however, be swayed into staying for dinner if she wishes it." Jin bowed to Viper.

Qing stepped between them, jealousy radiating from his flickering glamour. He thrust out his right hand. Thick pillars of water blasted toward Jin. The spear-sized stakes could impale a man at that velocity. Jin had seen Qing do it. If not for the blunt end, his brother's strike could kill. This attack was meant to sting and humiliate.

The water burst forward, coming dangerously close to striking Jin's torso. He twisted away, pulling the tendrils of air about him. Breezing around the frozen figures of his brother and the guards, he came to stand unscathed beside Qing. An expensive painting, Monet, he guessed, had taken the brunt of the attack. Jin stabbed a fingertip to Qing's head and pressed it hard.

"Too slow as usual, Big Brother." He cast a quick glance at Viper, whose excitement was evident. "Jealousy is very unbecoming."

Renee clapped his hands and laughed. "Bravo! Bravo! The Zhao Clan never fails to entertain or impress."

Jin turned away from Qing and took Viper's hand. She pretended to be gracious as he kissed it. "My apologies, Mademoiselle Girard, my brother and I were just catching up on old family news."

He observed the amused glint in her eye. She was making fun of him. Their last parting had been...unpleasant. Ever the cunning beauty, Viper had manipulated her way into his affection. Now he understood why. Qing had been her true target. Finding her way into the bed of a Clan leader's heir would normally be impossible at her level. Using the rivalry between brothers had been a stroke of cunning genius for dear little Viper.

Qing definitely didn't share her amusement. Mistrust crossed his face for a moment before he carefully tucked the emotion away. Brother Qing was the Zhao Clan's obedient lapdog. He would never dishonor their father by striking out at Viper and risking offense to another Clan. Not in plain sight.

"Come along, Mai Ling. We're late for dinner. Monsieur Girard will think us very rude." Qing lifted the child from her hiding place behind the nearest chair and into his arms. Mai Ling hugged his neck tightly, hiding her face in his shoulder.

"Don't be frightened, Mai Ling." Jin reached his fingers out, impotently stroking the empty air. He prayed she wasn't frightened of him now, after what she'd seen. And he prayed she would forgive or better still forget what she had heard.

Clutching at the diamond pendent with one hand, she reached out to him with the other. "Jin?"

"We will see each other again soon, my darling." He swallowed hard and forced a smile. "I promise."

"That isn't your decision, Jin." Qing threw him one last look after his entourage exited the room. "Perhaps Mademoiselle Girard will show you to the exit. Renee, would you be so kind as to escort my sister and me to the dining room?"

A strange sort of glee flashed in Renee's eyes as they met Jin's stare. It faded quickly. Then he turned and followed Qing out of the room.

Chapter Two

Jin's fists jammed deeper into the pockets of his jacket. Qing wasn't about to listen to any warnings coming from him. He'd rather let the world burn first. A dull ache began to form at the base of Jin's skull. Qing had been right about one thing. Their father would be furious Jin had shown up uninvited. Handing valuable evidence over in the first place had been a mistake. He'd have to produce proof of tonight's Vento Clan mischief.

"I should have picked Qing's pocket when we were playing sibling rivalry." That text message was the solid proof his father would need. Five-million Euros was a sizable amount of cash. The job they were being asked to do didn't sound like an observation-only duty.

"You won't challenge your brother for inheritance in the Zhao Clan, but you'll fight over childish slights? What you hold as important I don't understand." Viper's humorless laugh brought Jin's attention where it should have been. Deep in thought, he hadn't noticed they'd left the sleeping quarters. She'd taken them to the landing of a staircase he didn't recognize.

"Yes, so you've said many times. I have to get the...my mobile phone back from Qing." Trusting Viper with information was always a gamble. She liked to collect juicy bits of scandal to use for her many intrigues. At one time, he'd been foolish enough to share with her. Some life lessons were learned the hard way.

He stopped her at the top of the staircase. "So, where are we going? It's been a while since my last visit, but as I recall the main portal is in the other direction."

The Laws of Clan Hospitality dictated a visitor would only enter an estate in the designated greeting area. Portal magic, however, would actually take its passengers anywhere they desired to go, a benefit for those like Jin who preferred making their own entrance unobserved. Exits were an entirely different problem, though. An Otherworld home entered easily didn't necessarily guarantee an easy exit.

"This way." She arched her eyebrow ever so slightly and gave him a slow grin. Black silk swished against her bare skin as she descended the stairs.

Taking the small smile as an encouraging sign, Jin hurried after her. "I must speak with Zhao Long. You can help me reach him."

She shook her head and laughed. "Oh no, I can't. Don't pull me into another of your contests with Qing."

Jin took her hand. "This is no game, Viper. Something's not right about tonight. I was attacked outside the safe house by Vento Clan thugs. I think they're planning more trouble. Why else would they be watching the entrance?"

He opened his jacket and let her see the dried blood. Fingertips smoothed along his chest and down to hover over the injury. Memories of her touch, a lover's gentle caress, brought forth the aching wound her spurn had wrought. Viper's eyes lifted from his stained shirt.

"What happens to me if I help you?" She stepped away from him, hugging her arms about her body. "I'm with Qing. Gaining his trust was nearly impossible. Now his suspicion grows because of you. What would he believe if his pariah brother appeared at dinner tonight after he made a formal request of me to have you removed?"

"You'd have to find another mark to manipulate."

"Even in disgrace you flaunt your station at me! Standing on your moral high ground is so easy for you. You're Zhao Long's gifted son by the one woman powerful enough not to cower before him. He showered you with privilege, while my sire barely recognized me as part of the Clan." She looked away. "I do as I must."

Jin ran a finger along her bare arm. "You don't have to play these games. There is life beyond Otherworld."

"What are you saying? Leave my Clan, my family, to wander around the human world like you've chosen to do?" Viper pushed him away. "You're such a child. Unlike you, I know where I belong."

Footsteps came closer on the floor above them. Viper hurried Jin down the steps to the next landing where they both pushed through an entryway onto a floor lined with more rooms. This section of the manor was darker, and missing was the tasteful decor of the main house. Gloomy wood paneling framed a worn burgundy carpet. Dated light fixtures flickered dimly as they passed. Jin slowed his pace, sniffing at the stuffy air. His ex-lover was taking him to a deserted part of the house after dark. Bookshelves were lined with murder mysteries containing scenes like this.

"We have many visitors in the guest quarters tonight, but this floor is closed for repairs," she told him. "We'll be safe talking in one of the empty rooms. We don't want one of the others finding you, do we?"

His heart lifted. "Does this mean you've decided to help me?"

"Perhaps." She brought a hand to his cheek, inches away from his lips. He resisted the old habit of kissing her fingertips as he once had when they were together. Rattling the handle behind her back, she threw open the nearest door and pulled him further into the darkness. "I've missed you, Jin."

"How long did you wait after I was banished to go to my brother's bed?"

Laughter, low and rich, purred from her throat. She stepped away from him, her spicy perfume lingering behind. Jin heard silk gliding to the floor. "Jealousy is unbecoming, no?"

Her voice had grown harsh, grating as if the muscles around her vocal chords were squeezing tightly. Jin tensed. Only a fool would allow himself to relax this close to Viper. Against the backdrop of the twin moons, her body began to coil like the snake she admired so much.

Jin disappeared in a burst of self-preservation. He landed close to the door. Her body twisted, coming further into the thin strip of moonlight. Deadly fangs shimmered like ivory between full lips. He could smell the venom dripping from her exposed incisors. Viper enjoyed using many types of weapons in her assassinations, but for special prey she used her venomous gift. The poison would either kill an adult male in seconds or render him immobile, depending upon her mood.

"You have a talent for being in the wrong place at the wrong time. How troublesome you are! We've spent months planning for tonight. Every possible eventuality has been painstakingly plotted out. All the necessary players have been assembled." Viper darted quickly to the left, knocking a large piece of furniture against the door. "Then you decide to make an appearance."

"Renee made a deal with the Vento Clan, and you helped him." Jin pushed the furniture away from the door, careful to keep it between them. "He's plotting a coup. Why now? He had plenty of chances to challenge his father before Monsieur Girard remarried." Jin remained on high alert.

"These questions are pointless. You aren't leaving this room!" She lunged forward in a strike at Jin's midsection. But he evaporated just as she crashed into the door, smashing it off its hinges.

The scales on her back began to undulate. Strands of black hair disappeared under large scales as her head stretched wider. The thrust of her newly formed tail pierced the back of a discarded settee.

Sharp claws scraped down the wood paneling as the last of her transformation took on a life of its own. Staring at her hideous shape, Jin entertained a thousand unpleasant thoughts. He leapt over the thick, scaly tail. He'd heard rumors of her transformation into this beastly figure. None of them had been confirmed. Not many witnesses lived to describe the nightmarish visage.

"I won't allow you to ruin this chance for Renee or for me. Together, he and I will rule the Girard Clan." Ablaze with hatred, those serpent eyes held murder in them.

In the silence of the hall, Jin heard distant popping. Then screams of pain and terror filled the manor house. He pulled the tendrils of air about his body and raced past Viper. The darkened hallway and its abandoned rooms streaked by as he accelerated to his full speed. A large piece of the ruined door flew out and struck at the wall beside the entrance. Jin came to a momentary stop. Viper's large body raced toward him. She was fast, but not faster than an air elemental. He opened the door, slipped through and pulled it closed. Her body slammed against the wood. Then he heard a loud thud.

Jin cracked open the door again. Viper, back in her humanoid form, lay stretched out on the carpet. Her face was bloodied a bit, but the small moan from her lips confirmed she'd survived the head butt. It wouldn't keep her down for long.

More shots echoed against the walls of the staircase. Killing magic. Holding firmly to the pull of destructive energy, Jin raced down the stairs to the third floor. The noises grew louder. Years had passed since his last invitation to the Girard Estate. It gave the impression of a home filled with many corridors leading in an oval around the structure. A central foyer hosted entry to multiple ballrooms and parlors. Likely, the formal dining room would be situated among them.

A woman's screams brought Jin to a stop. Absolute fear and hopelessness sounded in her voice. Jin knew in that instant someone was dead. Images of Mai Ling's terrified face spurred his furious pace. Luck helped him to find the main corridor leading to the foyer. Heavy doors slammed open below him. He leaned over the railing in time to see frightened servers trampling each other to escape the bloodshed.

Jin didn't have time to find the stairs again. He swung his legs over the railing beside the nearest pillar. Palm-sized leaves had been sculpted into the wood centuries before. His fingers gripped at their shape. He was out of time. Without much to hang onto further down, this was going to be sloppy. Touching a toe lightly against the rail, Jin leapt toward the base. He landed hard and rolled across the marble floor. Ignoring the jar to his body, he pushed against the small crowd running from the dining room.

A residual sulfur-like odor from killing magic mixed with the scent of seafood and garlic. The stench escaped in sickening waves through the open doorway. Another short blast of power struck the door frame. Jin dove through the entrance, throwing his body to the ground. More screaming guests came at him in a rush. Jin rolled to the side behind the serving station. Refusing to look among the dead, he tried to find his family amid the rushing bodies. Chaos had been painted in gore upon the wall of windows looking out over the trees. Otherworld's two moons hung blood red in the sky, an unheeded omen of despicable murder.

Standing in the middle of gruesome bodies was Renee Girard. Sweat rolled off his bald head to gather upon the collar of his ruined silk shirt. Monsieur Girard lay at Renee's feet, his pretty young wife cowering beside his dead body. One hand gripped protectively at her pregnant belly, while the other extended in a frozen plea with her stepson. Their security team was sprawled uselessly across the dining room floor. One of the dead faces close to Jin wore an ugly expression of panicked surprise.

"Crying won't help you or the whelp in your womb, Madeline." Renee slowly extended his hand toward her belly. Ice from his palm formed to a sharpened point. Wild eyes watched her with the coldness of an exterminator.

"Enough of this, Renee!" A distinguished middle-aged Asian man dressed in spotless Armani stood unruffled in the midst of the macabre scene. Zhao Long! Flames danced around his hand ready for release. Qing stood next to his father. Spikes of water undulated from his fingertips. They were ready for battle, too focused to care who got in the way. Jin scanned the smoky, debris-filled room for the little pink dress. Mai Ling was missing.

"Lower your weapon," Zhao Long warned. The perfect features of his smooth face remained serene.

Jin's father minutely raised a razor-sharp eyebrow, the only sign he ever showed of irritation.

"You were meant to be a witness as per Clan Law, Monsieur Zhao, not to interfere in my coup." Renee's unnatural eyes turned to the Zhao Clan. "Don't pretend you give a damn about her life."

"Do you tell me my duty?" Zhao Long let the flames spike. "For century upon century, I have guarded the balance of power! Do you think a speck of dust may tell a mountain how to stand against the wind?"

Jin fought to stay put and not cower like the other remaining witnesses. His father was the living embodiment of the Clans. He had withstood war and famine in his very long life and was always there to guide his people. In fact, many a Zhao heir died off waiting for the dragon to fail. Qing, too, would likely never rise to his own glory.

Power, fearsome and terrible, shook the room. Darkness began to diminish the light. Jin saw the silhouette of a mighty beast rise up behind his father. Zhao Long had good reason to maintain his human glamour, for his true form was too horrifying for most eyes. He was the last of the mythical guardian beasts to walk the Human Realm. He was the last of the dragons.

"Balance of the Clans must be maintained. Girard named that child as his heir." Zhao raised his hand and a ball of fire erupted into creation. "I will not allow a crazed lunatic to upset the balance."

Jin held his breath as the fireball lifted out of Zhao's palm. It expanded and contracted in time to his father's furious breath. What madness had possessed Renee? He was one ice elemental against the great dragon and his water elemental son. The insane idiot wasn't even a threat.

The hairs at the back of Jin's neck bristled as a stagnant cold filled the air about him. His breaths came in shuttering gasps as if he were caught in the throes of a nightmare. He turned around slowly to face the presence haunting his right shoulder. Gray skin stretched taut over sharp, bony cheeks. Long wisps of snow silk hair fell in icy ribbons across its shoulders and chest. White orbs with faded-ash pupils stared at Jin from behind a pillar. Dark elf. Its very presence was tainted and wrong.

The nightmare raised a pale finger and pulled away the storm-cloud-gray fabric hiding its mouth. Teeth, filed down to jagged points, flashed Jin an expectant smile. The dark elf opened the folds of his cloak. Practiced hands brought out a shimmering weapon, a dagger of ice. The very air about the blade crackled as frigid temperature met the warmth of life. The cold ache in Jin's chest began to grow. He recognized the sensation for what it was, terror. Frozen in place, Jin could only watch as the blade of ice sailed across the distance, headed toward his father.

Ice met fire as the blade lodged in Zhao's chest. His father's ageless eyes met Jin's gaze for an eternal moment. Then the fireball in his hand flickered out. Zhao Long, the mighty dragon, sank to the floor. Time started again. Shouts of confusion and fury filled Jin's ears. He became conscious of the movement around him. Qing dropped to his knees at their father's side. Zhao Clan security circled about them, blocking Jin's path. It was pointless to argue. He'd stood by like a useless coward as his father had been struck down.

A portal tugged anxiously from the darkened corner of the dining room a few feet away. The dark elf leapt through its misty opening, leaving behind chaos and blood. Jin chased after him, slamming against the empty wall as the portal closed. A dark elf in the Girard Estate? He spun around, watching Renee Girard revel in the gore and destruction. The madman had invited the Unseelie into his family home. Nothing could close that door now. The only being powerful enough to banish this new evil was bleeding to death on the dining room floor.

The coup's timing made sense now. They were only weeks away from Midsummer's Eve at the end of June, the time of year when the barrier between Otherworld and the Human Realm grew weaker. The misty portals of the Unseelie Court would once again open upon the earth, bringing terror and chaos into a world that hadn't seen their like for generations.

Why? That was the big question. After these many centuries, what could a madman like Renee have promised the Unseelie Court? What could possibly entice them to risk open war with their Seelie cousins? A Sidhe War would bring about the destruction of both worlds. The conspirators had to be stopped. Jin ran his eyes along the lines of pain on his father's face. Perhaps the Seelie Descendant and their human neighbors were the real target. If that was the case, the

Unseelie had won the first battle. They'd just taken out their greatest opponent.

"Stay where you are, Qing, and tell your men to do the same." Renee had both hands raised. Ice spikes stabbed into the distance between them. "You've seen what I can do. A fight between us now would be very costly. Would you really let Daddy die for the sake of revenge?"

"I will hunt you down for what you've done, Renee!"

A vicious sneer formed beneath the cold eyes. "I'll be right here, ruling my clan. And when Daddy Zhao recovers...if he recovers...he'll tell you that I'm untouchable as leader of the Girard Clan. Go home, Qing. Go home to mourn your dead."

Qing clutched at his bleeding father. His rat eyes twitched with indecision. He looked from his father to Renee. An eternity crept by while they waited for the heir of the Zhao Clan to make a move. None of them had seen the dark elf. Jin marched toward their group. It was time to set the record straight. He wondered how pleased that thing of evil would be with Renee taking credit for defeating the mighty Zhao Long.

"Pick up my father," Qing finally said to the Zhao security team. "We must get him medical care."

The killing energy subsided noticeably as several of the guards gently picked up their fallen leader. Qing and the remaining security kept their weapons on Renee, itching for a chance to strike. The entourage backed out of the room, away from Renee Girard and his victims.

"Wait, Qing!" Jin found his voice at last. "You heard our father. We have to stop Renee."

"My first duty is to Father and my clan." Qing turned his back on Jin. "You've never understood or cared about either, Pariah." Qing hurried out of the room following the still form of their father. The drones who covered his back kept their eyes on Renee. They were angry enough to kill, but they wouldn't question an order from the heir of the Zhao Clan.

The door slammed shut, leaving Jin alone with a killer and his weeping victim. Renee gave Jin a dismissive shrug. "My sister was supposed to kill you, too. I do hope you haven't harmed her. Then again, you wouldn't, would you? Not the man who allies with unaffiliated freaks and humans."

"Your coup has failed, Renee. I saw the dark elf and I have proof of your alliance with the Vento Clan."

Renee took something from his trouser pocket and tossed it to Jin—the mobile Jin had taken off a Vento thug in the alley. Someone had crushed its surface and completely destroyed the SIM card. Jin lifted his eyes to Renee's triumphant face. The bastard was well informed. Qing wouldn't knowingly help Renee hurt their father, which meant someone on the Zhao security team had liberated the mobile to betray them.

"How did you get this?"

"I don't answer to you, Pariah. As a son of the Girard Clan, it is within my rights to challenge and defeat the current Clan leader."

"I don't think the law covers help from an Unseelie assassin."

Renee formed another ice shaft and pointed it at Madeline Girard's temple. "Zhao Long's favorite son, trained by full-blood elementals to become the Hand of Justice. Well, Zhao justice anyway. Tell me, Jin, are you fast enough to save her?"

Madeline Girard's pleading eyes turned to Jin. Her tears came harder as she covered her unborn child with her arms. Renee was ruthlessly ambitious. He wouldn't risk leaving the child alive. Both lives depended upon Jin's speed. He vanished in a gust of wind and reappeared within inches of Renee. Jin's roundhouse kick made crushing contact with his opponent's jaw. Renee's head snapped back, and he staggered, dropping the ice shaft to shatter upon the ground.

Jin pulled Lady Girard to her feet. "Run!"

Manic laughter echoed against the walls of the ruined dining room. Renee spat out two broken teeth. "You're as fast as they say you are, Jin. But I know your weakness."

He reached into his pocket and pulled out a strand of black hair with a single rosebud attached. Something imploded in Jin's heart as he looked at his sister's hair, yanked violently from her head. Renee had touched Mai Ling. He had hurt her. Even Clan Law wouldn't protect the lunatic now. He'd taunted Jin, calling him Zhao's Hand of Justice. So be it. Justice was coming for him.

"Where is Mai Ling?"

Behind Jin, Madame Girard screamed. He turned and saw Viper, clothed and in her humanoid form. Cold eyes glared at him with fury. No words were exchanged. They weren't necessary. Both of them knew it was too late for negotiations. Viper preferred to get her point across with a well-aimed weapon. She flicked her wrist, and a moment later Madeline dropped soundlessly to the ground. A slim blade jutted from her throat. Dead eyes stared up at the ceiling of her once beautiful dining room.

Viper suddenly rolled to the left. Too late, Jin saw the weapon lying in the dead hand of a guard, an infusion gun given only to Clan Security Forces. The weapon, made by magi, was designed to infuse the bearer's gift and focus it with the accuracy of a bullet. The nasty weapon was a good fit for Viper's deadly skill. She fired at Jin. The blast struck on his left side, knocking him off his feet. He struggled to catch his breath. The hit had torn into his jacket and found the silver cigarette case he'd stolen earlier.

The weapon swung around toward Renee. She pulled the trigger. A neatly formed hole appeared in her brother's forehead. "Poor, mad Renee. There can only be one leader. It's time I took my rightful place."

Jin jumped to the far wall before Viper could aim at him again. He took cover behind one of the overturned tables. Easing an empty serving platter out from under a fallen chair, he positioned its reflective surface for a better view. Viper's mirror image was spinning madly around the room trying to find him. Her weapon was at the ready.

"I knew you were ambitious, but I hadn't imagined you'd kill your brother. Tell me, Viper. How do you expect to get away with this with over a dozen witnesses?"

"A dozen witnesses who will testify they saw Renee go mad." Viper swung the weapon in a searching pattern. She wasn't about to let him leave the manor alive. "You're the only one who knows of my involvement and of my new ally from the Unseelie Court. Everyone else will hear my truth. I found Renee here, standing over the dead bodies of my father and stepmother. They'll understand I had to kill him. Even the Zhao Clan will support me as Clan leader. There is no one else."

"Jin!" Mai Ling screamed.

Her small fingers grabbed at the golden curtain fabric a few feet away. Mai Ling timidly pushed aside the drape. Her little dress was dirtied, but she didn't look hurt. He held out his arms to her. Mai Ling darted out from the golden folds of fabric, past the window toward her brother. She reached out for his embrace. A shot shattered the air. Mai Ling gave a tiny cry and fell against him lifelessly.

"Mai Ling?" He clutched at her limp body. Sticky, hot blood escaped the wound in her back, covering his hands. Too young. She had been too young to be mixed up in Clan betrayals. He blamed his father for bringing her here. He blamed Qing for leaving without her, but most of all he blamed the ruthless bitch who had taken her life. Jin slowly lowered her small body to rest upon the tiled floor.

Hatred. It flooded his soul and blinded him until he could only see Viper. "The moment you murdered Mai Ling, you signed your own death warrant," he said.

He sprang at her, hungry to kill. Any restraint he'd retained began to slip away. But she was ready for him. Her strike burned across his upper arm, drawing blood. Pain slammed him to the floor. Blood from the wound soaked through his right sleeve.

"Why must you always meddle, Jin? I will be made Girard Clan Leader. Qing and I will be mated, then even Zhao Long must respect me." She aimed the weapon at him again. "Your death will ensure the inevitable."

Viper had him pinned down and completely exposed. Even with his gift, Jin wasn't fast enough to take her out. He pushed the pain from his arm aside. Mai Ling was dead. He'd see her avenged even if that meant he'd die beside her. Then the door to the dining room burst open. Other Clansmen were coming in, a few Jin recognized from the Wainwright Clan.

"What is it? What has happened?" The murmurs rose like angry waves in a stormy ocean.

Viper hesitated, but only for a moment. She put on a mask of false horror and grief. "Renee has gone mad! He has murdered my father and conspired with Jin to take over the Girard Clan! They've killed Zhao Long!"

"She's lying! A dark elf stabbed my father," Jin began, but he saw the suspicion on their faces.

"A dark elf? Do you expect us to believe such tall tales?" Viper shook her head. Still playing the grieving daughter, she clung to an envoy from the Wainwright Clan. "My family is dead, murdered by his hand and he speaks of the impossible."

Jin took a step away from them. He was a pariah. No one trusted his word. He'd need proof to make them see the truth. It was time to retreat, recover and get revenge another day. Using all his focus, he concentrated on the window overlooking the forest floor. In a lightening moment he was at the latch, just missing Viper's next shot. He used a rough kick to break the latch and leapt outside, catching the breeze in his air elemental form.

"Come back and face me, Jin!" Viper screamed from the window ledge. "Nothing you can do and nothing you can lose will be payment enough for what you've done!"

Disappearing, reappearing, his body evaded their bolts of power as the others followed him into the gardens. One last leap, and he was gone from their sight, another shadow among the trees. But the forest wouldn't keep him safe for long, and Seelie Descendants were forbidden to cross the border into Otherworld proper. He was running out of space to flee.

Ahead, the steady pulse of the border's power drew near. Angry shouts permeated the trees behind him. Jin found no sign of his carefully planned exit strategy. It was time for drastic measures. He took a deep breath and jumped into the power of the border though no one to his memory had ever tried such a suicidal action. He closed his eyes, waiting for the punishing magic to seize onto him.

"That was not a very wise thing to do."

He who had spoken stood illuminated in the glow of the border's power. A circlet of moonlight rested lightly upon pale blond hair. Silver adorned his arms and belt. Wrapped in long robes of deep forest green, the elf lord's lean body towered over his squirming catch. Fists held firmly onto the scruff of Jin's jacket, pulling him forward roughly.

"You cut that a little close, Bryn!"

"Every alarm along the veil has been activated." Bryn pointed to the twin moons. "Death hangs over this house. As a lord of the Seelie Court, my duty is to ensure this violence doesn't cross over into Otherworld."

"So you saw the dark elf then?"

"The Unseelie Court may not set foot in Descendant Otherworld territory and neither may I. You know this."

"You doubt my word?"

"Certainly not. You are holder of my life debt. I could never doubt your word," Bryn said emphatically. "I'd hoped you might have been mistaken. Come, we must go. I'm not the only Seelie Lord watching this estate tonight."

Soft crystal bells announced their passage into a vast cavern where countless stone staircases stretched out before them in the endless distance. Each set of steps led to levels of rune-covered gateways within the rock. These openings seemingly framed solid stone, but the power behind them told Jin they weren't there for display.

"Welcome to the crossroads." Bryn led him past dozens of gateways, finally stopping at one that stood away from the rest. It was suspended in the shadows just past a massive fountain of blue crystals. "This is the safest gateway for you to use."

"Where does it lead?" Jin smoothed his hand along the ancient wall. The gateway didn't appear to be well used.

"Anywhere you wish," Bryn told him. He positioned Jin directly in front of the gateway. "Mark this gate's location in case you need it again. Think hard where you desire to go. Someplace safe where you can hide. No, don't tell me. You know if I'm asked I will have to speak the truth. Ready?"

Bryn's shove was quick and decisive. Those eternal elf eyes watched Jin as he fell backward into the gateway. Rock and crystal closed about him, twisting his body with a jerk. He fell into a whirlwind of stars and the distant unknown.

Chapter Three

Sometimes it just happened with no warning.

Waves of tingling energy raced up Gracie's spine, paralyzing her body. Reality began to fade into a frightening haze. Then visions of the future burned into her mind. She gripped the edge of her desk. The experience was like having cable wired to her brain. The channel she'd just seen looked like a sitcom she definitely wanted to miss. She spied a family fight on the horizon.

Reality returned as the mist of future moments faded and the vision released her. The faux wood grains of her desk came into sharp focus, and she blinked hard to clear her eyes. Wiping the drool from her cheek, she muttered a little curse at the messed-up gene giving her the Sight. These trips to futureland were rarely fun and almost never convenient. This particular preview had been short and to the point. Time to go hide.

It was half-past-two on a Saturday afternoon. Everyone else was enjoying their free time, leaving the other offices surrounding Gracie empty. Gawd, what she wouldn't give to be at the beach right now, June Gloom and all. But Doug Berry, owner of Berry Wholesale Office Supply, had devised other plans. He'd surprised her with a triple check of their inventory that promising weekend. And if Doug Berry worked a weekend, so did his daughter.

Gracie looked out over the windowless office space. Sneaking away wouldn't be easy. Talk about regretting a decision. The half-walls of glass she'd chosen weren't working out the way she'd hoped. They were supposed to keep people from feeling boxed in. Instead, the new look made everyone feel like guppies in a very small fishbowl. Despite the bright colors and cheery artwork, the remodeled business office still looked like what it was—desks stuffed into storage space over the warehouse.

Impatient fingers tugged a wayward strand of dark blond hair behind her ear. She tapped the toe of her boot against the desk, waiting for her company laptop to shut down. The mind-numbing task of checking inventory was more her dad's speed. He'd gone through the whole warehouse once already while she took care of payroll. Dad couldn't complain too hard about her leaving if their employees were getting paid on schedule.

Good old Dependable Gracie had done her job. It was time she did something completely impractical. Thoughts of her half-packed suitcase and the drawer full of travel brochures at home fueled her excitement. It was about time she had some kind of an adventure. She sure wasn't about to stick around and give Dad the chance to talk her out of another vacation.

Sliding the desk drawer open quietly, she grabbed her purse. The drawer clicked shut with a tiny thump. She made for the door and stuck her head out into the hall. She peered down the rows of empty offices. No sign of Dad or anyone else. Then she remembered the glass walls and was grateful to be alone. Nobody could accuse her of being the secret agent type.

She crept by the closed doors as quietly as any girl could in work boots. Knowing her own office was finally as empty as the others gave her an encouraging surge of hope. Yeah, hope was a good thing. Hope equaled happiness in Gracie's book.

The heavy steel door leading to the warehouse screeched on its hinges. Its familiar noise deflated her balloon of hope, but Gracie wasn't willing to give up yet. She ducked behind a row of overflowing filing cabinets. Invoices and shipping receipts flooded out of the drawers.

After months of his protests, she'd finally convinced her dad to move into the modern age. He'd purchased an expensive new computer system that she'd promised to get up and running. The guilt stabbed at her every time she walked past the full-to-the-brim cabinets. So much work had to be done. She pinched the side of her wrist. Someone else could do it for a week. For Pete's sake, she hadn't had a vacation in three years. Her guilt could take a back seat for once.

A mountain of a man moved through the emptiness of the offices, instantly filling it with his larger-than-life presence. Though he was in his early fifties, Doug Berry remained fit and muscular. Dark hair streaked with silver tumbled out from under his Chicago Bears cap. He was a force his employees and competitors instantly respected.

Nobody worked harder than Gracie's dad, but somehow he never lost his energy. The man was a machine when it came to the business. He'd built the company from nothing and turned it into the fourth largest supplier of office products in Southern California. Dad hadn't missed a day of work since the doors opened. He expected the same dedication from everyone on his payroll, especially Gracie.

Dad stopped at the garbage can a few feet away from her hiding place. His large fingers crumpled up the wrapper of a thick cigar. He never actually lit the things. Brenda, Gracie's stepmom, would raise a fuss if he came home smelling of smoke. Any hint of Dad enjoying something other than work and his TV time brought Brenda out of her suburban housewife stupor.

An appeased Brenda meant a peaceful home life for Dad. He tossed the plastic wrapper into the can and put the stogy in his mouth with a long hum. Dad then took off his cap and ran large fingers through his thick hair. He grinned. A hint of suspicion wormed its way into Gracie's thoughts until he walked down the hall toward his office.

The breath she'd been holding sputtered out in a mix of relief and victory. Clear. It might have been childish to hide like this from Dad, but she was beyond desperate. Darting behind the paper shredder bin a few doors down, she spotted her salvation among the maze of offices. The heavy steel door leading to the warehouse was in sight! She chewed her lip nervously. This was the tricky part. Dad had sharp ears. She'd need to open the squeaky door without being heard.

Gathering up her nerve, Gracie hurried to the door. She slowly turned the handle and then tugged at the heavy steel. Inch by inch, she pulled slowly until the opening was wide enough for her to squeeze her body through. Easing the door closed again, she waited. No noise. Nothing. She did a victorious fist pump. Almost home free! One more obstacle.

Her rubber-soled work boots danced down the stairs in a quiet ballet. She eased open the door to the main warehouse. Beyond the massive stacks of paper and crates of supplies was the loading dock area. The exit sign burned its reassuring neon green. She hurried past the empty bays. Her body plunged through the final exterior door, which clicked shut behind her. She sucked in a huge breath, happy to finally be outside. The little company car waited for her like a super-cheery white beacon of hope under the dreary clouds of overwork.

"Going someplace, Punkin?" Her dad stepped out of the nearest bay doorway. His dark eyes sparkled with humor beneath the brim of his hat. "I take it you know Brenda has a barbeque planned."

Gracie rolled her eyes. Why did she even try to fool her dad, for Pete's sake? He swore up and down that he didn't have her gift of Sight. Yet there he stood with that smug smile on his face, an expression she'd seen many times growing up. There he hovered like an overprotective ghost whenever she tried to sneak out with her friends or skip class.

Gawd, she'd never forget the memory of his fist slamming against the car window when she'd tried to get cozy with her boyfriend in high school. Doug Berry didn't like anyone fooling with his little girl. It was almost sweet in a suffocating way.

A short, thick stump of wild black hair and large teeth stood beside him. Ape, Dad's best friend and constant shadow, lifted a meaty hand up in greeting. "Brenda ain't that bad of a cook, Gracie."

"Hey, Ape." She waved back. "You sure you want to come over? There's going to be a huge fight this afternoon."

Dad tucked the cigar into the front pocket of his work shirt. "What's the fight about?"

Gracie shrugged. Maybe if she stayed calm and rational, she could still stop the argument. "I just saw angry exchanges. Nothing specific. I think I'll pass, Dad. I don't want to start my vacation off on a negative."

"Vacation?" Ape laughed, shoving his hands into the pockets of his denim overalls. He was the best mechanic Dad had. The way Ape fussed over their trucks, it was no wonder they never broke down. "Last time you took a few days, you sat on your ass at home and drank beer. What do you need a vacation for?"

Gracie shot Ape her coldest glare. Convincing her dad was going to be hard enough without a blow-by-blow commentary. But Ape was part of their family, and she was very fond of him, even if sometimes he took the role of Uncle Ape a little too far. Sometimes—like now—she needed him to keep his big mouth shut.

"Now is not the time to be going on vacation, Gracie." Dad shook his head. "We have that big shipment of paper coming in, and then the accounts need straightening out. And what about that new computer system you had to have?" He put his large hands on her shoulders. "I just can't spare you right now."

"You never can spare me, Dad, and that's the problem." Gracie took a deep breath, trying to hold her temper in check. Calm, she had to stay calm. If she let him fluster her, it was over.

Ape started to open his mouth again, but Gracie cut him off. "You need to be on my side in this one, Ape. If you take Dad's side, I won't tell you who's going to win the game today. Good luck explaining to Brenda why you can't pay your rent again and need another loan."

"There's no need to take your bad mood out on Ape." Dad ruthlessly chewed on the cigar. That was a bad, bad sign. "So, what are you going to do on this vacation of yours?"

She shrugged her shoulders. "I haven't decided yet. I might go to the beach or...or maybe even out of town."

"Oh no, you're not." Dad let the parental tone leak into his voice. "Going to the beach is one thing, but going to a strange town on your own isn't safe."

She rolled her eyes. Every time she even mentioned thinking about leaving town, Dad would give her a million used-up reasons why she shouldn't.

He was going to try to talk her out of going on vacation this time too. Why wouldn't he? It had worked every single time before.

"I'm not a child." She leaned against the warehouse door. Here we go. Family argument about to start. "I'm an adult who can make her own decisions. A woman with her own home doesn't ask her dad if she can go on vacation or not."

"It's a one-bedroom condo in a shitty complex. I still say that place isn't safe." He pulled the cigar out of his mouth and shook it. "What good is that big house if it's just Brenda and I? It doesn't make sense to keep it anymore when you're halfway across town."

"It's two miles away. I want to be within walking distance of my classes when I start college again."

Her dad shook his head. "I don't know why the hell you bother working on a degree. The business is going to be yours one day. You've got all you need right here. Why this sudden desire to wander? You used to be happy with the business and being with your family. Hell, you even dated that mook Brenda liked so much. What happened there? I thought you liked him."

Good old Glen. She shifted uncomfortably. They'd been together almost six months. Then a few weeks ago, she'd caught Glen playing tanning booth bingo with some slut from Del Mar. Gracie had kept that little secret from her folks. Dad would go absolutely ballistic if he ever found out.

Gracie cleared her throat. "I don't want to talk about Glen, okay? I'm going on vacation tomorrow, and where I go is up to me."

Dad frowned as his eyes wandered across her determined face. The gears were turning in that wickedly intelligent brain. He wasn't going to let it go, and she'd run out of time to convince him.

A familiar white sedan pulled into the parking lot. Brenda had arrived. This was epic. She rarely put in an appearance at work.

"Look, Dad, let's not make a big deal out of my vacation. Maybe we can still avoid the blow-up this afternoon."

"When was the last time one of your visions didn't happen?" Dad shook his head and gripped her chin gently in his hand. "Punkin, I know you're all grown up and want your own life. There's nothing I want more than to see you happy. It's just that I...hell. You know what I mean."

"I love you too, Dad." Gracie grabbed onto him and hugged him tight. She could never stay mad at him for long.

"Remember when we used to take you up to Shasta Lake? Why don't we do that again, just the two of us? I can rent a cabin and a boat. It'll be fun. What do you say?"

Gracie smiled. "Sure, Dad. I'll think it over." Damn it. Hopes for a new adventure were evaporating fast.

Dad stood away from her and nodded toward the sedan. "Brenda says she has a surprise."

"She's going to put in a full day's work for a change?" Ape murmured in Gracie's ear. "That would be a big surprise."

A man crawled out of the driver's seat. Gracie immediately recognized the broad shoulders and those baggy surf shorts he liked to wear. His shaggy blond head tilted as he studied their group. It was a gesture she used to find endearing. Now that tick made her want to strangle him.

"What's Glen doing here?" She turned on her dad.

"Geezus, Brenda," Dad grumbled. "Punkin, I didn't know he was coming here and in the damn car I paid for."

"She went behind my back and invited Glen without asking me first?" The crimson waves of fury smash against her let's-be-polite ceiling. This family argument was on in a big way.

Mr. Wonderful waltzed toward them with a handful of flowers. Glen loved making an entrance. He had an uncanny knack of choosing the exact moment when the conversation revolved around him. Tall, tanned and handsome, he turned heads when he entered a room. His green eyes sparkled when he saw her. Glen smiled that sheepish grin he always used to get around her anger. It wasn't working this time.

"Hi, Gracie. You look great. How have you been?"

"How have I been? Really? That's the best you can say to me?"

Glen cleared his throat and extended the flowers toward her. The twelve-dollar price tag was still attached to the plastic container. What an idiot. He waved the petals at her with a grin. She didn't take them.

"Mr. Berry, It's good to see you again." Glen shifted uneasily as three cold stares met his smile. "Brenda...I mean Mrs. Berry asked me to come and pick you up in her car."

"She let you drive her new car? Aren't you the smooth talker. Did you really think a grocery store bouquet would smooth over the fact you cheated on me? My friends saw that video of you two together on the internet. I've never been so humiliated in my life!"

A hush fell over the group. Gracie struggled to breathe in the horrible silence. Gawd, what had she been thinking just blurting out about Glen's infidelity like that?

A fist slammed against the metal warehouse door, making her and everyone else jump. She twisted around. Storm clouds were indeed forming over the warehouse. Dad's fury burned from beneath his cap. She took a step back. It was a good moment to duck and cover.

"You miserable little prick! I gave you business because you were friendly with Gracie."

Glen dropped the flowers. Backpedaling toward the sedan, he kept his eyes on Gracie's dad. Doug Berry wasn't a guy you wanted to have mad at you. Two men had tried to rob them once. Dad had put them both in the hospital. Right now, Gracie was having serious mixed feelings about letting Dad and Ape kill Glen. Not wanting to see them go to jail, though, she decided to try and calm things down.

"He's not worth it, Dad." Her hands came to rest on her father's chest and pressed firmly on a solid wall of muscle. Age hadn't affected his body or calmed his temper.

"I told you that little peckerwood was a jerk, Doug." Ape smacked a big fist into his baseball mitt hand. He took up a position to support his friend. Good old Glen wasn't coming out of this exchange in one piece.

Dad lifted Gracie off her feet and placed her to the side. The look on his face was ugly as he pointed a finger at Glen. "Start counting down the seconds you have on this earth because there aren't many left!"

"Now do you see why I didn't tell you? Gawd, Dad, you can't go all crazy on me!" She threw her arms around his waist and planted her boots on the asphalt. It slowed him down a little.

Glen, no doubt realizing he had no allies in this fight, darted past Ape and leapt behind a dumpster. A six-foot fence lay behind it. A coward like Glen could clear it no problem especially when he had two pissed-off guys after him.

Dad pushed away from Gracie and slammed his fist into the bay door, which shook wildly against the violence. "What the hell is wrong with you, Gracie? Why would you go out with that loser? He didn't treat you right. I raised you better than that!"

"So this is my fault?" Gracie blinked back angry tears.

Dad shoved the cigar into his mouth and chewed. His hard stare told her everything she needed to know. She'd lost any respect he'd given her as an adult. Right now, she was his bubble-headed little girl who couldn't make good choices on her own. Feeling like the child he thought she was, she turned away from him and ran toward her car.

"Gracie, you come back here!" Dad shouted.

"You both need to cool off, Doug." Ape gripped his friend's arm and pulled him inside the warehouse.

Fumbling with the keys, Gracie found that her fingers refused to cooperate. She dropped her key chain and it clattered to the asphalt. She bent over, grabbed it up again and unlocked the car. Just then a hand pressed against the door, forcing it closed. Green eyes surrounded by a shaggy head of blond hair stared at her in the reflection of the window. She tugged as hard as she could, but Glen put his weight against the frame.

"Get away from me, Glen."

"Honey, you have to listen to me." He brought a hand inches away from her face as if he were going to smooth her cheek, the same loving gesture he'd made a thousand times when they were together. Her sobs came harder. Damn it! She hated when she couldn't control her tears. Especially when she suspected Glen got off on seeing them.

"I don't have to do anything!" Gracie tugged again.

Glen put a hand on her shoulder and smoothed it down her arm. "We belong together, honey. You know that. Look, I made a mistake. Why can't you forgive me? Haven't I been understanding about your little episodes?"

"You have to get the hell away from me right now, Glen, or I'll let my Dad have you."

He stepped away in a hurry and allowed her to get into the car. The engine started with a vroom as she stomped on the gas. Her little hybrid lurched forward, smoking the wheels. She looked into the rearview mirror and saw Glen watching her car drive away, a stupid, desperate look on his face. The jerk had expected her to forgive him. Fat chance. He'd be waiting a long time for that to happen.

Gracie headed toward the one oasis where she always found a friendly face and a stiff drink of comfort waiting to welcome her. Rolling over the curb and onto the sand, she stopped the little car in her usual parking place just off the beach. The Rusty Grotto Cafe was an odd mix of beachfront shabby and Latino quirky. Its white stucco walls were covered in murals of seabirds eating tacos. The food wasn't anything special, but their Monster Margaritas were local legend.

Obnoxious cowbells over the door announced her arrival. She scanned the engrossed faces of the lunch crowd as they munched while sitting around lime-green plastic tables. Kay, the cafe's owner, bartender and maintenance team, stood behind the small bar. A master at multitasking, she was mixing margaritas and talking on her cell. Her ruffled turquoise uniform plunged off Kay's shoulders, coming dangerously close to violating California law. A thick magenta braid swayed in time to mariachi music playing over tin speakers.

Kay waved Gracie over. Her round face turned troubled when she noticed the state Gracie was in. Dark eyes moistened with sympathy. "I've gotta go.

No, I'll call you later." She hung up the phone and pushed a wad of napkins into Gracie's hand. "What happened? What's wrong, sweetie?"

"Brenda invited Glen to our barbeque."

"What?" Kay hissed between her teeth. "Gracie, you have to tell your folks what really happened. If you don't, they'll keep pulling crazy shit."

"I did tell them, well today I told my dad. It didn't do any good. Dad tried to kill Glen. He told me Glen's cheating was my fault! Well, he implied it." Her angry tears threatened to spill over again. "Dad can be such a jerk sometimes."

Kay came around the margarita station and pulled Gracie in for a hug. "Let's go sit in your spot while you sip on this. The lunch rush is almost over." Kay handed her one of the fresh Monster Margaritas she'd been making.

The sweaty smell of tequila and lime penetrated Gracie's stuffy nose. She took a long drink and shivered as the tart flavor hit her tongue. Kay was making them extra strong today.

Gracie followed her best friend past the lime tables and out onto the covered patio. The gentle ocean breeze brushed at her hair and face. It was early summer. The "June Gloom" had arrived. Gray and cloudy at this time of the year, San Diego was in its periodic funk; its sun was on break. Gracie sat down on her regular stool, facing out onto the beach. She took another deep drink of the brew as Kay waited.

"Better?"

Gracie nodded and leaned her elbows on the driftwood counter. "I can't believe Dad and Brenda.

It's like they think I'm twelve years old." She twisted the glass around. "I run the business, and it's Dad who gets to go to all the conventions and business trips. He's still living in the fifties for Pete's sake."

"Isn't it about time you showed him that you're a grown-up professional with a brain? If you don't, he'll never take you seriously." Kay poured more of the lime-green concoction into Gracie's glass.

"You're right! I'm my own person." She slammed back the drink. Margaritas on the rocks went down way too smooth. "It's time I showed him I can be independent! I don't need him interfering in my life all the time." She put the glass down and gave Kay a determined grin. I'm going someplace out of town on my vacation."

"Now you're talking," Kay said. "Where are you going?"

"Where? I don't know. I've never been anywhere."

"Kay! Where the hell are my drinks?" Sherri, one of the Grotto's waitresses, stomped onto the patio. Her face turned sour when she saw Gracie. They exchanged cold nods. A few months back, Gracie had caught Sherri flirting with Glen. Well, she could have him, and good luck. Gracie wasn't doing jealous anymore. Life was too short to follow around an idiot guy, worried he would go off with someone else. This was a new phase in Gracie's life. She was going to look out for herself from now on.

"Okay, relax, I'm coming." Kay patted Gracie's shoulder and hurried after Sherri.

Gracie turned her attention beachside where seabirds dove toward the water, darting over the waves. It was beautiful. The beach was always a good choice. Maybe her dad wouldn't be so ticked off if she stayed close to home. She rested her chin on her palm. Yeah, the beach again.

Her gaze drifted lazily to the tin napkin holder on the counter. Oh crap! Her face looked like a beach ball. Crimson patches flared beside the startling blue of her irises. Her nose was red and irritated from the rough napkins Kay had given her. She pushed away from the counter and hopped off the bench. Feeling shattered, she walked to the bathroom to wash her face.

The door leading to the back was stenciled with a giant seagull wearing a sombrero. She rolled her eyes and pushed through into the dark little hallway. The light was out again. Kay knew better. This was a lawsuit waiting to happen. Gracie flipped at the wall switch. Nothing. Grousing like the grumpy mess she was, she made a mental note to remind Kay to hire another handyman. The last one had quit after Kay dumped him.

Gracie heard a faint scrape somewhere in the darkness and stopped as a prickle of fear touched her neck. Her attacker grabbed Gracie from behind, gripping a sweaty hand firmly over her face. She kicked at his legs and twisted her body wildly. Her screams were muffled, but the noise was bound to attract some help. She wasn't going to make it easy for the creep.

"Stop." It was a single word in her mind, projected with absolute confidence. Gracie's limbs dropped to her sides and her body grew still. Her brain, however, was very active. She shouted desperately at her body to fight, but the control she once had was simply gone. It had been taken by her mysterious attacker.

A door opened in front of her. The acrid smell of cleaning chemicals and wet mop pierced through her stuffy nose. Oh God, he was going to rape her in the utility closet, ten feet away from the kitchen! She wanted to scream for help. She wanted to kick and hit until he let her go, but her body remained motionless. What the hell had he done to her?

"I must have a little chat with you, my dear," the man's voice said beside her. He was English and well educated from his accent. That didn't sound right. Gracie had expected some drug addict, wandering in off the beach.

He pushed her body forward until her knee struck one of the shelves in the closet. The door shut and the lock clicked home. An overhead light flooded the small space. Hands spun her around. Gracie blinked her stinging eyes. Eventually, her attacker came into focus. He was an older man, probably in his sixties, with a perfectly bald head and gray eyebrows. His dove-gray blazer looked sharp over a white turtleneck. Nice slacks and black leather shoes told Gracie he wasn't the average tourist. Nobody wore a blazer on a California beach. But his intense eyes were what captured her full attention. Great power lay in them. She'd been frightened before; now, she was terrified.

Lifting up his right arm, the man held it before Gracie's eyes. Ribbons of emerald ink twisted to form an elaborate triangle on the inside of his wrist. Golden letters spelled "Past. Present. Future." Two stars had been inked under the two-inch tattoo.

"You don't recognize this tattoo or the stars, do you?" He waited, watching her face intently. The slight smile on his face made Gracie's skin crawl. "Excellent. I'm called Druid. You are doubtless wondering why I have you restrained in this closet."

Blue flooded his eyes. He took in a long breath and then smiled fully. Something touched her mind, something insistent and intrusive. This creep shared her gift. Druid was just like her, but was much more powerful. What that meant for Gracie was the million-dollar question.

"Yes, I can see it. You've started to question your reality. I understand you better than you may think, my dear. Whoever has been hiding you is content to let you stay in mediocrity. You've grown bored." He brushed a strand of hair out of her face. "The familiar can be a comfort, but it can also be mundane."

Mundane. That was a good word for her whole life. The shelves disappeared. Images took their place. Gracie's future stretched out before her like a really boring 'to do' list: Get up, go to work with Dad at the warehouse, come home and watch television. She could almost see the middle-aged Gracie doing the same damn thing even after Dad passed away. She couldn't envision one different moment in the whole scene. The shelves appeared again, and she was back in the here and now.

"Hiding from life is the same thing as being dead, my dear. I need you to be strong and fearless." Druid was looking at her again with those unnerving eyes. The tip of his index finger touched her forearm. "You'll need all your courage where you're going."

The familiar tingle of her own power raced up her spine. Then the closet disappeared. She saw herself standing on a busy street with neon lights everywhere. It was warm here and full of excitement. Druid's hand squeezed her arm harder. She turned obediently toward him.

"You aren't alone, Gracie." His eyes found hers. Those orbs were hypnotic, compelling. She wasn't able to turn away. "I came here at great risk to tell you it's time for you to come out of hiding. You must become what nature intended. Don't let anyone stop you from leaving the mundane. Say it."

"I won't let anyone stop me from leaving the mundane." Gracie repeated the words like a mantra. They gave her such courage! The neon lights faded until all she could see were Druid's eyes. Nothing else existed.

"Very good, Gracie. You'll leave on the next flight to Las Vegas tonight. Airfare and a hotel have been arranged in your name. You're very excited to visit the Strip. There you will seek out a Columbian gentleman named Raul Vento."

Somewhere, deep inside her mind, the voice of fear shouted for Gracie to wake up. That fear struck out against the power in Druid's voice. Warnings and shrill alarms rang in her brain. She began to shake. Sweat drenched her hair and face. Too strong! Druid was too strong, but something told Gracie she'd stopped him from going any further into her mind. That was where her memories lived. She wouldn't, couldn't, let him see. Those precious memories of family and friends belonged only to her.

"I shall call you 'Titania,' yes that's an appropriate name for you." Druid let his hand drop to run along the front of her t-shirt. "Your appearance will have to change. This outfit is far too masculine. Raul prefers—I believe the American term is `trashy blondes.' Your friend Kay will help you with the details. I planted a suggestion in her mind after we spent a pleasurable evening together." A smug grin crossed his face at the memory. "She was very spirited and eager to please me."

"You son of a..." Gracie's words were strained, painful. She used every ounce of will to kick at Druid. The strike connected with his shin. She choked out a laugh when he hissed in pain. Steel-toed work boots might not be feminine, but they sure got the job done.

Druid wiped water from his eyes. "You're protective of your loved ones. How maternal. I'll remember that little piece of information for our times together." He stood up straight again and let his power pulse angrily about her.

"Listen, creep, I'm not going anywhere with you!" She kicked out wildly again with the only part of her body that wanted to cooperate. "I could kill you for what you did to Kay!"

"My dear, you'll quickly learn not to waste your concern on Normals. They are inferior to us in every way. She was there to use for my pleasure. I threw her aside when I grew bored. The silly cow doesn't remember any of it, but I could change that if you continue to fight me. I could compel her to be my willing slave. She would turn against you to please me."

Gracie lashed out again with her foot. This time it didn't move. Druid had her back under control. She was a prisoner in her own body, and she couldn't do a damn thing about it. Angry tears spilled down her passive cheeks. Dad had tried to keep her safe from the dangers in the world. Gracie wondered if he'd ever imagined anything like Druid.

"You continue to hesitate. Someone has put a block on your mind." Druid gripped her chin in his hand. Squeezing hard with his fingers, he forced her attention.""I may not be able to enthrall you completely, but I can still force you." He mentally pressed his will harder against her. "Your fear is gone. You will get on that plane, and you'll find Raul Vento. I need you beside him. Midsummer's Eve is less than a week away. You must be in his good graces by then."

Druid released Gracie's chin and allowed her to fall away from him. Those piercing orbs began to fade into the hazy darkness. "Disobedience shall be severely punished if you fail. We will meet again, my dear. Until that time you will have no memory of me or our conversation. You will only remember your excitement and the visions you saw of the Strip. My voice will be in your thoughts, and you will follow my instructions exactly."

Gracie screamed as her mind sank into the muddy darkness of his power. Helpless and alone, she grabbed onto her sanity with all the strength she had.

Chapter Four

Thick columns of bamboo jutted up from the Mexican sand before him. Taped to each stalk was a crude printout of Viper Girard's face. The bamboo rustled in the ocean breeze like crimson flags waved before an angry bull. Jin took in her many faces and focused his mind. The side of his hand struck the bamboo with a powerful left-handed whack, followed in rapid succession with a right. Then another left strike. The images of Viper's face fluttered as the bamboo swayed. Her two-dimensional visage appeared to be laughing at him. Jin twisted his body in a blur of bare skin, slamming his heel against the columns at full speed. Bamboo exploded into shards of kindling.

Twisting back into a combat-ready stance, he spun too sharply. Healing skin tightened across his ribs. He bit down on the curse aching to escape. Stepping into the waters of the Pacific, Jin bent over and waited for the pain to ease.

The portal had dropped him on the Cozumel resort's doorstep nearly two weeks before. So far, the escape had worked. He'd chosen this place for its remote location and its owner's predilection for dishonesty with the Clans.

He hadn't taken long in finding the most isolated part of the fifteen-acre grounds. This small stretch of beach was a perfect place to pursue his obsessive pastime. Someone had created a wooden platform in the midst of a white-sand base. It gave the illusion of floating upon the sand, while in the distance the crashing waves soothed the mind. The platform with its pillows and linen blankets was a welcome bit of comfort. Jin fell on the bedding, panting with exertion.

He swept his shaggy black bangs behind one ear. Reaching down over the choppy waters, the heavy clouds of June threatened to burst open. They reflected perfectly his mood. Hoping to ease his mind, he forced his breath to slow until his chest rose and fell in perfectly measured durations. He spent every waking moment either training his body back to health or plotting his revenge upon Viper. Troubled images invaded his dreams each night, robbing him of sleep. He could think of little else but her blood draining into the earth.

Giving up on his meditation, Jin poured a cup of tea from the small pot beside the platform. He turned the simple, white tea cup slowly in his fingers. The amber liquid shuddered, sending ripples against the porcelain surface. His wounds were healing rapidly. It was almost time to leave this place. Jin smoothed the scar where Viper's weapon had sliced his right arm.

Physically, he was on the mend. His heart and his head were another matter. He'd never felt so lost. A kind of grief had come to him when he'd been banished from the Clans. Still, he'd retained some form of hope. Thoughts of seeing Mai Ling had kept him going. Now she was gone. Revenge was all that he had left. It wouldn't wait much longer.

In the long hours of the night, he'd relived that evening over and over again. Neither Viper nor Renee had the political pull or power to negotiate with the Unseelie Court. Someone else must have brokered the dark elf's aid. All the facts led his mind to one logical conclusion. The Girard coup had been a ruse to cripple or kill Zhao Long. They needed him out of the way for something bigger. Jin suspected the plot had something to do with Midsummer's Eve.

"Jin! You've broken the one condition of sanctuary in my house! Again!" Dressed in billowing traffic-cone-orange robes, a bald-headed monk blustered toward Jin. The man was of Chinese descent, but his accent was most definitely American. When his sudden intruder tumbled on his saintly backside in the sand, Jin managed a quiet laugh, his first in weeks.

His host struggled for a moment, arse lifted in the air. Turning his attention away from the twisting robes still sprawled out on the sand, Jin managed to get his laughter under control. He was an unwanted guest in this peaceful little retreat. These human monks might not be affiliated with any Christian or Buddhist organization, but they had their own fascination with solitude. The gates were closed to outsiders unless the outsider had enough money to open them. Jin let out a long sigh of resignation and got up to assist his host out of the undignified position.

Putting on his most repentant expression, Jin helped the monk to his feet. "What brings you down to the beach?"

The agitated monk spread his arms wide over the shards of bamboo scattered on the sand. He picked up one of the pictures and shook it at Jin. Viper's face had been ripped in two pieces by his anger.

"It saddens me to see that you still pursue your road of self-destruction." The monk tugged at the folds of his orange silk wrap. "I had hoped that these weeks spent in isolation and quiet contemplation would help you balance your chi. You're a child of two worlds and until you master both, you will never find peace."

"What can I say? I am my father's son and my mother's biggest disappointment. Ask her—she'll tell you."

Eleanor Wainwright was a politician first and foremost. Blood or no, she wouldn't risk her station or the honor of her Clan to save her son. To be fair, she hadn't gone out of her way to help find him either. His mother, in fact, had remained oddly silent. According to the reports, Lady Wainwright had been unavailable for comment. Jin reminded himself those reports were carefully monitored and scrubbed to send the right message to official and non-official readers.

"Don't forget why you've come to me. I've kept you hidden from your enemies so that you may find your true path," the monk went on.

"And for my generous donation to your facility. Let's not forget that part." Jin let the flicker of a smile cross his lips. "Drop the disappointed holy man act, Murray. I remember the days when you were relieving rich old ladies of their jewelry." He tapped Murray's chest. "And taking a sizable cut of Zhao Clan profits from my father's gambling houses."

The monk glared. "I remember one lesson I learned well from those days. Never broadcast your whereabouts or intent! You've been trying to track Viper's movements on my computer system again." Murray waved his billowing mass of orange in an unenlightened fashion. "What if the Clans find out about this place? If your father knew I was helping you..."

"Yes, Murray, I understand. I'm out of favor with the Zhao Clan and by helping me, you put yourself at risk."

Jin could only imagine what his other friends and associates were going through right now. The Council wasn't above using their powers to persuade their subjects to tell the truth. Jin had stayed away from everyone the Clans could possibly associate with him. If they didn't know anything, his friends wouldn't be hurt. Reports on the manhunt for the "bloodthirsty conspirator" were filled with colorful lies. Viper's plan to frame him appeared to be working. He was being painted as a power-hungry monster out for revenge.

News of his father too filled the communication channels. Zhao Long was still in a mage-induced sleep. He was said to be healing, but the reports were vague. Jin scratched at the stubble on his chin. He'd stood by and let his father and his sister perish. Guilt and grief were his constant companions.

"You don't need to remind me the Clans have labeled me an anarchist and murderer. I've explained to you how Viper set me up." Jin rubbed at the scar on his right arm where Viper's strike had penetrated his flesh. "I'll be leaving soon. It's time to pay Viper a little visit. She's been very active over the past few days. It could be she has renewed her efforts to start trouble."

Murray gazed down at the sand. "Do as you will, Jin, but think on this proverb— before you set out for revenge, be sure to dig two graves."

A dark shadow of cold emotion moved over Jin's face. He let it pass before he gave Murray a curt nod. "Out of respect for your home, I'll try to stay away from your computers and be a polite guest."

"That's all I ask." Murray tucked his arms inside his garish robes. "We've known each other a long time, Jin. I want you to remember that I believe what you've told me. You're not like the others. I remember how you helped me escape Zhao Clan slavery. You're no murderer."

"Yes, I'll remember if it pleases you." Scooping up his sandals, Jin turned to Murray. "Coming?"

"Thank you, no. I want to take a walk along the beach."

"I'll come with you. Taking luncheon alone has grown dull."

"No, Jin, I prefer quiet contemplation in solitude," Murray said quickly. Tiny droplets of dew had formed on the monk's forehead. Or was it sweat? Murray's facial features remained calm and controlled. He'd been a con man for many years and was used to hiding his lies. Jin brushed away the specks of white sand on his forearm. His gaze never left Murray's face. He could be lying for any number of reasons. Jin let his predator smile escape to his lips. Betrayal had better not be one of them. That lie would see Murray to his grave.

"Enjoy your walk," he said at last and followed his own footprints in the sand. The uneasy feeling of suspicion stayed with him until he rounded the thick shrubs that acted as a gateway to the main garden.

Once there, he dropped his sandals on the stone path and stepped into them. A short walk brought him to what the monks lovingly referred to as "the junction." Several paths sprouted off the main walkway, making their way through a forest of thick bamboo and tropical foliage. Marked with ornate stone signs, each path took its visitor to the various gardens where the monks paid homage to the retreat's more ardent supporters. Rather than being appealing, Jin found the mishmash landscaping gave the grounds a feel of organized chaos.

He opted for a path leading to the far left. Stretching under a bamboo canopy, it brought him to an open stone courtyard with a Zen garden in the center. Two black granite stones brought over from China had been carefully placed on a base of white sand. Meant to convey harmony, they looked awkward in the Mexican sunshine.

Jin rounded the pool of white sand and came to a gravel pathway. A rusted sign missing most of its letters marked the path as the "walk of contemplation." It was appropriate. Jin liked spending his afternoon hours in the peace of the small garden beyond. Free from garish statuary, the simple little garden was the perfect place to plot his reunion with Viper.

He made for his usual spot. A comfortable hammock hung across from a small pond. Water lilies decorated the surface of the still water. Koi swam beneath them, circling the clumsily hidden pump. A bird feeder was suspended on the other side of the pond directly across from his hammock. He quieted his steps when he noticed a tiny sparrow pecking delicately at the seed in the feeder. Then suddenly it pushed away from the ceramic bowl and took flight.

The strike came at his head. Jin caught the nunchuck in his right hand a few inches above his shoulder and yanked it away. His attacker stumbled forward as he was pulled off balance. Jin didn't recognize him. He wasn't a Seelie Descendant. Someone had sent a human on this disaster of an ambush. Wide, terrified eyes stared at him. The human looked half starved.

Jin brought his heel to the attacker's chest, sending the man's body crashing into the bamboo unharmed. They'd timed their strike while he was in his human glamour, when his powers were reduced. Unfortunately for his attacker, he no longer adhered to Clan Rules for using his powers in front of humans.

Two more attackers came at Jin, brandishing Chinese fighting staffs. They thrust the slender six-foot poles at his legs. Jin easily blocked the attacks and stood back watching them hesitate. No sharp weapons or guns? They wanted Jin alive, but why?

He stood his ground, waiting for the first man to make his move. It was possible they'd been hired by the Clan Council to distract him until more powerful beings arrived, but humans? If they truly believed him to be the dangerous killer Viper had painted in her distorted picture, then why wouldn't they send Clansmen?

Another thrust came swiftly toward his torso. He caught the pole and twisted his body, ripping the weapon out of its owner's hands. The wood dropped to the stone. Its deafening echo sounded obscene in the serenity of the garden. Keeping his eye on his opponents, Jin stood calmly waiting for them to attack again. Neither man made a move.

The garden was silent again as each waited for his opponent to strike. Jin shifted his weight slightly. He didn't want to kill these humans. Using his power to jump out of sight seemed the best option. Maybe that was the point? The Clan Council wouldn't waste the chance for a surprise attack on what they considered a vicious killer. They'd send their most powerful hunter. Whoever had sent these humans knew Jin wouldn't kill them. In fact, he'd do everything in his power not to hurt such clearly underfed and terrified creatures.

And Jin was certain they'd had inside help. These humans knew exactly where to strike on his body, information they could only possess if they'd been told. Someone who'd been spending time with Jin over the past few weeks would have that knowledge. Murray's behavior on the beach made sense now. Jin would have to ask the monk about his new friends when he was finished cleaning the rubbish out of the garden.

A sharp point punctured the skin on his neck. Stinging like a wasp bite, the venom spread in hot waves up and down. He pulled the yellow feathered dart from his flesh and brought the tip to his nose. It was a tranquilizer dart. Not poison.

Jin's eyes scanned the thick bamboo surrounding the garden. The owner of the dart remained hidden. Cowards usually did. Jin disappeared with a short burst of air and reappeared in the thick bamboo behind his attackers. The drug was starting to affect his movement. He jumped again before its effects paralyzed him completely.

Landing clumsily at the head of the walk of contemplation, Jin fell face first onto the stone. His muscles grew limp as the drug invaded the rest of his body. A thick haze began to cross his vision. He was very close to losing consciousness.

"You're as fast as the stories claim." Deep laughter assaulted his throbbing ears. A man stepped out of the shadows cast by the morning sun. Platinum blond hair surrounded square features. His accent branded him as Russian. The slaughterhouse build and savage dark eyes marked him as a killer. "You've hidden yourself well for these many days, but we never had any doubt we would find you."

"Who are you?"

"I'm the warrior who will defeat you in battle." He thrust a thick wrist in Jin's face. The Trinity Badge had three stars below its outline. He was with the Girard Clan. Not good.

"Viper wishes it so. You're to be the guest of honor at a get-together Raul Vento is arranging." Viper and Raul Vento together? That was a dangerous and brutal combination. The Clans had found Jin at last, but he'd fallen into the hands of the wrong side. It was a safe bet they'd keep his capture quiet.

The man's features began to blur in the wake of the drug. A massive palm slapped Jin's cheek. "No Council trials for you, eh, murderer?"

Jin felt tiny rocks press against his cheek as he was dragged along the path. It had been sheer folly to think Viper hadn't been looking for him as intently as he'd been looking for her. He let out an incoherent gurgle. Revenge. It had become a deadly match between them. Only fate knew who would survive the game.

Chapter Five

Gracie frowned at her reflection twisting in the full-length mirror. She tossed the empty container of golden glitter hairspray into the trash can. Gawd, her hair was lit up like a sparkler. It matched her outfit at least. Held up with spaghetti straps and a prayer, the slinky dress didn't quite fit her body. She smoothed at the golden bead patterns sewn into the silk fabric and then looked over her shoulder at her backside. It showed every little bump.

What had she been thinking, borrowing this dress? She didn't own the right lingerie to wear underneath a skimpy little thing like this piece of barely-there. For Pete's sake, she didn't own anything that wasn't cotton and you couldn't buy in an outlet store.

No way was she wearing this. Maybe the other one she'd borrowed from Kay would be better. She opened the wardrobe and shook her head at the short, metallic cocktail dress hanging off the padded hanger. It fell in wispy folds to about six inches above the knees. A single strand of rhinestones thrown over the shoulder was the only support holding it up.

Shoving the dress back in place, Gracie hurried into the bathroom and leaned against the counter. The dress, the makeup and the awful glitter weren't her.

Rather than being a fun adventure, this trip to Vegas was turning into a hellish nightmare.

"I'll never be able to pull this off." Her eyes lifted to the mirror. A shadow passed over them. She staggered back as the dark outline rested in the depths of her irises.

"You will wear the dress and carry yourself as if you were a goddess. Do as you're told, and we won't need any more unpleasant lessons in obedience." The voice, insistent and cruel, echoed within the recesses of her mind. A sharp memory of stabbing pain made her shrink away, but it was impossible to run from the voice.

She stood up straight and lifted her chin. "I'm going to find out who you are. Then I'm going to find a way to get you out of me."

"I'm your new master, my dear. I may not be able to enthrall and control you completely now, but never assume I won't be able to eventually. We'll have our time together, either way. But rest assured I'll find a means to destroy that block in your mind." The shadow grew darker for a heartbeat and then faded into the blue of her eyes. *"I will break you, Gracie. Then your mind and your power will be mine to control."*

She wrapped her arms tightly about her trembling body and closed her eyes. This strange voice inside her mind represented every fear she'd ever had of being violated. He'd forced his presence into the shower with her earlier, watching through her eyes as she bathed. Things had grown dangerous when he'd wanted her to perform for his amusement. Somehow she'd managed to force the pervert out for a short time. Being able to fight him off, if only momentarily, had proven his hold over her was tenuous. The little glimmer of hope kept her from losing her sanity altogether.

Urgent buzzing from her bedside pulled Gracie's attention back to the present. Turning away from the mirror, she picked up her epileptic cell from the nightstand. Dad's picture smiled at her on the tiny screen. He must be worried sick about her. Yeah, he should be. Her finger hovered over the surface of the phone. She wanted to jump on the line and scream for his help, but Dad couldn't protect her this time. She'd have to fight her own battle with the bastard living inside her.

The sharp stab of pain came without warning. Falling against the bed, she clutched at her head with a small cry. "I wasn't going to answer it!"

The attack came like a wild thunderstorm. *"No distractions! I'm beginning to think you enjoy being punished."* Blinding flashes of light assaulted her vision. Hot bolts of power stabbed the tender flesh of her brain until she thought she would die from the pain.

"No more distractions. Don't make me punish you again. Now, get up. Raul will be at the rendezvous point soon. You must be there before him. Leave your mobile here."

Shaking from an excruciating mixture of pain and fury, she threw her cell on the nearest bed and grabbed her purse. Her electronic door key along with her ID and credit card were already tucked into the pocket of the gold-beaded belt. She stashed some cash for the taxi in her little gold purse and headed out the door toward the elevators.

The Styles Hotel and Casino was Las Vegas' newest off-Strip attraction. Chic and modern, the Italian design gave guests the illusion they were in Milan. Their grand-opening celebration was attracting curious tourists from all around the globe. Gracie had never seen so much glitz and glamour in one place.

Flashing neon bombarded her vision as the elevator doors opened in the middle of the casino. Dings of short-lived victories called to her fellow guests like sirens' songs. It wasn't long before Gracie was the lone traveler upon the path to the front desk. Ash granite encased a white runway stretching from the entrance hall of the hotel to the casino entrance. Amazing pictures of famous models peppered the walls in a stunning tableau of elegance and Italian flare. The whole lobby looked like a photo shoot from some high-concept cable show.

Rising up like a white marbled altar, the front desk towered over its worshippers. Gracie stopped to stare for a moment despite having witnessed the effect before. Close by, the concierge desk was a lesser beauty, but still impressive. A moderately handsome man in a sharp-looking suit stood behind the counter. His slicked-back hair and smoothly shaven face complemented model-quality features. He lifted his eyes and scanned Gracie quickly as she approached. Taking special notice of the beaded design on her chest, he gave her a well-practiced smile.

"Good evening, Signorina. How may I help you?" His Italian accent flowed over the desk, charming the other women within earshot. Several of them gave the young man smoldering looks.

"I need a taxi."

"I am Clayton. It is my pleasure to be of assistance to you."

Gracie jumped back when he oozed around the desk like Italian cream. She caught a whiff of his expensive cologne as he came closer to kiss her hand. The scent was probably a gift from some grateful female patron. Gracie let his smarmy behavior go. The way he was looking at her—like she was biscotti and he was hungry—made her feel a thousand times better about her stupid dress.

"I'd hazard a guess he's expecting something other than money for his gratuity."

Clayton took her arm and wrapped it around his. She allowed him to usher her out of the lobby while several jealous stares watched them exit through the massive glass doors. He waved a manicured hand at the valet. A few moments later, a sleek black limo pulled around to stop before them.

"The limousine is courtesy of the hotel. If I can do anything for you, Bella Signorina, find me and I will help."

"Yeah, thanks, I'll do that." Gracie hurried inside the limo half expecting him to pinch her backside. No. He was way too smooth. She wondered how many female guests got the limo treatment. It must have worked for him in the past. Concierge seemed like his side job.

The limo pushed through the streaming line of tourists walking along the Strip. Their outfits ranged from sparkly cocktail dresses to denim shorts and tank tops. Both modes of dress seemed to suit the city.

Gracie leaned back in the plush leather of the backseat and looked up through the moon roof at the cityscape. Neon flashed in manic pulses, drawing the eye.

The energy of the Strip hummed through the vehicle walls. It was exhilarating and overwhelming at the same time. Massive LED images of major headliners dazzled pedestrians along the way. Peppered between the more expensive advertisements were playbills for "topless dancing vampires" and nude circus performers. Sin city. She now totally understood how Vegas got its nickname.

A facsimile of the Eiffel Tower came up on her right. As the driver pulled over and helped her out of the limo, she shivered with a serious case of déjà vu. The sights and sounds, even the feeling of intoxicating excitement were coming alive again. She stood dumbly in the middle of the sidewalk for a moment, staring at the beauty of the Bellagio and Caesar's Palace. She'd seen this moment before, but not by her own command. Someone much more powerful than she had shown it to her. A name lingered just out of reach in her memory.

"I have it on good authority Raul has been visiting one of his mistresses this afternoon. You'll wait at the lobby bar until I point him out to you."

"He sounds like a real charmer. Why are you so interested in him anyway?"

"I warned you. No questions."

"Go head and zap me right here in the middle of the sidewalk. I'm sure it'll be easy for you to find another body after they take me to the emergency room."

"*Very well*," the voice murmured after a tense moment. "*I want him watched because I don't trust him to keep his word to me. Having you by his side will help me to make certain he fulfills his part of our bargain. Now, you must hurry inside. We don't want to miss our friend.*"

Walking into the Paris Las Vegas was like walking onto a movie set. Quaint bistros lined a realistic Parisian boulevard. A sunny afternoon sky stretched overhead. Gawking like the tourist she was, Gracie almost tripped up the stairs of Le Central Lobby Bar. She caught her fumble on the ornate iron rod. The bar wasn't busy, but it was still early on the Strip.

Craving a beer, she ordered a nerve stabilizing glass of chardonnay instead. She was supposed to be playing a part. This wasn't the kind of dress to drink beer in. Several of the men were casting glances her way. She pulled at the hem of her dress, which was working its way up a little too much for her comfort. How did Kay manage to keep her clothes in place? Pushing up on the bar stool, Gracie caught her heel and smacked back down again. Her wine glass toppled over onto the bar, sending a stream of chardonnay toward the bartender's tidy stack of orange slices.

"Well, that was smooth," she said, fiercely trying to mop up the spilled wine with her napkin. "Too bad there isn't a rock close by for me to crawl under."

"*My God is this what passes for sophistication in the desert? You'll need to do better if you're to convince Raul.*"

"I've told you. I'm not a femme fatale. Your little plan isn't going to work." She pushed the sticky wet napkins into a messy pile on the bar. The bartender didn't bat an eye as he cleaned up the mess. It was Vegas. He'd probably seen worse than a clumsy woman talking to herself.

"Damn your antics! He's gotten past us. Over there! He's exiting the doors at the front of the casino. Hurry!"

She pulled out a ten and threw it on the bar with an apologetic nod to the bartender. Weaving between the crowds of tourists and tipsy gamblers was a challenge in high heels. She finally reached the casino entrance and hurried out through the glass doors.

Water pulsed in time to classical music, claiming Gracie's attention across the street. The fountains of the Bellagio danced for a moment against the backdrop of the Las Vegas night; their beauty was stunning. The water of the fountains fell back to earth, and the crowd across the boulevard began to leave. It wasn't how she'd imagined first seeing the famous fountains. She'd daydreamed of taking a romantic stroll beside them with someone she loved. The bastard in her mind fell way below the mark there. She shrugged unhappily. At least she'd gotten to see them.

"This isn't the time for sightseeing. There! Head to your right."

She fell into the same pattern as the rest of the tourists crowding their way along Las Vegas Boulevard toward Bally's. Racing pink lights announced the Flamingo just ahead of her. Caesar's Palace shone white and gold on the other side. Shiny eye candy lit up the night. Every inch of Gracie's skin was tingling. The excitement of the Strip was contagious, so when the next vision came it hit her by surprise. She stumbled. Staggering out of the crowd, she leaned against the wall of the casino.

She Saw an older Latin man dressed in an expensive suit waiting on a curb. A cigar smoldered in his mouth as he concentrated on some sort of electronic device in his hand. Tires squealed behind him when a car turned onto the road from the busy boulevard. He didn't see the vehicle racing toward him. She knew he had no chance of getting out of the way in time.

The vision released her. She was standing at the corner of the road where the man was going to be run down. He was in fact about twenty feet away from her, sucking on his cigar. The voice would punish her if she didn't find its target, but she couldn't let the man die. Pushing aside her mission to follow Raul, she charged forward.

Angry honks and shouts thundered behind her from the boulevard. The car was coming toward her at a crazy speed. She flew around the corner as fast as her high heels would take her. It was going to be a race between her head-start in high heels and the car fighting traffic on the Strip. Blood pounded in her ears as her heart pumped wildly. Gulping in air, she tried to ignore her aching feet.

Tires screeched when the car took the corner onto the road behind her. Out of breath, she managed a warning yelp at the man. He ignored her cry, completely oblivious to the coming danger. Gracie threw her body into the man's side and they rolled away a few feet to safety. The car zoomed out of sight, its driver not touching his brakes as he flew onto Flamingo Road.

"That guy could have killed somebody!" She sat up, watching the taillights disappear into traffic. He could have been some drunk in a hurry, but the car hadn't weaved at all. It had gone straight for its intended victim. She rubbed at her aching elbow and shook her head. What had happened hadn't been an accident.

"I believe that was their intent," the man said, struggling to his feet and waving off the many hands that had suddenly appeared to assist him. He reached down to help her up. "Are you okay, miss?"

Gracie brushed at her dress. It didn't seem to have taken any damage. The California sun had negated her need to wear pantyhose. No harm there. She lifted her eyes and really looked at the Latin man for the first time. He was no victim. This was a predator, sizing her up with hungry interest. Oh, Gawd! She'd ruined the plan. The voice wasn't going to be pleased.

"Stay calm. He isn't going to hurt you, my dear. You're much too valuable," The voice said with a hum of pleasure. *"You're completely inept as a seductress. Thank your own luck the opportunity arose for you to save his life. Now he owes you his protection. Remember what I've told you, Gracie. Keep your eyes open."*

"I am Raul Vento. Because you saved my life, you may call me Raul." He grabbed Gracie's left wrist and turned it over. His puffy lips frowned at the tan skin. "Are you unaffiliated or hiding?"

She pulled her arm away. "I don't understand what you mean."

"Don't you?" He laughed and gestured to one of his Latino henchmen. The expressionless young man marched toward them and handed Raul a tiny device that looked like a flash drive. Two men grabbed Gracie's arms, holding her still as Raul brought the little device to touch the skin of her left wrist. A moment later she heard a tiny beep and the device flashed green.

"What was that?" Gracie tried to struggle out of their grip, but they weren't letting her go.

"Soon we'll find out who you are and which Clan owns you. What's your name?"

Every cell in Gracie's body warned her against telling him the truth. Pretending to be someone else might just keep her alive right now. Besides, she'd made a promise to...she couldn't remember. A strange name came to her as if it were a well-practiced role. "My name is Titania."

"Well, Titania, as I have said, I'm Raul Vento, head of the Vento Clan." Raul held up his left arm and pulled his sleeve up to expose the inside of his wrist. Gracie saw a tattoo of a strange sort of triangle. Four stars were inked underneath the base. She'd seen that tattoo somewhere before. "You are my guest."

"I think I'll pass, thanks. Someone's waiting for me."

"They will be disappointed." He gave her a savage grin. The threat behind it communicated more than any words could. "I would be foolish to allow such a powerful pre-cog loose. Your Clan leader will pay dearly for your return. And if you're unaffiliated, then you will soon join the Vento Clan. Take her to the car."

Someone whistled. An engine roared to life. Then a long, sleek limousine materialized out of the night. Struggling between the two Columbian gorillas, Gracie was as helpless as a paper doll. They lifted her up off her heels and into the street toward the car. She kicked and screamed, until a cold metal barrel pressed against the skin of her shoulder. Behind them, the Strip's flashy display kept all eyes focused on its seductive beauty. No one noticed her struggle. No one heard her scream.

Chapter Six

Cold water smacked Jin's face with the subtlety of a right hook. He reeled away, gasping for air. Still groggy from the drug, he struggled to get his eyes to cooperate. A second wave of water helped shock his body into motion. His backside scooted along some cool surface until his vision began to clear. He raised his hand to block the harsh glare from the overhead lights.

Several figures were silhouetted against the padded walls and ceilings. He blinked hard until their faces came into focus. Five Normals dressed in cheesy silver suits stood around him in a half-circle. Their dull eyes regarded him with unfriendly interest. He stared at the stone faces, not recognizing any of them. One thing was certain: He was still in the Human Realm. Humans weren't allowed into Otherworld.

"Easy now, sleepyhead," said a voice strained by too many years of smoking.

"Two-touch Tommy," Jin answered, rubbing at his eyes. "How delightful to see you again. And where are we?"

With a snort, Tommy let the silver bucket he'd just used to dump water on Jin drop to the ground. Sausage-sized fingers gripped at the suspenders holding up his straining slacks. He was a big man with a bigger belly. It appeared those "all you can eat" buffets he loved so much had taken their toll.

There had been a day when Tommy was a prized competitor in the underground Descendants' fight clubs. The remains of prominent muscle were still visible under his ill-fitting jacket. Middle-age hadn't taken the thunder out of his strike though. Jin knew Tommy could still lay a competitor out with two punches or less. For Tommy, like most Descendants given the gift of brute strength, loyalty was bought by the highest bidder and quickly lost again when an even higher bidder came along.

"Welcome to the Temple of Forbidden Pleasures, the best time in Vegas!" Tommy threw his arms wide and motioned over Jin's shoulder. "I think you'll like your accommodations."

The concrete floor of Jin's cell had been covered by thick gymnasium padding. A punching bag hung at the side of the room. Several kick pads and weights lined the far wall. The place looked like a martial arts training studio. Jin didn't like the direction his suspicions were headed.

"Vegas? As in Las Vegas, Nevada?" Jin rubbed at his temple. That was unpleasant news. He loved Vegas with its many entertaining distractions to be found on the Strip. Unfortunately, it was also located in the United States, which meant he was back on the grid.

The United States, like other young countries, was neutral territory. For any Seelie Descendant to enter these lands without permission was against Clan law. The Clan Council had signed a treaty centuries before with the Humans to keep these fledgling countries safe. A group known as the Enforcers—humans who had developed special skills—guarded the borders. They used a form of ancient magic to track down Seelie Descendants who broke the Treaty of Neutrality. Theirs was a law outside the human justice systems. Realistically, if Descendant magic failed, Humans could crush the Clans with sheer numbers.

Jim pushed to his feet, swayed a bit and then stabilized. The half-circle of Tommy's gang fell back a few steps when Jin stretched his arms over his head. He grinned. Having a killer's reputation might not be a bad thing under the circumstances.

"A rather large Russian told me Viper is my host."

"She'd like to think she runs things here." Tommy ran a thick thumb under his suspender. He shook his head and spat. "Raul Vento and Lou Fong own this club. They're doing pretty well too. Lots of rich, bored Descendants looking for sin. You know the type. Hell, you've ripped enough of them off."

"You mean this guy is just a punk thief?" One of Tommy's goons spat, a thin, nervous-looking thug. His fingers compulsively stroked the handle of the .38 sticking out from under his jacket. "Then why the hell does he get the royal treatment?"

Jin regarded him coolly. "I prefer to be called a procurement consultant."

"You're a fucking thief, Jin, among other things." Tommy snorted and poked a finger at his captive's chest. "But that's not why you're here."

"Enlighten me. What is this place?"

"You've never been to one of Raul's traveling shows before?"

"The Vento Clan as a whole doesn't appreciate my more endearing personality traits," Jin answered coolly.

"Raul's temple is a week-long party of adult entertainment. His guests come from all over the world to scratch their itch." Tommy unconsciously scratched at his big belly and shrugged. "Some come for the show. Others come for the kinky party favors, but everybody loves the element of danger."

A faction of Clan society missed the "good old days" of war and conquest. They liked to indulge their more savage side with fighting matches. These bouts weren't Marquis of Queensbury rules. Rather the crowds insisted upon the bouts not stopping until the fighter had maimed or murdered his opponent. Tommy was right. They'd want the full show. Raul's arena would most likely be in Otherworld so the fighters could use their full powers. That was why Raul's parties were by invitation only.

"Raul opens a temporary portal in a different human city every year. The spectators get to feel rebellious for a week, and the Clan Council is none the wiser."

That explained Jin's waking up in Vegas. Seelie Descendants couldn't cross the borders of Otherworld because of their curse. Traveling from one estate to another required the use of the Pillars of Power within the Human Realm. Somehow Raul must have found a way to create temporary portals to his estate. These side doors would be highly illegal as was his fight club.

Tommy leaned forward, eyes sparkling over his puffy cheeks. "You've just entered the underground fighting circuit."

Jin met Tommy's gaze with a cold scowl. Men and women fighting for sport was a loathsome pastime. These racketeers had no idea of the brutality he'd endured growing up in the Seelie combat training schools of Otherworld. The thought of using violence for someone else's entertainment dishonored the children who hadn't made it to adulthood.

"And if I refuse the job?"

"You don't have a choice. Your capture has caused a big fucking stir. We have at least thirty sponsors who will pay large for the pleasure of getting their fighter in the same ring with the Hand of Justice." Tommy let the yellow-stained grin cross his face. "I have faith in you, buddy. I bet you'll take out five before one of the other fighters kills you."

"I'm flattered, Tommy. You always were a friend." Jin swept his eyes over the room again. Even the door was padded and it had no handle. No escape.

"Yeah, well, all bets are off if Viper wins the auction. She really wants you dead." Tommy shook his head. "You should be more careful where you put your pecker. I hear open warfare has begun between Clan leader hopefuls. Viper's here to get Raul's support. Zhao is still unconscious, and your mother is too refined to lower herself to our level."

"Mother wouldn't, would she?"

Lady Eleanor Wainwright made it a practice to distance herself from lower life forms like unconnected Descendants and her son. Jin shrugged off the years of resentment. His mother was concerned with maintaining the status quo. Not for the sake of balance among the clans, however. That was his father's obsession. Her fanatic mission was to ensure that the Wainwright Clan's influence over Normal governments continued.

The Wainwrights were fond of considering themselves sage guides to the hapless masses. They would ensure their advice was taken, whether or not that meant shoving their will down someone's throat. Advice not taken meant a loss of status. Eleanor would do anything to keep her clan's reputation intact, even if that meant letting her son die. The thought of her desperate efforts to cover up where Jin had actually met his end cheered him a little.

The strength had returned to Jin's muscles, and his head had lost most of its fuzziness. It was time to make an exit. Taking out a handful of Normals would be easy enough. Tommy would pose more of a challenge. He called on his gift. Nothing happened. The half-circle of Normal goons took a step back and pulled their weapons. Fear radiated about them. These men were ready to kill at the slightest suspicious movement. He eased his hands down to his sides.

"You got no juice here, Jin, not yet." Tommy burst into laughter. The hoarse guffaws were beginning to grate on Jin's nerves. "All these rooms have power suppression devices."

"Don't worry. I'll get my chance." Jin kept his angry glare on Tommy. "And I won't forget your part in this either."

"Such tough talk," purred a woman's voice from behind the far wall of pillows. The padded barrier dissolved in front of Jin and was replaced with a sheet of thick glass. Viper's heartless predator eyes were trained on him. Triumph swam in their depths.

In her human glamour, she was an elegant vision. Black tresses fell upon slender shoulders of smooth skin. Diamonds dripped from her ears and wrists. More of the precious stone were weaved into the fabric of her black gown. Time hadn't changed her features, but the light of madness had grown in her eyes. Viper took a long drag from her cigarette holder and gave Jin a self-satisfied smile.

Once upon a time, he'd craved her fire. Love was uncommon in the world of the Clans. Jin and Viper had never learned to care for each other in that respect, but he'd deluded himself into believing she was fond of him. Her betrayal the night Mai Ling had been murdered killed any affection he'd had for her. Now Jin only saw a hateful enemy. Pain had stayed his hand from slaying her that night, and now his heart longed for her death.

Beside her, standing head and shoulders above Viper, was the Russian brute who had ambushed and drugged Jin in Cozumel. His short platinum hair jutted in spiked chaos on his head. Shark-like eyes stared at Jin through the glass. The weight of his visual probe made Jin uneasy. He turned his full attention back on the one who clearly had the brains in their little duo.

"Viper," Jin said. Her name was bile coming from his lips. "I understand you're working with Raul now, sharing his climb from number four to number one."

She gave Jin a slow smile, reveling in his hatred. "Jealous, my love?"

"Hardly," he said, the bile rising further up his throat. "What about your new Unseelie friend? Is he helping you become Clan leader or has he made the bargain with someone else perhaps?"

"What's he talking about?" Tommy shook his finger at Viper.

"Don't be a fool! Unseelie in the Human Realm?" Viper laughed and glared hard at Jin. "The death of his sister and the attack on his father have addled his mind."

"Perhaps I'll just ask the dark elf when he arrives on Midsummer's Eve. The real question is where he'll be arriving. It can't be Vegas. There aren't many wooded glens here, now are there?" Jim waited for her answer, but was met with a stony glare.

The dark elf's entry point into the Human Realm was an important missing piece of information. In Otherworld, Midsummer's Eve was the same night each year. It was, however, celebrated on different days in the Human Realm, due to traditions and beliefs. The difference was a slight deviation of a day or two, but the Sidhe needed to time their entry at the most opportune moment. They used the beliefs of the humans to increase their powers.

Jin decided to take another tact. "Why bring me here? Why not have your lapdog kill me in Mexico?"

"I'm no one's lapdog!" the Russian barked.

"Have a care, Kazakov," Viper said, running her hand along his bare arm. "Jin is goading you. He's cleverer than he looks, no?"

Kazakov pulled his arm away from Viper's touch and stepped closer to the glass. "You brought me here to fight, Viper, not to parade around at your side."

"Like a lapdog," Jin said. He gave the Russian a condescending smirk. "You drugged me with a dart while hiding like a cowering dog in the bamboo. I can only assume you're too afraid to fight me directly."

"If you want a fight, let's go right now!" Kazakov's fist swelled to three times its natural size. The fist became stone. Kazakov had earth elemental powers. Those were deadly if the fighter could impact on his opponent. Jin forced his body to remain still. The key to victory against an earth elemental was to avoid physical contact. Kazakov hammered the massive piece of stone against the glass. The transparent wall buckled with a groan. He struck at the glass again and gave a growl when it began to crack.

Jin took a ready stance and waited. Very soon, Viper would understand just how much he hated her. He made ready to jump through the shattered glass and pin her to the ground before she could scream. His fingers would wrap around her throat, squeezing hard. The violent anticipation must have shown in his eyes. Viper grabbed Kazakov's arm, pulling at him.

"Keep your fighter under control, Viper," Tommy warned, drawing his gun. "You know the rules. Bidding for Jin takes place tonight. Nobody touches him before then. Those are Raul's orders."

Several Seelie Descendants came at Kazakov in a rush. Arms wrapped around the Russian, pulling him to the ground. Their warm brown skin made a sharp contrast with his pale flesh. One of them delivered a brutal kick in Kazakov's ribs, while another held a machete to his throat. Even the hot-tempered Russian wasn't stupid enough to resist the Vento guards.

Jin winced when he hacked a glob of blood onto the floor. The Vento Clan was brutal in its discipline. Jin took a step behind Tommy as one of the Vento threw a glare at him. Jin was very close to the top of their most-hated list. It wouldn't be a good idea to provoke them while Raul wasn't around.

"Careful, you fool!" Viper slapped at the man with the machete. "He has to fight tomorrow. Get up, Kazakov. Wait for me in my chambers."

The Russian pushed aside from Vento's guards and gave Jin a look filled with angry promise. He stormed away from the group, striking the wall opposite Jin's cage with his massive fist.

"He seems lovely," Jin told Viper. "You two make a cute couple."

"We've gone to a great deal of trouble and expense to have you found." Viper stroked the long black cigarette holder as she contemplated him. "The least you can do is ensure everyone has a good time watching you die. Kazakov will have the pleasure of fighting you. I'll see to that."

She turned away from him with a laugh. The padded wall appeared again, blocking Jin's view of her departing back. It was a Clan illusion. They were taking extra pains in keeping him inside his fluffy cage, ensuring he wouldn't escape from his cell. Jin would have to find his opportunity when they took him into the ring. It wouldn't be easy. He knew Viper. She'd be ready for an escape attempt.

"Crazy bitch. That Russian is a dangerous killer too. You always did have balls, Jin. Well, we'd better let you rest for the auction. Try to look presentable." Tommy nodded to his boys. "Help yourself to all the bottled water you can drink." He kicked the silver bucket toward Jin's feet. "Feel free to take a piss in that."

The padded walls parted and the goons disappeared. Jin circled the room slowly, testing the pads for any other openings. He finally came to a stop at the large tub filled with ice and bottles of water. Bending to his thirst, he opened one of the bottles and drank it with greedy gulps.

His mind turned back to the Vento Clan. They were ruthless, getting what they wanted by torturing Normals in the villages of Columbia. Raul encouraged this behavior as they expanded their operations. He wasn't a man content with his status in life. It was no secret he coveted Zhao Long's chair. Jin threw his empty water bottle against the wall. The Clan Council was watching Raul. Not even his hungry nature would make him risk Clan justice. No, Raul would remain patient, subversive until he had some sort of leverage or something to give him an edge.

Jin shook his head. The Clans could fight their own battles. He had his own skin to think of at the moment, and Tommy did have a point. If Jin had any hope of surviving his opponents, his body would have to be ready to fight. But he had no intention of giving Viper sport by beating another man to death in the ring. He would use his skill in order to escape. Jin began the slow movements of his Tai Chi routine. Sharp body. Sharp mind. He had to stay patient and wait for his moment.

Chapter Seven

Their limo followed the flow of traffic up the Strip. The neon lights lessened in luster as they drove past Circus Circus and the Stratosphere. A few turns later, they were on an industrial road parallel to busy train tracks. Away from the Strip, north, Gracie thought, the buildings were all square and plain. They were boxes the color of sand, melting into the desert. Competing with the constant swimming neon of the Strip and its themed casinos and dazzling crowds would be difficult. The rest of the city seemed content not to try.

"Not much of a view." Gracie kept her voice steady and hid her shaking hands under her purse. "Where are we going?"

"I'm taking you to my club. Don't worry—I'm certain you'll find it entertaining."

"I have my doubts." She shifted her eyes toward the expressionless faces of Raul's henchmen. Gawd, what a mess she was in! She'd never been in this much trouble before. Her dad had always been there to watch over her, but Dad wasn't here. She'd have to keep her head and get out of this mess on her own.

"Come now." Raul patted her on the knee. She yanked her leg out of his reach. He chuckled. "My little club moves all over the world. It's a favorite meeting place for Seelie Descendants from all Clans. We have so little sport in this age."

"Seelie Descendant? What is that?"

"How quaint you are." He shrugged and pulled out another cigar. "If it's true that you're unaffiliated, I warn you, life for a lone Descendant isn't safe, especially a pre-cog. You need the security a Clan can offer you."

"You called me a pre-cog before. What does that mean?"

The cigar paused inches away from Raul's lips. His bushy moustache twitched as he watched her. The intense gaze was that of a killer. She felt as if she was being measured, analyzed. This whole farce was about to blow up in her face after less than an hour. The voice had miscalculated. Raul Vento was no fool.

"I warned you not to ask foolish questions. You are meant to fit in with his entourage, not behave like a dimwitted child!"

Her bitter comeback came close to escaping. She clutched harder at her purse and tried to look a little more sophisticated. The jerk in her head did have a point. She was suppose to be playing the part of enchantress looking for a slightly illegal good time. He'd certainly picked the wrong person. She'd always been a horrible liar.

"What an amusing little game you are playing, Titania." Raul shrugged and shook his head as if she were purposely being thickheaded. "A pre-cog or precognitive is a Seelie Descendant, like you, who can see the future with one hundred percent accuracy. They are rare. That naturally makes your kind very valuable. In fact, I haven't heard of a new pre-cog coming into power since poor Jessica."

"What happened to her?" Gracie asked nervously.

"She was a very kind and beautiful young woman. I met her once at a party many, many years ago. She fell in love with the wrong man. The Wainwrights protect their property you see. They tried to sway Jessica to abandon her lover. Instead she ran away with him." Raul shook his head. "It was a great sadness when word came both lovers had been killed."

He returned from the past and scanned Gracie's face again. "That's why I'm surprised you aren't locked in a gilded cage somewhere. Jessica's death was a lesson for all of us."

They weren't going to lock her in a cage. She was nobody's property. If the irritating voice thought she'd roll over and let him win, he had a huge surprise coming. There had to be a way to break the hold he had on her. Once she found it, then she'd head back home and forget this whole nightmare.

"So what's your gift?"

Raul let a wide smile cross his face. His dark beard rustled against the aging skin. Then his face seemed to change. The tan skin faded and turned gray. It hardened with what looked like large pieces of armor. Raul nodded to one of his men and in a quick movement the man stabbed a knife at his cheek. The blade broke with a loud snap and fell to the floor.

Gracie sat staring at him, speechless. Her mind wouldn't believe what her eyes had just seen. His skin changing like that had to be a trick. A trick was the only logical explanation for what she'd just witnessed.

They pulled into an industrial park. The limo swayed and bucked over the bumpy asphalt. Abandoned warehouses stood rotting about them in the arid night. Gracie gripped the expensive leather seat. This didn't look like the location for a club. It was the perfect setting for one of those crime dramas on TV. She just hoped she didn't end up as a chalk outline on a warehouse floor.

The limo stopped in front of one of the old buildings in the back of the park. Raul patted her arm. "My club is best hidden. We wouldn't want any uninvited Normals in would we? You won't be disappointed, I promise."

He took Gracie by the arm and hustled her toward the shabby building. She wasn't a Vegas native, but Gracie had seen her share of rundown. This shack was the worst sort of place in the worst neighborhood.

"It doesn't look like much, but trust me, you'll love the inside."

The slate steel door flew open as they approached. A burly thug from every Mob movie ever made held open the door, waiting as they passed through. She thought she saw a flash of metal—a gun maybe?

Don't panic. As long as you stay with Raul, the others can't harm you.

Gracie clutched her fist tight, trying to stop her body from trembling. Raul and his men thought she was someone else, one of these Seelie Descendant people. She had to stay in character, pretend she belonged here. Maybe she could find a way out. Yeah right, if she could escape the building, how would she make it back to the Strip? No cab would come into this neighborhood in the middle of the night.

Inside, rich red, gold and purple fabric draped every inch of the lavishly decorated club. Golden columns circled an area littered with bistro tables. Several bartenders hurriedly poured drinks, shoving them into the hands of beautiful servers dressed in short saris. Red paper lanterns hung from the ceiling and glowed merrily over the crowd. Raul's club had the feel of a palatial Chinese restaurant mixed with the set of a Bollywood movie. Definitely more than one culture was represented here. Then again, iniquity had no recognized boundaries.

Expensively dressed men and women paraded their togs. Chanel, Giorgio Armani...the procession of fabulous evening gowns made Gracie's borrowed dress look like a gunny sack. Jewels sparkled from every perfectly shaped neck. The women made it a point to pass close to them. Their eyes swept over Gracie's outfit before giving Raul a polite smile. Rude behavior aside, these women were all sporting odd wrist tattoos. Gracie had just walked into a freaking cult. Perfect! Her first night in Vegas and she was already in with the lost weekend crowd.

"You're impressed, I can tell." Raul smiled. "I'll find something to entertain you here. Anything you wish. I've given my word. No harm will come to you. Remember that when the time comes for you to accept your mark."

Accept her mark? That couldn't be good. This guy was serious about keeping her in his fantasy group. She had to find a way out, and fast, before things got really serious. And she had to get that device away from Raul. He'd said he could find out about Gracie's family with the sample he'd taken. It sounded like something out of a science fiction movie, but what if it wasn't just crazy talk? What if Raul could find out her real identity with that device? She couldn't risk putting her family in danger. The voice would just have to do his own dirty work.

"Raul, my dear, dear friend!" A man with abnormally sharp features rushed over to greet them. He bowed low to Raul and threw his arms wide in exaggerated excitement. Orange tigers pranced across the crimson fabric of his Chinese-style robe. Jade rings decorated each of his long fingers. From his snow-white hair to the golden slippers on his feet, he was playing the part of flamboyant club manager.

"And who is this lovely creature, Raul? Your next ex-wife?"

Oh, he was hilarious. What a jerk. The man had an air of spiteful subservience, which could have been the role he was playing that evening—or maybe he actually worked for Raul. Either way, he didn't seem to like Raul very much. Resentment sprang into the man's eyes when he was sure Raul was looking the other way.

"No, Mr. Fong! This is Titania, my very special guest." Raul pulled the blinking little device with Gracie's sample out of his pocket and handed it to

Fong. "Put this in a safe place until we have an opportunity to have it analyzed."

Fong accepted it with a bow to Gracie. "It's a great honor to have you in our humble establishment." The smile he gave her seemed genuine, but didn't quite make it to his eyes.

"Raul." A stunning woman waltzed toward them. Her jewel bedazzled black floor-length gown swept about her in waves. It spread open at her neck plummeting to her belly button. Perfect skin rose gently against the fabric at her breast, barely covering what lay beneath. The slit up her legs didn't leave much to the imagination, either. A long cigarette holder dangled between her fingers bobbing in time to her quick pace.

"Viper, you look ravishing this evening." Raul took her hand and kissed it. The old villain's eyes followed the hem of her neckline to its soft end. As he turned her hand slightly, the tattoo upon her wrist was exposed.

Viper smiled slowly and cast her poisonous yellow eyes on Gracie. For a moment, Gracie imagined she saw the irises narrow into a snake-like slit. Then Viper's eyes looked human again. Her smile widened, exposing two abnormally long canines that glistened in the flashing lights. Gracie turned away from Viper and pretended to admire the gaudy decor of the club. It was official. She wasn't too crazy about the members of Raul's group.

"You've arrived just in time for the auction." Viper tugged playfully at Raul's collar. "I thought perhaps you had forgotten. You will like our show tonight, no?"

"Of course. I'm most anxious to attend! Come, Titania, I'll escort you to the entertainment." Raul took Gracie's arm again. He leaned close and whispered into her ear. "I ask that you remain in your human glamour this evening. If the others find out you're a pre-cog, we'd have trouble on our hands."

They walked through the other partygoers milling toward a set of plain, putty-colored doors. Gracie let her gaze drift over the crowd, hoping to catch sight of anyone who might be willing to help her. The faces remained cold. But as she drew nearer to the doors, a strange feeling began to build in her heart, a sadness and longing she'd never before experienced.

Raul kept his pace, pulling her into the steel door. One moment her nose was dangerously close to its surface and then the next she was floating in a vortex of warmth. Strong emotions, not necessarily just her own, wrapped about her with loving arms. It was like coming home to a place she'd never been. Then, abruptly, she was at the top of a carpeted ramp that led down into the bowels of the building.

Golden columns lined the red carpet. They rose to a dizzying height above her head to touch the ceiling of a glass dome. Two moons shone down upon their heads. That was impossible. The warehouse hadn't been that tall—and Gracie's brain wouldn't wrap around the sight of the twin moons hanging above her.

She took a step forward and felt a wave of dizziness. Stumbling on her high heels, Gracie fell against Raul. She heard Viper snicker behind them. Gracie looked up to snap at Viper, but stopped mid-growl. Viper wasn't Viper anymore. She had speckled scales under that beautiful dress. Raul stood beside Gracie, completely encased in the armor she'd seen on him earlier.

"Are you well?"

"Calm down. You've just gone through a portal and are at the Vento Estate in Otherworld. You are no longer in the Human Realm, Gracie. Now is the time to call upon all your courage. Your life depends upon it."

"Yeah." Gracie let Raul guide her along as she stared. Plush, stadium-style seats made a half-circle around a stage at the center of the room. It was surrounded by garish red curtains. Sturdy railings blocked the stage from the audience or vice versa.

Raul helped Gracie to a seat beside him in a large boxed area. He snapped his fingers. A server appeared with a porcelain jar. Raul poured Gracie a glass of what he explained was mead. She sniffed at the beverage and took a tentative sip. It was very sweet and tasted good. The stuff probably went down pretty easy, but drinking large amounts of alcohol would be a mistake. She had to keep her wits about her if she was going to get out of this mess in one piece.

Above their heads, acrobats in brightly colored costumes performed. Dressed in glittering feathers, they swung in the air. Gracie gasped with the rest of the audience as one acrobat made a daring leap only to be caught by his teammate. Their act was an amazing aerial ballet. She guessed from the loud cheers, this troupe was a favorite with the tattoo club.

"Wow, I can't see the wires or swings." She clapped, forgetting for a moment her predicament. The acrobats made one final swing, and suddenly bright-colored, tropical birds were flying over the stage. "I can't see the performers anymore. How did they do that?"

"Appear to turn into birds, you mean?" Viper gave her a condescending laugh. "They're Sylphs of course. It's like watching with a child, no?"

"Maybe they'll do a fly-by and sprinkle on your head, then we can all have a good laugh." Gracie held her furious gaze as Viper pounced toward her.

Raul caught Viper on the chest and pushed her back. "Don't think I won't put you both in a corner somewhere until you can behave like adults."

It wasn't often Gracie took an immediate dislike to someone, but Viper ranked right up there. And from the dagger looks she was giving Gracie, the feeling was mutual. It might be jealousy. Raul and Viper seemed awfully chummy. Then again, who cared? Gracie was going to escape their company the very second she could manage it—no matter what the voice did to her.

The stage lights flashed twice. Excited murmurs came in hushed tones around the arena as the crowd began to quiet down. Their faces—all eager for the show to begin—had transformed. None of them looked human anymore. Some were unbelievably beautiful as if they were drawings of creatures from fairy tales. Others were awkward and put together wrong. All of them turned their hungry attention to center stage when the lights dimmed and a single drum began to beat.

Fong twirled out on the stage, his red tiger robes catching the air. He beat the strange drum in slow, deliberate strikes with his hand, or rather his paw. He slowly lifted his face to the crowd. Gone were his human features. A tiger, wild and beautiful, stared back at them. His jaw opened wide to expose sharp teeth. Then against all logic, he began to speak.

"We Seelie Descendants are a powerful foe. The humans understood this millennia ago, in the age before treaties and the industrialization of man. They once feared and worshiped us. But those days are no more." Disdainful cries came from the audience. Fong lifted his hand. "Woe to the Descendant who may no longer feel the thrill of the hunt! Woe to the Descendant who can no longer satisfy her blood lust!"

Deafening roars rose up from the audience. They began stomping their feet, hooves and other appendages Gracie didn't recognize. She shrank in her chair against the impassioned rage. What had the voice been thinking? These creatures were ready to start trouble, and things weren't looking too good for the sole human in a room full of pissed-off beasts with big teeth.

"As we join together in celebrating Midsummer, let us honor times gone by in the old ways. My lords and ladies, I bid you welcome to the Temple of Forbidden Pleasures! Let me introduce for your delight a new fighter to our club. The Temple bids welcome to Banan!"

A man walked out on stage from the shadowy recesses of the red curtain. He was neon yellow from head to toe with no visible muscle she could see. Only his eyes differed. They were awkwardly large and orange colored. Dressed only in a metallic g-string Speedo, he strutted on stage and raised his fists, growling at the audience. Several of the Descendants began waving white little cards in the air.

"What are they doing?"

"Those are bidding cards," Raul told her. "Current bid is fifty-thousand dollars American."

"You mean people are buying these men?"

"Don't be obtuse. They belong to their Clan. These people are here to bet on the fights. Only the very powerful and very rich may sponsor a fighter." Viper gave her a condescending sneer. "I sponsor two."

"I suppose some people do have to compensate for their shortcomings," Gracie shot back and earned another murderous glare.

"Are you interested in wagering on him? No?" Raul shrugged. "Perhaps another fighter will suit your tastes. We have many to choose from."

Raul wasn't exaggerating. Men and women strutted across the stage, showing off their muscles under multi-color and multi-textured skin. The crowd cheered or booed the fighters as they made their wagers. Gracie gripped at the glass of mead and drank a deep gulp. She was growing impatient, sitting here and watching this parade of flesh waltz by. And no way would she watch the fights either. It had always upset her when Dad and Ape ranted at their favorite fighters on TV. Seeing creatures beat each other live would be worse.

A massive man with platinum blond hair and bulging muscles swaggered out to the stage. He waved his arms until the crowd cheered louder. Viper lifted her chin and returned blondie's bow with a princess's nod. The fighter turned his eyes to Gracie and stared blatantly at her chest. She brought her right hand slowly up along the line of her breast and then jutted her middle finger in the salute position. The arrogant smile dropped from his face and he twisted away. Jerk.

"Let me guess. He's your fighter. Why am I not surprised?" Gracie rolled her eyes at Viper when the bulky blond disappeared behind the curtain.

Shouts came from backstage. Then the crowd gave a collective gasp when an unconscious Vento henchman flew through the curtain, ripping the fabric. Three more henchmen struggled to pull a man in chains onto the stage. Their prisoner looked human. He was dressed in filthy, loose-fitting trousers, almost like a martial arts uniform. His shaggy black hair fell in straight strands across his face. The guards managed to hold his restraints, but they gave him plenty of distance.

"Damn it! What is he doing here?"

"Who is he," she whispered. He must be someone very dangerous if the voice was frightened of him.

"He's the fly in my ointment! Bloody Viper and her games."

"And now for the highlight of the evening," Fong cried, waving his arms with great flourish toward the prisoner. "I give you a fighter who needs no introduction!"

The room exploded with cheers and chanting. Gracie couldn't make out what they were saying, but their tone suggested violence for the prisoner. They began to stomp their feet again, waving the bidding cards above their heads like mad. Several members of the audience grew impatient and started shouting their bids.

Gracie looked across the arena at the hunger on their faces. These weren't bored rich people looking for something exotic on their vacation in Vegas. They appeared dangerous, and they definitely wanted the man on the stage. She focused her attention back on the prisoner. He had lifted his gaze to regard the audience. She saw defiance on his face that warned he wouldn't be easy to master.

"The bid is up to five-hundred-thousand American already!" Raul hugged Viper.

"This is the infamous conspirator?" The fighter named Banan roared above the crowd. "He doesn't look like so much to me."

Banan marched away from the other fighters standing to the side of the stage. Taking huge breaths that made his neon yellow body bulge like a toad, he opened his mouth wide. Then he did something that challenged Gracie's view of reality. Banan spit out a long tongue with two sharp looking blades on its tip. The prisoner shook his head when the sharp points landed just short of his feet.

Banan, enraged by the prisoner's dismissiveness and the crowd's laughter, rushed forward. He came too close. In a lightening move, the prisoner struck at his attacker with a well-placed foot. It happened so fast the crowd took a moment to realize Banan was down with a dislocated knee. The crowd roared its pleasure.

"Death! Death! Death!" they demanded.

Banan held his hands up to the prisoner as if he were silently pleading. He looked terrified. Though he'd gone at the man like an obnoxious twerp, Gracie was worried for him too. She held her breath with the rest of the crowd, waiting to see if the dangerous man in chains would stomp the life out of his attacker.

The crowd issued a great groan of disappointment when the prisoner shook his head and stood away. He wasn't going to kill Banan. As a stranger in their strange world, Gracie didn't understand very many things. This act of compassion was perhaps the only thing she did understand about tonight.

One of the guard swung his night stick at the prisoner's stomach. He sunk to his knee with an angry groan. As the guards moved to circle about him, their captive pulled at his chains, striking out again with his feet. His hands yanked desperately at the collar around his neck. It looked painful.

"He doesn't look like he wants to be here, Raul!" Her own anger and disgust rose up in her throat.

"He'll fight," Viper said, smiling her snake-like grin. "He has no choice."

As the guards stood back, Gracie saw the man more clearly. Sharp cheek bones and an aquiline nose accentuated startling green eyes. He had a small scar along his jawline and a few scars on his torso. The nastiest one appeared to be a fresh wound across his rib cage.

His gaze finally rested on Viper. The loathing Gracie saw in his eyes gave her a jolt of hope. Her dad frequently quoted a Chinese proverb: "The enemy of my enemy is my friend."

Then his gaze fell on her. She began to tingle as the power raced up her spine.

"No! Turn away from him!"

The warning came too late. Her fear intensified until she struggled to breathe. Oh God, not now! The arena disappeared and Gracie found herself in a forest. The trees were taller than any she'd ever seen. Forest ferns covered the ground and surrounded their trail as he and she ran. She was afraid. Someone was chasing them. A warm hand squeezed hers as the prisoner pulled Gracie to a stop. He gently touched her cheek and then pulled her in for a long kiss. Her heart was breaking as he stood away and turned to leave.

"Jin, be careful!" When she blinked again, the arena was back. She was leaning over the railing with her hand held out toward him. The room was completely silent. Everyone was looking at her as if she were a wounded rabbit in a room full of rabid dogs.

"I knew there was something off about her!" Viper hissed and lifted a weapon, waving it toward Gracie. "I say we kill her now!"

Raul knocked the weapon out of Viper's grip with his arm. "That is not your decision. Stand down or you and I will have a problem." He gripped Gracie roughly by the shoulders. "How is it that you know Jin, Titania? Tell me right now! No more games."

"I've never seen him before," Gracie told him. She tried not to flinch as he raised his hand to slap her.

He let it drop down as others began to approach them. "Why is it that I don't believe you?"

"She's ruining everything!" Viper stormed. "I want Jin and will have him!"

"Why don't you stick that roach where the sun don't shine?" Gracie snapped.

"That's enough!" Raul turned to Fong who had popped his head out of the curtain. "Take silent bids for Jin. He fights tomorrow. And as for the rest of you, Titania is mine. Do not insult the hospitality of my home by trying to take her from me."

"Raul, you stupid fool!" Viper shot back and stormed out of the arena.

"This entire affair couldn't have happened more to my liking if I'd hired someone to arrange it!" The voice's laughter echoed in the recesses of Gracie's frightened mind. *"It appears for once Jin has been a help to me rather than a hindrance!"*

Gracie looked down at the stage. Jin was staring at her. His face was unreadable. Wonderful. She hoped she hadn't made an enemy of him.

"Come, Titania. You'll be taken to a safe location, and tomorrow we will see who you really are." Raul took her by the arm and pulled her out of the dining room. Tomorrow. That gave her tonight to find the device while everyone else was busy debauching.

Gracie tried to pay close attention as they walked down the hallway. This didn't look like an empty warehouse. Warm colors on plush walls had the feel of a home. A gentle breeze upon the air brought with it the smells of the ocean. This place was nowhere near Las Vegas.

Raul stopped at a door and pushed it open. A bedroom suite decorated in rich Spanish design wasn't what she'd been expecting. Large windows overlooked an ocean with two moons shining over its waves. This was like a five star hotel. She wished she could enjoy it.

"I must see to my guests by the laws of hospitality. You'll be safe in here until I've finished." His severe face leaned over her own. "Think very hard about answering my questions. I'll have the truth no matter the cost to you."

"I've told you! I don't know that man."

"A ridiculous fiction! You'll change your mind after a few minutes of my questioning, Titania. I hate to ruin that pretty face." Raul ran a finger up her arm and then chuckled when she backed away from him. He left her, pulling the door shut behind. The lock clicked home with a vicious finality.

Gracie plopped down on the oversized bed with a huge huff and fell back onto its feathered mattress. She was trapped in a strange world with no clue how to escape. Tears of frustration rolled down her temples and into her hair. She had to get the device with her DNA sample or whatever it was back from Fong before he could analyze her information. They'd find out about Dad and use him to force her into joining their little freak show. Gawd, she'd really screwed up this time. She should have listened to her father and been more careful. But now he was in danger too.

Chapter Eight

The chain snapped taut with a loud clink. Choking, Jin gripped the collar around his neck. His body was pulled backward forcibly, sending him staggering off the stage. Jin kept his eyes on the pre-cog. He didn't recognize her, but then again he wasn't exactly welcome among the Clans. Skin sun-kissed and smooth accented the athletic curves under her gold-beaded dress. She'd apparently tried to disguise herself by staying in her human glamour. But why? Had someone sent her to help him escape? Or did she have another reason to come on her own? Intriguing.

Titania, as he had overheard she was called, must be well connected. She was giving Viper heartburn without any concern for the ramifications. That must mean her handler was more powerful than Viper. Or Titania was simply an inexperienced fool. Either way, her handler would be in trouble with their Clan leader for leaving such a powerful pre-cog without protection.

That she had walked into one of Raul's parties alone was very unusual. Pre-cogs were rare. Jin had met only one, and that one, a male, remained under the watchful eye of Jin's mother at Wainwright Clan headquarters in London. She didn't often let her pet pre-cog out of his cage. Loathing crawled its way up Jin's spine whenever he thought of Druid. The bald-headed bastard. That unnerving third eye had tried many times to read and manipulate Jin without success. Their interactions constituted a mystery they both shared, along with a mutual and intense dislike of each other.

Jin had been surprised Titania had been able to do what the Druid could not - use her power on Jin. It was a puzzle for another day. When a pre-cog has a vision about you, it was best to pay attention. They were never wrong. His list of priorities was getting larger. Revenge upon Viper and escaping the temple alive had a new, competing priority.

He had to speak with that pre-cog and convince her to tell him about the vision he'd seen in her eyes. Her attempt to reach him had failed. As Raul gripped her arm and pulled her out of the arena, she'd given Jin one last look with those pleading blue eyes. Fear was in them. His attention had been riveted upon her until his view was obscured by the curtains hiding the backstage area.

An impatient club smacked into his ribs. Reeling away from the painful blow, Jin let out a growl. The forceful love tap hadn't broken anything. It did broadcast as much payback as his guards were willing to deliver. He didn't share their sentiment for the unlucky men he'd incapacitated on the stage. Maybe they'd think twice about putting a chain around another man's neck in the future. Life lessons learned.

"Stop stalling. Time to go back to your cage." His attacker lifted the club again in warning.

"Careful, you moron! Jin here belongs to Raul. Besides, I have money riding on him." Tommy put his thumbs under his suspenders and shook his head. "You are one lucky bastard. I saw that blonde waving her beads at you."

The third guard chimed in. "How do you figure this scrawny thing has two beautiful women after him?"

"I'm a good listener."

Tommy chuckled and pushed his prisoner down the hall. "Jin here has got what you'd call a taste for trouble."

On cue, Viper swept down on them like an ill wind. Three members of the Girard Clan stood behind her in a half-moon. Jin recognized them. Viper had brought some serious firepower with her. Perrin, strangely absent the night of the coup and the eldest of the three, had been one of Monsieur Girard's trusted body guards. Twin gingers, Harbin and Henri, stood beside him. They were much younger, but their killing skills were already well known among the Clans.

"Stand away from him, you idiots." Viper's voice was shaken, enraged. There was no reasoning with her while she was this angry. She waved a finger over her shoulder to her Clansmen. "Take him."

"Sorry, Viper," Tommy said, bringing his own power up. "You heard what Raul said. Jin goes back to the Human Realm for safekeeping."

"He can have Jin's body when I'm done."

Viper nodded. Her three Clansmen swept forward. Harbin and Henri moved as one, passing through Jin's guard with incredible speed. The whisk of their blades against air and flesh sounded like a razor scraping on leather. Streams of coppery blood fell onto the floor. Tommy and his friends hadn't had time to utter a cry or understand they were about to die.

Jin lifted up his fallen chain, ready to use it as a weapon. A titanium quill pounded in the ground at his feet. Perrin kept his open palm aimed at Jin in warning. The tip of a quill poked out of his flesh, ready to fly into Jin's body. Jin lifted his eyes to the unsmiling face of a traitor. He'd tried to kill Jin the night of the coup. Perrin had stood aside and let his honor die along with his Clan leader.

Viper smiled as Tommy's severed head rolled inches away from her foot. "Raul's food budget has just been drastically reduced, no?"

"He won't like you killing his hired help. Or taking me."

"Raul can be managed." She kicked the head away and brought her full attention back to Jin. "Your blond pre-cog lover has forced my hand. Make no mistake. I will risk anything to see you dead."

"You're the one who is mistaken. I've never seen that pre-cog before." Jin stared defiantly at Viper.

"Are you trying to protect her? You'll fail just as you failed to protect Mai Ling."

She pulled out a golden chain with a small diamond, heart-shaped pendant, the birthday gift Jin had given Mai Ling the night she'd died. Feeling the heart-wrenching loss of his sister ripped open the wound again. Hatred for Viper brought a fresh wave of fury against the wall of his calm. He struggled with his chains in his eagerness to get at her, but the ginger twins had a tight grip on them. Viper laughed and licked her fangs with the tip of her tongue.

"I thought the point of this little party was for your pleasure. Having me beaten to death on stage, now that would be a spectacle." Jin stopped struggling. It was a wasted gesture. "You were always impatient. These men with you, what did you promise them for their help? Do they receive riches and power once you're named Girard Clan leader? I've heard the infighting isn't going in your favor. Pity that."

"We can all thank your father for delaying the inevitable." Viper's smile disappeared. "The Council claims we have no clear heir to the Girard Clan. They won't make a decision on a new Clan leader until Zhao Long wakes. Foolish. The longer our Clan goes without a new leader, the more likely my takeover. It's inevitable."

"Some may not see it that way," taunted Jin.

The tips of her fangs parted frowning lips. "Why? You think because I'm a bastard female child, my sire had the right to shun me and ignore my natural talents for leadership?"

"No, I think it's because you're insane."

The strike to his ribcage came without warning. Then Perrin ground a fist in his palm, advising Jin to mind his manners. Viper must have promised him something other than money. Perhaps the fool believed she would make him her consort? Clearly Perrin had forgotten her brother's fate.

"I managed to convince the tribunal Renee acted alone. Any part I may have had in the affair was due to the blind affection a sister has for her brother."

Her shoulders tensed as she hesitated. "The Zhao Clan still rejects my innocence. Qing's pride had to be satisfied, and he insisted I be punished." Viper took off the diamond clip earrings. Both ear lobes were missing. The job hadn't been done neatly.

"The Council's priority is to keep the peace. As long as Raul Vento is around to lead, he can help stabilize the flailing Girard Clan. It's a dangerous time," Viper added.

"And what is Raul's reward?" Jin asked blandly.

"Ah, the price for Raul's cooperation is you upon the open market. What a bad boy you are, Jin, stealing a shipment of emeralds from the Vento Clan." Viper laughed and came closer.

Oh, yes. "That was an honest mistake. I didn't know I was stealing emeralds from Vento operatives." Jin shrugged at his chains. "They really shouldn't have paraded around such a tantalizing treasure."

"Don't expect the Zhao Clan to come to your rescue this time, my love. Qing has agreed not to intervene or help you in any way," she said, running a finger along Jin's chest.

He kept his features calm, betraying nothing. Qing turning against him wasn't the shock she'd hoped. He and Qing had never gotten along. His brother's brutality toward his lover, however, did come as a mild surprise. Qing wasn't one to disregard potential allies or enemies.

"We'll continue our conversation later on. I have to make an appearance at the festivities tonight. That pre-cog bitch is next on my list. Maybe you'll die together, no? Who can say?" Viper turned to her lackey holding Jin's chain. "Get rid of the bodies and hide Jin."

That pre-cog apparently had shaken up Viper's world. Clearly, this Titania wasn't a member of the Girard Clan, unless she was on the side that opposed Viper. She didn't seem fond of Raul either, and the Zhao Clan wasn't a good fit for an outspoken woman. That left the Wainwright Clan, his mother's people. Perhaps Jin had some hope of escape after all. He risked a smile as Viper stormed off. Oh yes, he would have to meet this pre-cog who so haphazardly pissed off the deadliest assassin in the Girard Clan. He was left with only one minor problem. He had to lose his escort.

Perrin followed Viper down the hall, leaving behind the ginger twins. With slicked-back hair and matching goatees, they circled Jin like hyenas tormenting their prey. Henri gripped Jin's neck chain and gave it a brutal tug. Jin stumbled forward. Both of his tormentors laughed as they watched him choke.

"Come along, *petit chien*," Henri said. "You have no bite now."

Jin fell to one knee and put his tethered wrists to his throat. He dug in with his bare feet. Pulling against the young man's tugging, he shortened the chain, link by link. If he could come within striking distance, they'd see this stray dog still had teeth.

A practiced fist thrust into Jin's kidney with a powerful blow. He sank back down to his knees, gagging at the stale air. Harbin slapped the back of his brother's head and grabbed Jin's chain. He laced it around one of the pillars.

"You aren't leaving me to deal with these bodies, you lazy shit." Harbin shoved at his twin, and they began to drag Tommy's body inside one of the cells. Harbin, the smarter of the two, reappeared with the keys to Jin's chains swinging on his finger. His twin, Henri, continued to struggle with another body. They weren't used to doing the heavy work. When they were done, Harbin came to unwrap Jin's chain.

"Do both of us a favor and take these chains off." Jin lifted up his wrists and clutched at the heavy collar. "Come now. In my condition I don't stand a chance against the two of you."

"Did you hear a dog barking?" Henri snickered and came to join them. "Do you think we're foolish enough to let you free, *petit chien*? I welcome you to try and escape. If you were as good as they say, I don't think you would have lost to a stump like Kazakov."

Henri pressed a powered-up hand against Jin's temple while Harbin increased the tightness of the collar. The harsh metal cut into Jin's skin. He gagged, choking as the metal squeezed. A small clink of hope came as spots began to dance before Jin's eyes. Keys jingled as they shifted in Harbin's pocket. Jin fought his urgent need for air and let his bound hands drop close to the man's side. Expert fingers lifted the keys out of the pocket and palmed them.

"Speak again, and the collar will tighten, *petit chien*. Come, Viper wants you safe until she can kill you." That set the two musclemen laughing again.

Jin walked silently between them, waiting for his opportunity. Frustration strained his patience with each tug of the chain. He'd make them eat every last link. Then would come Viper's turn. He gripped the keys tightly in his clenched fist until the metal began cutting into the skin.

They rounded an unadorned corner into the darkened recesses of an empty corridor. The click of the lock bursting loose from his wrists echoed against bare walls as the heavy chains fell. Jin tugged at the collar, but it wouldn't release. It appeared Viper didn't trust her lackeys with the key. Using what speed he had, Jin rolled forward into the shadows. He turned to see his two jailers staring at each other in shock amid the abandoned chains.

Using their momentary confusion, Jin struck. He banged their foreheads together with a vicious growl of triumph. He pounced on the cheekier of the two first, striking Henri on the back of the head and knocking him unconscious. Jin wasn't gentle with his remaining tormentor. He sank a heel deep in Harbin's stomach and then swung his other heel in a roundhouse kick to the chin. The redhead snapped backward and fell across the unconscious form of his twin.

Jin doubled back the way they had come, stopping just before the curtains. The fighters' portal to the human realm remained open and unguarded. Raul wouldn't want to risk any of the fighters being discovered on his property in Otherworld. A quick escape was essential. And sabotage between sponsors was a possibility. Poisoning another sponsor's fighter or making him disappear until after the match wasn't unheard of.

Jin made a note of his location and set off to explore. The Vento Clan Estate was situated on the warm shores of the sea. Few were invited to enjoy the mansion's luxurious beaches during the year. Midsummer was a special time, a time when Raul swung his doors open wide for his select guests. His hospitality and generosity during this one week of the year was well known. Every room was decorated to cater to his guests' comfort. Even the beaches were groomed for the occasion.

A faint whiff of the briny air from an air vent brushed against Jin's face. Grinning, he'd just found his private highway around the mansion. It was time he turned the tables on Viper. He didn't have much time before his real host realized he was missing. Soon the halls would fill with bloodthirsty fight enthusiasts wanting his head. It would take surprise and cunning to beat Viper at her own game. Jin had to take advantage of these few quiet moments to scope out the building.

He pushed the ornate metal screen aside and shimmied his body into the air vent. It was cramped and filthy, but passable. Thin plaster over ancient wood creaked angrily. It hadn't been designed to hold a man's weight. He'd have to keep moving or risk falling through into a room.

The majority of the Vento mansion was a ground-level structure offering open doorways out into the gardens or the sands of the beach. Dungeons far under the main floor were where Raul kept his unlucky prisoners. Jin and the other fighters had been temporarily kept in freshly renovated cells, but he could still smell the deaths of those who came before him. He'd have to climb out of hell and then return again.

Motivated, he began his ascent. Darkness was a suffocating reminder he could be trapped under rubble or fall to his death. He kept his breath even, choking down the feeling of claustrophobia until he came to a junction. The sounds of laughter and silver tapping on china drew him to the right. If Raul and Fong stayed true to the laws of hospitality, they'd host a feast for their guests. Then the private parties would begin. The halls and public rooms would be deserted, a perfect time to quietly set his trap. Of course, his work would be much easier without this damn power-suppressing collar around his neck. He scratched at his irritated skin under the thin metal band.

Following the smell of food, he crawled toward a small box of light. Several heads bent in polite conversation a few feet beneath him. His passing wouldn't go unnoticed, if he was even able to squeeze through the hole. Stray bits of light found their way down to him from a shaft above his head.

Continuing his climb, he found the large ventilation screen hanging over the mansion's dining room. A massive wall of windows overlooked the sea. It was an impressive view. Blue and terra cotta mosaics lined the sandstone room. Golden plates filled with exotic food came out in streams. Raul spared no expense for his guests.

Their host sat at the main table, speaking low with Fong. Viper sat on his other side, sipping her drink. She seemed in a merry mood and very pleased with herself. The pretty pre-cog wasn't with them.

Several excited conversations centered around the fighters. It was obscene how excited the crowd was to see their fellow Clansmen kill each other. Well, they were about to get a show. It would take less than a minute. With or without his gift, he'd pounce on Viper and part her head from her shoulders. That was how you killed a snake.

He pried open the vent cover, carefully pulling it inward. The nearest handhold, a sea-blue drape hanging behind the main table, was at least five feet away. His power would have made the jump simple, but he was restricted by the collar. As a youth training with his teachers, Jin had been stripped of his powers for the better part of a year. His masters had prepared him to face any circumstance with or without his power. They'd shown wisdom on that occasion, and he was grateful now. Bracing his feet against the lip of the vent, he pushed off and sailed over their heads. His hands eagerly gripped at the curtain. Nobody seemed to notice the acrobatics above them.

After carefully sliding downward, he sank to the floor in a low crouch. Parting the fabric, he kneeled behind his host and captor. It was time at last for him to get his revenge upon Viper. He moved closer to her chair. An arm's length of open floor separated him from her stiff back. His fingers longed to feel sweaty skin and the pulsing of blood in treacherous veins as he squeezed the life from her body.

The cold tip of a titanium quill touched at his bare ear lobe.

"Viper wants a private word with you," Perrin whispered. "Don't be a rude bastard."

Jin's gut folded in upon itself with nauseating disappointment. He'd been so close! So close to ending the nightmares and painful memories of Mai Ling's death! Forcing the calm to come to him once more, he murmured quietly, "We wouldn't want to disappoint her, now would we?"

Chapter Nine

"*W*himpering *like a little girl isn't helping. Pull yourself together.*"

The sob choked in Gracie's throat. She sat up with an indignant growl. He actually had the brass balls to pretend this was her fault! Gawd, she'd never loathed anyone more in her whole life. This creep had ambushed her in a closet, and then he'd taken control of her. She'd tried to fight him, but her fear had been her worst enemy. Now she didn't give a damn. Raul was going to kill her, and she'd make sure this bastard went down too.

"You're the one who got me into this mess! Raul is going to torture me or something, and guess what, I'm going to talk." The sharp stab of pain pierced her mind with the violence of a brutal attack. She screamed and clutched her head. "I hope Raul finds you and kills you! I'm telling him everything I know."

"*I don't think you will, my dear, not if you want to keep your father safe.*" The smug laugh bounced against her last nerve. "*That's right. I know who Daddy is and where your family can be found. Raul would forgive anything for that information.*"

She stopped struggling. Of course he knew about her dad. He probably knew everything else about her whole life. This creep would have had to follow her for months before abducting her. He'd known about

Kay and the Rusty Grotto. He'd used Kay without remorse to get at Gracie. And Dad? What would he do to Dad?

"I can't just sit here and wait for Raul to come back."

"Do you honestly believe I'd trust you to keep up the charade for long? This is going according to my plan. Though it would please me to see you humbled a bit, you are of no use to me broken. I will do that myself when we next meet face to face." The uncomfortable pause was full of horrible promise. *"I'll guide you to Fong's chambers. His safe is there. You'll find the device inside."*

She pushed off the bed and kneeled down by the thick, wooden door. The lock looked ancient, like something out of an old movie. She tugged at the handle. Old or not, it wasn't giving an inch. The lock might have pins inside. If she'd wiggle them with some kind of metal tool, maybe it would unlock? It worked on television.

"What are you doing? Must you be stupid? Get up and go to the armoire. Run your fingers behind it. No, fool! To the left side."

Her fingers touched adhesive tape. She tugged it free. A small, tightly wrapped paper bundle fell into her hand. The tape had yellowed with age, as if it had been stuck there for maybe a year or more. She unwrapped the bundle it had been holding. A key was inside.

"Wait. How did you know this key would be here?"

"I put it there of course. Now hurry."

"How did you know I would be here in this room at this moment?" The tickle of a memory touched her mind and vanished just as quickly. "You're a pre-cog too."

"Let's discuss it with Raul when he returns, shall we?"

Jerk. She'd have to trust him. What choice did she have? She stuck her head out into the hall. No sign of stragglers or guards. She crept through the doorway, lingering to listen for footsteps. If she went back in the direction they'd come from, she might run into some of the wait staff or partygoers. They might not help her escape. Gawd, they might just turn her in to Raul or worse. The other, unexplored direction might be her better bet. Of course, it might lead her deeper into the mansion.

A door closed nearby. Its echo sent Gracie ducking back into her room in a rush. She kept her own door open a tiny crack. Viper tiptoed down the hall. Well, that was interesting. It appeared Viper was sneaking around the temple without permission too.

"What is she up to?"

Gracie slipped off her high heels and threw them on the bed. Waiting until Viper passed by, she crept out after her. The voice didn't object. Viper slid down the hall on silent feet, not making a sound. Gracie froze again when Viper hesitated. She held her breath, hoping Viper couldn't hear the whisk of beads every time she moved her damn legs. Her quarry went on again, faster now. Gracie hurried after her. Viper stopped at one of the doors. She twisted suddenly toward Gracie. Pushing her body flat against the wall, Gracie rested her head against its painted surface. She listened for any signs that Viper had caught sight of her.

"There's something behind that door blocking my power." The voice hesitated. *"Viper is playing one of her games again. I don't like it, but I must know. Follow her."*

Gracie crept quickly to the door and put her ear against the wood. Either Viper was being very quiet or nobody was in the room. She turned the knob slowly and pulled open the door. The portal's magic sucked her in without warning. Any sign of the hall or her suite was gone. A large library lined with old books and comfortable-looking chairs replaced them. Gracie staggered forward against a shelf to steady her body.

"You've gone through a hidden portal. We're still in the Vento mansion, but it appears someone has taken us to the family's private living quarters. Raul will be very unhappy."

One of the chairs swiveled slowly around to face her. A man with shaggy strawberry hair sat quietly looking at her while the fingers of his right hand touched thoughtfully at his cheek. He wasn't much to look at, but something about him drew Gracie's attention. His pale gray eyes held a weight of knowledge in them that unnerved her.

"Run! He's much too dangerous! Hurry, Gracie, you must escape."

She tried to move away from the man, but her body seemed frozen in place. Her mind began to panic with a familiar terror. She felt almost as if she had been through this nightmare before. The man gestured with a single finger. Gracie moved toward him, unable to stop herself. Terror struggled for attention, but the longer she stared at the man, the more her resistance faded.

"You're Raul's lovely pre-cog friend. How careless of him to let you roam about on your own for anyone to take." The man's French accent washed over her, drawing Gracie closer. He rested a fingertip on her exposed arm. The simple touch sent shock waves down her body. She couldn't move. She couldn't breathe. His hypnotic gaze was all she could see.

"I find your innocence intoxicating. I shall have you for my own, no matter what Raul says." His hands drifted down her hip. "I am called Puppet Master. Let me into your mind completely. You must not be afraid to live, to experience the pleasures of life. I can show these to you."

An image of shackles burned against her consciousness. It gave her the strength to shout, "No!"

"Come now. I'm a member of the Girard Clan, not a monster as some of the rumors say. I can help you release your inhibitions."

The pressure of his presence pushed harder on her mind. This time it was stronger, trying to dominate. His gray eyes opened wide with surprise. He laughed.

"Someone has put a block on your mind. Interesting. And what is this?" he said, closing his eyes. "Well, well! It's my old rival hiding in your mind already. What game are you playing this time?"

"She's mine!" The voice's presence grew stronger in Gracie's mind, pulsing with anger. *"I warn you,*

Puppet Master. Do not interfere. I would be doing the world a favor ridding it of a depraved insect like you."

"You call me the insect? I walk about as I please. Does your good lady know you're off leash?" Puppet Master laughed as they both felt the voice's fury in Gracie's mind. "I've been longing to test my metal against you, old man. Let us see who wins this prize."

The Puppet Master's repulsive presence pressed harder still. Gracie resisted his invasion, pushing back in desperate mental shoves. She fell to the ground, screaming as both invaders twisted and pulled at her mind. Suddenly, something popped inside of her. Power, raw and uncontrolled, burst out of her like a flood. It knocked both intruders out of her mind. Puppet Master flew across the room, his body striking the bookshelves and sending them tumbling to the floor.

Gracie clutched at her head. The pain was terrible! Hot tears streamed down her burning cheeks. Her throat constricted with silent screams. She collapsed in on herself, hopelessly searching for comfort. Then the blue haze fell across her sight. Incoherent images streaked past her mind. A woman with kind eyes, her mother. Dad rocking her to sleep in his arms, weeping. She wondered why. Grief. The word whispered against her ears. Then she saw a bald man in gray, grabbing Gracie's face. His blue eyes were pulsing with incredible power. He shared her ability.

Abruptly, the foggy images dissolved and she Saw Puppet Master. His dead body sprawled broken on a carpeted floor. One eye was missing. Good riddance.

She knew she Saw him for what he was, a sick little man who enslaved others for his own sexual needs. Gracie opened her eyes and was back in the present. Puppet Master's strange control over her was gone.

"You sick creep!" She kicked him in the stomach as he lay trying to recover from her power. "I Saw your future. You're going to die soon."

Then she hurried away from him, running wildly through the chairs. Even now, she could still feel his slimy thoughts in her brain. She kept her eyes in desperate contact with the wall, hoping to find another exit out of the library. She had to get away from him and the other one, the first bastard who had gotten her into this mess in the first place! She hoped he was feeling as much pain as she was right then. But at the same time an uncomfortable thought struck her. He'd been her guide in this strange world. Now she was here on her own.

All at once, her fingers found salvation. Cool metal extended out from a wooden door to welcome her inside. She squeezed the knob and turned it. Power grasped her body, pulling hard. Another portal! She tumbled into a dimly lit room with candles lining black velvet walls. Her bare foot kicked the door closed with a desperate shove. This room was quiet at least.

She just needed a moment to calm down. Her head was pounding. Wetness dripped out of her nose. She wiped her hand across her face. Blood. Leaning against a velvet wall, she took deep breaths to calm her shattered nerves. The mental battle between her two captors had taken a harsh toll inside.

Still shaken, Gracie didn't notice the intense, predatory eyes watching her until she was inches away from his body. Chains rattled and pulled taut as he reached for her. She jumped back with a yowl. The prisoner, Jin, had been tied spread eagle to the wall. Dark strands of shaggy hair whipped forward as he lifted his chin for a better look at her. She noted a sharpness to his facial features that suggested he too was one of these Seelie Descendants. Startling green eyes blazed in fury as he glared directly into her gaze. Apparently, he didn't like being stared at and yanked against his restraints again.

"You scared me to death! I don't want to be scared anymore."

She remembered the vision she'd had of him in the forest. He had kissed her. Was it a vision or was it now? Her head hurt. She rested her forehead against his bare chest and wrapped her arms around his waist. Jin's body stopped struggling. He remained very still. Closing her eyes, she let the pain subside as his breath slowed.

Suddenly, and without its usual warning, her gift came to her. Black satin and diamonds. That ridiculous cigarette holder. "Gawd! Viper's coming."

Strange the vision hadn't crippled her this time. Her head still ached from the epic battle, yet she felt as if her mind was clear for the first time. She twirled around to get a better look at their surroundings. She noticed a few chairs, but no bed. Whips and harnesses dangled from steel pegs affixed to freestanding metal racks. Hell only knew what kind of games they played in this room.

Grabbing the first thing she could get her hands on, Gracie rolled her eyes when she saw it was an erect male fertility statue. She hurried behind the folds of black velvet. Peeking through the curtain, she watched as Viper swept in with a somber-looking man following quietly behind her. The smug grin she gave Jin made Gracie wonder what other horrors she'd have to endure tonight.

"Leave us," Viper commanded. The man dissolved out of the room, leaving Viper gazing at Jin's body. Obviously amused, Viper dropped a set of keys on the floor beside her. The little witch didn't like to lose.

"Well, Jin, you have nothing to say to me? How proud you are." Viper let the silk fall from her body. She was naked underneath. Gracie sneered at the suggestive bob of Viper's breasts. Fake. Probably. Viper brought her body to lean on Jin. She kissed him hard and bit down on his lip to draw a tiny stream of blood.

"How about now?" Viper laughed when Jin spit blood in her face. "I have hours to play with you, while Raul takes his blonde whore. He won't miss you." She playfully walked her diamond crusted nails up his bare chest and in a vicious move, brought them down again, to etch deep, red wounds in his flesh. "You'll never leave here alive. You're at my whim, Jin. Say hello to your personal angel of death."

Two long fangs appeared out of Viper's mouth. They were dripping with some kind of liquid. Gracie had seen a lot of pretty bizarre stuff tonight, but nothing like this. Okay, that was it. Gracie wasn't about to watch while Viper got her jollies torturing Jin. She took the fertility statue in both hands and came up to a good position beside her.

"Say hello to more plastic surgery!"

Gracie swung as hard as she could and smacked the statue in Viper's face. The snake-thing's pretty nose snapped with a sickening crunch. One of the fangs broke in half and fell point first to the ground. A foul smelling liquid sprayed down the woman's speckled front. Viper dropped to the side, unconscious. Jin's green eyes—and they were gorgeous eyes—stared at Gracie in surprise.

"You and I have the same problem," she said. "We both want out of here. If we work together to escape, we'll have a much better chance." She watched his blank expression as his eyes studied her curiously. A sudden realization occurred to her. "You don't speak English, do you? For Pete's sake, isn't that my luck!"

Jin was dangerous. Why else would they keep the man in chains? She'd be no match for him if he wanted to break her neck. She had to find a way to avoid any misunderstandings between the two of them. Gracie ran frustrated fingers over her face. Well, she'd just have to figure out how to communicate with him. It was obvious, based on her vision, that they'd found some way to speak to one another.

"Look, I'll let you go if you promise not to kill me. Deal?" She tossed the male statue when she realized what piece she'd been clutching. Using her fingers as puppets along with hand movements to get her point across, Gracie didn't hold much hope that he understood her. "Now, where did that freak drop her keys?"

She kicked at the dress with her bare feet. The fabric was still warm. Gracie flipped it away. The broken piece of fake fang fell out of the folds of gown. It landed close to Viper's leg. Still oozing with liquid, it seemed to have taken some of Viper's blood as well. Gracie crinkled her nose at the fang. That was one of the grossest things she'd seen in a while. Careful to avoid the mess, she picked up the keys.

"I don't know what you did to tick her off, but I'd choose my enemies more carefully next time." She reached up to unlock his wrists. "Look, we've got to get out of here now. Can you walk?"

The little upside down finger scissors weren't getting her message across. She knelt beside him with a shrug and began working on the shackles around his ankles. The key was sticking, hurting her fingers. His hair touched her shoulder as he bent down and took the key. She was suddenly very aware of the warmth as his arm brushed against her shoulder. Her eyes drifted up his lean, muscular form. A large bruise colored the side of his body. It looked painful.

"I wish you could understand me." Gracie stared into those deep green eyes as he turned at the sound of her voice. "How am I supposed to get us both out of here in one piece and get that stupid device back?"

Jin frowned. She saw no use in blaming him. That wasn't fair. It wasn't his fault they were in this mess. "Never mind. I'll think of something."

A loud bang on the door made Gracie jump. Her hands flew to grip Jin's arm. She let it drop quickly, blushing like a teen fan girl. Gawd! First she'd hugged him when she was half out of her mind and now she was acting shy? She wasn't sending mixed signals. The warning was quite clear. Beware of the crazy lady in the gold dress.

"Ho! Viper! You are needed," a man shouted from the other side of the door. The furious knocking came again. "Raul has discovered Jin has gone missing. He is calling for you! Viper? What are you doing?"

"I don't do impressions," Gracie whispered and shook her head at Jin.

He put a finger on his lips and then wrapped an arm around her shoulders. He hurried her to the folds of velvet beside the door and pushed her inside. His body moved as if he were a prowling cat to the fabric just beside the door. Shimmering eyes waited in the shadowy folds. Gracie imagined for a moment that he winked at her. Then the room fell into total darkness.

Chapter Ten

A bolt of power shattered the door, sending shards of wood into the darkened room. Jin held his position behind the fabric, waiting for Viper's allies to come inside. The curtains moved where the pre-cog, Titania, was hiding. He hoped she had the common sense to stay quiet until he took care of their mutual problem.

Harbin and Henri, looking a little battered, entered the room slowly. They swept their weapons across the dark recesses of the room, taking halting steps. One of them fumbled around for the light switch. A low moan from the corner stopped his search. Viper was waking up. Her allies abandoned caution and hurried toward the noise. Jin was on them in an angry surge of speed. His strikes quieted them quickly. In a few blazing strokes they fell in a heap next to each other.

Jin lifted Harbin by his shoulders and began dragging him to the corner to join their stunned boss. The overhead lights blazed on. Titania hurried to the man's feet and lifted him by the ankles. The lean muscles of her arms and legs tensed with the effort. A pre-cog used to heavy lifting? He was definitely beginning to like this girl.

They dropped Harbin's dead weight beside Viper. She stirred again. This time Jin brought a fist down on her jaw. Viper was out for a good long while now. A tiny shimmer caught his eye as Mai Ling's diamond pendant fell across speckled skin. Viper had put it on a new chain, sending the sparkling heart to hang between her treacherous breasts. He ripped it from her body and threw the chain at the wall. His shaking fingers tucked the little pendant in the small inside pocket of his trousers.

He stood up again, contemplating Viper's unconscious form. Murderess. Her death was overlong in coming. His fingers gripped the air, aching to squeeze the life from her body. He'd imagined himself doing the deed so often, now that he had the opportunity why was he hesitating? It would be a simple thing to take her worthless life. Hadn't his father trained him to be the Hand of Justice? Such an uncomplicated task. Jin looked down at his hands. They were shaking. He couldn't lose his nerve now, not with Mai Ling's killer here at his feet. Damn it! He hadn't been able to protect his sister that night, and now he was too weak to avenge her.

"Jin," Titania called. She was standing over Henri's body, trying to lift his shoulders. "A little help?"

He lifted up Henri and dumped him with his friends. Titania handed him three pairs of handcuffs with a crinkle of her nose. She folded her arms and shook her head at Viper's still form. Blonde waves swept across her bare shoulders. The dislike was evident on her expressive face.

"I hope one day she gets what she deserves." Titania lightly rested her hand on Jin's bare shoulder.

The touch was soft and reassuring. "My dad always says when you act like an ass, you're treated like an ass. Someday someone worse than she is will come along and teach Viper a lesson."

Jin clicked closed the last handcuff and sat back. Titania was right. Killing Viper now was too risky. Proving his innocence and her guilt would be the smart move. Perhaps he could get his life back then? It was a tiny ray of hope in an otherwise dark circumstance. Now he had a fresh plan, thanks to his pretty new pre-cog companion. He'd prove his innocence and make certain Viper and Raul experienced the anguish he had over the past few days. Then he'd finally see Viper to her death.

"We should go." Titania step forward to lead the way, but Jin pulled her behind him and kept a tight grasp on her hand. Having her handler come to their rescue would be helpful. In the meantime, keeping her safe was mutually beneficial. Besides, Titania had rescued him from Viper's torture chamber. Helping her escape from Otherworld was the least he could do.

"No, not that way." She shook her head and began to tremble as they passed by the small door she'd come through earlier. That confirmed his guess. Titania wasn't an experienced agent—but was she here on her own? Either someone was very eager to get his hands on Jin or this pre-cog was telling the truth and had fallen in with Raul by mistake. Perhaps remaining silent was the best strategy until he was sure of her identity and intent. He'd let her think what she needed to think in order to remain close to her.

He carefully watched his footing over the broken shards of door so that the bottoms of his bare feet escaped the jagged edges. Titania wasn't as fortunate. She began hopping up and down, finally coming to rest against the wall. A splinter had found its way into her foot. Anymore such outbursts and she might experience worse injuries from their captors.

"Ouch! For Pete's sake!" She wiped at the tiny piece of wood and stepped gingerly on her foot. An experienced agent she was not.

Jin put a warning finger to his lips and kept a steady pace forward. He'd taken careful note of the direction his captors had used after leaving the dining room. This side of the mansion was quiet. Viper had chosen a place where she knew no one could hear him scream. Not that he would have given her the pleasure.

They'd taken the quickest route from one side of the mansion to the other. Raul, lazy ass that he was, had commissioned a portal. It would have been a much shorter trip if they'd gone back through, but Titania had been frightened to enter the library. He was inclined to trust her judgment there. Warnings from a pre-cog were best heeded.

"I hope you know where you're going. Seriously, I can't take much more of this." Titania whispered in a steady stream. "One minute I'm at the Rusty Grotto, the next some creep is forcing me to buddy up to Raul. Listen, I have to find something he took from me and then I really need to get home. Is any of this getting through?"

He pulled her into his body and covered her mouth. Holding in a curse after her well-placed elbow struck his bruised ribs, Jin managed to duck behind a pillar. Perrin came around the corner at a quick pace. Viper's dangerous bodyguard passed them without stopping. It wouldn't be long before he found his friends and raised the alarm.

Titania must have come to the same realization. She stayed quiet and kept to his pace as they made their way through the empty halls. He hoped they'd at least make the dining room before the fury of the Vento Clan was unleashed.

"Wait!" Her body came to a stop as the mist of blue covered her eyes for a moment. "We have to be careful."

He stuck his head around the corner. She was right. They'd almost run into the glass atrium joining the two sides of the mansion. One side faced the front gardens, the other looked out over the swimming pool where several party guests were drinking and swimming. Granted most of them were paying rapt attention to their naked companions, but there was always the possibility he and Titania would be spotted.

Tugging at his restraining collar again, he wanted to unleash all the strength he had on the Vento Clan. But wishing for his powers wouldn't bring them back. He'd have to find another way. The quickest route to the dining room from here was through the atrium. He dropped to his knees and pulled Titania with him. She nodded with a frown and started crawling forward. Her beads swayed wildly as she zipped ahead. He followed close behind, grinning as they crawled. The view was nice. He might be a gentleman, but he wasn't a saint.

He helped her to her feet when they reached the other side. In the hallway, the lights had been dimmed. They were close to the fighters' portal. First things first. He had to get some fuel if they had any chance of escape.

"I recognize this. Why are we going to the dining room?" She tugged at his arm. "We're going to get caught."

Jin pulled her inside and closed the door after them. Glorious smells permeated the room, sending his stomach into a manic craze. He let go of her hand and pounced on a platter of cold pheasant. Stuffing the flesh in with one hand, he gulped from a water goblet with the other. Ignoring her questioning look, he grabbed up a basket of muffins. Greedily, Jin stuffed one in his mouth. It had been baked with rosemary and cheese. Absolute heaven! Say what you would about Raul, the man knew how to throw a party.

"We need to keep moving," Titania said, hugging her arms about her body. "We really can't spare any time to stop for a bite. Gawd! It's a good thing you're easy on the eyes."

She was watching him gorge. Not one of his finer moments and certainly not a way to impress her. Titania's eyes softened. Such concern for a total stranger, honestly—

what was she doing roaming around with this crowd on her own?

"I'm sorry. They must have been starving you for days. Why don't we bring some food with us?" She snatched up a linen napkin and laid it on the table beside the platter. She began putting pieces of pheasant on it, hoping he'd get the idea, no doubt.

It was time to end the ruse. If he was going to get them out of this in one piece, she'd have to do exactly what he told her. "Titania..."

"No, I'm Gracie Berry." She tapped her nicely formed chest. "Titania is just a stupid name I came up with back home. I think..." Her mouth made a little frown. "Anyway, I didn't want to give Raul my real name. Do you understand?"

Jin considered encouraging her to tap her chest again, but decided against it. Right now, he needed some answers from her. First on his list was the vision she'd had of him back in the arena.

"Gracie," Jin said, putting his hand firmly on her shoulders. Her bright blue eyes filled with curiosity and anticipation. Then suddenly her body went rigid. Her irises bled blue, covering the whites of her eyes. Another vision. Jin let his fingertips hover over her arm. He gently turned her wrist. No Clan tattoo, or not one that was visible anyway. There were ways to hide the tattoos, but that took a lot of power as well as skill. Whatever her reasons for helping him, she had inherited his powerful enemies.

He lifted her little gold purse from around her neck and opened it. Inside, he found forty dollars, a lipstick and a folded-up map of the Las Vegas Strip. No ID. He left the money in her purse and put it back on her body. Gracie swayed forward with a gasp. Her eyes went wide with fear, and for a moment, Jin thought she knew he had searched her.

"We need to hide!" She tugged at Jin's arm and hurried under the long banquet tables. Jin followed, sitting beside her as she kept watch on the entrance.

The door flew open, and Raul marched in, roughly pulling Viper along with him. Fong followed meekly behind like a little lapdog. White hot anger flared up in Jin's heart. Partners in Clansmen trafficking. He'd have to make sure the three of them got their just deserts before he left town. Keeping the balance of the Clans was his father's problem.

Raul swung Viper around and threw her against the far banquet table. "Did you really believe I'd forgive this childish obsession you have with Jin? You've put my reputation at risk. We've promised Jin to the crowd by my word. Now you've let him escape and with a valuable pre-cog."

"What does it matter how Jin dies?" Viper pushed away from the table. "The death mark on him only requires we produce his head."

He had a death mark out on him? That was disturbing news. The Clan Council typically called upon its unstoppable bounty hunter, the Griffin, for runners like him. He had been labeled a conspirator and murderer. The Griffin must be searching for him by now. He and Viper were the only ones left who knew the truth about the Girard coup. The true conspirator must have grown nervous.

This same person who had gained the Unseelie Court's help in attacking his father had now turned to another unholy bargain to have him killed. The death mark took powerful magic from the Unseelie Court. It was against Clan Law to enter into any agreement with them. Evil in nature, the death mark could only be brokered through a horrible sacrifice. Usually an Unseelie practitioner of magic demanded the blood of the innocent.

"And have you stopped to consider who put the death mark out on him and why?" Raul lit his cigar and flicked the lighter shut with a snap. "Word of his capture was announced this evening, almost to the very second the message was sent about the death mark on Jin's head. I don't believe in coincidence."

Jin turned his attention to Viper's cold, blank face. He'd assumed Raul was privy to the details of the Girard Clan coup, perhaps even its mastermind. It appeared Viper was keeping secrets from her benefactor. Or perhaps Raul Vento wasn't her true benefactor after all. Someone else was pulling the strings for her. Maybe their aspirations went higher than the Girard Clan.

Midsummer's Eve was only days away, the time when the veil between Otherworld and the Human Realm was at its weakest. The Unseelie Court could enter the Human Realm in power and numbers. It could signal the end of the Clans—and the Humans.

"Titania could be working with the person who put the death mark out on Jin. She could be spying on us. I say we kill them both." Fong shrugged. "Single women have disappeared in Vegas before."

"Let me do it! Let me do them both, Raul," Viper spat. "She broke my fang."

"And embarrassed you, my dear." Raul shook his head. "No, I want to ask her a few questions, like the identity of the person behind the failed assassination attempt on my life. It was quite the coincidence she happened by just as the car came at me." He took a long drag from his Cuban cigar. "She has to be a pre-cog from the Wainwright Clan. She has no Clan tattoo, but that bitch Eleanor could be hiding it. Why else would the girl be so interested in Jin? It can't be a coincidence."

Raul stared across the empty room, his cunning eyes glistening. "I don't believe in coincidences. Of course if she is an as-of-yet undiscovered pre-cog, I want her. The Wainwright Clan won't be so high and mighty if we have our own pre-cog."

Jin gave Gracie a quick glance. If the Vento Clan was able to capture Gracie and use her gift, then that would give them a major advantage. The balance of power would shift in favor of Raul, which would be a very bad thing for Seelie Descendants and Normals alike. Jin wasn't a crusader by any means, but he wasn't completely oblivious to the world around him, either. Gracie must be kept out of the hands of the Vento Clan. Besides, Raul wanted her, and Jin was in the mood to ruin his day.

All his speculation might be unnecessary if she'd been sent by the Wainwright Clan. He hadn't heard news of another pre-cog, but that was easily explained. Gracie was American. She was from neutral territory, which meant her indoctrination into a Clan would have been kept very quiet. Still, sending a pre-cog, new or otherwise, wasn't something his mother would do. She wasn't one to risk resources.

Raul took a small flashing device out of his pocket. It was used to measure a Seelie Descendant's power. Someone like Raul could also use it to find out the identity of the Descendant. It would tell him the individual's ancestry several generations past. Gracie tensed beside him. She looked ready to bolt out of hiding and grab the device.

"I need to go to my offices in Summerlin to run an analysis on Titania's sample." Raul's face turned to stone and he stuffed the device back in his pocket. "She'll cooperate once we have her family. I don't care how long I have to torture them, Titania will be mine."

"Dad!" Gracie cried in a whisper. Jin pulled her into his arms quickly and covered her mouth. She was trembling. Anxious tears rolled over Jin's fingers.

"But, Raul, we need your help to capture Jin." Fong kneaded his clasped hands. "He's worth a lot of money to us. Our guests will be very upset if they don't see him fight in the arena."

"I have twenty of my best men just outside. That should be enough to help you capture Jin again. He'll fight tomorrow night with the others," Raul said firmly. He grabbed Viper by the throat. "Find him, and do it quietly. I warn you. Don't harm Titania or Jin. If you go against my word again, I'll crush that lovely throat of yours."

He dropped Viper on her ass and walked out. Jin recognized well the venomous glare she gave his departing back. Raul had just made her "most wanted dead" list. Viper got to her feet again. Fong stood away from Viper, sensing that he could easily become her whipping post. Then she moved out the door with Fong following closely behind.

Jin considered using his remaining speed to rush up behind her and snap that treacherous neck, saving Raul the trouble. But he had Gracie to consider. Getting her out of Otherworld before those Vento thugs found them would be best. He'd have his chance with Viper again. Gracie's gift could tell him the right time when he was the one with the greatest advantage.

"Oh God, what am I going to do?" She pulled his hand away, turned and pressed her cheek against his chest. Gracie let the tears splash against his skin. "They're going to hurt my dad. And how helpful is it that I'm having a breakdown right now! Gawd, pull it together, Gracie."

He could feel her heart beating wildly against his body. She was like a frightened sparrow, trembling in a windstorm. Jin stroked her hair gently. Right now, the girl in his arms wasn't a powerful pre-cog from the Wainwright Clan. She was a victim of circumstance in a brutal world. Or was she? Gracie, if that was her real name, could be playing him. Yet, he hadn't seen any deception in her eyes. And these crocodile tears were real enough. He held her tighter.

His problems, though, were piling up. Raul and Viper had joined forces to find and kill him. If they failed, he still had a death mark out on his life. And his family— both sides—wouldn't protect him. Yet, he couldn't leave Gracie behind for Raul to find. She wouldn't last long. He'd get her back safely to her handler. And if she was an unaffiliated Seelie Descendant, well, he'd figure that out later. She needed him, and for now, he needed her. Jin had just become her shadow whether she liked it or not.

An explosion of glass and tile shook the ground. In the midst of falling debris and shouts of terror, the high-pitched screech of a predatory bird thundered through the Vento mansion, a sound every Descendant prayed he would never hear. The call of the Griffin signaled certain death for any it pursued.

"What the hell was that?" Gracie cried.

Jin grabbed her hand and pulled her out from under the table. "We have to go."

"You speak English!" Gracie slapped at his hand. "I've been doing scissor puppets, and you speak English?"

"Yes, I speak English in the Human Realm, but right now you're speaking Elfish. You don't understand," he hissed. "We really have to get out of Otherworld right now!"

The deafening screech pounded against the walls of the mansion again. "I have come for you, murderer! Show yourself, or I will topple this dwelling asunder."

They were knocked to the floor when another explosion shook the foundations of the mansion. Jin covered Gracie with his body as pieces of ceiling tiles and lights rained down upon them. The Griffin was getting closer.

"That thing is going to bring down the whole house! Who is it looking for?"

Jin rolled to his feet and picked her up. "It's looking for me."

Chapter Eleven

The doors to the dining room burst open. Viper and Fong along with Raul's men surged inside. Stumbling over one another, they hurried to block the doors. Tables and chairs were overturned in their haste. Jin froze against the far wall as they began to power up. Then, as if she could sense his animosity, Viper turned to the back of the room. Her eyes found his across the chaos.

"Jin! Get him and the girl!" The twisted hatred on her face was focused at Gracie. Viper lifted her hand, exposing the sharp point of a dagger. She brought her hand back in a quick movement. Then suddenly, Viper's body was propelled into a pile of discarded chairs by a large block of flying wood. Massive talons shredded the door and walls of the dining room. The Griffin had found him.

Part lion, part golden eagle, the Griffin was an ancient creature from myth and legends. Its single mindedness and loyalty to the honor of the master it served made the creature a trustworthy bounty hunter. The Griffin couldn't be bribed, and it couldn't be swayed. Its talons welcomed the blood of its prey, guilty or no. Large wings expanded from an elephant-sized frame to pound the air with gale-force thrusts and blow any barriers out of its path. Scanning the room with the sharp vision of an avian predator, the Griffin came to rest its attention on Jin.

"Murderer! Conspirator!" The screech of triumph rang around the room, dropping the Clansmen to their knees. "I have come for you!"

The Griffin was an unbeatable agent of the Council. It had served the Seelie Descendants for centuries and never to Jin's memory had it failed in its objective. Even at full power, he'd lose this battle. Escape was his only option. The Griffin was free to roam within Otherworld, but it wasn't allowed to set paw in the Human Realm. He must escape Otherworld.

First he'd have to find a way out of the dining room. A small crack in the wall at the back of the room caught his attention. Two frightened eyes stared in terror at the Griffin. One of the serving staff must be hiding at the entrance to the kitchens. Raul wouldn't want such common practicalities as a server's entrance ruining the aesthetics of the room.

"You haven't been invited into my home, creature!" Raul shouted behind its huge body. Bolts of power struck the Griffin's side, rocking it minutely. Jin whistled. That was just going to make the creature angry, but at least its attention would be on someone else.

"You dare attack me?" The Griffin lowered its head to get a better look at the lesser being who had struck its side. "I'm here at the will of the Clan Council. Interference from anyone—Clan leader or no—will not be tolerated."

Raul hesitated. He was obviously aware of the consequences if he should continue his rebellion. But Viper made up his mind for him. Stumbling out of the broken pieces of furniture, she grabbed an infuser from the nearest member of the Vento security team and fired at the Griffin. Raul hurried to her side, joining her attack.

Following their leader in his folly, the Vento Clansmen struck at the beast. They were wasting their time. The unstoppable creature coming toward them could easily devour the Descendants standing between it and its prey. It swiped its talons at the Descendants, striking their bodies. Several fell away, bloodied and unconscious.

Jin pulled Gracie behind him toward the door. They'd been handed a miraculous opportunity to escape while Raul and his followers were distracting the beast. He pushed into the kitchen with an extended arm sending the frightened servers staggering back against the wall. Jin had no idea where they were in relation to their exit. Supposing his guess was correct based on his trip through the ventilation system, they were headed in the wrong direction. He'd have to change course if they were to find the fighters' portal.

"Do you know where we're going?" Gracie's feet slapped on the tile beside him.

"I have an idea, yes." He kept a tight hold on her hand as they ran toward the pantry past two massive ovens. A small door led out to the kitchen herb garden. The scene of fresh basil and rosemary filled the gentle sea breeze. They hopped down the gravel path in bare feet, following as it brought them back toward the mansion. The glass domes previously suspended over the stage had been smashed. A few twisted steel frames were all that was left of the once beautiful ceiling.

"Raul has some major home repairs since that creature used his roof as a pet door." Gracie shook her head and gave Jin a sideways glance. "It seems pretty interested in finding you."

"The Griffin is a kind of bounty hunter. It's sent by the Clan Council to track down people like me—whether they're innocent or not."

"And you're innocent?"

"Viper framed me. She wants me dead in the worst way." He turned to Gracie and saw her expressive face now contorted with indecision. "I promise you. I'm no killer."

Screams erupted in the yard behind them. The Griffin had followed Jin's scent. Jin tugged Gracie forward again onto a small patio off the mansion. A wall of glass framed in place with ornate iron rod exposed a quaint parlor. Glass double doors appeared to act as entry into the once peaceful garden. Jin yanked at the handles and found them unlocked.

More falling stones and breaking glass signaled the creature was getting closer. Racing through the parlor, Jin burst into the hall at a reckless pace. The spot was decorated in a feminine style with fresh flowers in vases and low lighting. Damn! He didn't recognize this room. They were lost with a massive killing machine only minutes behind them.

"Are you absolutely sure you know where we are?" Gracie frowned at him and shook her head. "Tell me where we're going and then let me try something."

"We're looking for the portal Raul brought the fighters through. It should be near here down one level."

She nodded with fierce concentration, allowing the blue to flood her eyes. He took an impatient step toward her, very aware of the Griffin's pounding steps growing closer. Then Gracie blinked and took Jin's hand again. They turned left back in the direction of the dining room. A few more turns and they were at a small staircase leading down. The reassuring tug of the portal's power was waiting for them at the bottom.

"Nicely done." He gave her a smile and was glad to see it returned.

They crept down the stairs, but stealth was unnecessary. It seemed every available Clansmen in the mansion had gone to fend off the Griffin. Escape would be easy from here. He gave Gracie a nod and then they ran into the portal's mouth.

Its magic thrust them back into the Human Realm and right into the small handful of Tommy's Normal guards. The men stared blankly for a moment at the fugitives. Then the jittery Normal with the .38 startled them into action by reaching for his gun. Jin rolled into their midst and kicked the weapon out of the guard's hand. Then he thrust his heel into a rushing guard's stomach for a solid hit.

Mr. Jittery charged toward his fallen weapon. Jin struck at the running legs, sending the man sprawling headfirst onto the floor. His head struck the ground with a loud smack. Jin stood away from the guards when he was satisfied he and Gracie were the only ones moving.

Her jaw was open in surprise, and she gave him an appreciative nod. He grabbed her hand, taking the lead again as they passed the empty cells once holding the fighters. He put a finger to his lips, and she nodded. Jin stared at her for a moment in surprise. She trusted him, a complete stranger? Even the Griffin's presence hadn't shaken her trust in him.

Then she stiffened behind him, pulling his body to a stop. He turned to see the blue had covered her eyes again. She blinked. Pulling him quickly behind a stack of empty boxes, Gracie shushed him. Two Normals with guns exited one of the rooms down the hall in the direction where Jin and Gracie were headed. Jin nodded in approval. This pre-cog was handy to have around.

After the Normals moved past them, the two escapees continued to creep around the boxes lining the hall, heading toward what Jin hoped was the exit. The arid breeze with a faint smell of hydraulic fluid told him they were close. Traversing a stack of empty boxes, they saw their goal. A patch of sunlight burned through the open door to the outside. Gracie quickened her pace. She was a caged animal who has noticed the gate open. The little pre-cog ran faster until she was taking the lead. Jin didn't blame her for being eager to escape. He had tired of Raul's hospitality as well.

Safely under the early morning sunlight, he sucked in the dry air. Time spent in his gilded cage had made him wonder if he'd ever breathe free again. Stored heat from the previous day rose up from the asphalt, burning his toes. No shade beckoned across the sea of hot black tar. They'd have to find shoes soon.

A belligerent shout took Jin's attention off his footwear problem and onto the two Vento Clansmen running toward them. The Griffin must have abandoned its hunt when it discovered Jin had left Otherworld. Jin's foot flew up and snapped the first man's head back. Jin dropped, spinning with his other leg to sweep the man's limbs. The Vento Clansman's comrade pointed a human weapon toward the fray. Jin disarmed him in one fluid move. Bringing his knee up into the man's gut, he followed with joined fists down on the guy's back, knocking him cold across his friend's stunned form.

"Whoa! You're fast. I mean Kung Fu movie fast."

A martial arts fan? Well, that was one more point in her favor. Gracie got another point for being even prettier in the light of day. He took her hand and led her around the outside of the building.

The parking lot behind the warehouse looked like a parking lot at a mortician's convention. Black limousines and sedans lined the blacktop under the morning Vegas sun. Jin passed them by with a derisive grunt. Then hope sparkled as a blue gem among coal. A blue Lamborghini Aventado Roadster glittered like a rock star at the end of the line of bulky sedans. He hurried over to run his hands along its sexy lines.

"Daddy like," Jin hummed under his breath. He lifted the door up and slid down into the sleek leather seat. The owner of this beautiful piece of automotive perfection hadn't locked it. In Jin's book, that meant the super-car wasn't being properly taken care of—an egregious sin. The cretin didn't deserve to own her. It was time she had someone behind the wheel who truly respected and adored every inch of her fine carbon fiber frame.

"Oh no, we are not stealing a car!" Gracie's bare feet danced on the hot pavement.

Jin pointed at the group of Seelie Descendants running toward them. Gracie yelped and raced around to the other side of the Lambo. Her fist banged on the door with an unacceptable level of disrespect for the super-car. For a brief moment, Jin considered leaving her and then motioned up with his hands. She got the hint and lifted the car door. The golden fabric crept up her bare thighs as she fell down into the seat. Her hand tugged at the hem when she caught him looking.

The engine fired up and gave that distinctive Lambo roar. The engine echoed among the abandoned warehouses, waking up a few stray birds unlucky enough to call the rooftops home. The blue bullet shot out of the parking lot, knocking over the Seelie Descendants as they ran for their own cars. Jin dove into the early morning traffic on the nearby, busy industrial road.

The Lambo zipped around the other cars at a jet's pace. One of the sleepy drivers spilled his coffee and shook an angry fist at the sports car's departing tail.

"Gawd! I'm going to die today," Gracie cried, gripping her nails into the leather seats. The sounds of crashing vehicles and angry honking made them both look in the rearview mirror. "They're after us!"

"I've figured that out on my own," Jin said with a grin.

"I think I liked it better when you didn't speak English. Who are you anyway?"

"That's a complicated question."

"Let's start with an easy one. You're English, not part of these Seelie Descendants then?"

"I was raised in London by my mother and spent the summers in Hong Kong with my father. Both of them are Seelie Descendants. Better?"

"That doesn't tell me anything. Who are you? Why were you being held a prisoner by those guys?"

"It's safer for you if you don't know." He talked while carefully focusing on his driving.

"Safer? Have you forgotten what we've just been through in Raul's club?" Gracie gripped the seat harder. "Forget it. We'll get these creeps off our backs and then you're going to the police with me."

She was naive, for sure. "The police are no match for these people." He shook his head. "I need you to understand the danger you're in right now. The Clans are powerful. They have ties in every government and criminal organization in the world. Do you get what I'm trying to tell you?"

"And you're part of these Clans?" She pointed at his left wrist.

"Sometimes," he said with a shrug. He couldn't completely disavow his heritage.

"Sometimes? And what about the other times?" Gracie shook her head. "You haven't been straight with me since the second we met. How can I trust you?"

Well, it would seem her trust in him had stopped at the doors of the warehouse. He didn't blame her really, though. Everyone was out to use her for her powers. It was bound to make her suspicious if she was wise. And their meeting with the Griffin when it so helpfully proclaimed him as a murderer had doubtless put the seed of mistrust in her mind.

"Very well, but remember that I warned you." Jin took them into the left lane around a much slower car. "The Clans are made up of four families, the Zhao, the Wainwright, the Girard and the Vento. They're all powerful. Each Clan leader is duty bound to maintain the balance of power between the Clans. It would be very dangerous for the inhabitants of our little planet, otherwise. A few weeks ago, Viper and her brother tried to take over the Girard Clan, resulting in many deaths."

Jin paused for a moment and swallowed hard. "I was there when the attack happened. Viper's brother died. I know the truth of what really happened, you see, and that's why Viper wants me dead."

"Can't you warn the other Clans?" she asked, reasonably.

"I'm not in good standing with the Clans, so they won't believe me without evidence. I have to prove what happened before the Griffin finds me again." He shrugged and shifted lanes. "I've been in hiding for the past few weeks at a meditation retreat in Mexico trying to figure out how to get that proof. One of my enemies found me and brought me here."

"Where I saved you from Viper." Gracie's wide eyes held him in their gaze.

"Viper wants me dead, and now she has reason to hate you as well. Stay away from her," he warned.

"Fine by me," she said.

"Now it's my turn to ask questions. Why Titania?" Jin asked.

She shrugged, sending the golden curls swaying over her bare shoulders. "No idea. It's just a name that came to me."

"Really?" Jin grinned and chuckled harder when she glared at him. "Titania is the fairy queen and consort of Oberon from A Midsummer Night's Dream. You know the story. Puck sprinkled magic in her eyes and she fell in love with a human who had the head of an ass." He laughed again.

"Well that explains why everybody was giggling when Raul introduced me." Her face paled and she turned to look out the window, ignoring his unspoken question.

Three black sedans appeared in his rearview mirror. Typical. Raul's security had rather limited imagination. He wasn't too worried. The Aventador could reach from zed to sixty in less than three seconds. And with a top speed of two-hundred-and-seventeen miles per hour, it would leave those Mercedes sedans in the dust. Assuming Jin and Gracie could reach the highway.

"Jin! Red light!" Gracie stomped her bare foot on the passenger's side floor. Her eyes were clamped tightly shut.

Instead of putting on the brakes, Jim pressed his foot down harder on the gas pedal. The Lambo roared and rocketed forward. He took the on-ramp to I-15 at seventy miles per hour. Swinging among the thin freeway traffic, he moved to the fast lane. He wanted their pursuers to think he was making a run for it, but Jin had no intention of leaving Vegas yet. He had a little matter of revenge to take care of first. He needed to lose his playmates though. The Nevada desert was a big place. He'd take them on a nature tour and then hit the freeway back south to the city.

A streak of red shot by them and the familiar roar of the Lamborghini shook the windows. The second Lamborghini glistened in the morning desert sun like the dawn. The driver whipped in front of them and stuck an insistent hand out the window. Two black sedans began to pull up to either side of Jin, trying to block him in.

Gracie yanked open the glove box and then slammed it again when she found nothing inside. She shifted in her seat, finally bending over. The positioned offered Jin an unintended look at her bare thigh. With a cry of victory, Gracie pried a full bottle of strawberry daiquiri mix from under the seat. She rolled down the window and threw the bottle for a direct hit on the sedan's windshield. Oh yes, he liked this girl.

Jin darted out in front of the sedan as it swayed in traffic. His Lambo took the lane change like the beautiful professional it was. Gracie made an unfriendly gesture toward the driver as they jetted past their red twin.

Somewhere to his right were Nellis AFB and the speedway. He would love to have pulled off and given the Lambo a run on the track. Being chased could put such a damper on a good time. Jin began searching the flat skyline. Strange they'd run into no highway patrol cars trying to intercept them. He wondered how Raul had arranged that one. No matter. He had to lose his red twin and get back to Vegas.

Jin took an obscure exit onto a utility road, spraying gravel as his tires caught the shoulder. His twin followed. Dust flew up behind them in sprays of dirty red. This was going to take a "hands on" approach. He headed for some sandy mounds and turned the Lamborghini to watch his red rival come head on. The two cars stopped and stood staring at each other, engines rumbling in expectation.

"You guys are going to ram each other in the middle of nowhere? Unbelievable!" Gracie gripped the seat with one hand. She muttered something else about male ego and tugged her seatbelt tight.

Red shot forward, aiming to take them head to head. Jin grinned viciously and pressed on the gas pedal. They'd see what red had. The two Lambos roared toward each other, accelerating at a wild pace, a game of super-car chicken. Jin had no intention of giving way. He accelerated faster, ignoring Gracie's scream.

Then an uninvited guest interrupted their play. A Bugatti Veyron's sleek black form zipped in between the two cars like a jet fighter. Jin slammed on the brakes and shuddered to a stop, but red wasn't so lucky. He yanked the wheel too hard, and his beautiful Lambo rolled several times. Sand and sage sprayed into the air, giving the ballet a dramatic backdrop. The ruined super-car teetered to a stop in the sand.

The Veyron rolled slowly toward the crippled Lambo. Its shape began to change. The vehicle's sleek lines thickened. It grew wider, while growing skyward. The hulking mechanical form shifted until a Peterbuilt Diesel stood within a haze of heat. The big truck let out a ravenous growl. Then it rammed the defeated Lambo and rolled over it, as if it were feasting upon the super-car.

"I did not just see that," Gracie whispered, shaking her head. "I'm having a nervous breakdown. Who could blame me?"

Jin turned their Lambo back toward the freeway. Figment or not, that powerful Seelie Descendant would be coming for them next. He gave their car full throttle once they hit the on-ramp. Somehow the Seelie Descendant in the Veyron had transformed the vehicle around him. Jin searched his memory, but he didn't recall ever meeting or even hearing of anyone who could do that little trick. Someone in the Clans had a new toy. He hoped whoever held its leash wouldn't let it lose on him next.

Chapter Twelve

They sat in silence for a moment, watching the open spaces of the Nevada desert zip by the Lambo's windows. The dangerous implication of his situation was beginning to sink in. He had to prove his innocence, yes, but that wouldn't matter if the Unseelie Court stormed through the veil between Realms. They would invade with unstoppable powers the Human Realm hadn't seen for centuries. The Clans were in upheaval. They wouldn't be able to assemble in time.

He had to warn Bryn. Of course the Seelie Lords wouldn't get off their pampered asses to help if they didn't have proof. He turned his gaze to the pre-cog sitting next to him. Gracie leaned against the seat with her head back and eyes closed. Strands of blonde hair whipped wildly about her face. The image reflected both their lives at the moment. Somewhere in her head could be the key to this whole mystery.

"How did you come to be with Raul?"

She sighed heavily. "Do we have to talk about this right now?"

"Yes, we do," he said.

She turned her head away and stared out the window. "There was a man. I don't remember much about him or how he came to be in my mind. I just know he took control of me."

"Are you telling me you, a pre-cog, were enthralled? I didn't think that was possible. Your power would have protected you."

She turned to him, face creased with worry. "Puppet Master told me someone had put a block on my mind. Now it's gone and for the first time I can call the visions whenever I want."

Puppet Master was the worst sort of predator. He'd probably licked his lips when he'd seen Gracie. The vicious little toad had doubtless tried to enslave her and found someone living in her mind already. Her battered appearance and fear when she'd found Jin in the chamber made sense now.

"I think you should start from the beginning."

"I don't remember much about what happened. I'd had a huge fight with Dad and went to see my friend Kay at the Rusty Grotto. That's a cafe she owns in San Diego." Her blue eyes grew distant and clouded over. "I remember images of a man. He attacked me in the dark. Then I remember entering my room at the hotel here in Vegas. Everything else is a blur."

Her hand made a fist and she slammed it against the gold fabric of her dress. "He hurt me when I didn't do what he said. I wore this awful dress, put glitter in my hair and went to the Paris to follow Raul. A car tried to run him over, and I saved his life. The voice in my head told me that I was to spy on Raul and his cronies. They had some deal going on and the voice was worried Raul would cheat him. That's all I remember. Gawd! It's so frustrating."

He reached over and grasped Gracie's hand. "You're very lucky to escape his enthrall. Puppet Master and the voice fought over you, did they?"

She nodded. Her voice cracked as she spoke. She sounded worn to the bone. "When they fought something broke free in my mind. I think it may have been the block on my power. Whatever it was threw them both out of me and I escaped. That's when I found you."

"Your memories will come back in time." He turned the Lambo onto the Strip much too fast for the traffic. This magnificent feat of engineering was too conspicuous even for Vegas. He gripped the steering wheel with a deep breath.

"You can drop me off at the Styles Casino." Gracie braced herself against the car's door.

He wasn't ready to leave her yet. Raul did have a valid point. This girl wasn't what she pretended to be. Jin knew next to nothing about her. But she was telling the truth about being enthralled. He'd recognized the signs. If she could remember who enthralled her, then he would have a good idea as to who was behind this entire affair.

Only a handful of Descendants had the strength and ability to enthrall a pre-cog. Each of them was equally dangerous. Gracie wouldn't last very long on her own. If she turned out to be an unaffiliated pre-cog, she would be a target for every Seelie Descendant with ambition. They'd fight over her until she was forced into a Clan or killed. Jin would stick with her until he knew the truth. He owed her his life.

He pulled into a car park at one of the many malls and positioned the Lamborghini as far away from the tourists as possible. They made for the entrance and followed the monorail signs. There was a stop within walking distance of her hotel. He'd driven by the Styles Casino the last time he was in Vegas. It wasn't his first choice, but the construction site had looked like a grand affair.

"We can't go in the mall without shoes."

He shook his head and pulled her through the doors. Gracie may have been a powerful Seelie Descendant, but she thought like a Normal. Descendants did as they pleased. If that meant walking into a mall nude, so be it.

The chill of artificial air struck his bare chest. He involuntarily shivered. The aroma of baked goods mixed with the smell of expensive perfume and new clothes. Walking quickly, Jin plucked two pairs of flip flops from an oddities shop and handed one to Gracie. She rolled her eyes and snapped off the string tying them together.

They followed the signs up the stairs and out onto the monorail platform. Jin pulled Gracie onboard, hurrying her to a seat before the car moved forward. They sat in silence as the smoothly moving train transported them along the Strip. Gracie watched out the window, her eyes wide as they passed casino after casino.

Jin took her by the shoulders and ushered her off the monorail when they reached their stop. Several gray-haired ladies gave them furtive, disapproving looks as they left together. He gave the ladies a wink and wagged his eyebrows.

It was approaching late morning when they walked the final stretch toward the Styles Hotel and Casino. Jin let out an approving whistle. The casino was everything the hype boasted it would be. Not bad for an off-Strip property. Grand gardens with tasteful modern deco statuary surrounded the drive up to the portico. The clean, stylish lines modeled Milan in an ostentatious tribute. Sharply dressed attendants waited to serve the bustling crowds.

Gracie began fussing with her dress and hair. "I look like I've been wandering the streets all night." She frowned at Jin's bare chest. "Will they even let us in the door the way we are?"

Jin slipped an arm around her waist and walked her toward the lobby. Practiced fingers eased a jacket off the handle of a busy tourist's bag as they walked past. Pulling on the garment, he wrinkled his nose at the fabric. Polyester from the rack. Well, it would have to do. In fact, no one noticed or gave them a second glance. It was Vegas. Nobody cared what you did as long as it didn't ruin their good time.

They rushed past the front desk and into the noisy, everyday business of the casino. He took in the electric atmosphere with sharp, thief's eyes. A face he recognized schmoozed a group of young ladies beside the Concierge desk. Typical of the man. Jin's luck was changing for the better. He would see Gracie to her room and make contact with his old acquaintance later.

A serious-looking attendant eyed them as they approached the guest elevators. "Key please."

Jin nuzzled Gracie's neck as she dug into a pocket strategically placed under the bodice of her dress. Clever girl. Her obvious paranoia had saved both their lives. They entered the elevator and she pressed three. He was a little taken aback as they waited for the elevator to reach her floor.

Gracie hurried out and walked down the hall toward the guest rooms. She was staying in the cheap rooms? They stopped at the end of the hall and she opened the door. The room was clean and tastefully decorated, but it wasn't up to the standards he'd expect a powerful pre-cog would enjoy.

Bryn—or Rogers as he liked to be called in the Human Realm—could have feasibly set them up in the cheap rooms if she was a hired consultant on a job. Image was everything to portray a role. This was indeed the room of a single young woman on her holiday. Then again, if the person who had enthralled her made the arrangements, he hadn't been trying to hide her very well. Interesting.

Two full beds called invitingly from against the wall. Gracie passed by them both and walked to the window. "We have to talk. I need you to understand some things."

Jin sat down on the bed in front of her. He was all attention, looking deeply into her eyes. The look she gave him held genuine concern and reluctant regret. This ought to be entertaining. How should a young woman handle a strange man in her bedroom? He put a hand over his mouth to stifle his laughter.

"Listen, Jin, I want to help you. I really mean that, but having you stay with me in my room is...well, it's just not a good idea." She returned his gaze, running her eyes along his form. "Wait. Where did you get that jacket? You can't take things that don't belong to you."

She tugged at the back of the garment, pulling it off him. Muttering fiercely under her breath, Gracie began searching through the pockets. She lifted out a wallet and shook it at Jin. "Never mind, I'm too tired to think about anything, but a shower and room service."

Gracie picked up the phone and hit the front desk button. "Yes, this is Miss Berry in room...yes, that's right. I found someone's jacket and wallet in the hallway. They must have dropped it. Okay, I'll listen for the door. Oh, can I order room service too?"

She ordered a hearty breakfast—steak and eggs—with plenty of coffee on the side. Jin's mouth was already watering. She forced a smile as she hung up the phone. "There. No harm done. Breakfast should be here soon. Then you need to go."

He stood up and walked over to the window. "Have you stopped to consider why all this is happening?" They'd given her a view of the parking lot. Her captor had been on the cheap side.

"I don't care," she said, slumping down on the other bed. "I just want to get that device back and go home."

"You should care, Gracie. I believe war is coming." He sat down on the bed across from her again. "Millennia ago, there was a civil war. Our ancestors chose the wrong side and were cast out of Otherworld. The Seelie Court granted each Clan a strip of land on the outskirts of Otherworld, but most of the time we are banished to the Human Realm. The Unseelie Court are bitter rivals of the Seelie Court. They didn't want to give up the Human Realm. I believe they're plotting to take it back with the help of a powerful Seelie Descendant."

She looked at him blankly. "But, why now? If what you say is true, they've had hundreds of years to start a war."

Jin shrugged and shook his head. "I have no idea. The day and month makes sense though. Midsummer's Eve is a few days away. That's the time of year when the veil between Realms is at its weakest. Given help, the Unseelie Court could pass through and easily conquer this world. They have great power and are ruthless. There would be no bargains or mercy for the humans I'm afraid."

Her face paled. "Can't we warn someone? Can't we find a way to stop all this?"

"Not without proof."

The knock on the door startled them both. Breakfast had arrived. They ate a silent meal in their exhaustion. When the plates were licked clean, Gracie pushed at the rolling table with their empty dishes. Jin jumped up to help her and she shivered as his skin brushed her bare shoulder.

She stepped away from him and hurried to her suitcase. Pulling out a bright pink t-shirt, she disappeared into the bathroom. He heard the water turn on. Gracie hadn't seemed to make up her mind about him. He felt the deep attraction between them, but she was resistant for some reason. Perhaps she was the wise one. Even thinking of attractions right now was rather foolish. His life was out of control. He needed to stop playing Viper's fool and start on the offensive. Finding out Gracie's identity might be a good start.

He crept soundlessly across the floor, looking for the gold belt containing her ID and money. Damn it. The belt wasn't out in the open. He came to the bathroom door and opened it a crack. Gracie's golden belt was on the counter resting on top of her ruined dress. She might have trusted Jin with her life, but she wasn't willing to trust him with her money.

Smart girl. She was learning. His eyes drifted to the shower. Gracie stood behind a wall-length panel of glass. Water and soap washed down her bare skin. He forced himself away from the view, which was a little too exhilarating at the moment.

Sitting down on the edge of his bed, he scanned the room. There had to be a clue to Gracie's identity somewhere. He'd find out who she really was, contact her handler and then get the truth. His eyes rested on the mobile phone Gracie had abandoned. Jin leaned back against the pillows and began looking through her contact list. The typical entries popped up, family and friends. He found one number for work with a San Diego area code. In fact, all her contacts were located in San Diego. Either this girl was very sheltered or her identity was a complete fake.

Jin went to her inbox and got an "inbox full" error. Over fifty unopened messages were waiting to be read. All of them had been sent within the past twenty-four hours. He opened the oldest message from Dad.

"Need to talk about BBQ. Call me."

Jin opened another about an hour later from Dad again: *"Damn it! Answer your fckng phone right now."* The next one he chose was from early that morning. *"Please call me, Punkin. I'm worried. Can't find you at your house or with any of your friends. Call me."*

Now that sounded like a worried father. Unless he was Gracie's handler. Either way, "Dad" should be worried. Jin was about to hack her voicemail when the water stopped running. He stuffed the mobile under Gracie's pillow and hurried under the covers.

He rested on the pillow with his eyes closed, listening to her get ready for bed. Whoever her dad turned out to be—father or handler—it was imperative they contact him whether the girl wanted to or not. She needed someone to look after her. Then again, he needed Gracie along while he flushed out the unknown person who wanted him dead. Her handler might not like that plan. Musing on the possibilities, he drifted off to sleep.

Chapter Thirteen

"The temple of what?" Dull, bored eyes stared at Gracie over a large pile of files. This detective they'd pushed her off onto wasn't listening to her any better than the sergeant at the front desk. For three hours, Gracie had tried to convince the LVMPD she'd been kidnapped in their city and no one seemed to be taking her seriously.

"The Temple of Forbidden Pleasures," Gracie said, tapping on the paper in front of him. "I've told you twice already."

He sipped lazily from a stained coffee cup and glared at her. "So let me get this straight. You saved some guy's life, but you don't remember his last name. Then he kidnapped you, trying to make you part of his cult. This guy and his buddies drove you to his private club in a limo where people were being sold as fighters to rich investors."

"That's right," she said, watching his stone face. The nameplate on his desk read "Detective C. Rollins." Clearly, the detective didn't believe her.

She'd left Jin sleeping in the hotel room. They needed help from the authorities, and Jin wasn't exactly on board with the idea. After braving the afternoon heat and slow traffic in an overpriced cab to tell her story, she'd expected at least a little emotion. The policeman across from her didn't look the slightest bit outraged or even simply shocked. He just looked bored.

"And were these people being sold against their will, ma'am?"

"No," she said, hesitating when she thought about Jin in chains. "People were bidding on them, not buying them. They seemed pretty happy about it."

"I see. And were any of the other guests there against their will?"

"Well, no." She gripped the chair's uncomfortable seat in frustration. Now she was lying to the police for Jin. He so owed her. "But I certainly wasn't there by choice."

Gracie watched his calloused fingers type slowly on the computer. Each key clack struck at her frayed nerves. She turned away from him and looked out over the room of other clacking keyboards. No one in this building was going to believe her crazy story.

They probably listened to hundreds of wild alcohol-induced tales every day, though most of them didn't hear about acrobats turning into birds or women with fangs. And she wasn't about to share Jin's cockamamie story about the Seelie either. Talking about elves and pixies would get her locked up for sure.

Then she saw them. A group of blue suits were headed into the squad room, looking very official. Lou Fong, white hair neatly clipped and styled, was at their head. He stopped a uniformed police officer, flipping a badge at him. One of Fong's men showed the officer something on a tablet device. Fong lifted his hand to indicate someone's height. Gracie was pretty sure she fit that bill. She couldn't see any guns, but they were still dangerous without them. Grabbing her purse, she lifted off the chair.

"Look, let's just forget the whole thing. I've changed my mind." Gracie spun around and headed toward the back of the room, past the line of computers, moving toward a hall of offices. She risked a look over her shoulder and saw Fong speaking with Detective Rollins.

Perfect! She'd heard Raul's orders to find them, but she hadn't understood how determined this cult could be. Risking being caught posing as policemen in a police station ranked right up there on the desperation meter.

She ducked behind a vending machine and snuck a quick look. Fong was still standing by the officer's desk, chatting as if he had nothing better to do. Two of his men stood beside him, waiting. She gulped in a few more panicked breaths. More men had been with Fong earlier. They must have started their search. She had to find a way off this floor. Gawd knew where this hall would take her. She could be headed right for the holding cells.

Deciding to risk running into caged criminals, Gracie darted down the hall and hurried deeper into the bowels of the station. She skidded to a stop when a blue suit stepped into the hall in front of her. He gave her the smile of a jackal at feeding time. Gracie inched away as fast as she could on the slippery tile floor. Her back thudded against a brick wall of blue suits. All of them grinned in unison and then they grabbed her.

"Let me go!" Gracie struggled against the iron fists that held her. "I'll scream and every cop in this building will be on you in a heartbeat!"

"That would not be so good for them," one of the suits said. His Latin accent added to the threat of his words. Gracie looked down as he opened his jacket. A serious looking weapon hung beneath the fabric. While Gracie didn't know much about weapons, all she really needed to know was that they could kill police officers as easily as they could kill anyone else. One wrong word, and she might start a bloodbath.

"There you are, Miss Wainwright. Telling stories again, are we?" Fong shook his head and gave Detective Rollins a long suffering sigh. "We've been searching for this woman for the past thirty-six hours. She's a potential witness in a kidnapping, but uh, doesn't want to be cooperative. Who knows, she's probably lying again. We have to question her anyway. You understand how it is."

Another agent handed Rollins a stack of papers. He glanced at them quickly and then gave them back. "Glad she's yours." Detective Rollins shook his head.

Gracie shifted uncomfortably in their grip. Special Bogus Agent Fong took her arm, yanking it sharply and then twisted. She winced with a hiss. Now that they had her, these guys wouldn't give her up easily. Fong loosened his grip when she stopped resisting. She knew what they were capable of. No cop in the building could stop them from taking her now. Fong pulled her away from the desk, and they headed to the elevators.

"Listen to me, my last name isn't Wainwright. I'm not who you think I am."

"Don't give me any trouble, Titania. We wouldn't want your wrist sore from the handcuffs, now would we? Not this soon before you're marked." He pulled her forward into the elevator. "You're going to take us to Jin now. Believe me when I say I'll hurt you in other places if you don't cooperate."

Gracie's mind raced while they headed down to the lobby level. She was no match for these guys; nobody was, well, except Jin. They certainly were afraid of him. Gawd! She'd made another stupid move coming to the police station alone. But one bit of luck was in her favor. Detective Rollins hadn't blurted out her real name.

They moved into the parking garage of the large gray building. Each step into its depths felt to her like another foot closer to the gallows. Gracie couldn't see a way out of this. The men with her were zealots in their cult. They'd dared to march into a police station and kidnap her again. For them, she was a valuable tool to get to Jin.

Gracie began to shake. She wasn't a fearless heroine in some movie. They would hurt her, and she'd take them back to the hotel eventually. She wasn't a fool either. When Jin woke up, he would run as fast as he could out of Vegas and away from her. No matter what they did, she'd keep them busy until he had a chance to leave that hotel room. Jin had saved her life. She owed him that much.

Suddenly, the lights flickered and died. Dimly lit by the sunbeams crashing between the parking garage's pillars, the structure became a bizarre maze of blacks and grays. Fong stopped. He pulled his weapon, brandishing it close to her arm. The others spread out a little, looking sharply into the darkness. Gracie saw it first, her scream warning the rest.

A massive shadow reached from the ground, spanning up toward them across the ceiling. Someone or something was hovering between the cars. Gracie shook her head in a daze. No one could make that big of a shadow with no light source. It was impossible. Then again, she'd seen a great many impossible things in the past few days.

An orange-red circle glowed in the darkness. Then a strange whirring sound echoed against the walls of the parking garage. The circle shot out of the darkness, growing in size as it approached. It hit one of the men to Fong's right. The orange-red light of the circle struck him at his nose and his torso. Three large pieces of the man slid to the pavement. Gracie saw no blood. The man's body parts seemed to have been cauterized from the heat of the circle.

"Holy fuck! What was that?" one of the men yelled.

"It would appear we're not the only ones looking for Jin." Fong dropped Gracie's arm and pointed his weapon at the shadow. Then the dark mass was gone. The strange whirring sound echoed among the bumpers again. This time Fong ducked behind a Land Rover, leaving Gracie standing in the middle of the garage with her mouth open. She stood frozen, watching the deadly circle of light approach. She stood there with the silent scream still on her lips, her feet refusing to move when the next man was cut in pieces by the circle.

Shots rang out to her right. Fong was firing wildly into the darkness. He was down to two henchmen, and he was scared. But what remained of his blue-suited crew had chosen to stand their ground. Gracie stared at the men shooting at the nothingness. What she saw didn't make sense to her already-rattled nerves. The men stood in a straight line, firing without weapons. A part of her mind suggested she was in shock.

Gracie covered her ears, backing away from the fallen body parts. Hands grabbed her and pulled her behind a vehicle. She turned to face her new captor and looked upon a nightmare. His massive form was completely covered in an ash shroud straight from an old horror movie. On his head was a wide-brimmed black hat that hid his face. He looked like death. God, he was terrifying.

"Run!" he said in a voice that rocked her to her bones. He pushed her away from him and raised his finger up at the same time. The orange-red circle shot out from the tip, striking another of Fong's henchmen. Gracie saw the light come from his finger, but she still couldn't believe it. That didn't register as real. It was impossible.

Gracie's legs took over. She leapt over the short wall of the garage and ran as fast as she could away from the violence. A crowd of police officers started pouring in from the station. Fong's gunplay had begun to draw a crowd. The other man, the nightmare, hadn't made a sound. Gracie trembled when she remembered the death she saw in his eyes.

She plunged toward the busy street and threw her body at the side of an empty cab pulling out of the station. Then she climbed inside without waiting for a greeting and watched the garage through the open window as the cab pulled away. A pair of dark eyes under a wide brim hat watched her leave. Whoever this strange man might be, he'd known where she was and when she would be escorted outside. Either he'd planned to take her for his own prize or force her to take him to Jin. She couldn't be sure if he was friend or foe. Either way, he scared the hell out of her. She'd see those horrible eyes in her nightmares.

She leaned back in the plush seat and the tears came in heavy sobs. Gracie pressed her sweaty palms over her eyelids. She was on her own now with no idea what to do next. The police didn't believe her, Jin was long gone and she couldn't go to her family, not if she wanted to keep them safe.

Something tapped against Gracie's hand. She lowered it and saw a hanky box poking toward her face. Gracie accepted the box from the driver and took out a few tissues. She nodded her thanks, but he pulled the collar of his jacket up around his cheeks and sank down in the seat. That was odd. Who wore a coat during summertime in Las Vegas? Gracie tried to get another peek, but they were pulling up to the Styles Casino.

Gracie got out and leaned next to the driver's window. She grabbed a ten from her purse and was about to hand it to him, when her brain caught up with her. "Hey, how did you know where I was staying?" The cabbie sped away without answering and without his fare.

She stuffed the ten in her pocket, watching the back of the cab as it hit the Strip. Its rear end shimmered from yellow to a bright green as the shape began to change. Gracie turned away. She was losing it. The cab hadn't changed colors or shapes, and the desert had played tricks with her eyes when she thought she saw that sports car turn into a diesel truck. Those men in the police station garage hadn't fired shots without any guns. And the deadly circles of orange...well, she couldn't explain those yet.

Her head was pounding by the time she got inside the hotel. The loud dings from every square inch of the casino didn't help as she walked toward the elevator. Denying that these Seelie Descendants were real was getting harder with each passing moment. Whether through weird luck or some sort of genetic mutation, she had become one of them.

What was she going to tell Dad and Brenda? A cold beer would really go down good right now. She needed to think things through in a quiet place. Stepping into the elevator, she closed her eyes to block out the headache trying to settle in her temples.

Two hands grabbed her waist from behind. She let out a scream and thrust her elbow back hard into the attacker's gut. Throwing herself at the elevator buttons, she began pushing them like a crazy person.

"Damn, Gracie, it's me!" Glen fell against the back of the elevator, rubbing at his stomach. His shaggy blond hair and tan skin looked green under the dim light in there. He stood up, adjusting his baggy surfer shorts. The amusement in his eyes grated on her last nerve.

"What the hell are you doing here?" The elevator doors swung open and she hurried onto her floor. Glen followed, trying to take her arm. She batted him away. "How the hell did you know where I was?"

"I went to see Kay, but she wouldn't tell me where you went." Glen gave her a slow smile. His fingers smoothed at Gracie's collar. "Sherri told me where you'd gone after I bought her a drink. She heard you and Kay planning the trip."

"A drink? Are you sure that's all it took?" Gracie made a grand gesture of pulling the key card from her bag, hoping Glen didn't notice her confusion. She had no memory of Kay helping her plan her trip.

"You've come a long distance for nothing, Glen."

"Come on, Gracie, you can't just leave me standing out here. I came all this way."

Yeah, he didn't seem worried about intruding on her phony vacation. The thought she might not want him with her hadn't occurred to the arrogant jerk. "Look, Glen, I can't deal with you right now. Go home."

"What?" Clearly that wasn't the answer Glen had expected.

Gracie turned on him, angrier than she had ever felt before. "You cheated on me. Now you come crawling back, butting into my vacation and expect a warm welcome? You probably thought I'd share my bed with you too, right?"

Glen's vacant expression told her that was exactly what he'd thought. "Gracie, you know we belong together. I just needed to sow a few wild oats before we get married." Glen gave her that condescending smirk. "It's not as if you have anybody waiting in the wings. You can't do without me, Gracie, and you know it."

"Oh I can do better, Glen. I have me and I like who I am. I like my life without you!"

"Yeah right, if you can do better than me, then why haven't you?"

And then something much better opened the door of the hotel room, dressed in nothing but a towel. Jin's green eyes narrowed as he looked at Glen in warning. He took Gracie's hand and gently pulled her behind him.

"Who the hell is this?" Glen barked, the red veins popping out all over his face. At one time, Gracie would have loved for him to be jealous. Now, she could only think of her own anger and what she and Jin had already endured over the past twenty-four hours. Glen had about four inches on Jin in height and at least fifty pounds. And Glen was used to being a bully.

"It's none of your business what Jin and I are doing." She was shaking now, angry and scared at the same time. "Get out of here."

"Jin?" Glen spat and looked the smaller man up and down. "You're playing around with this... Damn it, Gracie, you have no idea what you're getting involved with. I'm not leaving here without you."

Glen poked at Jin's chest. Bad move. The muscle on Jin's arm tightened, not in fear, but he seemed to be preparing for something. His response came with shocking speed. Jin grabbed Glen's finger in mid-poke and snapped it like a twig. With the same hand, he smashed his fist into Glen's nose, dropping him to the floor. Jin put an arm around Gracie's waist and ushered her inside, shutting the door like a punctuation mark.

"Listen, I'm sorry about Glen. He's a bigot and a bully." She sighed and leaned against the wall. "I'm sorry about everything, Jin. I went to the police, but they wouldn't believe me. And then Fong and his goons showed up."

Gracie went to the mini bar and opened a ten-dollar bottle of beer. She sank onto the end of her bed and gulped the liquid down in a few quick swallows. When she lowered the bottle, she saw Jin watching her.

"What are you still doing here anyway? I was pretty sure you'd want to leave as soon as you could." She gave him a tired grin and gulped the last swallow of beer. "Gawd, the police practically laughed me out of the station for making up stories. They were eager to hand me over when Fong and his goons came." Gracie put the empty bottle on the floor and massaged at her aching neck.

"They almost had me, Jin. I'd be in Raul's hands right now if it wasn't for that strange man who helped me. At least I think he helped me. He killed those men with some kind of orange light. I don't know. Things happened so quickly. I thought he fired the light from his finger. I must sound like a totally crazy person." She shook her head.

"Well, if you told the police you went to a party in the suburbs of Otherworld, then, yes, I'm sure they thought you were a crazy person." He joined her at the end of the bed and took her hand in his. "You shouldn't have taken the risk. We stick together from now on, right?"

Gracie lifted a pair of wire cutters out of her purse. "Here, I liberated this from a maintenance cart downstairs. I think it may work on that collar." She leaned in close. "You're starting to rub off on me and not in a good way."

She touched his skin with gentle fingers and smoothed around the collar, looking for a place to cut. The metal was tight against his throat. Jin's fingers touched hers, softly caressing them. They moved up her arm and came to rest upon her cheek. He lifted his face toward hers, bringing his lips closer.

The practical side of Gracie counseled her to put a stop to his line of action right then and there. Hadn't she promised herself to stay away from bad boys? Not to mention that an ass-kicking Seelie from another world did not a good boyfriend make. Her eyes closed as his hand caressed the small of her back, pulling her closer. Tensing with anticipation, she waited for the contact.

A strange whistle from the hall pierced through the door. Jin's advance stopped. The whistle sounded again. He suddenly lifted up away from her and roared a feral growl. The quick pinch at the base of her neck brought the peace of darkness and took her toward sleep.

Chapter Fourteen

Another distinctive whistle pierced the silence. Its owner was close to their room now. Jin pulled open the door. A young man with strawberry hair and a ruddy complexion jumped in surprise, then entered the room. He was dressed in a hideous Hawaiian shirt and linen pants. A bushy moustache quivered over the grin on his lips. Myles Wainwright was Jin's favorite cousin. They'd been close friends since their boarding school days, which was why Jin had called him, asking for a little help.

Myles was a Normal. His lack of Seelie power dropped him to the Wainwright Clan's unacceptable list. As a bastard, Jin shared the same status as his cousin. Tired of being treated like a second-class citizen, Myles had moved to Vancouver, British Columbia where Jin had helped him get started in a small import and export business.

"Hello, Cousin. I'm happy to see you, but your timing is horrible."

"You're a bit underdressed. I'll pass on the embrace." Myles grinned and handed Jin a shopping bag. He looked at Gracie's unconscious form. "Sorry, I've interrupted whatever this is. Oh and by the way, you have an unconscious man in the hall. A rival perhaps?"

"It isn't like that." Jin brushed the lock of hair out of Gracie's face. "Do you recognize her? I was thinking she may be from the Wainwright Clan or one of Bryn's people."

"I've never seen her before." Myles shrugged and sat down on the other bed. "He's eager to speak to you. Bryn, I mean. And he sent this."

Myles handed Jin a Seelie universal key guaranteed to open anything once. Jin took the little key from his cousin and smiled. Dropping the shopping bag on the bed, he touched the key to his neck. It popped open the collar with one quick twist. A thousand and one blessings upon Bryn's head! Jin groaned with relief and rubbed at his irritated skin. The key sputtered, expelling the last bit of Seelie magic. Then it disintegrated into small pieces of metal along with the collar.

Myles rubbed his hands nervously on the bedspread. "You were right not to try to contact us. We've been watched while you were on the run. Of course, Bryn has been monitoring the Clans too. When he heard that you'd been captured, I came to Vegas straight away."

Jin took the ice bucket from the desk and went to the bathroom. He filled the bucket with water and yanked open the room door. Glen was still sprawled out on the rug across from their room. Why Gracie had wasted time on a Normal, he couldn't guess. Her station as a pre-cog would afford her the choice of any lover who caught her fancy. Men and women would die trying to win her favor. Instead, she'd chosen an arrogant prat who had no idea of her worth.

Shaggy blond hair fell above the two eyes that were starting to blacken. Jin sneered at the sloppy lout and his insufferable baggy shorts. What an ass. He threw the bucket of water and waited for Glen to stop sputtering. He grabbed Glen's throat, pulling him to his feet, and squeezed. Ignoring the slaps of impotent anger, Jin kept up the pressure until he saw the glint of another being behind those frightened eyes.

"And who's enthrall are you? Let your master speak now!" He received no answer, but power swirled in anger behind the Normal's eyes. "I am a son of the Wainwright Clan. I know you're there. Tell me what you want with Gracie or I'll kill your enthrall right now. That won't be very pleasant for you while you're joined."

"Have a care, Jin. You've stumbled across a situation that's none of your business. Leave Gracie, and be on your way. I warn you. I will have her back." The voice coming from Glen's swollen lip held power now. His master was finally ready to talk.

Only a handful of Descendants could enthrall a pre-cog. Fewer still had such hatred for Jin. One primary candidate topped the list. Druid, his mother's pet pre-cog, had the power and skill to trap another pre-cog. Jin shook his head. No, Eleanor Wainwright kept a close eye on her former consort after he'd tried to take her Clan from her. It had to be someone else.

Jin let a hard smile cross his face. "My pre-cog friend is very popular and in high demand. I think it best she stay with me for the time being."

"Damn your insufferable interference! You're about to be very sorry."

"Oh, I'm sure."

The power disappeared from behind Glen's eyes as his master fled. Glen sat rigid on the floor, staring up at Jin. Then he staggered to his feet. He showed an arrogance normally absent in enthrall victims. Gracie's ex-lover might have been one of those foolish humans who sought out Seelie Descendant masters. They entered into a contract expecting to gain something from the relationship, but soon learned the harsh realities of being a slave. And once the contract was voluntarily signed, nothing would break it. Death became their only release. The catacombs under the London Pillar were full of disappointed Normals.

"Glen, I want you to listen to me carefully." Jin held up a fist to get his point across. "Come near Gracie again, and I'll put you in a body cast. Do you understand?"

"Where did she dig you up, some dive bar?" His smashed nose made Glen's voice nasally. "Whatever, grasshopper. Just send the leftovers back to me when you're through. I'm in it for her share of daddy's business."

Jin was on him in a furious volley of fists. Glen dropped unsteadily to his knees, slightly more bloodied than before. His eyes went wide for a moment as he stared up at Jin. Then he laughed. "You wait until my master catches up with you. You think you've won? He always gets what he wants. Gracie is no exception."

Jin threw Glen down the hall toward the elevators. He kept his murderous glare on the bastard until Glen's baggy shorts disappeared from view. They had, Jin was pleased to note, a large wet spot on the front.

Myles was holding the door for Jin as he turned back toward the room. An amused smirk was on his face. "Well, that's a first. I was only kidding when I suggested he was a rival."

"I'm not jealous, if that's what you're insinuating." Jin shoved the ice bucket into Myles' arms. "I don't do jealous."

Jin moved to the curtains, pretending to be very interested in the view while he calmed down. He wasn't the possessive sort when it came to women. It wasn't any of his business who Gracie wasted her love on. His anger was out of concern for their safety. The last thing they needed was another complication. His urge to throw Glen off the top of the hotel was simply frustration, not jealousy.

"Adventure isn't really your forte, Myles." He turned away from the view when he'd found his serenity again. "I'm grateful to you."

"My coming to join you wasn't entirely saint-like. I need your help. Someone has been sabotaging the business. They began hijacking and vandalizing cargo. It's gotten ugly. We've had deaths." Myles set the bucket down on the bathroom counter and leaned against the door frame. "The police don't have any leads. I've asked the Wainwright Clan for help. I think you can guess their response."

"Yes, I'm afraid Mother hasn't forgiven you for being my business partner." Jin walked over to the shopping bag. "I think the same person who put a death mark out on me may be sabotaging the business. They want me utterly destroyed. I'm sorry you've had to get involved in this. I know how much the business means to you."

"I'm glad we can solve this together then," his cousin said with a half-smile. "Well, nothing will be solved if you insist on staying in that towel."

Jin laughed and leaned over to dig through the bag. Myles was blood, and a faithful friend. Whoever targeted him would soon wish he'd never had the idea. Jin lifted up a black t-shirt with a "Welcome to Las Vegas" sign on it and made a face. Well-intentioned or not, his cousin had lousy taste.

"Listen, it was either that shirt or a red 'I love the Strip' polo with lips on it."

Jin opened the shopping bag again and pulled out a pair of jeans, a t-shirt and underwear. A pair of cheap tennis shoes fell out of the box on the chair. Jin pulled on the shoes and moved to stand in front of the mirror. A tourist fresh from the nearest mall stood glaring back at him. All he needed was a camera around his neck to complete the picture.

"Ghastly," Jin murmured.

He took the second key out of Gracie's purse and put the "Privacy Please" sign on the door. She'd be safe enough for the short time he'd be gone. He and his cousin headed down the hall toward the elevators. The décor was tastefully done. Someone had taken great care in making sure the ambiance stayed consistent throughout the hotel. Even the cheap rooms had been handsomely decorated to match the theme. Jin looked forward to seeing what the high-roller area offered.

Myles walked silently beside him, trying to suppress a laugh. He caught Jin's sour look and shrugged. "Sorry, Cousin, I've never seen you looking so dumpy. The infamous Jin walking among the common tourists. It's funny." He shoved Jin's shoulder. "So, what's our plan?"

"Someone has put a death mark out on me and I want to find out who. I'm tired of running. I want my life back. I'll take it by force if necessary." They stepped on the elevator and Jin hit the casino level button. "We start with the people who captured me. Raul and Viper said they didn't know who was behind the death mark. I don't believe them. They have to have an idea."

"You can't just ring Raul's doorbell. Besides, he's probably moved the temporary portal to some other location. How will we find them?"

"It seems I'm to be the star attraction in their fight club this week. Don't worry. They'll come to us."

Myles gripped his arm. Worry showed on his face. "You don't know if that death mark specifies your capture dead or alive. They may put a bullet in your skull rather than try to capture you again."

That was a point Jin hadn't considered. "We have a backup plan. The girl, Gracie, is a pre-cog with no Clan markings. Either she's unaffiliated or she's hiding to get at me. Raul wants her in the worst way. She's our bait." Jin rolled his eyes when Myles frowned. "They won't hurt her. She's too valuable. Listen, you can't tell anyone about Gracie. She's important to me. I mean she's necessary to the plan. You and Bryn are the only ones I trust right now. Promise."

Myles raised an eyebrow. "Of course, Jin, you can always count on me."

The elevator took them to the casino floor. Jin nodded politely to the attendant.

The two men wandered for a while among the flashing lights and mesmerized tourists anchored to their slot machines. Lining the bright runway style walkway to the lobby, craps, roulette and poker did their best to pull Jin away from his mission.

He passed the gambling by without giving into temptation. He had business to take care of, and the clock was ticking. In only a matter of time his enemies and Gracie's suitors would find them. They needed to be prepared with the upper hand.

Jin stopped in the center of the lobby, staring up at the ceiling. It really was incredible and elaborately done. Tugging at his shirt's cheap fabric, he wished he didn't have a massive red sign on its front marking him as a tourist.

People passed by without even acknowledging his presence. Jin shrugged. Maybe the simple tourist persona was more effective than he'd thought. It definitely wasn't his typical style.

"I'm going to say hello to an old friend," Jin told Myles. "Why don't you meet us in the parking garage. We'll be there shortly."

"I don't even want to know what you're really going to do." Myles chuckled and headed toward the exit.

"Get out of the way, you moron." A very white, very blond man spat at Jin. His accent marked him as South African from the brutal twist of his vowels. He pushed Jin out of the path of the brass luggage cart and turned his back as if Jin were nothing. Gold rings dripped from his fingers. The cut of his clothing was expensive—a rich foreigner leaving for the airport. Perfect.

Jin brushed lightly against Blondie's back and then moved casually to a corner of the lobby where a cappuccino café waited. He opened the man's wallet and thumbed through the cash. Several hundred-dollar bills were tucked into the expensive leather. Somebody had been a lucky boy.

Jin plucked several bills out of the back, leaving the smaller currency amounts close to the front. It was easier to hand out the twenties to airport vendors. He folded a few paper napkins into thin strips and tucked them back between the one-hundred-dollar bills, Jin knew the man wouldn't look at until he got home. Exchange rates outside the US were much better.

Jin turned his attention to the rainbow of credit cards stuffed into the man's wallet. A *Dubai First Royale* jumped into his fingers. Blondie had taste if not common sense, but then again, the rich didn't need to worry about such things. Real gold and diamonds decorated the card. Jin, his heart breaking, put the card back. Such a theft would be much too obvious.

"Sorry, darling, Daddy would miss you right away. We need your plain sister."

"Centurion or platinum?" Jin bit his lips as he smoothed over the titanium surface of the centurion. No, it was best he show some restraint. From the rubbed marks on the titanium surface of the centurion, it appeared that was the card the man preferred. The platinum card looked like a newer issue and very untouched. It would get Jin through the door in style. He tucked the other cards back in the wallet and stuffed the platinum into his pocket.

He made his way through the revolving door to stand by the porter loading bags into a limo for the South African. After several warnings from the belligerent guest, the young local looked as though he wanted to beat the idiot with his own luggage and then quit.

Jin moved up behind the man and lightly put his wallet back. He winked at the porter, who kept his mouth closed and his eyes on Jin. The departing guest didn't tip the porter, and the limo drove away. Jin came to join the porter and handed him a hundred-dollar bill.

"Beautiful afternoon, isn't it?"

"Yes, sir, it certainly is." The attendant stuffed the money away quickly. "Anything you need, sir, just let me know. "

"Thank you. I'll remember that."

Jin entered the hotel again. This time the door was held open for him. He moved to the concierge desk, pleased to see a familiar face among the chic suits and perfectly coiffed hair.

"Hello, Clayton," Jin said.

Shoulders stiffened in unhappy surprise. The concierge turned around slowly, keeping a practiced, neutral expression on his face. "How nice it is to see you again, sir." The classy Italian accent oozed out of him, causing stirs among his female co-workers and the pretty guests within earshot.

"I wonder if you could assist me with a private matter, Clayton," Jin said, putting a little furrow in his brow. "It's in the garage, you see."

"Of course, sir." Clayton's words oozed with helpfulness, but the look in his eyes shot daggers.

They walked together to the hotel parking structure, chatting pleasantly about the weather. When Clayton was sure they were alone, he pushed Jin into a pillar and put the tip of a very sharp knife against the elf's kidney.

"What the hell are you doing here, Jin?" Clayton's Liverpool accent grated against the concrete walls. "I thought you were dead. And now you show up here dragging your shit with you?"

"Drop the knife, friend," Myles warned behind Clayton. "I wouldn't want to ruin that pretty suit with a bullet hole."

Jin threw an arm up to knock away the blade, grabbed Clayton's arm and twisted it behind his back. He held Clayton's face against the concrete. "Now, is that any way to treat an old friend you owe fifty-thousand pounds?" Jin twisted a little harder until Clayton cried out and then he let the wrist go.

Clayton staggered away and began straightening his suit. "I don't have the money. It took everything I had to buy a new identity when that last job went south."

"So, you skim off the top here then?"

"No, the general manager watches the books." Clayton's face grew worried. "Listen, Jin, this is a legitimate job. If I can stay clean, I have a real chance to make something of my life. They're talking about opening up one of these in Monte Carlo."

"You've gone straight?" Jin shivered. "What's happened to the world since I've been away?"

"That's right, mate, and I don't need any of your kind of trouble here. I've heard a nasty rumor going around all the Clan-friendly organizations. Someone high up in Clan society has a hit out on you. Anybody who helps you is screwed."

Jin observed the animal terror on Clayton's face. The two of them had done jobs together before. Clayton was no coward and didn't scare easily. Jin's new enemy had taken great care to close any avenues he might look to for help. It would make the job of staying alive much more difficult.

"Very well. Do me this favor and we'll mark the books even." Jin reached in his pocket for the credit card and handed it to Clayton. "I want the high-roller suite for a few days. We need a place to lay low until we come up with a plan. I'll want the full treatment of course, new clothes, champagne, the works. The lady I'm with..." Jin gave Clayton a sour look when he snorted. "The lady I'm with, Gracie Berry, will have the finest of everything while she's here. Do you understand?"

"Wait, Gracie Berry, the dye-job blonde with the nice arse? You're together? But she's not even rich. What are you playing at?"

"That's not your affair." Jin folded his arms, stuffing down his irritation. "You'll treat her like a duchess, Clayton, or I'll stick that knife so far up your butt, you'll be able to whistle through your belly button. Understand?"

"Yeah, mate, I've got the picture." Clayton looked down at the credit card. "Shall I take you gentlemen to your suite, Mr. ...Amherst?"

"Yes." Jin grinned. "And then I'd like to have a few things sent up to the room."

Chapter Fifteen

"What do you mean we've been upgraded?"

Gracie rubbed at the back of her neck. It felt sore. The last thing she remembered was holding wire cutters against Jin's collar. He'd been about to kiss her. She, against her better judgment, was going to let him. Then she'd felt a pinch and the world went dark. Her eyes opened again to find the Italian concierge, Clayton, shaking her awake. Jin was gone.

"Yes, Signorina, your companion has already taken care of your things." The concierge brushed at an imaginary spot on his sleeve. The gesture communicated his disapproval of the questionable activities that had taken place in her room. "I will show you to your suite."

He cleared his throat with a touch of impatience and rocked from toe to heel, waiting. She noticed he very carefully avoided looking at her. The guy was a good candidate for a nervous breakdown.

"So is Jin in the new room?"

"Yes, Signorina, I will take you to him now." She noted a slight tightening of his lips and the burning fire of resentment in his eyes. That was pretty telling.

They headed out into the hall where Clayton ushered her into a waiting elevator. He swiped a key card and hit the button for the penthouse. She backed up against the wall as the elevator rose sharply. Clayton faced away from her toward the door. His shoulders tightened. He hadn't said why she'd been upgraded. It might have been some hotel contest, but Clayton's manner didn't exactly exude happiness. This was one ticked-off concierge. She decided not to press him for answers.

The elevator doors opened onto a short marble-encrusted hall. Two sets of suite doors were positioned at each end. Clayton hurried to the one on the far left. Gracie followed him, tiptoeing over the cold marble tiles on her bare feet. He pushed open the double doors and escorted her into a lavish suite. Expensive black furnishings filled the rooms. A massive television screen broadcasted the night's weather on one side, while a well-stocked bar stood against the other.

Floating over the scene like a beautiful cloud of crystal was an ultramodern chandelier. Its style was similar to a Chihuly sculpture. A wall of glass framed the chandelier against the backdrop of Las Vegas. Taking a deep breath, Gracie hurried across the sea of chilly marble to the full-length window. This suite overlooked the casino's grounds, statuary and gardens. Just over the rooftop of another hotel, the lights of the Strip shimmered in the night sky. Her afternoon had fallen away into evening.

"I didn't know they made rooms like this."

"You are indeed fortunate." The concierge clicked his heels together and bowed again. "If you need anything, please just call and I'll take care of it personally."

"That will do for now, Clayton. Thank you." As Clayton withdrew, Jin descended the stairs dressed in an expensive black suit. His hair had been trimmed into a collar-length cut she'd seen on a few celebrities. He smiled, watching her reaction with those deep eyes. The fleeting smile faded as he tugged at the sleeves of his black silk shirt, pulling the fabric in place beneath the suit jacket. He looked sleek, sophisticated and hot as hell.

"Where did you get those clothes and this room? Who's paying for all this?" Gracie put her hand to her forehead. "Oh, gawd, they have my credit card number."

He came at her in a gust of charm and style. Taking her hand, he kissed it softly. Spicy cologne, expensive no doubt, wafted toward her. Wow, he smelled good. The aroma certainly didn't come from a drugstore shelf. Her nose took another covert whiff. Might as well enjoy the experience. She was paying for it.

"Our hotel and these clothes are a gift from a benefactor. Now, are you going to tell me what you Saw in your vision when we first laid eyes on each other?"

Jin's body shifted a little. Now he looked alert, interested. So that was it. He'd stuck close to her this whole time to find out what she'd Seen. The realization stung a bit, but she supposed she didn't blame him. A glance into the future was an advantage they both could use right about then.

"We were in a forest and someone was chasing us."

"Were we lovers?" He wore an insolent grin on his face that she was coming to recognize all too well.

"Really? That's what you want to ask me?" She threw up her hands. "How about asking why we were in that forest and where it is? Obviously it wasn't in Nevada."

"That sounds like a yes to me."

Just then a Tommy Bahama poster model came out of the bathroom. She guessed this stranger was in his late twenties or early thirties. Carmel hair was neatly trimmed against sunburned ears. A bushy mustache wiggled as he smiled at her.

"Who the hell are you?" Gracie asked.

"This is my cousin, Myles. He's a Normal, or human, if you prefer."

"Welcome aboard," she told Myles. A dull ache began to creep up her neck to her head. She rubbed at her temples. "So, guys, why am I here? Why didn't you leave me in my room and run?"

"I want to find out who put that death mark out on me, Gracie. In order to do that, I need to draw out Raul and his friends. We'll trap one of them and convince them to take us to the person behind my death mark."

"Convince, huh?" She folded her arms again and watched Jin's expectant look. "A pre-cog would come in handy trapping one of Raul's goons. Especially one he wants so bad. Is that it? You want to use me as bait." She felt disgusted with Jin—and with herself.

"Did it occur to you that if you help us, you may be able to get the device back and protect your family?" Jin scanned her face with a cat-like intensity.

"Do you think you can return home and go into hiding?"

"Oh right, I'll sit there and wait for Raul to find my family once he analyzes the device. I need to get it back, Jin. They'll hurt my dad if I don't!"

"Then help me lure Raul out. He wants you just as much as he wants me."

Gracie rubbed at her temples again. All this running and danger was way out of her ordinary experience. She'd just started feeling a little safe again. Now he was asking her to face their attackers. She wrapped her arms around her body with a shiver. But what choice did she have? Raul wouldn't simply give her the device back. Jin was right. She'd have to take it. Besides, she'd found a powerful ally. If anyone could help her out of this mess, it was Jin. The tiny bit of hope eased her headache a bit.

"What do I need to do?"

"Gracie Berry, you are a godsend!" Jin gave her a quick kiss on the forehead. "Myles and I are going to meet a friend of mine to see if he can help us. Stay here until I get back."

"What do you mean stay here?"

Gracie grabbed his lapel before he could turn away. She was a part of this now. No way would she be left out of the decisions like some lost puppy. Jin was her only hope of sorting out this mess. She needed to stick with him to make sure that device got back into the right hands—hers.

"I'll be moving in dangerous circles this evening." Jin turned away, walking to the bar's countertop. Keeping his back to her, he stuffed his wallet and a few dangerous-looking items into his pockets. "I can't have you there complicating things."

"You think I'd be in the way, like the time I saved your ass in Raul's temple with my gift." She was hot now and more than a little tired of people treating her like a child. First Dad, then the voice and now this guy who clearly had forgotten what they'd been through and her part in it.

"If it weren't for me, you'd be Griffin kibble right now."

His body stiffened and his hands paused in their work. He turned slowly to face her. The utter lack of emotion in his manner reminded her Jin was no one to anger. And his cousin moved judiciously behind the bar counter, pretending to be engrossed in examining the liqueurs. But she stood her ground. Jin was dangerous. Yet whether it was her gift or from the brief time they'd spent together, she was convinced he wouldn't hurt her.

"I'm grateful to you." The steady gaze of determination was in his eyes. "Please understand. I'm tired of hiding from these people. I want my life back. That means I have to take some risks. I can work faster and better on my own. You're staying here where it's safe."

The door to the suite crashed open. Three men pushed through the ruined wood. She recognized them. They'd almost been captured by the older man leading their group as she and Jin were trying to escape Raul's mansion. The others were the red-headed twins they'd left unconscious beside Viper.

Both twins eyed Jin intensely, waving their blades toward him in steady arches.

"How'd they find us?" She stepped back almost on Myles' feet.

Clayton stuck his head around the doorjamb. His eyes held a mixture of anger and shame when he looked at Jin. Gracie saw no signs of violence against him on his face or suit. He'd betrayed them. Well, that answered her question.

"Clayton, you bastard!" Jin growled, stepping between her and the men. "Myles, take Gracie upstairs."

Jin's cousin gripped her arm, pulling Gracie backward. His hands were rough and calloused. Dad would have called them working hands. Now they were pulling her away from a fight in which her only ally was outnumbered. She had to be able to do something. She began to resist. Myles gently, but firmly insisted.

"He doesn't need our help, Miss Berry. You're about to see why they call him the Hand of Justice."

The twins moved forward, their blades slicing the air in perfect unison. Each brother kept his sword active as they branched out to circle Jin. Gracie winced at the rapid whirring of the blades. Speed formed them into the illusion of a solid circle of iron. Jin remained motionless, a vessel of pure serenity in the very center of the deadly tornado.

"Have a care, Harbin. We're about to do battle with the Hand of Justice. Rumors speak of his speed. He's untouchable in a fight, or so they say." The twin on the left snickered. "Or at least he used to be. Big Daddy Zhao has shunned him."

"Oh yes. What is it they call him now, Henri?" Harbin tilted his head slightly, dropping his lips into a pout. "Pariah? Yes, that's it. He turned coward. Well, coward, we've come to collect that empty head of yours."

Jin's serenity dissolved. The hard, emotionless look returned to his face. Myles tensed behind Gracie, unconsciously gripping his fingers deeper into her muscle. They waited together for Jin to make his move.

"This is about to get bloody. We need to get out of his way." Myles dragged her toward the stairs.

Clayton came at them in a rush, blocking their path. He held a gun. Sweat stains soaked his collar. He wiped at the droplets threatening to run into his eyes. Gracie recognized desperate fear when she saw it. Hell, she'd experienced it every moment the voice had kept residence in her mind.

"Not so fast, my little bird," he told Gracie, eyeing her as if she was his salvation. "I've been promised a sizable reward for your capture. You're about to get me back home in style."

"Jin is going to kick your ass, Clayton." Myles gripped Gracie's arm harder.

"He's a bit busy just now."

The quiet man in the back of the room had slowly taken off his jacket. Gracie screamed when his face began to change. His nose grew bigger, smashing in upon itself like a pug dog. Fabric in the man's shirt ripped. The glimmer of overhead lights caught the long steel quills sprouting from his tail.

"I've wanted a chance at you since that night in Paris," said the man, aiming his tail toward Jin. "I seldom miss."

"I owe you a strike, Perrin." Jin touched the fading red line on his jaw. "I'm afraid you won't find me an easy target now that I'm free of my collar."

A burst of air struck Gracie, bringing with it a puff of expensive cologne. Jin had vanished. Seconds later he reappeared behind Perrin. He brought his clenched fists down upon the back of the man's neck. Perrin fell to his knees. Jin's leg was a blur as he swung it in an arch. His heel smashed against the man's head. Perrin collapsed in a heap of flesh and metal.

"Fast," Gracie said in an awed whisper.

Myles used the distraction to throw his shoulder into Clayton's body. The gun flew across the marbled floor, coming to a stop against the large window panel. Gracie stumbled backward as they struggled. Myles was holding his own, but Clayton the betrayer had desperation on his side.

The twins were moving toward her now. Their swords had stopped the deadly motion. Henri had traded his blade for a set of handcuffs. They had different plans for her. Gracie looked for something to defend herself with, but she saw nothing heavy enough.

"Jin! A little help here!"

He crossed the distance in a few seconds, smashing a fist into Harbin's jaw. Twisting sharply, Jin threw the heel of his right foot at Henri. Both men staggered back.

"Behind you!" She waved wildly at Perrin. He was reaching toward his tail. Jin pulled Harbin against his chest at the same moment Perrin threw the quill. It penetrated deep into the young man's chest. His eyes opened wide as the life left his body.

"Harbin!" Henri pushed Jin out of the way and clutched at his twin. Crazed eyes found Perrin. He bolted forward at his brother's killer in a rage. Two quills punctured Henri's body just as his sword met flesh. Perrin collapsed on the floor in a puddle of blood. Henri fell beside him.

"Stay where you are, Jin!" Clayton cried from the window. He was holding the barrel of his gun toward Gracie. She hadn't noticed him moving as she watched the horrific drama with the twins unfold. Fear collapsed her lungs as she shrank away from the barrel. Her arms stretched out toward the shooter, an instinctive response to protect her own life. She'd never felt a terror so profound.

"Put the gun down, and I'll let you walk away," Jin said.

A shot rang out and then another. The glass behind Clayton shattered as a bloodied rose blossomed on his chest. He fell backward, out into the Vegas night. Myles came to stand by Gracie. The gun in his hand lowered slowly toward the floor.

Jin hurried toward them. "I think it's time we checked out of this hotel." He prodded Gracie up the stairs. "Grab something chic. Don't worry about the rest right now."

She paused at the top of the stairs in a daze. A massive loft hung suspended overlooking the bright lights of Vegas. The luxurious accommodations seemed surreal when her mind remembered the dead bodies downstairs. She hurried forward. Her suitcase had been emptied. Hanging in the wardrobe on one side were several expensive suits for Jin. The other side hosted the dresses that Kay had lent her. Nothing from her humdrum life at home remained.

Gracie opened the drawers situated between their clothes. Jin's undergarments were folded neatly inside. She closed the drawer with a thud and caught a whiff of his spicy cologne. She breathed it in. Then she remembered the smell as it mixed with the copper odor of blood. Her stomach lurched.

Breathing in gulps of air through her mouth, she checked in the next drawer and found lacey things. Expensive, sexy and barely there. Her own underwear was missing. "Where's my underwear?"

"If you're referring to those adult diapers, I threw them out," Jin said behind her. Damn he was quiet. Jin had that slinky dress hanging from his fingertip. Its metallic fabric shimmered in the light of the bedroom. One shoulder bare and one flowing sleeve to the elbow, it looked like a skimpy kite waving on his hand.

"I can't wear that."

Jin held her chin with his fingers. "Modesty is a luxury we can't afford right now. You're a beautiful, intelligent woman with an amazing spirit. I would suggest you start behaving like your true self for all our sakes." He moved a hand down her back and pulled her closer. "Grab appropriate shoes. Hurry, darling. We'll have unwanted visitors any moment."

Gracie clasped the straps of her borrowed black pumps. Jin moved an arm around her shoulder and ushered her to the elevators without giving her a chance to grab anything else. Myles handed Gracie her purse. He looked a bit shaken. Her guess was Myles wasn't used to this type of action either.

"We need to split up." Jin exchanged a look with his cousin. "Gracie and I will draw as much attention as we can. Tell our friend to hurry."

Myles nodded with a frown. The doors opened into the casino. Its lights seemed gaudy and terrifying now. Gracie blinked against the brightness. Myles gave them one last nod and was gone.

"Stay with me, Gracie," Jin whispered in her ear. "We're being followed. You must keep up."

They were being hunted again. Raul wasn't giving up easily. Any rational person would have steered clear of her after Fong and his men had been ambushed by the walking nightmare in the police parking garage. His terrible eyes were imprinted in her memory. She'd never forget his overpowering presence or the cold precision he'd used to exterminate Fong's men.

Warm air spread across her body in a rush as they hurried out of the casino's entrance. A white limo sat at the curb. Its uniformed chauffer stood waiting with the passenger's door open. The young man tipped his hat to Gracie. He stepped aside to allow Jin more space to nudge her inside.

"Caesar's Palace, driver." Jin eased into the limo seat with a practiced move. That told her about the kind of lifestyle he was used to more than words ever could. This wasn't a beer-and-football guy sitting next to her.

"We couldn't take two seconds to let me change in the restroom?" Sirens answered her question. "Okay, close your eyes then."

Jin pressed a button that raised the divider between the front seat and the back. He put both hands over his eyes. She took the opportunity to look at his face. It was calm and stony. No one would guess he'd just beaten the hell out of three guys and watched them die a few minutes before.

Gracie pulled off her clothes as the bright lights of the Strip passed by the limo windows. They were approaching the heart of the Strip. Gracie recognized the Paris and the little road where she'd first tangled with Raul. The limo floated past and then fought through the traffic of cars and humans to turned into a long driveway. She tugged the dress down over her hips, gawking out the window at the iconic Las Vegas Casino.

Brilliant lights illuminated the grounds of Caesar's Palace. Several valets rushed to open the door for them. Gracie pulled on her shoes and took a deep breath. Ready or not, they were here. Stares followed as they walked from the limo to the casino. Jin was getting what he wanted. All eyes were fixed on them.

He stopped at the entrance of the casino to let her take it all in. She'd been impressed by the Styles, but it couldn't compare to the marvel of Vegas design they stood in right now. Overwhelmed by the glamour and sounds, she allowed him to lead her deeper inside.

"What's your taste, darling? What games do you prefer?"

"Games? Do you really think we should be playing some stupid game when..."

He pulled her closer and pressed his lips to her ear. "We're meeting someone here who can help us. Discretion would be helpful. Can't you pretend you're having fun?"

Gracie shrugged. "I've never gambled before."

"Let me enlighten you on the pleasures of Vegas."

"Seriously? Shouldn't we be hiding or something?" She faked a quick smile when Jin cleared his throat. Right. She'd play along, so he could meet his friend. Then she'd find someplace to hide. This was happening way too fast for her taste. She still needed that quiet minute to think things through.

Jin was in his element as he guided her around the casino. He pointed out gaming tables and the different kinds of slot machines. Several of the cocktail waitresses smiled at him as they passed by. Clearly, this wasn't the first time he'd been one of their customers.

Several minutes went by before Jin decided they were looking a bit suspicious. Craps tables lined the edge of the carpeted casino path. He chose an open one at the end, explaining the rules of the game to her in a rush. She rolled her eyes when he eased his way into the shooter's position. They were wasting time while he threw dice on a stupid table. The spectators around the table clapped when Jin finished his throw. He must have won. Great. Now she'd never get him away from the table.

Prickles of warning along her spine paused Gracie's hand. Then the vision came in a rush. Eyes. One set and then two moved among the penny machines, their faces hidden in a blur of color and lights. Something was blocking her power. Jin had his arm around her when her sight returned.

"Jin, I Saw…"

"We're being followed again. Yes, I know. It would appear my friend has been detained." His smile appeared forced as he raised his voice. "Perhaps it's time we stopped for a drink. "I know a nice little bar at the Bellagio I think you'll love."

Their driver was waiting patiently for them at the entrance. He pulled the limo away from Caesars and onto the Strip. It was a short drive to the Bellagio's entrance. Gracie leaned against the car door, watching the beauty pass by them. A small lake surrounded by a Tuscan countryside filled the window. Jin took her arm and guided her as she stared, transfixed by the Bellagio grounds.

"It's incredible!" Gracie breathed as they walked the halls of the Bellagio, away from the noise of the casino proper. The lights surrounding a beautiful pool area mirrored pictures she'd seen of Tuscany. She made a mental note to stay at this casino the next time she was in Vegas. If she made it out of this alive, anyway.

"This is one of my favorite spots in Vegas," Jin told her. They were holding hands with fingers entwined. He brought her in close and ran his lips against her earlobe. "Are you having a good time, darling?"

The embrace was a little too genuine. They were playing a part, but his closeness made the attraction between them that much stronger. Well, stronger in her heart anyway. Jin was using her as bait. She forced the harsh reality to the forefront of her mind and pushed gently away.

"I'll be right back." She left him staring after her, his expression blank. Hurrying into the ladies room, she washed her hands and caught a glimpse of herself in the mirror. Her cheeks were flushed and she was glowing like...like a woman in a state of serious infatuation. Gawd, what was she thinking? They'd been thrown together in a dangerous fight for survival. He'd get what he needed, and then he'd be gone, leaving her behind. They had made no promises for anything else.

Arms wrapped about her as she exited the restroom. "Hello, Titania."

Gracie struggled against his hold, trying to push away from the disgusting embrace. Sickening gray eyes met hers. Puppet Master pushed her against the wall and smiled down at her skimpy dress.

"You've opened up so much since our last meeting. I'd like to take credit for this transformation."

"You're wrong there, creep." Gracie shoved him again.

"I will have you, Titania. I will humiliate you as you humiliated me. Then I will kill you."

Chapter Sixteen

Gracie gave him a final glance before disappearing into the ladies room. Her look was smoldering. No wonder every man they passed looked at her as she walked away. Jin took a slow breath, still watching the door. She had no idea what she did to him or how she made him feel. Something about her gave him pause. He'd never met anyone without guile before. Cunning and manipulation were a way of life in the Clans, but Gracie didn't seem to have any ulterior motives other than keeping her family safe.

No one was without guile, he reminded himself.

A movement in the window's reflection pulled his attention back to matters at hand. He knew someone had been following them, of course, and had been waiting for them to make their move. Shaggy blonde hair fell over womanish shoulders. The diseased gray eyes blinked at Jin's back, and then he skulked toward the ladies room after Gracie.

Jin waited until he heard the door swing shut before following. Cool steel pressed against his back. No one seemed to notice the awkwardness of his stance or the impending danger. In fact, the Normals in the sitting area seemed disoriented. Jin shifted his shoulders slowly. A Seelie Descendant held that weapon.

"You're my prize now, Jin," a deep voice murmured low. "Turn around. I want you to see this coming."

Jin slowly turned to face his attacker. A black man, lean and muscular, stood with a misshapen limb pointing at him. Its working parts grew out of the Descendant's wrist, while the barrel sprouted where his fingers should have been. Wild green hair and dark glasses accented a broad grin. He wasn't one of the fighters from the Temple; most likely he was one of Puppet Master's enthralls.

"I don't have time to play quick draw with you," Jin warned him. "My lady friend is waiting." Gracie was in real trouble. Puppet Master was as dangerous as an asp. If he made his way into her mind the consequences were unpredictable.

"Piss off." Jin's attacker raised the weapon higher, grinning as he took aim.

Jin spun his body to the side and struck out with his palm. He knocked the weapon away and brought his heel up to the man's jaw in the same movement. His attacker dropped with a grunt. Jin maneuvered the Descendant's unconscious body into one of the plush chairs and hurried toward the restrooms.

He eased open the door. Puppet Master had his hands on Gracie, squeezing her face painfully. Jumping behind him, Jin snatched the fingers holding her chin. He yanked the digits into odd positions until they looked like bent prongs on a fork. The Puppet Master screeched in pain, turning toward Jin with a murderous glare. His other hand tugged at the handle of a pistol caught in the pocket of his jacket.

"You!" Puppet Master froze, his fingers hovering over the gun. Jin pulled the gun from the pocket and stuffed it in his own belt.

"We need to talk, Eugene." He smacked his hand on the vile creature's nose. Jin then threw the limp body over a shoulder and exited via one of the doors marked "private." Extra chairs and empty cardboard boxes littered the floor. Gracie followed.

Jin tossed the Puppet Master down on a chair and slapped him hard across the face. Puppet Master groaned. He came to slowly. When he saw Jin, his eyes darted across his captor's body, looking for the advantage. The bastard had survived many an angry adversary in his short life. He was most dangerous now that Jin had him cornered.

"You're a favorite with Viper, Eugene." Jin folded his arms, standing threateningly over the degenerate creature. "She confides in you."

"No, you're wrong. She doesn't care for me. I disgust her, or so she says." A fond memory seemed to cross Eugene's lecherous face. "I tried to break her once, you see. She holds it against me."

Gracie stalked over to stand at Jin's elbow. "I wonder why, you sick freak." She was shaking with violent tremors of fury. "Gawd, I just want to bash his head in right now."

"You might get your chance after I've questioned him." Jin regarded her closely. The look of absolute revulsion on her face confirmed what he had suspected in the temple. She had the right to hurt the revolting little toad after what he'd done to her.

Puppet Master's eyes began to swim in watery gray. His loathsome power reached out toward Gracie. Jin threw a lightning strike to Eugene's face, plucking one of the gray orbs from its socket. It dropped with a dramatic thump upon the floor. Gracie jumped back as it rolled toward her feet.

"Try to strike at my lady friend again, and I'll part your head from your shoulders."

Eugene rolled on the carpeted floor, clutching at his bloody socket with both hands. Silent screams caught upon the swollen lips. He was in agony. Jin stared down at the infamous Puppet Master. He had no sympathy for the wretch.

"You bastard! Viper doesn't trust me. Neither does Raul, but he likes the party favors I bring with me. He enjoys his toys subservient." Eugene pressed both hands harder to his empty eye socket. "While we were enjoying a little fun time in the play room, he admitted to me that he and Fong had heard about the death mark out on you. It was broadcast across every Clan communication channel in existence. The person or persons were very good at hiding their identity."

Jin lifted his hand to strike again. "You're lying. Those channels are closely regulated by the Council. No one could use them anonymously."

"Wait! I think Viper may have an idea who's behind the death mark. She's playing a power game with Raul. The old fool doesn't realize it. He thinks she won't dare strike at him, despite her plot against the Zhao Clan. Yes, I know about that night."

That made Jin pause. Whatever else she might be, Viper wasn't a fool. She wouldn't hand over such valuable information to a manipulative bastard like Eugene. Someone else had let slip her plot against the Zhao Clan. It might have been Renee Girard. Hell only knew what devilry that psychotic madman had indulged in.

Eugene apparently saw Jin's surprise and confusion. He made a living capitalizing on momentary flaws in strength. The Puppet Master regained some of his confidence. He smiled.

"Viper has been busy trying to save her own ass after she let you escape. She's convinced Raul to hold a safari on the streets of Vegas. The entrance fee is five-hundred-thousand US currency. You're the prey, and the trophy is Titania." Eugene's remaining eye grew hazy. Jin could feel the power seep into the gray orb again. "I can help you find out who's behind this horrible attack on you, Jin. You know I can find out anything I want. Let me help you."

Jin slapped Eugene hard, knocking away the power. "Don't be a fool. I'm a son of the Wainwright Clan. Your power doesn't work on me."

"A bargain then?"

"And what's your price for this help? Money? Power?" Jin shook his head and stood away.

"I want her." Eugene pointed at Gracie with a bloodied finger. "Give her to me, and I'll give you the person who wants you dead."

Puppet Master struggled to his feet, a sick, feverish hunger on his face as he shuffled toward Gracie. "I look forward to breaking you this time, Titania. Our fun ended much too quickly at the temple."

Gracie backed away from them. Her anger had faded into disgust and terror. "I'll kill you before I let you touch me."

She clutched at her head, screaming. Blood began to form in her nostrils. Puppet Master laughed, squeezing his bloodied hands out toward Gracie. Jin stepped behind Eugene, gripped his chin and twisted with all the speed he had.

The Puppet Master's lifeless body dropped to the carpet. As Jin stood staring down at Eugene's neck, reaching at an awkward angle away from his shoulders, something drained away from his being. This was the first life he had taken and by the sick, hollow feeling in his gut, he prayed it was the last. Eugene, no, he couldn't refer to Puppet Master as a person, the insidious creature had been trying to kill Gracie. Jin had done the world a favor.

He wordlessly picked up the body, dragged it outside and stuffed it into one of the massive garbage dumpsters. Stabbing the remaining gray eye with a piece of wood, he threw it in after him.

"I think it's time we moved on. Are you all right?" He reached out his hand to Gracie. She didn't answer him. Her face had taken on a pale, sickly pallor. Those blue eyes wouldn't meet his at first. He lifted her chin gently until she met his gaze. Then the tears came. He pulled her into his body, holding her as she wept. Any remorse he'd had about taking Eugene's life faded.

Gracie clutched at him. He smoothed his hand softly down her back in reassurance. Why hadn't she used her power to protect herself? It seemed almost as if Gracie had never learned to control her abilities. She was like an innocent child with newly discovered gifts, thrown into the fighting circle. Just as he had been.

Jin kept an arm around Gracie's shoulders as they joined the throngs of people at the Bellagio's fountains. The famous light and water show was already in progress. Couples held hands as they gazed up at the beauty of the fountains. Jin and Gracie moved between two clusters of tourists, trying to blend in among the crowd.

"It's beautiful," Gracie said. She was still shaking. Violence was a way of life in the Clans. Though Gracie was trying to keep it together, clearly she wasn't used to witnessing such things. She had a vulnerability about her Jin hadn't experienced very often in his life. He was dangerously close to becoming convinced she was telling the truth about herself.

He pulled Gracie in close again and rested his cheek on her hair. She was so soft under the thin dress. Her arms moved inside his jacket and held him too as they stood watching the dancing fountains. Gracie lifted her face and smiled up at him. Jin slowly, tentatively, lowered his lips to hers in a long kiss. He was rewarded as her fingers twisted at his shirt. When their lips parted, she rested her head on his shoulder. They watched the jets of water rise and fall in time to the music.

The hairs stood up on the back of his neck, and he finally noticed the shark-like eyes on them. Jin recognized the granite jawline and boxer's frame.

Slicked-back salt-and-pepper hair rose well above the crowd. Their ally had arrived at last. Jin was surprised it had taken his attentive guardian this long to find him. Jin pulled Gracie in tighter, protectively trying to keep her face hidden from the man, though that ship had sailed. Jin wasn't in the mood to answer awkward, probing questions.

Other faces were watching them too. Jin counted at least five. Puppet Master might have been Raul's ally, but that didn't mean Raul trusted the demented worm. Clearly he'd sent Vento security along to watch their slimy friend.

"Come, Gracie. I want to show you the gardens."

Jin kept their pace slow, two lovers enjoying the romance of the Bellagio. He guided her to the bushes lining the drive and pulled her into the shadows. "Gracie, I need you to do exactly what I say. Do you understand?"

"They've found us, haven't they? Of all the damn nights to wear stilettos."

"This way." He pulled Gracie toward the driveway and into the shadows of the alley joining the casinos. Here were no bright lights or curious tourists. He and Myles had plotted out the evening. Their plan was to lose his followers in the empty streets and back alleyways after he'd had the opportunity to question someone. He hadn't expected them to be waiting back here.

Two men stepped away from a pillar, brandishing chains. Jin motioned Gracie to stay back, and approached the two men. He stood waiting for them in a ready stance. The first came at him in a blur of steel. Jin sidestepped the chain and sent a kick to the owner's midsection. The man folded like a cheap chair and rolled away. The second man let his chain strike toward Jin's rib cage. Jin fell flat on the ground, letting the chain pass harmlessly over his head. His foot made contact with the attacker's knee. He twisted back to a standing position and let his palm strike at the wounded man's chin.

Behind him, Gracie screamed. A third man pulled on a thick clump of her hair. He had a tight grip around her torso.

"Stilettos, Gracie!" Jin yelled, flying toward them.

Gracie brought the heel of her shoe down as hard as she could against the man's ankle. He howled with pain and smacked the butt of his weapon on her head. She crumbled to the ground in a heap of metallic fabric.

"You just made your last mistake," Jin told her attacker. He brought his foot to the man's chin. The thug staggered backward, but he wasn't down yet. Jin aimed several hits to his torso until his fists had done the appropriate amount of injury. With one last kick to the chest, Jin sent the Clansman smashing into the dumpster.

He knelt down beside Gracie and lifted her into his arms. "Darling, open your eyes for me."

"Darling?" A long shadow fell over them. Jin looked up at the granite features and slender form. Cold eyes glinted behind the gun pointed at Jin's head. Two muted shots thumped in the stillness of the alley. Jin looked over his shoulder. He observed two dead bodies, bleeding out from perfectly executed shots to the head.

"Hello, Bryn." He lifted Gracie off the cold floor.

Lord Brynmor of the Seelie Court wore his mobster glamour like a favorite jacket. In truth it suited him, not that Jin would ever tell Bryn such a thing. Bryn delighted in the disguise a bit too much sometimes, even fooling powerful Clan Leaders like Zhao Long and Jin's mother. The one chink in the armor of his disguise was the accent. He couldn't quite pull off the Chicago mobster tone. Instead, he managed to sound like a man who was so well traveled, he'd lost any distinctive clues to his nationality.

"What a foolhardy plan. Of course they were able to ambush you. It wasn't difficult for every punk Descendant in the area to find you the way you've been throwing around the cash. In the future, I suggest you allow me to come up with the plans." Bryn ran curious eyes over Gracie's still form and the way Jin was gently holding her. "Where the hell have you been? You know I don't like it when you're out of contact."

"Sorry, Nanny," Jin said, carrying Gracie and walking out of the alley beside Bryn. "I've been at a remote meditation retreat. Where's Myles?"

"Here!" Myles came running up behind Bryn, breathless. "I was covering the alley. He motioned with his head at the rooftop. Myles holstered his weapon. Jin nodded and smiled. Myles wasn't much of a fighter, but he was still good people and someone Jin could always rely on for help.

Bryn took Jin's arm and pulled him to the left. "I think it would be better to continue our little reunion at the safe house."

"You bought a house here for the occasion?"

"Bought? You must be losing it." Bryn took them to a black sedan that looked just like every other hired sedan in Vegas.

"Take Gracie and see that's she's comfortable," Jin told Bryn. "I have something to take care of."

"Don't be long. Your mother has been calling me every freakin' hour wanting to know if you made it to the house." Bryn held open the back door of the sedan. He flicked a card with the address of the safe house at Jin, who memorized it and nodded with a disgruntled frown. "Don't look at me that way. I needed the Wainwright resources to find you. Making you call home when I found you was the price of her help. And you know how she is."

"Yes, I know how she is. Her concern now is rather unexpected, considering she refused to help me when I needed her most." The resentment bubbled up and he quickly stuffed it down again. This wasn't the time.

Gracie stirred in Jin's arms as he put her in the back seat. "Jin?"

"Go with Bryn, darling." Jin smoothed the strand of hair out of her face.

Two bullets pinged off the side of the car very close to Bryn's leg. Jin slammed the door closed. He pushed Bryn before the big man could take aim.

"Go!" he cried and hurried to cover.

"Come on, Myles. You're with me!" Bryn barked and Myles obeyed like a puppy.

Jin jumped in a burst of polluted air to a dumpster down the alley. He pressed his back against the metal container, watching the taillights of the sedan disappear. He tried not to think about what the surface of the dumpster was doing to his Armani jacket. Keeping still, he waited for the running feet to pass his location. The gunman stopped at the curb, gulping breaths, and rested hands on his knees trying to memorize Bryn's license plate number. It wouldn't do him any good. Bryn had a massive collection of stolen license plates he switched out every time he left the house.

The gunman cursed and turned, heading back down the alley. Jin followed carefully behind, keeping to the shadows. A black sedan was waiting for the man. He got in the passenger's side. From the wild arm waving, Jin guessed the driver wasn't pleased that his partner had lost their prey. The sedan pulled away and started for the busy traffic of the Strip. Jin hurried into the parking lot and found a motorcycle locked by the security door. It took him a few seconds to pick the lock and hotwire the engine.

He came up behind the sedan, which was stuck at the first light. Jin stayed back and to the left, away from the side-view mirror of the man who had fired at him. They were headed south. The car made a swift turn right off the Strip and got onto I-15, headed north. Jin stayed within sight of the car as it turned onto 95. The Clans were obsessed with having the best in every city they visited. That would mean these goons were headed toward the affluence of Summerlin.

The sedan cut across two lanes of heavy freeway traffic, taking the Summerlin exit on screeching tires. Jin gripped the brakes hard. The motorcycle shuddered at the unexpected deceleration. Then its engine roared again as he jerked the bike between a Toyota Corolla and a VW Beetle. Angry honks and a few crude gestures peppered the VW's windshield. Jin ignored the show and cut over to the next lane.

A thundering groan of truck brakes came from the lane behind him. The heat from the diesel's engine burned on exposed skin with the chrome grill only inches away. Gripping the motorcycle with his hands and legs, Jin jumped into the exhaust-filled air of the freeway. He couldn't take the weight of the bike far, a few feet. It was enough. He landed hard on the side of the freeway. The motorcycle struggled on dirt and rock for a few feet until he was able to go against traffic and up the Summerlin exit ramp.

The bike weaved between vehicles at a frantic pace. Losing these thugs wasn't an option. They were his only lead to Raul. Somewhere in Summerlin, the Vento Clan had set up temporary headquarters. Since the kind of magic it took to open a portal to Otherworld required serious preparation time, they needed a secure, fixed location to work from. Raul was too clever and security conscious to keep the source anywhere near his party guests.

Jin spotted the sedan as it slowed into the parking lot of a cluster of smaller, newer office buildings. Keeping the bike well back and out of their line of sight, he took a closer look at the complex. Typical cookie-cutter brick buildings. Nothing unusual to see, which was the point.

It was well after business hours as the sedan's rear lights disappeared into an attached parking garage. Jin could hear the car's engine in the empty structure. He dropped the bike behind the building's dumpster. Crouching in the shadows, he closed his eyes to listen. The squealing tires of the sedan told him the driver was still pissed and clumsy. They hadn't considered they were being followed. He caught the wind and lifted his body up to the second level of the structure.

Jin crouched low, watching the two men exit the car. Both of them were armed with human weapons. Whoever was holding their leash didn't want to draw attention. Using their Seelie powers in public would certainly be noticed by the wrong people. Even in Vegas. His arm burned with the memory of Viper's strike penetrating his flesh. He'd have to disarm them before they entered the elevators.

"What are you going to say?" the younger passenger asked. His face had lost the punk bravado now that he was back at Vento headquarters. Well known among the Clans was what Raul did to those who failed him. "We weren't expecting that other guy…"

"Shut up, Bennie!" The driver brought a hard slap to the kid's face.

Their backs faced the emptiness of the parking garage as they waited. Jin crept closer, forcing away the anxious tension of waiting a few seconds more.

Everything was riding on his next move. Raul would talk. He'd tell the truth this time or...the ugly thought hung suspended in the darkness of Jin's heart. He wiped sweaty palms on his trouser legs.

Extreme anxiety was an alien emotion he'd picked up in the last few months. Proof of his innocence and Gracie's safety rested with the ruthless man holding court in his office fortress. Jin would do anything to get his life back, even if that meant taking another's life. Desperation told him he must.

The elevator doors slowly rolled open. His quarry stepped forward, the driver first and then the passenger. Jin ran at them, tackling the passenger, Bennie, in the small of his back. This created a domino effect. The other man, the driver, slammed his head against the back wall. His body dropped in an unconscious heap on the floor. Yanking open his jacket, Jin grabbed the gun from its holster. He did the same to the dazed kid's weapon. Bennie twisted around and started to power up.

"Don't, unless you're faster than a bullet. Now, which floor are we going to?" He kicked the kid hard in the stomach when he received no answer. "I hate repeating myself."

"Five," Bennie said, hunching over to protect his gut. "You are so dead."

"I get that a lot. On your feet and face the door." Jin stood back as the young man staggered slowly to his feet. "Viper, Fong or Raul, which one do you work for?"

"Raul is my mother's cousin. Who do you think?" Bennie cursed when the warning smack struck him on the head. "He's got plenty of men waiting, Jin. They'll pop you before you can step a foot inside."

"That is precisely why you're going in first." The doors rolled open with a dull ding. Jin kept the gun against Bennie's back as they walked together down the dusty blue hallway. An uneasy feeling began to creep into the fringes of his senses. Something wasn't right about this floor. He should be able to feel the strong power of the Making Magic calling. He did sense remnants of that power, but no living energy. It was almost as if something or someone had killed it.

"I don't see any of your friends, Bennie."

The young man shook his head, appearing spooked. "Maybe they left?"

Trap or not, he had no choice. The death mark on his head had brought every supernatural hunter in the Human Realm to Vegas. He was a dead man unless Raul gave up a name. Then he would have a trail to follow and nothing this side of hell could keep Jin from finding the truth.

A set of glass doors awaited them as the hallway lead to the suites. The bright gold letters etched on the glass read, "Goodtime Enterprises." An average looking office space, cheaply furnished, had been staged on the other side of the glass. Just an average office with average employees doing dull work. Hardly worth a second glance.

"Let's see if anyone is home." He pushed the young man forward.

They were met by no bodyguards or security when they came inside. Dim emergency lights shone on empty desks. The office looked deserted except for a small sliver of light coming from under Raul's office door.

Bennie hesitated. Then knocked. "I'm coming in, boss."

Raul Vento was sitting at his desk. A perfectly formed bottle-cap-sized hole in his forehead tunneled to the back of his skull. Jin observed no blood or gore. It was as if the weapon used had been hot enough to cauterize the wound. Empty eyes stared straight ahead. Death had come for him so quickly he hadn't found time for surprise. Raul was gone, taking any hope of Jin's salvation with him.

He pounded a frustrated fist on the desk. The sudden violence knocked a smoldering cigar from Raul's dead hand. All the tips of his fingers were missing. The skin had blackened around each severed end. Whatever had done this was sending a message.

"*Ay dios mios!*" Bennie backed against the wall. His hand reached instinctively for the empty holster. "Who could do something like this?"

Gracie's story about the terrifying man in the police parking garage didn't seem like a fiction now. She had claimed the man could fire deadly orange circles with his finger. Jin looked down at the gun in his hand. It would be useless against someone who could do this to Raul. A new power had come to town, but whose side was he on?

Chapter Seventeen

Jin leaned in a little to get a better look at the perfect tunnel through Raul's head. The stranger who had helped Gracie at the police station might have performed the execution as a vendetta against Raul. Clearly her rescuer hadn't been happy with the Vento Clan leader. It was one possible motive. Jin didn't want to think about the other possibility.

"Shit!" Bennie started to back out of the room.

"If you don't want to have his murder pinned on you, then I suggest you help me hide the body." Jin's warning look froze the young man in place. "Don't touch anything and stay still."

"Bullshit! They have ways of finding things out."

"I could make sure your name tops the list of suspects if that works better for you."

Jin checked the desk and Raul's pockets, looking for the device Gracie sought. Resting on the desk were two wine glasses with fingerprints prominently positioned. Several familiar golden hairs had been carefully placed on Raul's jacket. Gold high heels sat askew by the couch as if their owner had playfully kicked them off. Gracie was being set up and Jin didn't have to make a great deductive leap to guess who was framing her. Viper was never one to let a slight go. If she'd allied herself with this unknown power, then they were all in trouble. She had no remorse and would use her new friend to take over all the Clans.

After Jin was satisfied he'd found all the incriminating evidence against Gracie, they wrapped Raul in one of the moving blankets lying around the empty office space. The sedan driver was missing after his nap on the elevator floor. Just the two of them were left to do the work. Raul hadn't been one to watch his weight. Jin's suit was forced to endure more hardship. The heavy labor of getting the bulky body to the car was slow.

"Time to go for a ride." Jin struck Bennie with a sharp tap to the temple. The young man grunted as his knees buckled under the weight of his limp body. Catching Bennie under his arms, Jin pushed his prisoner's unconscious body in the back seat. He swung the door shut.

Jin moved around to the driver's side and pulled open the door. A blackened circle against the far wall caught his attention. He moved closer for a better look. The circle had burned all the way through the wall. A huge chunk of concrete was resting on its side. On the ground were remnants of a small device. It had been cut with precision lengthwise up the center. Completely unusable. Jin picked both halves up and examined them more closely. The word 'Titania' flickered in faded lettering on the display. Then the device gave one last pop and died.

His foot kicked at the concrete in frustration. He hated being played. Gracie had masterfully manipulated him since the moment they'd first laid eyes on each other. That farm girl innocence had suckered him in just as she and her ally had known it would. He considered leaving Raul's body right where it was and dumping her things in the trunk, but maybe he was wrong about Gracie. She had some serious questions to answer when he got back to the safe house.

Jin raced out of the parking lot a little faster than he should have and headed onto the 95. The quickest way to get rid of Raul was to make him a permanent part of nature. He headed toward Red Rocks Canyon Park. Going past the entrance, he stopped when his headlights fell on a small dirt turnout. He shut off the sedan's engine and opened the car door. Constellations formed overhead in the infinite blackness of a desert night. No other cars were on the road, but that could change. Even now, he could see the lights of civilization sparkle in the distance. Sleeping beauty would need to dig a deep hole quickly.

"Get up," Jin kicked at the gunman's shoe. Bennie, disoriented and groggy, struggled out of the vehicle. His eyes took in their surroundings, then he turned to Jin and waited. Dry lips parted in silent anticipation.

"How very convenient for you there's a shovel in the trunk. Get busy."

The steady rhythm of shovel against sand and stone did little to ease Jin's anger. He wanted answers to his fast-building list of questions. He didn't trust the Puppet Master, but Eugene had shown honesty when faced with Jin's brutal questioning. He'd told them Raul and Fong were clueless as to who commissioned the death mark. Jin hadn't been sure of

Viper. She was the logical choice, but she'd denied knowing who it was in her conversation with Raul in the dining room at the temple. Of course she could have been lying to them.

"This is maddening!" Jin hit a fist against the car's side.

"Easy, I'm done." Bennie struggled up the embankment and threw the shovel in the trunk. "What now? You didn't have me dig two holes and you let me cover Raul. So does that mean you're not going to kill me?" Bennie brushed the dirt and sweat off his arms. "I'm Raul's man. Viper will want me eliminated anyway. Drop me at the next shit town and I disappear."

"Break your promise to me, and Viper will be the least of your worries." Jin held open the trunk for him to climb inside. "You understand that I'd rather you not know the direction I disappear in?"

Bennie got in the car without complaint and Jin headed off toward Vegas again. He pulled into the welcoming drive of the Red Rocks Casino and parked the car at the far end of the lot. It was time to switch vehicles. When Jin found a suitable car—a convertible Mercedes—he clicked the auto open to pop the trunk of the sedan. Let the guy hotwire his own ride to wherever.

Bryn had chosen a vacant house in Summerlin. After tossing Gracie's shoes in a strip mall dumpster, Jin navigated to the neighborhood. Then he parked his stolen ride a few blocks away and walked to the address he'd been given. The door opened wide as he stepped up onto the front porch. Bryn, still sporting his human glamour, stood fully dressed, arms folded and waiting.

"Welcome home." He looked Jin up and down, stone faced. "You look like hell."

"It's been an eventful evening." He followed Bryn into the kitchen where Bryn had been working on a laptop. An assortment of luncheon meats and cheeses were set up on the snack bar. Then Bryn poured Jin a healthy portion of milk. Jin gulped it down, waiting for the angry lecture. Instead, he got a wistful curiosity. Jin hadn't seen Bryn perplexed for several years.

They'd first met on one of the many occasions Jin had run away from boarding school. He'd managed to make it all the way to the United States on his own. He'd found Bryn being beaten up by a group of humans who had gotten the better of him when he was intoxicated. It had been Bryn's first visit to the modern day Human Realm. Swords had been replaced with handguns. The bar he'd chosen had no concept of a fair fight. Jin, at the age of nine, had fought off the humans. He helped Bryn to a cheap motel to heal. Bryn had been paying back the debt since by acting as Jin's occasional bodyguard.

"So, you've been in a meditation retreat," Bryn said as he constructed a large sandwich and pushed it at Jin. "Learn anything while you contemplated your belly button?"

"Yes, I learned I'm not as well loved by my friends as I once thought." Jin took a bite. "Where's Myles?"

"I sent him for Miss Berry's things." Bryn examined Jin with those eternally wise eyes. "Care to elaborate? Myles told me about Clayton, but does someone else need to be schooled on the finer points of loyalty and honor?"

"We have bigger problems." Jin smiled sadly. Knowing without question he had two people he could trust with his life, Bryn and Myles, was a comfort. "I think the Unseelie Court is planning to invade the Human Realm, and I believe they'll try it on Midsummer's Eve."

Bryn stretched his hands along the tiled counter and shook his head slowly. "I searched for signs of their coming while you were away. I found none. You know we can't approach the Seelie Court without proof."

"I had proof right in my hand." Jin slapped at the counter. "I took a mobile from one of the Vento Clan Security Team. I saw a text message. Like a fool, I handed it over to Qing. Renee crushed it. He was careful to destroy the SIM Card." Jin let his gaze fix on the blinking clock in the microwave. "What we really need is a confession from Viper. She'll admit they brought a dark elf into the Girard home that night or I'll..."

"Let me guess, you'll set your new girlfriend on her?" Bryn's eyes glistened with amusement as he stared at Jin over his glass.

"She broke Viper's nose." Jin smiled. "Gracie saved my life. I hope you've been treating her with courtesy whether she deserves it or not."

"I've kept Miss Berry unconscious until I can find out more about her. The potion should be wearing off soon."

"You've shown more wisdom than I."

Bryn passed over the potato chips when Jin motioned toward them. "The heart loses all wisdom when love enters it." Bryn chuckled when Jin hissed between gritted teeth. "That kiss by the fountain was pretty romantic. Had me convinced that you cared for her."

"You're getting soft." Jin shook the half-eaten sandwich at him. "I was using her to draw out Raul."

"Don't con me, kiddo. I've known you since you were in nappies." Bryn folded his arm in the condescending stance he frequently used on Jin. "You have feelings for her and pretty strong ones based on how defensive you are now."

"Where is she? I have questions that need answers."

"She?" An austere voice echoed in the kitchen. "Is this someone I should meet, Jin?"

"Damn," Bryn whispered low.

"Hello, Mother. How whimsical of you to eavesdrop at this time of night." The sour-stomach feeling was coming in full force now. He spun the laptop around to see a harsh-looking woman with jade eyes and a single band of silver in her dark hair. She could have kept the beauty of her youth if not for her severe temperament. The hair on his neck bristled at the sight of her. Jin knew perfectly well that his mother had no interest in his whereabouts. An inkling of suspicion crawled into his mind.

If anyone had a vested interest in finding and recruiting a new pre-cog it would be Eleanor Wainwright. She would do anything to keep her Clan's reputation intact. The Wainwright Clan viewed itself as a keeper of knowledge and beacon of guiding light. The Clan members fancied that world leaders came to them for governance advice. In reality, Eleanor spent much of her day force-feeding influence down their gullets.

"The young lady in question is just another of my dalliances as you put it. Hardly worthy of your notice."

"Indeed?" Her sharp, suspicious eyes narrowed as she regarded him. "It is very difficult to ascertain whether or not you're lying, Jin. I'm afraid you're too much like your father in that respect." She let a frown cross her otherwise emotionless face. "I could take the knowledge from you."

Bryn pulled Jin behind him. "That wasn't our deal, Eleanor. You saw him. He's recovered from the gunshot and being taken. Glad you asked. We're done here."

"I had rather imagined that you'd like the information I have regarding the death mark on Jin. Very well. You may contact me when you're willing to be civil and are prepared to give me something I want." She disappeared with a snapping bleep.

"That bitch hacked into my system!" Bryn growled, stroking the keys on his laptop like a worried mother. "She has all the information I collected so far on Miss Berry. Damn!" He yanked the device out of its USB port. "Well, she won't get to the rest of it. Unfortunately, neither will we."

"At least she didn't find out your real identity. That's a small wonder." Jin slapped at the counter. "What is it that we know about Miss Berry?"

"She's an unaffiliated Seelie Descendant. I'm in the process of checking the back story about her life in San Diego. I've searched all the Clan files. Nothing." He looked at Jin. "Did you find the device that Raul took from her? I wonder how much he knows."

"Whatever he knows he took to the grave with him. I found him dead a couple of hours ago with a nice large hole scored through his forehead." Jin shook his head and picked up the sandwich again. "Gracie's device had been cut in half by some laser-like power. We have another unaffiliated Seelie Descendant running around, Bryn and he's very deadly. He killed Fong and a gaggle of Clansmen at a police station."

"You think Miss Berry and this new powerhouse may be working together?"

"We'll soon find out. She has some explaining to do, and this time I won't buy into her innocent routine." He felt free of her enchantment.

"I'll run a background check on a clean computer. We'll see if she really is who she says she is." Bryn gave him a probing look. "And if she really is Gracie Berry, innocent victim?"

Jin let out an irritated sigh. "Then any record of her being in Vegas needs to disappear. Where is she?"

"Last bedroom on the left."

Jin fingered the gash in his dirty, sweat-stained shirt. Every speck on his ruined clothes, every bloodied knuckle had been for her sake. She owed him the truth this time. He raised a fist to pound on her door, but let it drop to his side. A chance still existed he was wrong about Gracie. God, he wanted to be wrong. He knocked softly, almost hoping she wouldn't answer. The knob rattled for a moment and then the door opened a crack. Gracie was dressed in a man's robe much too large for her. Rubbing the sleep out of her eyes, she shuffled forward.

"Jin." Her arms wrapped around his waist. "I was worried you'd been shot!"

The heat of her body burned through his tattered shirt. Thin fabric was the only barrier to her naked form. He lifted his hand to hover over her head, almost touching the sleep-tussled blond strands. Clenching the hand into a fist, he stepped away from her.

"Raul is dead, murdered by that mystery man you saw at the police station." He analyzed every inch of her face as he waited for the lie. "He destroyed that DNA sample for you. Care to explain why he did that?"

"I have no idea why he's helping me." Gracie folded her arms tightly about her body. She shook her head, eyes growing distant.

Damn it! Was she confused by this new killer? Or was she scrambling for another lie? He couldn't tell anymore. She'd gotten to him. Like a fool he'd let her inside when he should have shown caution.

"I should think that was obvious. You two are working together. Why don't you stop this ruse and tell me what it is you want from me?"

An array of emotions crossed her face. Anger finally won out. "You think I know that man? You think I've been pretending all this time?" Red spread across her cheek like a slap mark. Tears seeped out of her eyes. "I'm not the liar here, remember?"

"Stop the tears, Gracie. They don't work on me."

"I'm not crying!" She gave his chest a hard shove. "You are such a jerk!" She slammed the bedroom door, taking any chance of the truth with her.

"You're a master communicator," Bryn said behind him. "Come on, I want to show you what I found doing a background check."

The laptop was open with a picture of Gracie's driver's license. School records and social security number information were in the various windows. Jin leaned over and looked at Gracie's life story. All of it took place in San Diego.

"She's an unaffiliated Seelie Descendant, and she is also who she says she is, Grace Berry from San Diego." Bryn frowned at the screen. The windows began to flicker and the data started to disappear. "What the hell? Someone is erasing Gracie."

"What? What does that mean?"

"It means that someone doesn't want us to know who she is. And whoever is doing this is a real pro. Could be Clan doing this or her strange guardian angel. I can't trace it back." Bryn looked away from the screen. "What the hell is going on, Jin?"

"I wish I knew."

Chapter Eighteen

Morning light crept along the storm-cloud-colored bedspread. Gracie had been monitoring its progress for hours against the digital clock on the nightstand. Though it was still early, she suspected Dad would be up and on his way to the office. She rubbed at her swollen eyes. The headache wasn't getting any better. She was stupid to feel so crushed. Jin was practically a stranger. After all, he'd lived up to his end of the bargain. They had no plans or promises for after he'd helped her recover the DNA sample from Raul. She was on her own now. She was the one who had to figure out how to save her family.

Rolling over on the pillow, she clutched at the bedspread. Her things sat by the door. Someone had brought them from the hotel. *Here's your hat, what's your hurry?* She'd definitely overstayed her welcome here. She slid out of the bed. It was time to face the music with her dad anyway. He needed to know the danger he was in. She had to toughen up and explain to him why she couldn't go back home. Her turn had come to be the strong, responsible one for Dad's sake.

For hours, she'd tried to think of a way to explain what had happened to her. Finding the words to help her father and Brenda understand she was something not human seemed to be impossible. It didn't matter.

She'd have to leave once she'd gotten them to safety. Dad wouldn't want to let her go. He'd insist they stay together as a family, but they wouldn't be safe as long as she was around.

Time to quit stalling. She dug through her purse for her cell and tried her dad first. An obnoxious pre-recorded message told her the user she was trying to reach had been disconnected. She tried Ape. Same thing. An odd, frozen feeling was beginning to spread through her chest. She dialed Brenda at the house, close to panic. She got no answer. That wasn't right. Brenda was like a rabid raccoon when the phone rang. Her stepmother never let that stupid phone ring more than twice unless she...

Gracie's trembling fingers pressed the speed dial for their office. Someone at the warehouse would be able to put her through to Dad. He was always there. Maybe Brenda had gone with him today? They'd need all the help they could get if that big shipment of file folders came in. Sure, the file folders she'd forgotten to order before she'd left.

"Archibald Aquatics," chimed a perky female voice.

"Wait, this number belongs to Berry Wholesale Office Supply." Panic echoed in her own voice. She tried to calm down.

"No, I'm sorry. This is Archibald Aquatics. You must have dialed the wrong number." The perky voice was still trying to be polite.

"I've had this same number on speed dial for years. What happened to Berry Wholesale Office Supply?"

"I'm sorry, ma'am, you have the wrong number. Maybe if you told me where you are..."

Gracie hung up abruptly and stared at the cell. Her stomach knotted as the frozen feeling reached it. Maybe her mysterious stalker had been too late finding the device? Maybe the Vento Clan had already taken her family—or worse, this unknown killer had taken them instead.

Home was the place to start looking. She grabbed her airline ticket and called the customer service number. After she committed to pay an outrageous price, they put her on the first available flight that afternoon. It was still early morning. She had a few hours to spare. Gracie took a hasty shower. Throwing open her suitcase, she rummaged for comfortable clothes and sneakers.

Once she found Dad, they'd have to move fast, but to where? He might have some ideas, but he'd be a hard sell. She ought to have all the planning done before she got home. She'd get a map at the airport and start figuring out where to go from there.

Gracie zipped her suitcase, snapping the lock shut. She crept out of the room and down the hall toward what she hoped was the front door. The wheels of her suitcase clicked on the tile floor. Willing them to be quiet, she galloped faster toward the exit and her uncertain freedom.

"Morning. Want some eggs?" A man's tall form filled the hall, blocking out the early-day sun. Intense eyes pinned her in place. He was dressed in a black "Kiss the Cook" apron and held an empty plate in his hand. In the alley, Jin had called him Bryn. Gracie assumed they were friends, but didn't remember much after being put in the car. Someone had carried her inside and undressed her. The thought of this total stranger seeing her naked made her blush.

Caught between hunger and indecision, Gracie shrugged. "I could eat. Thanks." She followed his lean form toward the intoxicating smell of eggs and bacon. Bryn had the gait of a dancer, with graceful and purposeful movements.

They passed by the living room where Jin was making slow, methodical Tai Chi moves in the dim morning light. As his body turned, their eyes met. He quickly looked away. That communicated his feelings about her more than words ever could. Fine. He'd be rid of her soon enough.

Myles lifted a hand in greeting as Gracie entered the kitchen. He poured two cups of coffee and handed her one. Then she sat down at the breakfast bar with a nod of thanks.

Bryn put a plate of gourmet quality eggs and hash browns in front of Gracie. He gave her a proud smile when she hummed with pleasure. They ate in silence until Myles cleared his throat uncomfortably.

"So, Miss Berry, what are your plans now that your device has been destroyed?"

"I have a few ideas," she said, digging into her food and avoiding their eyes. "How about the three of you? I'm sure you're eager to leave Vegas after last night."

"We don't have any set plans," Bryn told her with a shrug. "Say, why don't you stay with us for a while longer. We have plenty of room here at the house."

She looked at Bryn in mid-bite. He appeared to be sincere, not joking. That was unexpected, considering the entire house must have heard her argument with Jin last night. These two didn't seem to mind her hanging out, but Jin was an entirely different matter. No way would she stick around when she wasn't wanted.

"I doubt Jin would appreciate my staying. He made that very clear last night," she said stiffly and took another sip of coffee to hide her hurt. "It's best that I finish breakfast and then go."

"You don't have to leave, Miss Berry. I have a feeling Jin will come around. You'll see." Bryn smiled. He was trying extra hard to be charming and nice. Now was the time to go.

"Thank you for breakfast. I've got to be someplace. Goodbye." She stood up. The two men gave each other uncomfortable looks. She hurried away before they decided to do something crazy. Jin was still entranced in his Tai Chi. His eyes remained glued on the far wall. He didn't even turn his head as she walked by. Gracie walked faster, trying not to cry. For all his surface charm, Jin was truly the cold-hearted killer others feared him to be.

She grabbed her suitcase and almost made it to the front door when a puff of air gusted before her. Gracie let out a scream as a bare arm pushed against the door. Jin stepped out of the nothingness, sweat dripping on his skin. He stared down at her with absolute confidence. Damn it! She was so tired of people pushing her around. This time she had more at stake. She had Dad and Brenda to think of now. Jin didn't care about them. He was only concerned about his own problems.

"Gracie, we need to talk."

"Get out of my way," Gracie told him and pulled at the door he'd blocked with his hand.

"We both know I can make you stay until you hear me out."

There it was, that insufferable arrogance. Well, she wouldn't give in to him this time. She had her own troubles. Jin could just suck it up and deal with his stuff on his own time. She was tough now, hardcore. No more weepy tears or cries for help. Gracie pinched at the scratch Viper had made on his chest.

"Ouch!" He chuckled and leaned against the door. "Please, Gracie. Let's talk."

"No, I have to go home." She turned away from him and headed toward the door Bryn had carried her through last night. Oh gawd! She shut her eyes as the sob choked her. Tears escaped and flooded down her red cheeks. A burst of air whooshed past her. Jin blocked her path again. He held a gentle hand to her chin and lifted it.

"My life is missing! I called the business. It's not there anymore. I can't find my dad or my email. I have to go home. I have to find them."

He pulled her in, resting her head against his chest. Then Jin's arm wrapped around her waist and she let herself be guided to the kitchen. He brushed at her hair after she sat back down at the snack bar. It was actually comforting.

"What's your plan? You can't wander all over San Diego looking for your family. It isn't safe."

Gracie pushed away from him. "I have to do something!"

Bryn lifted a cool glass of water toward her. She took it and gulped it down. It did seem to help calm her. Gracie took the wet towel offered next and patted her face, chasing the panic away. Hysterics wouldn't help Dad or Ape.

"I ran a background check on you last night." Bryn spun his laptop screen toward her. It was blank.

"I don't understand."

"I was showing Jin your life in San Diego and showing him that you really are an unaffiliated Descendant. We sat here and watched all your information being erased from every state and federal computer system. " Bryn pulled up the mapping software with satellite photos of Dave Berry's warehouse or rather where it should have been. They stared at the empty lot that had been demolished and resurfaced with pavement. Even if she did go back, she wouldn't even find a warehouse to search in.

"No. That can't be right. I practically grew up in that warehouse. We have twenty employees. They can't have all disappeared!"

"Most satellite photos are months old when they appear on search engines. A buddy of mine confirmed these satellite images were uploaded yesterday." Bryn slammed the laptop shut firmly. "Someone wants to make you disappear. They have the skill and the political power to make it happen."

"They can't just make me disappear! I'm a person with a life." Fear and panic had just been pushed to the back seat. Whoever was behind all this had crossed a line. "You guys think these Clan freaks are behind my family's disappearance, don't you."

"They seem the most likely suspects." Jin gripped her shoulders gently. "The Clans have the power, money and technology to make something like this happen. And they certainly are willing to fight over you."

Gracie nodded slowly. "Then it's probably time to ask Viper a few questions."

Jin gave her a slow, vicious grin. "I like how you think, Gracie Berry."

She returned his smile with one of her own. She almost forgave him for... Well, whatever she was angry at him about. "What's the plan?"

"Don't worry. I promise that we'll find your family. First, we need to deal with our hunters. I have an idea that will get them out of the way and humiliate Viper at the same time."

"And you have the advantage of having a pre-cog on your team." Gracie lifted her hand. "Count me in."

"You two need to slow down a minute," Bryn told them. "I've been monitoring Viper's communications. She's taken over Raul's little show and is broadcasting her messages on a loosely secure connection. It seems fishy to me."

"I haven't seen her do one practical thing since we met," Gracie murmured, letting the dislike creep into her voice.

"She's an unbalanced girl, our Viper," Jin said. "That's why we need to completely discredit her with Raul's party guests. A night in human jail and being tossed out of the country will certainly ruin their week and any hope Viper has of winning favor enough to take over the Girard Clan."

"Couldn't happen to a nicer snake."

Jin smiled at her. "You know, darling, you're much more pleasant than my mother's pet pre-cog. Druid is a complete and utter ass."

"That bald bastard." Bryn's face turned hard. "He couldn't die soon enough to suit me."

"Wait, there's another pre-cog?" A sharp stab in the middle of Gracie's brain propelled her forward against the snack bar. Its tile surface disappeared. Suddenly, she was in a broom closet with shelves and a flickering overhead light. Gracie recognized the cheesy mariachi music and the smell of taco meat. She was at the Rusty Grotto Cafe back home. A bald man with glowing eyes and a sinister face leaned against her. On the inside of his wrist was the familiar clan badge. He'd called himself Druid. He had been the voice in her head.

She came back to the present and woke up on the couch in the living room. Her head rested upon Jin's lap. His worried face stared down at her. A cool cloth patted softly against her forehead. Bryn and Myles stood over them, waiting anxiously.

"Druid," Gracie managed. "He found me in San Diego. He forced me to come here to find Raul. Somehow he took my memories."

Jin helped her up to a sitting position and exchanged a look with Bryn. "If Druid knows about Gracie, then so does my mother."

"Not necessarily," Bryn told him. "That son of a bitch has been trying to undermine your mother for years. He could be running some kind of con."

"What if he's the one behind the death mark on you, Jin?" Gracie clutched at his arm. "If he's trying to get at your mother, maybe he'll do it by killing you?"

Jin shook his head. "You don't understand, darling. My mother has a tight grip on Druid. She has ways of...correcting him."

The look on Jin's face told her that he'd been corrected a time or two himself. "Maybe we should call her and ask? Listen, Druid said he knew who my dad was and where we lived. What if he's telling the truth?"

Jin and Bryn shook their heads at the same time. "Druid's actions toward you are suspicious, darling, but we don't want to get my mother involved. It would be very bad if she found out any more about you than she already knows."

Bryn broke in. "Your gifts are very rare, Gracie. Clan leaders have been known to kill each other in order to win their rival's pre-cog. The last one to be born, well her life ended in tragedy." Gracie saw an unfathomable sadness behind Bryn's eyes as he spoke. "Jessica was a beautiful young woman who fell in love with the wrong man. They tried to run away together, but both of them were hunted down and killed by Jessica's own Clan family."

Bryn shook his head. "Such a horrible waste of two good people. I met Frank the Zed once. He was perhaps one of the most powerful Mercs I'd ever seen, but even his power couldn't save them from the covetous ambitions of the Clans."

Jin nodded his agreement. "Pre-cogs give their Clans the advantage. They're normally locked away from the public, protected from harm. Seeing you unaccompanied was a shock." Jin turned a solemn face to her. "My mother would take you by force, Gracie, just as Raul tried to do. You'd be her new pet and neither of us could do anything about it. We must keep you away from her at all costs."

Chapter Nineteen

The sun had disappeared behind the last towering structure on the Vegas skyline. Lights flickered on all along the Strip. Jin took a deep breath, inhaling the smells of exhaust and latent heat. This was going to be fun.

He turned away from the lights of the city and focused his attention on their rooftop command center. Bryn was surrounded by sound boards and other gadgets. His fingers were a blur as he clicked on his keyboards and slid levers along his toys. He was in his Zen state.

Gracie stood behind Bryn with a look of awe on her face. Gone was the golden glitter and borrowed dresses. Her blue jeans and a worn navy t-shirt were a better fit. Lived-in sneakers toed at a cable, pushing it out of the way. With her hair pulled back in a pony tail, she was a natural beauty. Jin was startled to find he preferred her this way.

Bryn handed Gracie two headsets. She shrugged and made her way toward Jin, hopping over the electrical cords and other equipment. He took one of the headsets and put it on. They were small and very high tech.

"Bryn says he can tap into all the outdoor speakers on the Strip," Gracie said, fumbling with her own headset. She looked up at Jin with concern. "Have I mentioned yet how crazy I think this idea is?"

"Oh at least ten times that I recall." He chuckled and shook his head. "Relax, Myles is ready with the truck and Bryn, well Bryn is always ready."

"The police aren't going to think this is too funny," Gracie said.

"That's precisely the point."

"Maybe I should come down there with you. I might not See the trouble coming your way from up here."

He shook his head. "I want you to stay close to Bryn. If the Clans got hold of you, we'd have a very dangerous situation."

"What about you, Jin? These guys are seriously trying to hurt you. Maybe even kill you. Viper sure will if she gets the chance." Gracie gave him a furtive look and then pretended to adjust her headset. "She certainly is determined to keep you from talking about something nobody believes anyway. Why does she really want you dead? Bad breakup?"

A strange mix of pleasure and hesitation struck him as he noticed her try to play it cool. Gracie had no mask to hide behind. Her face showed what she felt all the time. In a world with lies and intrigue, Gracie Berry was the first person he'd ever met who was truly honest. But, could he be honest with her in return?

"I was visiting my family at the Girard Clan's safe house. Nobody expected me to be there that night, especially Viper." He tugged at the clasp on the cloak he was wearing. "She and her brother, Renee, tried to take control of their Clan, wounding my father in the process. I ruined their plans.”

“Viper doesn’t seem to be the type who takes things like that very well.”

“No. You’re right. She shot my little sister in the back for revenge.” Jin lifted his eyes to Gracie’s open face and the shock and empathy he saw there. He swallowed hard. “Mai Ling was just turning six when she... I’d come to see her for her birthday. She was running to me, and Viper shot her. My sister bled out in my arms.” He turned his face away from her. Gracie’s hand took his and held it. Comfort. It was an alien concept for him. “I couldn’t keep her safe.”

Guilt rammed his conscience hard. This was the first time he’d spoken of Mai Ling and her death with anyone but her killer. He hadn’t allowed his heart to grieve for her. That would drain his strength from him, strength he needed to avenge her death.

“Well, that’s why Viper hates me. I took her Clan from her after she took my sister from me. For some reason I couldn’t make myself kill her at the temple. I’ve planned my revenge for so long, but I just couldn’t bring myself to kill her.”

“That’s simple. You’re not a cold-blooded killer. I mean you don’t just go around killing people.” Then she looked at him more closely. “Do you?”

Jin shook his head with a reluctant smile. Strange. He cared what she thought of him and didn’t want her to see him as a killer. Gracie touched his arm and gave it a little squeeze.

“You’re not a killer, Jin. You’re a good man who’s in a lot of pain. Somehow you’ve managed to find the courage to stop these jerks anyway. That makes you a hero in my book."

Relief washed over him, and he laughed. "Gracie Berry, you're the only one in the world who could see me as a hero." He kissed her forehead. "Thank you."

They both stayed close, looking into each other's eyes. Jin brought his mouth to touch Gracie's lips. Their kiss communicated affection and true want. He'd never experienced such honest tenderness before.

Bryn cleared his throat. "It's time, lovebirds."

Jin sat on the edge of the building and spun his legs over the side. Gracie's arms wrapped around his neck. Her look told him to be careful.

"I never thought I'd say this to a guy, but here let me fix your lipstick."

Jin puckered his lips as she touched up the blue liquid. He gathered the long black cloak in his arms as she stepped away. Then he jumped into the hot night air. Landing on a tiny foothold several feet below, he looked back up at Gracie. Her shocked face watched him jump again. She would have no more doubt now that the Seelie Descendants were real.

Having stopped his freefall to the street, Jin waited. A large truck with a flatbed trailer pulled into the busy intersection and stopped dead center. Myles jumped out of the driver's side of the truck, taking the keys with him. Nobody was moving it anytime soon. Jin jumped again, making his appearance on the ground like thick smoke beside the trailer. As soon as the smoke dissipated, the stalled traffic and spectators became visible. Some of them gasped and began pointing at him. Showtime.

He threw off the black cape he'd been wearing. Now he was dressed in a rhinestone vest and tight satin pants. The crowd gasped again and began to move closer.

"Wow, you're very sparkly." Gracie's voice came through the headset.

"Drink me in," he murmured in the headset's microphone. Flourishing his arms about, Jin danced from corner to corner. The crowds grew thicker, effectively blocking traffic.

"Don't just stand there looking like a burrito in tinfoil. Do something. You've got to keep the crowd's attention."

"Thank you, Bryn. I'm aware."

He made an elaborate show of smoothing at his bare arms, assuring the small crowd that he had nothing hidden there. With a wave of his right hand, Jin gripped his left wrist and shook it up and down a few times. Then he seemingly pulled a large tablecloth out of thin air. Jin shook the cloth and stretched it out as if he were spreading it over a table. It stayed in that shape and the crowd applauded. They couldn't see he'd used his speed to set up the prop table that had been strapped to the trailer.

A rather voluptuous young lady pushed her way to the front of the crowd. Perfect. Performing his arm shake again, this time on her, Jin pulled a sexy black bra and held it up for the crowd to see. The woman laughed and kissed him on the cheek.

"Oh that was hysterical," Gracie said in his ear. She wasn't laughing. Jealous? Jin smiled.

"I'll show you the trick when we're alone this evening," Jin said softly.

While it was true Jin liked attention especially from the pretty women in a crowd, he wasn't much of a performer. What looked like an amazing feat to a Normal, would appear as a cheap child's trick to his fellow Seelie Descendants.

"Jin, the police have a wagon and are three blocks away," Gracie told him.

"Any sign of our friends yet?"

"No—wait," Gracie murmured. "They're all coming for the intersection at once. It looks like they'll beat the police to your location. You have to get out of there!"

He looked out over the crowd and saw several Descendants moving closer, at least ten of them, some moving faster than others. They had him surrounded. Not all of Raul's original guests had joined the hunt, but enough to sink Viper's future. Just behind them, several angry red and blue lights flashed. The police were coming in full force. Gracie was right. It was time to leave the stage.

"Time for my finale." He was about to jump when someone tackled him from behind.

"You're mine!" Hard muscle shoved his face against the trailer. Icy fingers drew a frigid trail along his neck. "Where is the pre-cog? She's worth a lot of money to me. Tell me where she is and I'll deliver her to Viper in one piece."

The ice elemental didn't get long to savor her moment. Another hunter kicked her in the ribs, rolling the female's large body off of Jin. The new hunter's hand swept up. Sharp, dagger-like nails stabbed down at Jin. He rolled and heard the ping of those steel nails stick to the ground.

"Hold it!" Several guns were on them. At least twenty very normal and very angry policemen circled around the hunters. Jin's plan had worked perfectly. His exit strategy had not.

A slick-looking man dressed in black stalked past the police and stood before them. He didn't present a badge to identify himself and he had no marks on his clothes. Yet, every Descendant on the flatbed knew who he was just as certainly as they knew the man could kill them without any fuss. He was an Enforcer, a human given weapons to keep the peace when unruly Seelie Descendants came to town.

"Evening, folks," he said, pulling up a tablet device. "I have your permit for entry into the United States right here. Nowhere does it say anything about blocking traffic and using your special gifts in front of the public." He lowered the tablet again. "I think you all know what this means."

Jin knew exactly what it meant. They'd be taken to a special holding facility and would be the guests of the United States government for violating neutral territory. None of them would be allowed in the US again if they made it out of the facility at all.

"This is Viper's doing!" one of them growled. "It's that bitch you should arrest!"

"You don't see her here, do you?" another yelled. "She planned all this to get us out of the way! I'll have my revenge on her no matter what it takes!"

The troops of policemen seemed unconcerned with who was really to blame. They had a cluster of crazies blocking the intersection and causing mass chaos in the busiest place in Vegas. It was time to clean up the mess. They moved forward in a wave when the Enforcer gave them the signal. One of the policemen pulled the plastic strap tightly on Jin's wrists. Escape just became more difficult.

A crack sounded above the noise of voices and angry car horns. The ugly Descendant who had tried to skewer Jin fell backward. Blood began oozing out of his forehead. It took a moment for the crowd to realize what had just happened. Then all hell broke loose. People, Normals and Seelie Descendants alike, began running for cover from the sniper. Screams sprang up all around Jin as they ran, leaving him alone beside the trailer.

He took his chance and jumped behind the line of dark uniforms. Wrists firmly fastened together, Jin ran as fast as he could for the casino.

Chapter Twenty

Gracie gripped the edge, her eyes searching for any sign of Jin among the chaos below. Chaos. That had been her warning vision. She hadn't been able to provide more concrete information than flashes of bodies and horrific noise. The hodgepodge was all coming to pass just as she'd seen it.

"Come away from there before someone sees you!" Bryn finished stripping down his rifle and then shouldered the bag he carried the pieces in.

"What about Jin?" She reluctantly took his offered hand. It was sweaty, but reassuring.

He moved faster toward the door to the stairwell. "We have to make a run for it before the police lock down this place."

The handle of the door began to turn as Bryn reached for it. He dropped Gracie's hand and lifted a pistol from his holster, aiming the barrel toward the opening. Myles, who was just entering, lifted his hands in the air with a yelp. Bryn let out a curse and holstered the weapon again.

"Take Gracie to the rendezvous point," Bryn ordered as they all continued to run down the stairs. "I'm going to help Jin. He won't get too far with his wrists bound."

They pushed through the casino level doors and were immediately drowning in the constant dings and flashes of the games. Tension started to pulse in Gracie's temples and behind her eyes. The effect made her sick to her stomach. Breathing down the nausea, she kept close to Myles.

"Bryn!" she shouted. He turned a dark face toward her. "Be careful."

Myles took her hand as Bryn disappeared into the haze of lights and sound. "This way!"

Bright flashes of color and confusion struck at her consciousness. She became disoriented. Myles noticed her floundering and forced them to continue on at a normal pace. They didn't want to draw attention by running through the casino. Alarms started going off in Gracie's mind. She watched several of the security team talking rapidly on their radios.

"Myles," Gracie warned.

"I see them. We'll take the exterior doors leading to the parking garage. We're almost home free."

A large "Parking" sign above a set of glass double doors attracted Gracie's attention. They were pretty hard to miss, yet she'd managed it. An uneasy feeling gurgled in her stomach. After everything that had happened to her in parking garages since she'd arrived in Vegas, she doubted she could go into one again without feeling anxious. And her damn headache wasn't helping matters. She was starting to get really sick to her stomach.

Myles banked a hard left, narrowly avoiding the deadly orange circle coming from the shadows. It struck the concrete beside his head as they ran. He pulled Gracie along the front bumpers of the cars.

Then they stopped near a low point in the exterior wall of the garage. His frightened face looked oddly pale in the fluorescent light.

Myles pointed at their rented van parked in the street behind the casino. She nodded to let him know she understood.

"You have to make it to the van, Gracie," Myles whispered. His hand was shaking as he wiped at the sweat. "I'll draw them away."

"No, Myles," Gracie gripped his arms. "It's too dangerous. We have to stay together."

"I know you think I'm not as brave as Jin or Bryn, but I'm a hunter." Myles looked intently at her. "I can stalk this guy without being seen. Now, go to the van. Here are the keys." He pressed them into her hand and then he was gone.

"Myles, come back!" Well, that was just perfect. Myles was trying to play the hero. She thought about Dad's larger-than-life personality. He and Jin were similar in that respect. It must have been tough on Myles growing up in Jin's shadow. Setting out to prove he had courage against this enemy was suicide. She'd better go after him.

Another blast of power struck at the asphalt a few feet in front of her. Change of plans. Gracie ducked her head and crawled over the half-wall separating the street and the garage. She ran flat out toward their van waiting on the street. A taxi pulled up swiftly and jumped the curb. It came to a stop, blocking her path. Two Seelie Descendants got out of the car. They were on Gracie before she had a chance to react.

Powerful hands pushed her into the back. They crawled in on both sides of her. Viper, who sat in the front passenger seat, leaned over the headrest to regard her. Eager glee sparkled in her eyes. Gracie hadn't noticed the driver until Viper touched a fingertip on his shoulder. He took off his red baseball cap and turned in his seat to smile at Gracie. She recognized the familiar shaggy blond head. Glen? She couldn't fathom how he'd appeared in the middle of all this.

"We meet again, Titania, or should I say Gracie Berry." Viper's malicious eyes glared at her in the reflection of the glass. Gracie flew at the snake-woman, throwing a punch toward her face. But Viper was ready for her this time. She twisted Gracie's arm and threw her off. Out of nowhere, a swift fist struck Gracie's jaw. Gracie clutched at her mouth. Blood trickled down her chin.

"You don't know how many times I've wanted to do that," Glen said with a laugh. "By the way, Gracie, Druid says hello."

All the memories of their time together, good and bad, collapsed in shades of doubt. Glen knew Druid. Of course he did! Why slither out from under his rock when he could have just as easily sent someone like Glen to spy on her? Gracie recognized his essence now. He was inside Glen just as he'd been inside her.

How many times had it been Druid's words rather than Glen's when she'd been convinced to get a place of her own away from her family? How many times had Druid been watching through Glen's eyes as they made love? Gawd! She stopped that disgusting train of thought.

"Glen, you son of a bitch! How could you tell them about me?"

"She is very slow, isn't she? Don't try anything else. Jin isn't here to help you this time." Viper held her weapon on Gracie, following her with the barrel when she sat back. "Oh, but don't worry, Gracie. I've made certain Jin will come for you. He's the guest of honor at my party. One might say he's the main event."

A snake-like grin stretched across her speckled face. It was the hungry smile of a predator about to dine upon its unwitting victim. Bryn had been right after all. Viper wasn't the overanxious and desperate fool who was out of control all for the sake of revenge. She'd carefully planned all this chaos. They'd gotten rid of her other obstacles for her. Jin was the last.

Chapter Twenty-One

Jin gripped the cracked dashboard of the 1968 Dodge Charger. Bryn had "borrowed" it from one of the unlucky casino goers. The restoration job had been focused on the engine. It's 460 hemi was coming in handy getting them away from the bedlam. They passed the blockades of police and Enforcer vehicles circling around the casino. In another few minutes the entire downtown area would be cut off. Bryn floored the hemi, and the car disappeared into the night streets like a ghost.

Jin allowed himself a satisfied grin. They'd done it! The plan had worked perfectly. His hunters were out of the way, and Viper was completely discredited. She'd be answering some uncomfortable questions from the Clan Council soon, provided Jin decided to let her live.

"I think we've worn out our welcome," Bryn told him. "We ought to get the hell out of town tonight."

"I'll need the car after we pick up Gracie and Myles at the rendezvous point." Jin finished fastening his jeans and pulled on a dark t-shirt. After tossing the sparkly vest out the window onto the side of the freeway, he sat back and directed his thoughts to the second half of his plan. "I have one last chore here in town. You take them to a safe place. I won't be long."

Bryn took the next exit and headed north. "You're mistaken if you think I'm going to let you go after Viper alone."

Their rented van was parked behind the abandoned gas station. Bryn pulled up alongside. Myles came around the Dodge, leaning heavily on its side. His face was streaked with sweat and blood. Jin rushed out of the car and held Myles' shoulders to steady him. His cousin looked like a man who'd seen death up close and barely escaped.

"They have Gracie!" Myles gripped Jin's arm tightly. "Viper took her. I don't know where."

"What the hell happened?" Bryn looked at the cut along Myles' hairline. "It's not too bad. I've got a kit in the car."

They sat him down on the floor of the van, and Bryn went to work on the wound. Jin pulled one of Gracie's bottled waters out of the back. She'd told him they'd need a good drink of something after it was all over. He squeezed the bottle hard. Water exploded from the flimsy container, splashing down his front. He grabbed another and handed it to Myles.

"We ran into the parking garage as a shortcut to head toward the van. Someone was waiting for us." Myles brought his shaking hands up to his face. "I told Gracie to make a run for it. I thought I could handle the guy. God, Jin, I was wrong. All I saw was a dark shroud and fiery circles. Whoever or whatever this killer is, he can cut through concrete! He almost had me, but security came and we both had to run out of the structure." Myles looked down. "I saw Viper take Gracie, but I couldn't get to the van fast enough.

I didn't know what else to do, so I just came here. I'm so sorry."

"It's not your fault, Cousin. I've seen what he can do. You were lucky to escape with your life." Jin felt as shaken as Myles seemed to be.

"Damn good thing I put a tracking device in one of her sneakers." Bryn got in the car and sat behind the wheel fiddling with a small handheld device. Jin joined him in the front and Myles got in the back.

The handheld device glowed bright green in the dim light of the car. Bryn gave his friend a triumphant grin. "We have a signal. Let's go get your girlfriend."

The Dodge raced back onto the freeway and headed north toward the warehouses in the industrial district. Jin recognized the nondescript outline of the warehouse where Raul had thrown his party. Viper wasn't a fool. She'd picked this place for a reason. It was an obvious trap, broadcasting a clear message. One of them was going to die this evening.

"We'll get Gracie back." Bryn gave Jin a quick look. "Don't worry. She'll be fine."

Jin nodded. "I hope you're right. Viper hates Gracie. The catacombs under the Girard Estate are full of Viper's old enemies." Jin fidgeted with a loose wire hanging under the dashboard of the Dodge. "Gracie's not my girlfriend," he added carefully. "We're just friends."

"Bullshit. I watched you with her in the casino acting like an overprotective show-off. You have a thing for her."

Bryn was an elf lord, born with powers few Seelie Descendants could even come close to possessing. He saw through lies and tricks to reveal the truth. His supernatural powers made him a wise protector of the veil between worlds though sometimes his keen insights weren't as appreciated as he hoped they would be. It was true Jin liked Gracie very much. She was fresh and honest in a world tainted by deception. In the temple and on the Strip she'd shown courage and loyalty. She was someone Jin counted as a friend.

"She's my friend. I'm not going to let her down."

Myles leaned over the torn back seat and pointed to their right. "Black sedan at two o'clock."

The sedan changed lanes, easing over beside them. Its tinted window lowered. The driver held up a woman's purse, making sure Jin got a good, long look. He recognized it as Gracie's purse.

"They were watching for us." Jin gripped at the Charger's broken handle. He nodded to the driver and the sedan sped ahead of them. "It would appear they want us to follow them off the freeway."

"Let's make this count. Myles, pass up my duffle," Bryn instructed. He ducked when Myles lifted the large bag over the back seat. Jin took it and unzipped the bag. Electronics and weapons in neat compartments weighed down the container.

"There in the middle pocket. You're going to be wired when you face that bitch again. Do the smart thing this time, Jin. Get Viper to confess," Bryn advised. "That'll get you your life back faster than killing her will."

"I can't promise she'll come out of our conversation alive," said Jin steadily. He lifted his shirt and taped the wire to his chest.

"Just make sure you come out of there breathing yourself."

They followed their escort off on a North Las Vegas exit. The nearly abandoned warehouse complex was a quick drive up the road to the left. Jin had guessed right. Viper had returned to the temple's entrance.

Their escort was joined by another, matching, black sedan. The two vehicles stopped in front of the warehouse entrance and waited.

"What are we up against?" Bryn asked. He stopped in the center of the drive a few hundred feet away and let the engine idle.

"The warehouse is straightforward enough, but if Viper has taken Gracie to the Vento mansion, we have a problem." He closed his eyes for a moment and then shook his head. "I don't feel a temporary portal. This should be a Human Realm game."

"We'll find some high ground. How are you playing it?"

"Right down the middle," Jin told him. He was playing it as best he could. The drivers of the sedans got out of their vehicles and stood on either side of the warehouse door. "They're growing impatient."

"We're walking right into their trap." Bryn tapped Jin on the chest and gave him his most serious "watch your ass" look.

Jin pushed open the Charger's door and stepped out into the hot Vegas night. Diesel fumes and the odor of rusting metal flooded the air. He slapped a hand on the Charger's roof and began walking toward the temple. Bryn's tires kicked up gravel when he floored it. The headlights disappeared around the corner of the block of warehouses.

His escorts made no move to stop Jin as he pushed through the warehouse doors. Inside, remnants of colorful decorations hung in strips and tatters, exposing bare warehouse walls. An empty bar, covered with broken glass, stood like a relic in Raul's ruined club. All the partygoers were gone, but they'd left a hell of a mess behind. Too bad. Jin grinned slowly, not in the least regretting spoiling their fun.

Viper stood in the center of the warehouse bay, waiting for him. The look of cold vengeance on her face spoke of the bitter battle soon to come. Though they were in the Human Realm, she'd let her glamour dissolve. The match was to be full Seelie Power then.

"Hello, Jin," she said. The snake smile widened. "Are you ready to perform for my amusement now?"

"Where's Titania?" Jin took a ready stance as Viper's private squad blocked off his escape route.

Viper motioned to the right with her hand, and one of the men dragged Gracie into the light. Her wrists were bound and her mouth had been gagged. Jin saw the dried blood at the edge of her mouth from a split lip. Someone was going to pay for that. Their eyes met for a moment and Gracie nodded, indicating she was all right. The goon pushed her down roughly. She thrust her foot out, trying for a kick at his knee. He pushed her leg away, landing a slap across her face.

Dazed, Gracie brought shaking hands up to cover the red on her cheek. The goon laughed at Jin, mocking his impotent growl of rage. Then he fastened Gracie's wrists to the floor with a chain. Gracie yanked hard at her shackles. Her angry stare turned back on Viper.

"Do you think he's come for your sake? Don't be so naïve. Jin doesn't keep his toys for long, especially when they become too inconvenient." Viper clicked her nails on the handle of the weapon she carried. She turned her snake eyes to Jin. "He's come for me, for revenge. You see, Gracie? You see how much he loathes me? He will never feel anything that intense for you."

"She's not in this, Viper. Let her walk."

"You don't make the rules here! This is my place now. You'll fight or both you and your whore will die." Viper slapped viciously at Gracie's head.

"The temple looks a bit shabby under your new management. Are things falling apart now Raul isn't here to hold your hand?" Jin kicked at an overturned table. "How will you keep order with no respect? Better call your dark elf friend in again for help."

Viper laughed and pointed her weapon at Gracie's head. "Oh dear how hurtful! Are you trying for a confession perhaps? It's almost as if you were wearing a wire." Her thumb cocked the weapon. Gracie flinched as it clicked. "Take off the shirt."

Damn! How had she known? Jin pulled the shirt over his head and yanked off the wire. He threw it to the ground. Viper's shot came in a blinding movement. The little device exploded against the concrete.

"You have nowhere to run, Jin." Viper stood up straighter. Her crazed eyes were defiant. "Let it be decided in the ring. What do you have to lose? Only your life. I give you my word, if you fight I'll let the girl go and drop my grievance against her."

"Do you expect me to trust you?" Jin shook his head. "Tell me, Viper, was Raul surprised when he learned it was you and Fong who ordered the hit on him? I imagine he trusted you until your new ally made a hole in his forehead."

Viper laughed. "When I found Raul dead, I took advantage of an opportunity. Think, Jin. How was he killed? Someone really hated Raul. They took his fingers before he died. I'm powerful, but not more powerful than a Clan leader." Viper leaned forward a bit. "And what have you done with dear Raul?"

She didn't know about Gracie's strange protector? Provided she was telling the truth, they were no closer to figuring out who the man was, and why he was so interested in Gracie. Another problem that had to be handled.

"I think I'll keep that to myself, Viper. I do so love to make you worry. Wasn't it fortunate that I stumbled across his body? I was able to clean up the incriminating evidence you planted there. Gracie isn't going to take the fall for his murder." Jin gave Viper a slow smile. "The Clan Council will be interested in his whereabouts as well. Best to let us go. You're beaten, Viper. You're out of leverage."

"Oh, am I?" Viper's snake eyes glinted their terrible topaz. She waved a hand. Kazakov came from the shadows and stepped into the center of the arena. He was dressed in boxing shorts and was a mass of muscles and scars. He balanced Myles' unconscious body over one massive shoulder. The golden-tooth sneer he gave Jin told the elf he was hungry for battle.

Chapter Twenty-Two

Kazakov was a killer. Jin had known many, most of them in his own family—but Kazakov was a different sort of killer. He didn't operate in the shadows or in thoughtful acceptance. Rather, he was a showman, killing on command for the want of cheers and adulation. And what his kind lacked in finesse, they made up for in stupidity. They made good sport, but they didn't last long among the Clans.

Myles groaned low when Kazakov lifted his unconscious body roughly to the other shoulder. Jin's cousin was still alive. Kazakov had shown wisdom there. His death would come a little quicker and would be less painful.

A dot flashed at the concrete a few centimeters beside Kazakov's feet. The little red dot moved across the floor and came to rest on Viper's forehead. Bryn! Now the fight would be a fair one.

Viper pressed her weapon against Gracie's temple. "It would appear we are at an impasse."

"I have your word then, Viper? If I fight this prancing fool, you'll free Gracie and never bother her again?"

"Of course, my own true love! First, tell your nanny to lower his weapon."

Jin waved a signal, and the red dot disappeared from Viper's forehead. Kazakov let Myles slide off his shoulder and gripped him by an arm and a leg. He swung Myles and tossed him several feet away, over by the door.

"You should have let your friend shoot her, Jin. She's not going to let the girl go when I've killed you. Viper has promised me Gracie. I'm going to use her as my brood mare."

Gracie yanked at her chain in fury. She kicked out toward the Russian, striking his bare leg. Her muffled yelp confirmed she'd struck solid stone. Taking on this opponent was going to be like fighting granite.

"I don't think she likes you."

"She'll learn to obey her master. And she'll use her gift to make me rich." Kazakov thumped his chest with a massive fist. "Our sons will be strong."

"What makes you think you'll ever touch her?" Jin dropped his glamour and brought the full force of his power into the warehouse. Air pushed against the walls in great gusts of stormy anger.

"I see your true nature at last! Killing you will be a great victory and test of my skill." Kazakov extended his right hand. It morphed into a massive, rock fist. Kazakov threw it toward Jin's body. The fist passed through empty air.

"Too slow, big boy!"

Jin jumped again as another strike flew toward him. In his air elemental form, he saw the fist pierce the ether in a slow, clumsy line. Kazakov's face contorted in confusion and disappointment. Jin's laughter spun wildly around the Russian's head, making him stagger. Landing beside Kazakov, he kicked a lightening blow at the Russian's knee, collapsing it. Then he brought a fist down upon the man's granite jaw.

"High-pressured jets of air can cut through metal. That rock jaw of yours isn't a problem for the likes of me!" Jin jumped just as the fist came dangerously close to his torso, cutting a long gash at his side with its rocky surface.

Enough play—it was time to end this. Jin brought his elemental body to a faster pace, swirling and leaping until he was a blur. Each time he landed, he made a strike at the Russian. The big man staggered, close to collapse. Kazakov fell at last to one knee. Jin let his airy form dissipate and came to a stop beside the Russian. He raised a hand to make the final blow. A shot rang out. Something sliced his temple. Hot blood began to drip down onto his cheek.

Jin, dazed, jumped away from Kazakov and landed close to Gracie. Her fingers touched his shoulder, trying to encourage him. Viper had shot him, and she was lifting her weapon to strike again. Another shot rang out. This time a splatter of blood struck her hand. Bryn was still playing the guardian angel.

Large hands grabbed Jin's hair and yanked him mercilessly against the solid mass that was the Russian's chest. This wasn't the last memory he wanted—although, now if it had been Gracie's chest...

"You tell that friend of yours he's welcome to kill Viper, but I'm exiting here alive," Kazakov ordered. He held firmly onto Jin's hair and had his gun pointed at Gracie. Jin, still a bit dazed, was finding it hard to concentrate on anything except the pain in his scalp and Gracie's frightened eyes.

The air about them had grown heavy. It almost seemed to crackle with violent energy. Then an orange circle of burning light flew at them from the shadows. It struck at the chains holding Gracie to the floor. The energy circle cut through the steel and concrete with ease. Jin used the opportunity to elbow Kazakov. The large man released Jin's hair with a grunt. Jin rolled away and watched in fascinated horror as another orange circle punched through the Russian like a cookie cutter.

More orange beams struck at the walls and the ceilings. This new, unknown power was going to bring the whole building on top of their heads. Jin hurried to Gracie and freed her wrists. She pulled the gag out of her mouth, spitting out bits of fabric.

"Go help Myles out of the building. I'll meet you outside."

Her blue eyes were troubled as she regarded him. Pale eyebrows furrowed. He saw that she didn't like leaving him, but she nodded and hurried through the dust and smoke. He waited to make sure she reached Myles and then turned his attention to finding Viper. Moving among the drifting tendrils of smoke, he came to the spot he'd last seen her. He saw drops of blood. Bryn had winged her. He kept low to the ground, following the bloody trail.

Two smoldering orbs glared at him through the smoke and falling debris. Viper crouched in a corner, clutching at her bleeding hand. She was unarmed, but that didn't mean she wasn't deadly. Springing at him, she flew over a pile of burning beams like a salamander. The venom dripped from her intact fang. The other—courtesy of Gracie—had blackened in death.

Careful to avoid the deadly tip, Jin stepped to the side and brought his leg to her torso in a roundhouse kick. She tumbled to the floor and then twisted to right her body.

"A love tap?" she hissed in laughter. "I find your hatred intoxicating! I will miss you, my love."

"You'll be dead. When you are, I assure you that I'll never think of you again." He caught her wrist as she lunged forward to grab him. The bone snapped, and she howled in pain.

"I want to know who put the death mark out on me. Was it you?"

Angry tears of agony pooled in her hateful eyes. "Now, my love, would I pass up the chance to kill you myself? No, someone wants you dead even more than I do. Hard to believe, I know."

She looked into his eyes then. He found no lie this time, only the glee she felt when she saw how much the truth frustrated him. Someone else either hated him enough to want him dead, or simply wanted him out of the way for another reason. Whoever had put the death mark out on him was powerful enough to frighten old allies into betrayal.

"Sorry to disappoint. I can imagine how much you hoped for it to be me." Viper stood up and let both arms drop to her sides. "You should have looked to your family, Jin. Too late. I won't let you escape me this time."

Her body began to change. It thickened at the torso, and her arms disappeared. Viper's hair turned into scales and the large, scaly hood of a snake formed in its place. True to her name, Viper had become the snake her soul modeled so well.

"I promise you, Viper. You'll tell me who put that death mark out. Things changed on the night you murdered Mai Ling. I'm not the same person. I don't care how much I have to hurt you to get at the truth."

He stood ready. He'd escaped his last encounter with her full snake form with speed and distraction in the darkened halls of the Girard mansion. This time she was ready to strike. Her thick body undulated as a deep hiss echoed in the empty warehouse. Viper coiled. Her scales caught the light of an unexpected blast of fast-approaching flames as she prepared to strike.

One flame swung away from the main fiery body. It slammed down hard against Viper's hood, knocking her back into a pile of burning beams. Gracie threw the two-by-four she brandished into the fire after Viper.

Jin grabbed Gracie's arm. "I told you to wait for me outside!"

"You're welcome. Gawd!"

Jin gripped her hand tightly and rushed into the smoke toward the waiting door and safety. Gracie made a small fuss at being dragged, but followed quickly enough. He was beside himself with anger. She'd shut Viper up before he could question her further, killing her. And Gracie's mysterious protector had brought down the warehouse. Jin was starting back at square one. In the distance, he saw Bryn helping a stunned Myles toward the car. That calmed him a little.

"Why are you pissed off at me?" Gracie yanked her hand away. "I didn't ask you to come down here."

"Yet you knew I would. Strange that your protector just happened to show up at the right moment. And he's destroyed any evidence I could collect to prove my innocence." The blood drained from her face and anger burned in her eyes. "What's your game? Have you and your partner been after me the entire time? Is that why you saved me from Viper and stuck close, so your partner could take me out?"

"My partner? You sound insane right now. I told you. I have no idea who that man is!"

"I don't believe you! Not anymore." He kicked at the dirt and clutched his fists tightly. "Viper's confession was the only proof I had of my innocence, Gracie. You just cocked that up for me."

"Are you sure that's true?" She gripped his arm and spun him around to face her. "You wanted to kill Viper, is that it? Do you think it would make you feel better about failing Mai Ling?"

"She was my sister!"

"Yes, she was. How do you think she would feel if she could see how consumed with hate you are? Tell me, Jin, have you taken any time to mourn her? Or have you just been focused on your own hate?"

"Go to hell!"

"Fine! This is where you and I part company." She turned away angrily and started down the parking lot toward the exit. Jin watched her go. Every instinct he had told him he was wrong about Gracie, but the facts were overwhelming. Friend or foe, she'd gotten one thing right. Jin hadn't spared a single moment to mourn for the only soul he'd ever truly loved.

Suddenly, a black SUV burst from between two warehouses. Tires screeched as the vehicle stopped and two men in masks got out. They grabbed Gracie and pulled her inside before Jin registered what was happening. He jumped as far as he dared with his head wound, landing several feet behind the SUV as it sped away. He ran, using his full speed. An orange circle flew past him and struck just behind the vehicle. It cut one of the power poles.

Jin barely managed to roll out of the way as the pole fell. He sucked air back into his lungs and helplessly watched the van speed out of the parking lot with Gracie inside.

A shadow fell across the pavement in front of him. He looked up to find a man seemingly floating like a phantom, pointing his glowing orange finger at Jin. Jin jumped to the left, but the impenetrable eyes of a killer found him. Jin used his full speed, reappearing several feet back toward the warehouse. A hand grasped him before he could completely form his body. He stopped struggling as the massive fist held him in place. This destructive force of the unnatural was faster and stronger than Jin on his best day.

"So this is Zhao's Hand of Justice? All I see is a two-bit thief." The baritone growl shook Jin to his very core. "Tell me where that SUV has gone, and I'll send you home to your bitch of a mother in one body bag instead of three."

Bryn came up behind him with a shotgun and pointed it at the shadow's head. "Well, Frank the Zed. I'm not easily shocked. It's funny how some people think you're dead."

"You know him?" Jin choked, legs swinging as he tried to break free of the massive grip.

"This is Frank, the deadliest Merc assassin the Clans ever produced. Frank here was supposedly killed in an explosion along with two other Descendants from the Wainwright Clan. Tell me, Frank, where is your wife? Where's Jessica?"

A Merc? That explained why he was so powerful and wasn't claimed by any Clan. Then the second name Bryn had uttered registered in Jin's slow-functioning mind. Jessica. She had been the last pre-cog born and discovered by the Clans, well before Gracie. This nightmare of death gripping his throat had been her lover. They'd run away together, or so the tragic love story told.

"She's dead. The tales tell true for my Jessica, Lord Brynmor." The voice lost its harshness and grew softer. "Yeah, I can see you in that bad gangster costume."

"Drop it." A short burly man stood with a gun pointed at Bryn's head. "I never iced an elf lord before, but I sure would if you get any funny ideas."

"This is getting us nowhere! Let me go. I have to save Gracie." Jin pulled at the fingers around his throat as hard as he could. They didn't budge.

"You've been so keen to help us in the past, why won't you help me save Gracie now?"

Frank dropped Jin to the ground. His form shifted and he became a solid, middle-aged mountain of a man. "I'm not helping you two guys, you stupid little prick." Frank pulled out a cigar and chomped it between his teeth. "Those bastards have my little girl."

"Wait," Jin stammered. "Gracie is your daughter?"

"Yeah." Frank poked a massive finger in Jin's chest, knocking him back a few steps. "And this is one daddy who isn't afraid to pop a cap in your ass."

That explained a great deal, like why Frank would take out Raul Vento and destroy Gracie's device. Or bring down a warehouse to get her back. This was a father who would dare anything or kill anyone to save his beloved daughter. And Jin had the distinct impression Frank didn't approve of him. That was going to make their journey to save Gracie more than a little awkward.

Chapter Twenty-Three

Jin leaned against the pine tree, peering out between the branches with his binoculars. Frank's cigar smoke struck his neck in rapid bursts like the breath of a panting dog. Jin turned around and gave Frank a hard look. It didn't seem to impress Frank a bit. Gracie's father had taken a great deal of convincing to join them at the Canadian border in Idaho. Frank wanted to take the direct approach and invade Vancouver all on his own. Calmer heads had convinced him subtlety would be more successful.

"You'd better be right about this, kid. I don't like how you're gambling with Gracie's life." Frank puffed harder on his cigar. He lifted the Chicago Bears cap, wiped at his forehead and pulled it back on again. His stalking pace resumed.

"I've explained Druid's involvement and my mother's confiscation of Gracie's data. She'd do anything to capture another pre-cog."

The glow of killing magic burned in Frank's eyes as he turned to glare at Jin. "Wasting time on a fucking trip to Vancouver just to find an empty room will really frustrate me. I'll be looking to take it out on your ass."

"Easy, Frank. You have to calm down a little. We want to be careful, right? It wouldn't help Gracie if we all got shot trying to sneak across the border." Ape gave Jin an encouraging nod.

Jin regarded the surprising little man. Ape was five feet of simple wisdom, wrapped up in a constantly cheery package of denim overalls. Frank had resisted any arguments Jin could give on taking the land route to British Columbia. It was due to Ape's support, he finally relented.

"Border security has always been tight to and from the US for Seelie Descendants. It's gotten worse since the September 11th tragedy." Jin noticed Frank was listening and hurried on. "The Clans agreed to install magical devices that monitor the border for uninvited Seelie Descendants. If triggered, the magic will immediately notify the Enforcers. I'm sure I don't have to tell you how ready their teams are to get their hands on law-breaking Descendants. That's why we can't simply walk across the border or drive through the Normals' gate."

"So then what do we do?" Ape looked at Frank who appeared about ready to challenge the entire US and Canadian military.

Doug Berry's glamour may have stood in the trees, but inside was the uncontainable rage of a Merc. The worn jeans and work shirt had fooled everyone for years, but Jin knew a killer when he saw one. He certainly wouldn't make the mistake of underestimating Frank's abilities or his anger. He'd have to exercise every one of his diplomatic skills to keep their furious companion calm.

"I have friends who assist less-than-honest Descendants over the border when their need is great," Jin told the others.

"Well, our need sure as hell is great. Who are these people?" Frank came to block Jin's path to the van. Damn, he was fast. He'd crossed that distance in the span of a thought.

"Friends of mine. Listen, you'll have to trust me if you want Gracie back. I know my mother. She'll have her under lock and key by now. The Wainwrights like to control their pre-cogs."

"Your mother was always a bitch on wheels. If Eleanor did take my little girl, I'm going to put a hole in her chest where her heart should be."

"Easy, Frank, that's the kid's mom," Ape said.

"I have mixed emotions," Jin admitted. He kept his eyes on Frank. He was getting a little irritated at the constant questioning of his motives. He was very tempted to point out that Frank had been the one who'd lied to Gracie her entire life. He'd also been the one who'd never warned her about life in the Clans, preferring to keep her under his influence.

"Say we find Gracie. Then what? Are you going to put her in a cage and hope she forgets everything she's learned in the past 24 hours?" asked Jin. "You should have told her the truth so she could learn to protect herself."

"I can protect her!"

Frank's glamour wavered as the power pushed to escape. An eerie orange light glowed in the center of his fingertip. He leaned over Jin in a move meant to intimidate him. It was working. But Jin managed to stand his ground. Frank needed to hear the truth for Gracie's sake.

"Yes, you've been doing a stellar job so far, pushing her at nice guys like Glen. Did you know he was Druid's enthrall? Your hiding place wasn't as clever as you'd imagined."

The dark power was building behind Frank's eyes. Pushing him this far was dangerous, but Jin was tired of his bullying. Let him terrorize the poor bastard who married his daughter.

"Somebody got to that asshole," Ape grunted with a laugh. "He looked like road kill."

"You're welcome." Jin folded his arms. "What if I hadn't been there? And what about Puppet Master? She almost became his slave. Her power should have protected her, Frank. Instead he got inside her mind and hurt her."

"That pervert should have been put down a long time ago." Frank bit his cigar harder.

"He won't be bothering Gracie or anyone else ever again. His body's rotting in a landfill by now."

Frank slowly took the cigar out of his mouth. "You sound like a jealous lover." He pushed a massive finger in Jin's chest. "I know all about you, kid. You're just a punk thief who thinks with his dick. Why don't you find another winner like Viper and stay the hell away from my Gracie!"

In a mad act of anger, Jin pushed back. "Get this through your head. I'm helping your daughter because Gracie's not like Clan women. She isn't out to gain anything from anyone. I suppose that's why I trust her." Yes, he trusted her, but too late.

"What are you trying to say?" Frank folded his arms with a frown. Ape and Bryn were looking at him, too, as he stood squirming like an idiot. Damn! He didn't know what he was trying to say. He sounded like a complete fool.

"She's my friend. I'm not going to let her down."

"Friend, huh?" Frank searched Jin's face for a long time before he spoke. "All right, I'm willing to believe you about that for now. You help me find my daughter, and I'll help keep the hounds off your ass. But you've got to promise me one thing first. If you do run into Gracie before I do, you can't tell her about...about me. She was unsettled enough about being a Seelie Descendant. Can you imagine her reaction when she finds out her dad is a Merc assassin? I want to be the one to tell her."

"Very well, Frank. I'll keep your secret. I can vouch for my cousin Myles and Bryn, of course." Jin threw a hard look at Frank. "Then you disappear with your daughter and I get on with my life."

Frank spun around and hurried toward the van. "Let's go. We're burning daylight."

Bryn came up beside Jin and nudged his elbow. "I hope to hell your friends will help us. Frank is getting impatient and I don't want to be there when he blows."

Ape slapped Jin on the back. "Don't worry, kid. He likes you."

"I can tell."

He'd had plenty of powerful Descendants irritated with him, but Frank the Zed wasn't someone he could simply jump away from or charm. This mountain of destruction would be his death. He was more powerful than any Seelie Descendant Jin had met, perhaps even more powerful than Zhao Long.

"You're still walking, ain't ya? Just make sure these friends of yours come through, and you'll be fine." Ape gave them a massive grin.

"So, what are you to Frank? You stayed with him in exile all these years."

Ape shoved his big hands into the denim overalls with a shrug. "I was Frank's manager when he was still a Merc. You've seen for yourself he sometimes gets a little worked up."

A little worked up? That was a massive understatement. Jin wasn't sure he wanted to be around Frank the Zed when he really got mad.

"Jessica was able to calm him right down. He never lost his temper with her." Ape shook his head sadly. "When she died, nobody else was there to take care of Frank except for me. He needs me." Ape shrugged his shoulders again. "Frank's a good guy. Give him a chance."

"I'll give him a chance if he returns the favor."

The Unruly Pig was a greasy haven in the wooded landscape of Northern Idaho. Jin's friends had set up their barbeque joint about ten miles south of Eastport and the Canadian border. It was just outside the range of the border's magic. Their restaurant was a rundown red shack with hideous yellow trim and an enormous pig resting atop the roof. It was a bit of an eyesore considering the gorgeous views of the Moyie River and the forest. Most people would consider the place a shabby little diner with decent barbeque, but it was so much more.

Standing behind the bar made out of a large, solid, pine trunk was an alarmingly thin man with sandy hair. Long fingers pulled on the beer tap as he expertly poured a cold one for his single customer. He looked up with dull eyes when Jin and his friends entered. Then a broad smile stretched under the thin mustache.

"Well, look who the cat dragged in. Jin!" Vince turned around to shout into the kitchen behind him. "Hey, Lefty! Look who's here. It's Jin and he's brought friends."

The kitchen doors swung open and out stomped a dwarf with a pumpkin-sized head. She had pale blonde hair that had long since lost its curl. Her red-checkered flannel shirt was rolled up at the sleeves. One of her arms, the left one, was much shorter than the other. Lefty was a full Seelie dwarf, but her deformity had earned her a one-way ticket to the Human Realm.

"And where the hell have you been?" Her gravel laugh caused the flannel to pulsate.

"Oh, I've been on holiday. You're looking lovely as always, Lefty." Jin kissed her small right hand.

"Bullshit!" Lefty waved them to a table. "We eat first and then you can tell me what you guys want. Must be serious the way the big one looks." She licked her lips as she took Frank in. "And expensive."

Vince brought a pitcher of beer on tap to their table. Jin's large glass of iced tea came with a piece of printer paper. He read it through and then read it again. He had no need to verify the source. The protective runes on the top of the memo were official Clan Council markings.

Frank snatched it from his hand and read it with a frown. "You've got an illegal death mark on your head, kid. It says, 'Required: severed head as proof of completion.' Geezus, talk about bad timing. How'd you guys get this?"

"We got that off an official Clan transmission. Security level three." Vince stood a little straighter, pleased by Frank's surprised expression. "We have ways of listening in on the Clans. Keeps us alive." He gave Jin an apologetic grin. "Couldn't find out who sanctioned the hit though. The Council don't know either."

Frank handed the paper back to Vince. "Level three means they'll be examining your whole life to see who had balls big enough to break Clan law for revenge. You've pissed off someone very powerful, kid. In the old days, they would've handed that to me, and I'd have your head in a box by now. I've heard nowadays the less-than-law-abiding make deals with an Unseelie sorcerer to conjure demons to do the job. Nasty ones. The demon's reward is the blood of the innocent. Considering how hungry they are, demons rarely fail."

Jin gave the matter some thought. "The night of the failed Girard Clan coup, I saw a dark elf in their mansion. He tried to kill my father." Jin leaned across the table, lowering his voice. Not that it mattered. The only customer had taken one look at Frank, paid up and left. "Viper has a benefactor. I believe that person is the one who brokered the deal with the sorcerer. They want to silence me about what I saw that night. Bryn and I suspect the Unseelie Court may try to come through the mists into the Human Realm on Midsummer's Eve two days from now. We just don't know where they'll land."

"And what about you, Lord Bryn? Is the Seelie Court going to look into this?" Frank asked.

Bryn shook his head. "I can't go to them without proof."

"So we're on our own?" Frank snorted and lifted his glass. "That's fucking great. Well, kid, you're screwed. I have friends in low places too. They made Gracie's life in San Diego disappear along with my business, but I don't think even they can erase a death mark."

Ape cleared his throat and raised his beer glass. "Here's to today then!"

Jin lifted his tea glass and drank. Viper's words came back to him in a rush. She'd told him to look to his family. As Clan leaders, either of his parents could sanction a hit on their son and later hide their involvement. Jin was a known troublemaker, a rebel and constant source of inconvenience to them both. But, were they ruthless enough to kill their own offspring?

Jin's father had plenty of bastards. He seemed more amused than bothered by them. Jin doubted the great Zhao Long would allow himself to be wounded and lose face. His mother, Eleanor, on the other hand would do anything to keep the Wainwright Clan out of scandal. Had Jin become too much of a liability?

Pushing his mind away from the subject, Jin watched in open curiosity as Ape shoveled in spare rib after spare rib. The man was a bottomless pit. Frank and Bryn were close seconds. Apparently the powerful Frank's stomach wasn't affected by his worry over Gracie. Jin—disturbingly—couldn't eat. The others had no idea what Eleanor Wainwright was capable of. He'd seen her "punish" the Druid before, and the Druid was more powerful than Gracie.

"You don't like my cookin', Jin?" Lefty frowned as she put another platter of ribs on the table. "You upset about that death mark?"

"Girl trouble," Bryn said, between bites.

"You're shittin' me?" Vince laughed as he picked up their empty pitcher and delivered a new one full of amber beer.

Frank bolted up, fingers glowing. "That's my daughter."

"My apologies, mister!" Vince said, holding his hands up. "Is she why you need to get across the border? I mean, we can help."

"And just how do you plan on doing that?" Frank folded his arms, clearly trying to calm down.

"Come on, I'll show you. We've got ways of getting you across the border provided you can pay that is. We ain't running no charity."

Jin interjected quickly. "The usual amount, plus a little extra perhaps?" He lifted ten-thousand dollars in US currency out toward Vince's hands. "I suggest you take this and be happy, my friends."

A massive hand blocked the exchange. Frank's eyes glowed with their deathlike emptiness. Vince shrank away, but Jin forced his body to stay in place. "I pay my own way, kid. It's my daughter and my dime. I won't have any outstanding favors for someone like you to claim from my family. Understand?"

"Someone like me," Jin said. "A pariah and thief you mean? I'd rather be a thief than a hired killer."

"You just kill for revenge or when it suits you. Is that it?" Frank leaned closer.

Bryn stepped between them. "Okay, guys, I think there's enough testosterone in this room to fill Canada. Let's not lose sight of who really matters. Or have you forgotten Gracie?"

Frank looked away first, but not before an awkward sort of shame passed across his face. Jin recognized the look. Guilt. He'd carried his own guilt as a constant burden since Mai Ling's death. Jin stepped away and took a gulp of iced tea.

"Come on then," Lefty said. She stomped toward the back and all of them followed her into the kitchen where the smell of roasting chicken joined the aroma of smoked meat. Someone had fashioned a catwalk along the kitchen appliances for Lefty's use. She walked past the modern machines, leading them to a wall in the back. Large blocks of stone formed a hearth and chimney. Lefty stopped beside a massive pot of boiling sauce and pulled on one of the kitchen spoons hanging off a hook. The back wall slid open, revealing a set of stairs.

Frank gave them a wary look. Jin ignored him and walked forward. Frank was the first to follow. They descended several flights into the earth. Electric lights illuminated the steep staircase. Lefty had no use for them. Dwarves were born to rock and cave, but the man they had come to see loved his modern technology. Flat screens and computer servers greeted them like sentries as they finally reached the lair. The perfume smell of ink and new paper struck Jin as he stepped into the darkened cavern.

The Engraver sat on a barstool in the very center of chaos central. His eight arms worked frantically on several different forged documents at once. Jin contemplated the maze of papers and empty passport books from the multitude of countries.

"Hello, Bob, you're looking well." Jin waved a hand in greeting and was rewarded with a grin that parted a freckled face. Thinning red hair was held by an accountant's green visor against the man's abnormally small head.

"Jin! How's my favorite customer?"

"I'm in need, my friend."

"Of course you are. You don't come for the barbeque!" Bob laughed and when he saw the sour expression on Lefty's face, he laughed harder.

"We need to cross the border as Normals."

Surprise turned to suspicion on Bob's freckled face, but greed finally took center stage. This was going to cost some serious money.

"That's tricky. It'll take time and it's going to cost you."

Frank let his anger out in a great explosion of black. Both hands powered up and aimed square at Bob. "We don't have time for this bullshit! Now get us through the fucking border."

"No, Frank! Don't!" Jin called out a warning. Too late.

Vince and Lefty hurried toward each other. Vince lifted Lefty to his shoulders. Jin froze as their bodies began to morph. Lefty's legs joined with Vince's arms. Within moments, he couldn't see where Lefty ended and Vince began. Thick brown hair burst from their joined skin. Too late! Bloody Frank and his bloody temper!

Power, raw and fierce, began to fill the chamber. Burning yellow eyes widened to scope out the new intruders. A massive muzzle opened to show jagged teeth. Drool dripped from the vicious jaw, striking the ground. Its acid chemistry sizzled upon the rock. Then the gigantic werewolf from every monster horror story stalked toward them.

Chapter Twenty-Four

Gracie lifted a groggy hand to rub at her eyes. Her head and body were sluggish, as if she were trying to sit up in slippery syrup. She smoothed at cool linen on a comfortable bed. Reaching a hand for the lamp hanging on the headboard, she flinched as its light struck her eyes. Someone had dressed her in a flimsy hospital gown with cheery splashes of pink and blue. A cotton ball was taped to the inside of her arm. They'd drawn blood.

A block of light cut through the darkness across from the end of her bed. More lamps flickered on, illuminating the room. She was in a hotel suite, pretty pricey too, based on the tasteful contemporary decor. Double doors stood open, leading into a large sitting room. A cheery looking nurse in white greeted her from the doorway with a prim smile.

The odor of eucalyptus and other herbs slapped Gracie's nose as she walked past. Her new caretaker's skin had a strange tint. It was the pale color of a middle-aged Anglo-Saxon busybody, but as she passed into the light a sparkle of green, blue and purple surrounded her hands. She was a Seelie Descendant.

"Good morning, Miss Berry." The nurse put a pair of scrubs down on the bed next to Gracie.

"You'll want to dress." The woman's high-pitched voice was already grating on Gracie's nerves.

"Where am I? Who are you guys?"

"I'm sure I'm not the one you need to speak with, miss. I'm your nurse, not your cruise director." Her bright-white uniform moved quickly against the shadows to the wall. She briskly pushed a button, and the curtains began to open on an afternoon sky. Something in the distance flew across the blue. Gracie hurried out of bed and to the window.

The little bush plane landed in a harbor surrounded by tall evergreen trees. Marinas with boats and bush planes jutted out from the rocky shore. A grassy walking path followed the water's edge, going to Gawd knew where. Glass skyscrapers blocked her view of its destination.

"What the hell? Las Vegas isn't by the ocean!"

"Very astute, Miss Berry," A prim British voice, dripping with sarcasm said from the other side of the wall. "Please dress quickly. We must have a chat, and I prefer not to do it through a barrier."

Gracie grabbed the scrubs and hurried into the bathroom. Flipping on the light, she stopped to admire the palatial elegance that included a king-sized hydro tub with golden faucets. One of those expensive Swedish showers stood beside it. Both touches of luxury didn't make a dent in the sheer size of the room. The bathroom was bigger than Gracie's whole condo back home.

"Please exercise some haste," the nurse said entering and standing beside her. "Lady Wainwright doesn't like to be kept waiting."

"I think I'll call you Nurse Hoover, because your bedside manner sucks." The joke was bad, but the look of utter disdain on the nurse's face sold it. Hoover stepped out of the bathroom in a huff.

Gracie swung the door closed for some privacy and splashed water on her face. It helped chase the effects of the sedative away. After she'd pulled on the scrubs, Gracie opened the door. Hoover stood waiting for her as if Gracie were an invalid. The nurse twisted away with a little hop and led her into a sitting room tastefully decorated in white and gold.

A middle-aged woman sat on one of the comfortable-looking chairs by the window. She was beautiful. Dark, shoulder-length hair had been perfectly coiffed in a stylish fashion. A single band of silver intruded on the dark hair. Her sharp features were smooth and ageless. Startling green eyes lifted from the cup of tea. Their color and shape reminded her of someone she never expected to see again.

"What should we talk about?" Gracie said. "Oh, I know. Let's start with who the hell you are." Gracie put her fist on her hips. By the sharp intake of breath from Nurse Hoover, she guessed the woman sitting before her wasn't someone accustomed to being spoken to that way. Well, that was just tough.

"I should think that was obvious." The woman's eyebrow rose ever so slightly. It was the smallest of gestures, designed to intimidate. Gracie hated to admit it, but it worked.

"Not really. How about you tell me?"

"Clearly I was mistaken. I had assumed you and my son were...close."

"It's really none of your business, but since you're so worried about it, we're not romantically involved. He can't be the reason I'm here." She plopped down in the chair across from Jin's mother and helped herself to a cup of tea. "So, why did you kidnap me?"

"I do hope, my dear, that your lack of mental acuity is a temporary result of the sedatives." Lady Wainwright scanned Gracie with cold eyes. "You're a valuable Seelie Descendant. Pre-cognitives are very rare, so when one is born it is imperative she—or he—will be nurtured and protected. Eventually, the pre-cognitive is trained to hone her powers for the good of the Clans. I've brought you here for your own protection."

Gracie leaned back in her chair and shook her head. "It wasn't for my protection. You want to use me for my powers just like everybody else."

"Don't be childish. Jin has a skewed opinion of Clan life. You're allowing his poor feelings to sway you. The Wainwright Clan can teach you to use your powers. You'll be given great wealth, luxury, lovers..."

"I tell you what I do want. I want to leave right now." Gracie stood up and headed toward the outer door. "I'm going to tell the police about you, lady. The FBI frowns on kidnapping."

"As a high-ranking British official, I'm on rather friendly terms with the United States government, Miss Berry. When I explained what you were, they were very happy to get you out of neutral territory and safely across the border." A faint smile passed the woman's lips.

"Wait? What border?" Gracie ran to the window and its panoramic view. A red and white flag waved on the building next to them. The maple leaf greeted her good humouredly.

"Canada!" Gracie turned from the window to stare at Jin's mother. No wonder he had intimacy issues. "How am I in Canada? You can't just take people like this. I have a life! What about my family?"

"The Wainwright Clan is your family now. I have another matter to see to here in Vancouver. Once that's resolved, we'll return to England and you'll be marked as a Wainwright." She stood up elegantly and faced the door. "In the meantime, I've arranged for your mentor to join us."

As if on cue, the exterior door opened. Gracie recognized the face and those penetrating eyes. Druid was standing before her in the flesh, dressed in a very sharp gray suit. For all her angry promises to get even with him, she hadn't been ready to face the creep directly. The old fear returned as he passed her a warning look. He approached them with a wide smile and bowed to Lady Wainwright.

"Miss Berry, this is Druid. He's an experienced pre-cog and can teach you how to use your powers." Lady Wainwright moved away from them toward the door.

"We've met. I don't want his instruction!"

Lady Wainwright paused for a moment to regard Druid. A strange sort of smile crossed her face when their eyes met. It stayed there for the briefest of moments, before she turned away. The look of hatred on Druid's face when her back was turned told Gracie volumes about their relationship. It appeared Druid had kept Gracie's existence from Jin's mother. Neither of them looked very pleased. Good. Gracie was going to help that wound fester any way she could.

"Don't be absurd. Druid is the only one who can help develop you to your full potential. Listen to him well, Miss Berry, or should I say Titania? You are much too valuable to roam around on your own. Tell the nurse if you require anything else, and it will be provided to you."

The exterior door opened by itself. Gracie stared, and her jaw dropped. She'd seen some weird things during her time with the Seelie Descendants, but this...this was magic. Lady Wainwright passed through into the hall without looking behind her. She had given a command and expected it to be followed. Well, she could go to hell. Gracie was going to find a way out. She wasn't anyone's property.

"I can see the wheels turning in your mind, Titania. There isn't a move you can make without me knowing first." Druid stalked to the window, his hands clasped behind his back.

"Stop calling me Titania! Jin told me who that was, and I don't think it's funny."

Druid stiffened at the mention of Jin's name. There was obviously history between the two of them. Gracie was a bit curious, but not enough to stay put. Then again, maybe Jin's story was something she could use against Druid.

A soft knock on the door interrupted her train of thought. Glen came in carrying another pot of tea and a clean cup. He was dressed in a teal jumpsuit with matching sneakers; the spark of humor or life was missing from his eyes. Druid had him under tight control again. Gracie shivered, remembering the times the monster had taken control of her.

"You remember Glen. No need for introductions." Druid continued to gaze out over the harbor as Glen poured his tea.

"I could kill you for what you did to Kay and my family." Gracie raised a fist in an impotent desire to strike the man. His confident stance didn't waiver. He'd been playing some sort of a game, and it looked as though he thought he was about to win. "How did you know about me? I mean how did you know I even existed and was in San Diego?"

"Like you, I'm a pre-cog." He turned and gestured for her to take a seat. Druid sat in the chair across from her as primly as Lady Wainwright had. "Someone had taken great pains to hide you from the Clans. I wasn't able to See visions of you until you went to college. It was a delightful surprise."

"So why not come after me then? Why send Glen?"

"You may have been ready to explore your powers, my dear, but I was not." Druid waved his finger and Glen squirted lemon in his tea cup. Gracie was beginning to feel sorry for Glen. He had been reduced to being Druid's empty slave.

"I needed time to prepare for your entrance into our Clan. Glen was very eager to assist me. Some among the human race actually enjoy being enthralls. I find them useful. Glen here sought me out. I instructed him to keep an eye on you, and in exchange he'd be given a part of your father's business. He was very keen."

Any sympathy Gracie had for Glen faded at once. She should have let Dad kill him back at the warehouse. He'd been playing an angle the entire length of their relationship. What a jerk. Well, he was getting what he deserved now.

"I don't understand. You forced me into going to Vegas, so I could run into Jin? Is that it?"

"No. Jin, as usual, was a surprise element. You'll find he's unpredictable." That was interesting. Druid had just showed her an unexpected insight into his biggest source of irritation. Jin did have that effect on people sometimes.

"My plan was for you to be taken by Raul. Lady Wainwright's hand would be forced, and she would battle Raul for you. That would weaken both Clans long enough for me to put certain pieces into play."

"Wait. You want to take over the Wainwright Clan?" Gracie slapped her hands on her thighs. "You ruined my life, so you could be head freak?"

He leaned forward. She observed a wolfish grin on his face. "Don't you see? I can't overthrow her on my own. She's too powerful. But, you and I together could trap her. She will fall and the rest of the Clan will finally be free."

"Free under your rule, you mean." Gracie shook her head. "I get it. I just met Lady Wainwright, and I want to beat her to a pulp, but that doesn't mean I'm going to. I'm out of here. I'm going back home. You both can keep your Clan and your power."

Druid's eyes narrowed, and he leaned back in the chair again. "You don't seem to realize your position, Titania. No one leaves the Wainwright Clan unless by Eleanor's permission. She has claimed you and now you are hers unless..."

"Unless I help you." Gracie rose to her feet. "Why don't you just ask your friend from the Unseelie Court to help you? Or should I tell Eleanor about him?"

Druid slammed a fist on the chair in an unexpected surge of anger. "Jin has been telling stories! He's a pariah. No one's going to believe him or you."

"I wouldn't be too sure about that." She headed toward the door. "You and your Clan can go to hell. I'm leaving."

"You'll soon see things my way." Druid flicked his hand.

A sharp pain stabbed deep inside Gracie's mind. She fell to her knees, clutching at her head. The pain made her stomach wretch.

"I'm my own person! I'll never join you!"

Druid laughed low, watching her with his smug expression. "You're mine now, Titania. Soon you will learn to do as you're told like a good little girl, or I'll take your mind from you."

Chapter Twenty-Five

The massive werewolf moved on quick paws to intercept Frank. Jowls dripping with acid drool lowered, ready to taste flesh. A deep, ghastly growl rumbled from its furry throat. Frank stood to meet it. His body transformed into a shroud-like form floating under his wide-brim hat. He extended a glowing finger and held it toward the advancing werewolf. Though the werewolf had a height and weight advantage on Frank, Gracie's father was one of the most powerful Descendants Jin had ever seen. It would be a needless and bloody battle. Time to step in.

"Hello, Dutch," Jin called to the werewolf. "I'd hoped we wouldn't wake you on this visit."

Those yellow eyes glanced briefly toward Jin, but the teeth-baring muzzle stayed fixed on his opponent. Jin eased toward Frank, trying not to make any threatening moves. Dutch was a wild card. He retained the cognitive tactical abilities of a human, enhanced by the cunning of a wolf. Yet human emotions like empathy, affection or fear had been lost the moment Lefty and Vince joined.

"Bob, perhaps you can explain to Dutch that we're customers."

"What the hell is with your friend? He can't come in here threatening people." Bob raised all eight arms in protest. "I think it's time he left."

"Why don't you and your pet come over here and make me." An ugly grin stretched across Frank's face. Something in him was hungry.

"Listen to me, you have to calm down for Gracie's sake. We need Bob's help. If you try to smash through the human border, Enforcers will come down on all of us and then what chance does Gracie have?"

"Listen to the kid, Frank," Ape said, coming over to rest a hand on his friend's arm. "He's making sense. We gotta be quiet about this. Right?"

"Right," Frank grumbled and let his power dissipate. He turned dark orbs on Jin. "You made the right choice controlling your fear, kid."

"I don't understand." He'd spent his entire life learning to hide his fear. Showing emotions, especially fear to someone like Frank could prove deadly.

"How do you think I find my targets? I can see the energy signature around your body, and right now it's a dark blue neon sign telling me you're about to piss yourself." Frank snorted and straightened up. "I'm talking about your fear, kid."

"Are you telling me you can see my aura?"

"What do you think I am, some kind of fucking hippie?" Frank pushed Jin with a meaty hand. "Geezus!"

He let the shroud fall away with a laugh and marched over to take a seat by Bob's chair. The engraver stared as Frank dug in his shirt pocket and pulled out two cigars. He handed one to Bob. Seven arms dropped, allowing the eighth to hold the cigar under his nose. Bob nodded his thanks and leaned over to let Frank light it for him.

Ape gave Jin a shrug and patted his stomach. "Who else is hungry?"

Dutch shifted on his paws and then sneezed. The werewolf's shape began to transform until Lefty and Vince took his place. The dwarf hurried to join Ape by the stairs. He took her hand and kissed it. Lefty blushed. They started up the stairs, talking softly in easy conversation. Vince shook his head and then followed.

"What just happened?" Jin asked Bryn.

"Hey, you survived. Why ask why?"

Bob seemed very motivated to get them on their way. Several tense hours later, he handed them each phony passports and a tiny device that attached to their collars like an extra button. Jin could feel his power being drawn behind a veil. Frank seemed used to the feeling. This object or something similar must have been how he had hidden for so many years.

"That device is a one-way ticket across the border sensors, boys," Vince told them. "If that little light switches from green to yellow, you're screwed. You may as well put your arms up and wait for the Enforcers."

"So how do we get across the border without being stopped?" Myles asked, tapping at his own device. "I'm sorry, but we couldn't look more suspicious if we tried."

"That's my department. Get in the van," Ape said, giving Myles a hard pat on the back. "Hey, I thought you was a Normal. Why do you need one of these things?"

"I didn't want to run the risk of Wainwright DNA triggering the border's magic." The bushy moustache angled downward on Myles' lip.

"Good thinking, Cousin." Jin gave Myles a nod. His cousin was used to living with his lack of Descendant gifts. That didn't mean he was fond of discussing it with strangers.

Ape shrugged and headed toward the van. He stopped before Lefty as the rest of them piled inside the vehicle. She patted his stomach and handed him a large bag. Ape leaned over to kiss her cheek. His lips moved in a whisper that made her blush. Then he hopped in the driver's seat. Immediately, the smell of barbeque sauce filled the van, sending waves of nausea through Jin's stomach.

Jin took his seat and exchanged a look with Bryn. They were putting a great deal of trust in Frank's friend. Suddenly, the van rumbled and Ape pulled forward. It sounded as if they were right next to a big diesel. Jin looked out the window at Ape's side-view mirror. They were in a Mac truck! Or at least an illusion of one.

"You were in the Bugatti outside of Vegas after we escaped the temple." Sparkling eyes full of humor looked back at Jin in the rearview mirror. He returned the smile. They'd been watching over Gracie for much longer than he'd suspected.

"Gracie sure has bagged her one of them road scholars, Frank." Ape laughed when Frank's face turned sour.

He pulled them back onto the highway and entered the truck lane toward the border. The van followed the signs instructing large, loaded trucks toward the right. Cars swarmed beside them. The Normals were completely oblivious as they flew by. Ape's power was working, but could he get them through the inspection at the border?

Their vehicle pulled onto the weight scale. The fake airbrakes triggered, and they rolled to a stop. The van fell silent when Ape got out and walked around to meet an official-looking officer with a clip board. The two had a brief discussion. Then Ape shrugged and led the inspector toward them. Damn! The last thing they needed was a scuffle at the border. Jin would have to be quick, incapacitating the man before it turned lethal. But Frank grabbed Jin's arm and gave him a warning glare. Jin froze.

Myles stirred as the border patrol inspector opened what he thought was the rear door of the trailer. Frank was on the young man in a flash. He held Myles tightly with a hand over his mouth. Wild eyes full of terror found Jin's. Jin couldn't do anything for his cousin at that moment.

"Yeah, I'm just headed back to Ottawa empty. Boss needs the trailer for cargo to Calgary." Ape shrugged. "Nice not to have to rush."

The inspector gave the van a quick look, pausing on Jin's face. Jin forced his body to a calm and still state as the Normal continued to stare. What had

Frank expected to happen? One word, one shout would bring the Canadian authorities down upon the van. Then the inspector turned his attention to the clipboard.

"There's a true word." The agent shook Ape's hand. "Have a nice day."

Ape closed up and crawled back behind the driver's seat. "I like these Canadians. They're nice folks. Hey, Frank, we should stay up here awhile, you know, after we get Gracie."

"It's a little too close to Eleanor for my tastes."

Frank released Myles, who scrambled away, shaken. He fell into an empty seat at the back of the van. Jin left him alone to recover. He'd experienced the overwhelming fear Frank could inspire.

"We have to get over the border first." Jin leaned across the seat to get a better view out of the windshield. "The real challenge is coming up fast. The Seelie Descendant border is just ahead. I can feel its magic."

Normals couldn't see or sense the thick blue line of power created to deter illegal Seelie Descendants from crossing over the border, but to a Descendant, the borderline felt like a sharp jolt of electricity from an outlet. It was a gentle zap until you broke the law. Then the thrust behind that jolt strengthened to the point at which it could knock an adult Descendant immobile to the ground.

Spikes of biting power struck at Jin's legs. The tiny jolts raced up his torso and down his arms. He gritted his teeth against the wasp stings of energy. Gripping at his lapel, he brought their expensive new toy into his line of sight. The light on his small device continued to glow green. It was working. His heart beat in time to the little pulse of "green means go" beat. Then it turned red and shut down.

"Satisfied?" Jin asked Frank. Gracie's father grunted once and turned to stare out the window.

They headed west toward the coast, skirting along the US border. Jin stared out the window at the passing countryside. Getting Gracie back from his mother would be easier said than done. The Wainwright Clan had a strong security force, many of whom possessed mental powers. Even with Frank's strength and anger, rescuing Gracie was going to be an adventure.

The van swayed as Frank sank into the seat next to Jin. He pulled off his cap and rested it on the seat. Large fingers raked through his thick hair. Jin tensed beside him. The van had several empty seats, so why he'd chosen to sit next to Jin was an unpleasant mystery.

"And where do you plan to take Gracie when we get her back?"

"Why are you so interested?" Frank stared at Jin with those dark eyes.

"Listen, Frank, Gracie was using her powers to help me find out who was behind that death mark. That's all. We're just friends."

Frank stayed quiet for a moment and caressed the wedding ring hanging around his neck. "Gracie's mother, Jessica, was a pre-cog too. A pretty powerful one." Frank smiled a little. "She was the sweetest person I've ever met. It wasn't too long before I fell in love with her. For some reason she fell for me too."

Jessica, Frank said, had stood against the Wainwright Clan, refusing to end their relationship. It wasn't until they'd faked their deaths that they were finally free. "Our happiness didn't last long. God, it cost me. Jessica's death was too high a price to pay." Frank looked at Jin, who saw worry and love in those wrinkles. "I won't let Gracie be trapped in the Clans, kid. She deserves a better life."

"Yes, she does. But Gracie may not want to go back into hiding again. She doesn't understand our world."

"Yeah, I heard what that prick Raul did and took care of him." Frank chewed on a cigar and grinned. "You've made an enemy of that little psycho bitch, Viper. Are you going to handle that problem?"

"She's in fiery pieces back in Vegas."

"Did you see her dead body?" Frank shook his head. "You should know better, kid. Never take anything for granted."

"Guys," Ape shouted. He slammed on the brakes causing the van to sway wildly. "We got company!"

The van's side door slammed open. Asphalt streaked by at sixty miles per hour beneath Jin's feet. An invisible force wrapped around his waist and pulled him violently from the van. He tried to escape his human glamour, but something behind the magic was preventing his transformation.

He slowed abruptly and dropped to the road's surface in a painful heap. Shaking his head against the shock, he struggled to sit up. Immense clouds of midnight smoke darkened the Canadian sky. Hellfire burst from the ground, casting red stains against the black. It stood among the bloodied horizon, featureless and unfathomably dark. The demon had found Jin at last.

Chapter Twenty-Six

Gracie tugged on her shoe, hopping fast on one foot as she tried to keep up with Glen. He was taking her to Druid. Apparently neither of them understood the concept of rest. It was midnight in Vancouver, and all Gracie wanted to do was collapse into her bed. Druid had been grilling her the entire day, trying to break through her power. Though she'd never been trained, instinct was keeping her out of trouble for the time being.

"Hurry, Gracie," Glen called over his shoulder. "Druid's in a bad mood. One of his enthralls was caught servicing another Seelie Descendant."

"I don't understand."

The look on Glen's face was one she'd never seen before. He was terrified. "Enthralls are owned by their masters. We aren't supposed to sleep with another Seelie Descendant by choice or otherwise without permission."

In other words they were slaves. Everything she thought she knew about Glen, his charm and intelligence, had all been a lie. This submissive husk was someone she didn't recognize. It turned her stomach to see him like this.

"And you chose to be enthralled by him? Why would you give up your whole identity to that creep?"

"You don't get it, Gracie. I was a three-time loser headed to prison before I met Druid. He set me free and gave me things I'd never had before. You should see our apartments in London!"

"You're right. I don't get it. You didn't just betray me, Glen, you betrayed my family. What about Dad and Ape? What about Brenda who was always so nice to you?"

He turned on her then. His face contorted in resentment. "You don't know anything about real life. Daddy gave you everything you have. Now you're going to be a pampered pre-cog. The Wainwrights will give you anything you want. Money, houses, cars! God, it makes me sick. You get everything just because you were born with a third eye."

She shook her head. "All I want is my freedom. Help me out of here, Glen." She shrank back from the hatred on his face. Seeing such contempt from the man she'd thought she loved was unsettling. How could Glen have been with her, pretending everything was okay, when he secretly despised her so much?

"Look, Druid and the Wainwright Clan don't have your family." He turned away from her and began walking down the hallway again. "They sent a squad of Clansmen to the house. Somebody had emptied it out and your family was gone. It was like they disappeared. That's all I know."

The wave of relief was so strong, she almost cried. Dad and the others had escaped. Maybe Jin had found them? She clutched at the little bit of hope he'd just given her. Glen had softened a bit. A human being might still live inside his slave's body. Maybe he had some feelings left for her, after all. Somehow she'd have to convince him to help her escape.

Druid was waiting for them before a set of double doors. Beside him cowered a pretty young woman with chestnut hair and frightened brown eyes. Her jumpsuit was disheveled and she was barefoot. Druid ignored her as if she were a discarded piece of furniture.

"There you are, my dear. We're going to train in Otherworld tonight." He extended his hand to the set of doors. "Stretch out your senses, Titania. Can you feel the call of the portal? It isn't a Pillar of Power, but the magic is still strong."

"Pillar of Power?"

"Each of the Clan Families have estates in Otherworld. The Seelie Court gifted those estates with a permanent portal between Otherworld and the Human Realm. When the Seelie Court still ruled the Earth, we had many pillars. Now just four remain. Our pillar is in London." He stretched out his hand toward the door, passing his fingers through the wood.

"This is a temporary portal similar to the one Raul used in his club. Lady Wainwright had it commissioned for your training while we're here. It leads directly to the Seers Cave. Only Seelie Descendants may enter Otherworld through these portals. Only Seers may enter the Cave."

"What about me then? I'm at least part human." Gracie stepped away from the magic.

"A demonstration perhaps?" Druid turned to the young woman. She cowered away from him, bringing trembling hands to guard her face. He gave her a gentle smile and began to stroke her hair. His fingers coaxed her into an upright stance. The young woman's face lightened and her fear dissolved. Her master had forgiven her.

Druid's enthrall smiled at him and ran headfirst into the door. Fire consumed her body in a matter of seconds. The echo of her final scream hung in the hallway.

"You bastard!" Gracie cried, staring at his cruel face in shock.

Glen's hands shoved her from behind and she flew into the door. The burning fire didn't consume her. Instead, a familiar power wrapped around her body, calming her fear. She felt reassurance and comfort. This was Otherworld.

The portal had deposited her in a tunnel dimly lit by glowing blue crystals. Rune stones shimmered in golden lines at her feet. She felt different somehow, as if a heaviness had been lifted from her body.

Druid came through the portal behind her. "I think I've proven my point, Titania. You're a Seelie Descendant as were your parents."

"No, my parents were human." Something like an electric shock bit at the skin on her chest. She brought her hands up to cover the spot.

"This is a place for only truth. Lie, especially to yourself, and the magic here will punish you." Druid rested a hand on her shoulder, which she quickly threw off. "I am the only one willing to tell you the absolute truth. You are part elvin Seer, Titania. I don't know what the other part is, but I know it isn't human. Seelie and humans can't mate."

Gracie closed her eyes as the truth sank in. She'd been forced in Vegas to accept she was one of these Seelie Descendants, but had assumed it was by some sort of mutation. Accepting the truth Druid had just given her meant accepting her dad had lied her whole life. Gawd, she didn't even have the strength to be angry with Dad anymore. She just wanted him to be alive.

"Come along. I've more to show you."

"I don't think I can take anymore."

He gripped her shoulder and prodded her forward as he might a dimwitted child. If Druid was concerned about her ability to accept her new reality, he wasn't showing it. The creep was grinning with a pretty inappropriate glee. He stopped at a thick, golden band of runes circling the opening of a cave. Here, she could feel tremendous power waiting in anticipation. She extended her hand and regarded the lazy blue smoke dancing about her fingers.

"This is the Seers Cave. It exists neither in space nor time. Only true seers are allowed behind this line." Druid stretched his fingers out and the smoke embraced him as well. "This is the only place where members of the Seelie and Unseelie Courts mix with Descendants. The magic here is neither good nor evil. It simply exists."

Forests of blue crystal lined a stone walking path inside the cave. Purple and rose crystal stalactites hung down over their heads, adding a comfortable glow. Standing here was like being in the very center of a geode. Gracie took a closer look as she passed one of the blue crystals. These didn't seem like the kind of formations you'd find at a natural history museum or a rock shop. She felt magic in the structures about her.

Druid and she followed the path up a small rise. The floor of the cave dipped down to form a smooth bowl. In its center was a pool. Still water reflected the many colors of the cave while several fluttering creatures danced above its surface. The light of their expelled power sparkled against the mirror face of the water.

"Are those what I think they are?" Her eyes followed the tiny winged creatures that darted inches above the pool.

"Fairies," Druid said, waving them away. "Ignore them. I have little patience for their kind."

The tiny beings flew to the far side of the cave, eager to get away from Druid. Gracie knew just how they felt. The creep looked down on everyone. Someday he'd get his, and she hoped she was there to see it.

"This is the Scrying Pool. It helps to enhance our powers and shows us the truth of things." Druid pointed to a large, flat stone beside the pool. "Kneel down and look into the water."

She eased into a crouch at the stone's rim and stretched out a hand. The stone was warm under her palm. Energy pulsed from its form. The rock felt as if it were alive. Magic. It had to be. A rock wasn't warm unless it had been sitting in the hot sun for hours.

Sunlight didn't reach this place. Hesitating for a moment, she crawled forward toward the water.

"What am I looking for?"

"The pool will show you what you need to know." He stepped back away from her and folded his arms.

The look of expectant pleasure on his face sent shivers of foreboding through her body. She leaned out over the still water. As her gaze penetrated the surface, the pool began to stir, spinning faster and faster until it formed a slow whirlpool. Rainbow hues swirled in the depths of the pool. Then the waters became still once more. In the pool's reflection was a woman. Her golden curls framed an oval face covered with a fragile veil of gold embedded in her skin. The lacey lines surrounded all three of her eyes. The solid opal eye in her forehead blinked once and then closed. She was beautiful in a strange, otherworldly way.

Gracie backpedaled away from the waters. Her own arms were covered with the same delicate lace as those of the woman in the pool. The Trinity Badge pulsed in greens and gold on her left wrist. She grabbed a handful of hair and pulled it before her eyes. Golden curls. Oh Gawd, she was the woman in the water!

"What have you done to me?"

"The Scrying Pool shows you the truth you need to see. This is who you really are, Titania. Someone locked you away in that hideous human glamour. It's time to be your actual true self."

His voice drew her focus. In the center of his enormous forehead was a solid blue third eye. Druid's body was a sickly white. Black lines of unsettling patterns raced along his arms and neck. He wasn't a pretty sight, but then again, who was she to talk?

The cave fell away and Gracie was standing in the middle of Hoyt Plaza in San Diego. Smoke filled the air. Several of the buildings were on fire. They had massive holes in them. Windows were shattered and large chunks of asphalt had been blown from the road. Bodies littered the ground. It looked like a war zone.

"This is what happens if you return home to your old life," Druid said beside her. "You are known to the Clans now, Titania. Each Clan would do anything to take you and use your power to build their strength. That is how rare a gift we have. Do you understand?"

"I don't believe you. It's another trick to manipulate me," Gracie said, but she knew her uncertainty came through in her voice. "I won't go home then. I'll run someplace else."

"They'll find you, no matter where you run. Don't be a fool." Druid's hand came to touch her arm lightly. "I can help you become strong. No one will be able to use you when our training is done."

Gracie continued to stare at the carnage before her. No matter where she ran, innocent people would get hurt. There had to be a way out. She had to think of a way to escape Druid's control, find her father and then save them both. Until then, she'd learn what she could from Druid. She'd learn how to defeat him.

Chapter Twenty-Seven

Hellfire spread across the asphalt like a red carpet before the shadow demon. Its midnight body blocked the sun's light, absorbing any rays touching its physique. The demon stood twice the size of a man. Its featureless face remained focused on Jin sitting in the middle of the highway. Enormous leather wings, tattered and burned, stretched out longer than a diesel truck and trailer. They flapped once and then the thing charged toward Jin with a cry of ravenous hunger.

A hand yanked him up by the collar and swept him out of the way of the demon's strike. "Don't just sit there on your ass, kid. That demon is looking to make you lunch."

Frank floated beside him, his shroud form translucent in the daylight. He kept his eyes on the demon as it turned back toward them on rapid wings. Its scream of fury filled the empty highway with ear-shattering thunder.

"Stand aside, mortal! That is my prey." Its words twisted Jin's insides, grating against his eardrums like shattered glass. It took a fiery step toward them and stretched massive wings to fly again. A big diesel truck's grill hit it from the side and kept going for several feet. The demon roared, shaking the trees beside the road.

"Ape just bought us some time," Bryn said, rushing up to join them. "It won't hold that SOB for long."

"You could have sent that demon back to Hell with a thought, Lord Brynmor." Frank turned accusing eyes on him.

"And give that Unseelie sorcerer a reason to start a Sidhe war? You know I can't do that. Not even for Jin's sake."

Jin got to his feet. He twisted his torso, trying to stretch away the dull ache. Resting a hand on Bryn's shoulder, he looked down the highway. The truck's brake lights flashed as it came to a smoky stop.

"We kill it then?"

Frank snorted and pulled the cigar out from his mouth. "Demons can't be destroyed. They can only be sent back to Hell. We need to target the guy holding its leash."

"I can sense his presence, but this human glamour is putting a damper on my powers." Bryn closed his eyes again, concentrating hard.

Beating wings and furious growls announced the demon had recovered from his run-in with the truck. It slapped a hand against the cab and the diesel went flying. Jin hoped Ape and Myles had their seat belts on.

"You gotta give me something to work with, Bryn. Maybe I can see his energy signature if you can narrow down his location." Frank fired an orange circle at the creature from Hell. His strike would have cut through a mountain. The demon kept coming.

"I believe you're making it angry. Let's see if it can catch the wind." Jin stepped away from them and took on his air elemental form. He burst across the road toward the trees in a blustery gale. The demon changed direction to follow, bringing the midnight clouds with it as it came.

Jin dove into the trees, brushing past boughs and rock as he went. The demon matched him speed for speed. In fact, it was beginning to catch up. He rushed on faster, gaining altitude as he went. The treetops became a blur; still, the demon grew closer.

It reached out with clawed fingers and caught a tendril of Jin's elemental body, forcing him back to his human glamour form. Hellfire burned through his jeans as they plummeted toward the forest floor. He struggled desperately to unfasten his pants. The ground was coming fast. His zipper gave way. He yanked the fabric off his legs, robbing the demon of its prize. Jin's power wrapped about him once more, inches above the treetops.

The demon gripped Jin's pants with a howl. Fire engulfed them until little pieces of ash floated down upon the treetops. The unholy thing came at Jin again and rapidly gained ground. Jin was beginning to tire. The creature's not-so-gentle invitation to join it in Hell was taking a toll on his strength. Clawed fingers reached out again toward him, aiming for his throat. Then the demon stopped. Its featureless face turned back toward the road. In a burst of Hellfire, it was gone.

Jin followed the stench of Hellfire back to his friends. Bryn and the others were crouching behind the overturned van. Across the road was a dark elf. Thin strips of hair sticky with dark, dried blood fell across pale gray skin on an elongated forehead. He was dressed in dark robes encircled by rings of silver. Bones from the animals he'd sacrificed had been fixed to the fabric to form magical runes. The Unseelie sorcerer made a portal and dashed through it, leaving the demon to sink back into the Hellfire that had spawned it.

"What happened? That thing had me, but it just stopped."

"Frank drew blood on the Unseelie sorcerer," Bryn told him. "Demons are difficult to control. If the person who summons them is wounded and the demon smells their blood, it's over. All a demon needs is a drop to seek revenge upon the person who enslaves them."

"Nice legs." Frank snorted. "Come on, Ape, let's get this van straightened out. We need to get to Vancouver."

"It's over then?" Myles let out a frightened breath.

"That demon will keep coming back until we kill the sorcerer or Jin's dead." Frank put his hands on the van's roof. "Are you going to help or what?"

Chapter Twenty-Eight

" $\mathbf{A}$ re you going to live? That was a nasty tumble you took on the highway."

Jin nodded at Bryn and then leaned against the railing. He let his eyes drift to the approaching cruise ship on its way to dock at Canada Place. They'd arrived in Vancouver a few hours after luncheon. The scrapes and bruises from his rapid fall on the road were aching. He was running out of his normal calm.

Jin had required all his patience to coax Frank into walking the seawall pedestrian trail along the harbor. The view was beautiful and the moment of peace much needed. A bush plane took flight against the backdrop of evergreen trees lining the waterfront. Vancouver was a pleasant place to visit, but even the Canadian perpetual cheeriness seemed a bit irritating under the circumstances.

"What's on your mind, kid?" Frank put the last bite of cigar into his mouth and chewed.

"I was just wondering why my mother hasn't taken Gracie to London yet."

"Geezus," Frank slammed his hands down on the railing with a thud. "How do you know she hasn't?"

"We drove past the safe house. My mother and her entourage are still there. I'm certain she would insist upon accompanying Gracie to London.

Discovering a new young and powerful pre-cog will give her leverage over my father."

"I've never been to the Vancouver safe house. Where is it and what's the layout?" Bryn asked.

"Mother enjoys the perks her status provides. She insisted on a luxury hotel with a phenomenal view. The Wainwright Clan invested a large sum of money during the construction of the hotel. Naturally, they required the top floor be reserved for their exclusive use."

Jin led them up the stairs and to the platform that was home to the Olympic Torch from the 2010 Vancouver Winter Olympics. A breeze from the harbor swept across his face. Crisp sea air mixed with the residual smells of lunchtime fare. He ignored the sudden ache of hunger and entered the square where four massive steel and glass pillars leaned to join in the middle. The torch was held in their embrace. Ape whistled appreciatively when they stood before it, their backs to the street.

"So where is this hotel and how do you know Eleanor is still holding court?" Frank asked.

"There," Jin pointed behind them to a hotel on West Hastings Street. It stood like an immense glass tower keeping watch over the harbor. "Do you see the small purple flag under the Canadian Maple Leaf? That is an announcement and a warning that the head of the Wainwright Clan is in residence."

"She was always one to be overly impressed with herself." Frank spat and pulled out another cigar. "Okay, guys, we hit the hotel at midnight. I'll go in first and take out security."

"We can't go in with guns blazing. Innocent people are staying at that hotel," Myles cried. He shrank away as Frank's dark stare turned toward him.

"If you don't have the fucking stomach for this, stay here."

"Easy, Frank," Jin interrupted, bringing his attention away from Myles. "He has a point. If you go charging in with your firepower, more than Wainwright security will be involved. Gracie could be hurt in the crossfire, too. Besides, she wouldn't want any innocent people hurt, would she?"

"No, she wouldn't." Frank crumbled the cigar in his hand. "You got a better idea?"

"Listen, Frank, you were right about me. I am a thief," Jin told him. "In fact, I'm a damn good thief. I can break in anywhere without getting caught. Let me go in after Gracie. I can find her and get her out safely without being seen."

"How do I know you aren't in this thing with your mother?" Frank's dark eyes searched Jin's face. Jin saw vulnerability in them, a father's desperate worry for his daughter.

"You'll just have to trust me." Jin waited, observing the struggle behind Frank's eyes. This was a man who had no chinks in his armor. He had challenged the Vento Clan, Dutch and a demon all without fear. Now he faced a situation unfamiliar to the impervious. He had to trust someone he knew was flawed with the only precious thing he was afraid of losing. Gracie.

"You have until midnight. Then I'm coming in to get my daughter." Frank turned and headed toward the street with Ape following him.

Bryn slapped Jin on the back. "I get the feeling he loves your plan. Come on, Myles. We'd better start looking for a safe place to stay."

Jin walked toward the hotel. Its curving exterior was glass, much like most of the buildings along West Hastings Street. Their design focused on the fantastic view of the harbor. Unfortunately, that meant very few handholds. Entering from the exterior wasn't an option. Getting in was going to take a more subtle approach.

As a youth, Jin had entertained his mischievous nature by breaking into or out of every safe house the Clans owned. This safe house was new, an unknown. And it wasn't a joke this time. Gracie was at stake.

Searching the exterior with a swift visual scan, he found the security cameras around the hotel. Their location was well hidden, but predictable. He paused for a deep breath and then jumped across the street to land at the entrance of the hotel bar, a modern affair with bright-white floors and tasteful sherbet colors. He sat on a blonde wood bistro table beside the far window facing the street. On the other side of the bar was a solid glass wall looking into the lobby of the hotel.

Two men in linen entered the lobby. They looked like businessmen on their way to their rooms. Jin knew better. He recognized them as Wainwright security. Eleanor must have her full guard here based on the two powerhouses who'd just walked through the lobby. They weren't killers by any means, rather they exhibited the powers that the Wainwright Clan cultivated. Pretending to be with room service or maintenance was out. These Descendants had strong mental powers. They'd be waiting for him to use a disguise. It was better to take the direct approach.

Keeping to a casual pace out of the bar, he entered the hotel lobby. A cart full of luggage headed toward the elevators rolled close by his position, pushed by a swift-moving bellhop. Jin hurried beside the cart and kept the wall of bags between him and the visible security cameras. Inside the elevator, he nodded to the bellhop and waited for the young man to insert his key card. Jin's swift finger pressed twenty-eight.

The door opened onto the floor. Jin stepped out, patting his pockets as if he were looking for his key. The bellhop turned away. He wasn't eager to get entangled with a guest who'd been clumsy enough to lose his key card. The doors closed. Jin waited until the elevator car began to move before wedging his tool in the lock.

He pushed the doors open. The car had stopped a few floors below. He'd be safe enough as long as it kept heading down. Pulling air about his body, he yanked the wedge out of the door and jumped to the steel girder on the next floor up. The thin line of light from the hall disappeared as the door closed.

Small lights gave him enough illumination to plan his next jump. He pushed away from the girder and lifted up to the top floor. Balancing on the thin lip of the thirtieth floor, he was able to get the wedge into the door and force it open. Hovering against the door jam, he expected to see Wainwright security guarding the elevators, but the hall was empty. He crept to the nearest vending machine nook to get his bearings. Several suites were located on this floor. He imagined many of them would be in use while his mother was holding court. Finding Gracie without being spotted wouldn't be easy.

An absurd whistling approached from his left. Jin's skin began to crawl. He'd recognize that whistle anywhere. The sound had haunted him at every turn during his childhood. Druid. It would take the hope of recruiting someone like Gracie for Eleanor to let her precious bird out of his gilded London cage.

The Wainwright Clan's pre-cog might have been powerful, but he couldn't quite master a headstrong boy like Jin. Druid never could sense Jin's presence or predict his future. Jin had been rather surprised an untrained pre-cog like Gracie could See what was to come for him. That had to mean something.

Jin crept on silent feet as he followed. Druid's gait was buoyant and lively. He seemed happy. The icy hand of resentment grasped Jin's heart. If Druid was happy, the rest of the Clan must be suffering. Jin remembered that lesson well from the many intrigues during his visits to the Wainwright Estate.

The memories were still strong in his mind when they came upon a suite heavily guarded by Eleanor's personal bodyguard. Not all of them were there, just a few, but enough to make Jin wonder who he'd find behind those doors. Either Gracie was within his reach or he'd experience the worst-case scenario, coming face to face with his mother.

Chapter Twenty-Nine

Gracie wiped at her nose with the wash cloth. The steady stream of blood had finally stopped. Gawd, Druid was a cruel monster! She'd tried to call the nurse, hoping word of his brutal training methods would reach Jin's mother. Druid anticipated her plan. He'd kept her in his world of illusion all morning, pushing her mental barriers until her head felt as if it would burst.

She hadn't slept since the moment she awoke in the strange hotel. Druid sprang on her when she thought she was alone, or he'd tease her by not coming when he said he would. She didn't dare close her eyes for fear he would attack her in her sleep.

Whistling his unidentifiable song, he was at her door again. Gracie kept her tears in check. She was beyond tired, but she couldn't let him break her. Having him inside her mind again would be worse than any punishment he could concoct. The door popped open, and Druid came in looking refreshed. He stared down at her untouched meal with a frown.

"You've not eaten your luncheon. How unfortunate. Lady Wainwright will not be pleased you continue to torture yourself."

"I seriously doubt old Eleanor will approve of your plot to take over the Clan." Hatred swelled in her heart with an intensity she'd never felt before. "I can't wait to have another chat with her. I'm sure she'll be interested in what I have to say."

"Lady Wainwright rarely bothers with the insignificant details like you. Once she turned you over to my care, she moved on to other things." Those powerful eyes looked into hers. "By the time she calls for you again, I will have broken you, my dear. You will belong to me."

"That will be a cold day in hell."

Druid raised his hand as if to strike her. The hotel room with all its furnishings disappeared. He'd used his power again to torment her. This time she was standing in front of the Rusty Grotto Cafe. Her brain remembered the smells of taco meat and tequila. Gracie lifted her face skyward, letting the sun warm her cheeks.

She pushed the false sensations away. None of it was real. Whatever she found inside wouldn't be real either. She reached out her hand and pulled the door open. The cafe was empty. In this reality, the lime-green table and chairs were a nauseating pink. Gray paint covered the walls. She found no murals or mariachi music. Druid hadn't been able to force her mind to recreate her memory. It was a small victory.

The kitchen door swung open, and Kay walked into the room. Her friend's magenta braid swayed as she walked. The turquoise uniform blazed like a guiding beacon into the recesses of Gracie's mind. The last memory of Kay was still vivid, and Druid had found it. He had opened a tiny path through the protective barrier of her power. He could hurt her now.

"You think you're protecting your family from us, don't you?" His disembodied voice echoed in the haze. It was condescending and cruel like its owner. "I'm touched by your maternal streak, my dear. Perhaps I'll give you a child. Yes, I think I would enjoy seeing you carry my son. And won't we have fun trying?"

"I'd kill myself before I let you touch me!"

"You won't have much say in the matter. Well, at any rate, we don't need your family if we already have your good friend, Kay." Laughter, ugly and vile, echoed off the walls. "It would be a pity to kill her. I do look forward to enjoying her body again. She's very spirited."

Kay walked wordlessly by Gracie to the register. She began fussing with the cash in the drawer. An axe appeared over her head, suspended by Druid's will. Gracie rushed toward her, shouting and pulling at Kay, but her hands passed through her friend's body. Druid's laughter grew louder and louder until Gracie was forced to cover her ears.

"This isn't real!"

"It could be with one phone call unless you give me what I want. I'm the only one who knows about Kay." He let the threat hang in the air. "You can keep her safe, Gracie."

"You go to hell!" She had to save Kay in the here and now. If Druid could bring these images to life, then maybe she could control them. She concentrated her whole being on the axe over Kay's head. It began to quiver. Gracie concentrated harder, using her fear and her hatred in one last push to throw the axe away from Kay.

"A worthy effort," Druid said. The axe flew up again. This time it swung for Kay's neck and sent her head rolling underneath a nearby table. Gracie screamed. Something broke inside of her. Lashing out wildly with her power, she began to rip down the walls of the cafe. Druid's laughter, cruel and lurid, smashed violently against her ears. Her mind began to break.

Then Druid screamed. His world of illusion fell away, and the hotel room reappeared. Through the haze of her pain, she saw his body fly across the room. A man dressed all in black stood facing away from her. Jin. He'd come for her. Clutching at the sudden hope, she brought her power back under control. Her dazed and aching head couldn't reason out why Jin was in her hotel room. Seeing him here in Canada didn't seem possible. Was he just another illusion meant to torment her?

Power, wild and angry, gathered around him. He stood in the center of a sudden windstorm. Then he disappeared. Unexpelled energy lifted the hair on her arms. Impatient, its reentry into the room struck her like a sonic boom. Jin reappeared on top of Druid. His fists and knees struck at his enemy in a rage. The older man couldn't block the strikes. Jin was too fast.

"Stop it this instant!" A powerful voice shook the room. Eleanor Wainwright lifted a hand and flicked it. Jin was lifted off Druid's bruised and broken body. Eleanor slammed her son into the nearby chair and held him there with the power of her mind. Gracie clutched at her body with a shiver. She'd underestimated Eleanor's level of power.

Jin struggled in the chair, but she had a firm grip on him. "Mother, I promise if that bastard ever comes near Gracie again, I'll kill him."

Mother and son stared at each other for a long time. Gracie had come to know that look on Jin's face. He meant what he said. He would kill Druid if given the chance. Gracie got a great deal of satisfaction from that knowledge. Here was someone in the world Druid feared.

"Call an ambulance and have Druid taken to the hospital," Eleanor ordered. Two guards quickly complied. They picked up Druid and hurried from the room. Gracie watched his bleeding body disappear through the door. Relief flooded every chamber of her body and mind. She closed her eyes, letting the tears come.

"Perhaps you would like to go freshen up, Miss Berry?" Eleanor wasn't asking. "Now, Miss Berry. I would have a word with my son."

Gracie struggled to her feet, suddenly feeling an urgent need to leave the room. She threw her body forward, encouraging her legs to cooperate. The bathroom seemed a million miles away, but she made it and locked the door tightly behind her. Sinking down against the far wall, she put her face in her hands. She'd believed for a moment Jin was about to set her free, but then Eleanor's power had forced her into the bathroom with a single mental shove. Gracie finally understood how powerful Lady Wainwright really was, and now she knew Eleanor would do anything to keep Gracie with her. Even if it meant hurting her own son.

Chapter Thirty

The grip on Jin's body eased. He pulled his arms away from the sides of his body where they'd been pinned. Sitting upright on the chair, his eyes never broke contact with his mother's identical green orbs. They were in a battle of wills, but this time Jin wouldn't give in. Too much was at stake.

"I am going to walk out the front door with Gracie, Mother. Don't try to stop us." Jin stood up and took a threatening stance. His mother's lip curled ever so slightly in amusement.

"Don't be a fool, child. Who is this girl to you? A passing fancy perhaps?" Eleanor folded her arms and lifted a sarcastic eyebrow. "Must I list all of the hobbies you dropped after a few months?"

"I was a child then. You abandoned me at boarding school. I grew bored and lonely." Jin made a fist and let his frustration show. No one caused him to lose his calm reserve more quickly than his mother.

"I certainly hope you don't expect an apology for the superior education I wasted upon an ungrateful son. You were always a willful child, Jin. Time hasn't changed your temperament. Titania is too valuable for me to entrust her with you."

"That isn't your decision!"

"Oh? And who will protect Titania when so many hunt her for their own purposes? You?" When

Jin didn't answer, she lifted her chin in cold triumph. "Just as I thought."

One thing was certain, the sooner he got Gracie to her father, the better. Frank would be able to take her into hiding and keep her away from the Wainwright Clan and anyone else. He broke eye contact and began to walk past her.

"I'm not leaving her here with that bastard Druid!"

"How many times must I ask you not to refer to your stepfather with disrespect?" She shook her head and waved a dismissive hand. "I suppose after this unfortunate altercation there will be no repairing your relationship with him."

"God, Mother! Druid and I will never get on. I'm the bastard son of the man you shagged one drunken night while your husband was in his cage at home. Learn to accept it!"

An empty tea tray came at him without warning. It struck hard across the side of his face, stunning him and bringing him to his knees. His mother's eyes were directly on him. Her face had gone pale with rage. It was at this point he usually apologized and acquiesced to her. Not this time.

"Druid enthralled Gracie and threw her into Raul Vento's clutches. No doubt he's trying again to take over the Wainwright Clan by starting a Clan war." Jin rubbed his stinging skin where the tray had hit him. "Someone made a deal with the Unseelie Court to send a sorcerer and his pet demon after me. I'm beginning to think Druid's ambitions go higher than your Clan. Tomorrow is Midsummer's Eve. I believe the Unseelie Court will cross over the veil into the Human Realm during its peak."

Jin tried to read her cold face, but as usual she betrayed nothing. "You knew, didn't you?"

"I brought Titania here for her own protection, but that wasn't my only reason. I knew you'd come for her." Eleanor let her arms fall to the sides of her perfectly tailored suit. She rose to stand before him. "We have another matter to discuss. There is still the issue of who put a death mark out on you."

"Do you know who it is?"

She put a fingertip on her temple and smiled. "Jin, you don't let me into your life. How am I supposed to know who has it in for you? Think. Who benefits most from your death?"

"Well, Viper certainly hated me enough to do it." Jin shivered when he remembered her snake-like head disappearing in the fire. Another face full of hatred appeared in his memory. "Qing was still rather unhappy with me for having his lover first. Both of them were motivated to get revenge on me."

"That's not what I asked. Pay attention." Eleanor frowned and folded her arms as she often did when he was a misbehaving boy. "Think, child! Who benefits most if you die?"

"Do you know who it is?" Jin asked again, trying to read that impenetrable face.

Eleanor threw up her hands. "You are absolutely impossible." She walked toward the bedroom door. "In light of the demon attack this afternoon, which would seem to substantiate your claim of innocence for the Girard Clan murders, your father and I have appealed to the Council to call off the Griffin. You may stay the night and think about what I've asked you. Do not try to take Titania from this safe house. I promise you will regret it."

"We'll be going now!" Jin called after her. Eleanor waved a dismissive hand at him. Her guard snapped to attention and exited the room after her.

Jin seethed with anger and frustration. She knew who'd put the death mark out on him. Rather than openly helping him, she did what she always did, gave him little hints so he could figure it out on his own. Her first love, the Wainwright Clan, came before all. Its leader was determined to maintain her objectivity where he was concerned. She and her Clan could go to hell. He'd come for Gracie, not to beg for his mother's help. Moving over to the master bath, he tapped quietly on the door.

"Gracie? Are you all right?" When she didn't answer him, he tapped harder. "Gracie, I need for you to come out. Everyone's gone. It's just you and I."

Silence wasn't the response he'd expected. He bent down and easily picked the lock, swinging the door open. Gracie was leaning against the back wall, wedged between the counter and the toilet. She had her arms wrapped tightly around her body. Her eyes were red with broken blood vessels. He wouldn't forget the look of terror on her face as he stood before her now. In fact, he'd think of it as he slowly killed the Druid.

"I've come to take you out of here, darling." He held his hand out to her.

As she looked at his offered hand, the fire came back into her face. "Is that supposed to make me feel better? Why are you really here, Jin?"

Hurt, betrayal, mistrust, all of them crossed her face as she looked at him now. Despite her father's best efforts, Gracie had learned what being part of the Clan world was really like. He moved toward her, but stopped when she raised a hand.

"I'm here to rescue you."

"Who the hell asked you to come here? Since you believe everyone is a liar, how do I know that you're telling the truth? Maybe it's you who has been playing me, so I could come here and be your mother's guest as she calls it."

"I deserve that."

"Yeah, you do." Gracie pushed away from the wall, swayed a bit and righted herself against the counter. "You say you're here to rescue me. Well, okay, let's get the hell out of here. And then, I never want to see you again."

He wrapped an arm around her waist and pulled her in close. Jin's gentle fingers moved along her cheeks to chase the hardness away from her face. Those soulful eyes began to soften, exposing her vulnerability in them. He knew then how much his harsh words had hurt her.

"Please let me help you, Gracie. I know I don't deserve your trust, but I'm asking for it one last time."

"Gawd, please get me out of here, Jin. I'm so tired." She rested her forehead against his chest. He lifted her into his arms when her knees buckled. Her arms wrapped around his neck and she rested her head on his shoulder.

He grappled with the door handle and swung it open. This time the hall wasn't empty. Clearly his mother had made his entrance easy, but she wanted to dissuade him from leaving again. Her security team eyed him carrying Gracie in his arms. They weren't powering up yet, but their manner indicated it wouldn't take much to spur them into action.

Tingles of magic touched the edges of his senses. Someone had made a temporary portal. Its magic was like a beacon of hope. Their escape might prove to be less violent than he'd anticipated. He carried her down the hall toward the portal disguised as a set of double doors leading into a suite.

Two Wainwright security guards stalked up toward them. Jin put Gracie next to the faux double doors and stepped forward to meet them with fist and feet. This was no time for a fair fight. He wasn't about to give them a chance to power up. They collapsed on the ground. Another presence crept up behind him. He spun his heel around in a blur, stopping the attack inches away from Glen's frightened face.

"Glen? What are you doing here?" Jin dropped his leg and pushed Glen out of his space.

"Gracie, don't let him kill me!" He sunk down to his knees and started to whimper.

Jin kept his body between the cowering creature and Gracie. "Don't listen to him. His connection with his master has been severed. He'll say anything to be picked up by someone else. It's like a junky with his heroin."

"You know what it's like, Gracie. I had to do what he said." Glen pleaded, crawling on his knees toward her. Jin thrust a leg out, knocking Glen on his side.

"You chose this, Glen." She shivered and hugged herself. "This is your chance to escape. Run, Glen, get away from him while you can."

"Take me with you! I can be your enthrall, Gracie. I'll do whatever you want!"

She turned her face away from the pathetic creature. Jin put his arms around her. Glen was a pitiable fool. Most likely he'd be taken by another Descendant, or worse, he'd crawl to Druid's side at the hospital. Either way, Gracie was right. Glen had chosen this life.

The magic of the portal welcomed them. He kept his arm about Gracie as he concentrated on the crossroads. Soft crystal bells began to chime as the hotel disappeared. Then they were standing in a vast cavern of gateways and lights. His human glamour fell away and he stretched out his full being with a sigh. Gracie stepped away from him. Her hair was like ribbons of golden silk. Fibers of gold lace ran along her face and arms. Bright blue eyes looked at him shyly as her perfect opal third eye blinked closed.

"I look pretty different, don't I?"

He smoothed at her hair and smiled at her. "You were pretty in your human glamour, but as your true self you're simply gorgeous."

She smiled and the blush showed under her lace. "So where are we? I thought this led to the Seers Cave."

"This is the crossroads—it'll help us travel to safety."

They walked past several stone staircases leading up to layers of gateways carved in the rock. The openings went to places he could only imagine. They weren't for half-breeds like him. These gates existed for the Seelie and Unseelie Courts. He ignored them, concentrating on finding the massive fountain of blue crystals Bryn had showed him on his last visit. The gate was hidden in the shadows, seemingly lifeless, but when Jin touched the gate's surface it came alive. He took Gracie's hand and pulled her through.

They landed in the small kitchen of a dark cabin. The chilly air of night in the wild was a harsh shock to skin used to central heating. He stood still in the crisp air, listening. Wind danced gently with the leaves as it glided past. Somewhere in the trees beyond the cabin, an owl hooted its lonely call. Nature's night music. Nothing out of place.

Jin rifled through the kitchen drawers until he found matches. In circumstances such as these, he wished he had been born a fire elemental. Across the room, Gracie found a lantern. Its glow was comforting. Now that the cabin was filled with light, Jin noticed the lack of furniture. A queen-sized mattress sat on the floor, and nearby, a lonely rug. The kitchen looked as if it had been gutted. Its stove and refrigerator were missing. A short refrigerator fresh from a local college dorm room had taken its place.

"Where are we?" She rubbed her arms to warm up.

"This is Myles' cabin just outside Horseshoe Bay, about thirty minutes north of downtown Vancouver. It was in better shape the last time I was here. Not exactly the accommodations I had in mind, but you'll be safe until we can join the others."

"It's okay," she told him.

The red of her eyes looked harsher and more painful under the light. He turned away, unable to meet her gaze. It was his fault she'd been put on his mother's radar. If he hadn't been such a self-centered bastard, Gracie would be safe with her father. She could have had a real life again, away from the Clans and away from him.

"Gracie, I'm sorry. This is all my fault. I should have trusted you from the beginning. You were right about my selfish hatred for Viper. You were right about everything." He turned to leave. "I'll get some firewood."

Her hand touched his, stopping him. Gentle fingers touched the cuts on his face and neck. He closed his eyes, basking in the warmth of her tenderness. The fingers moved to the back of his head, lowering his face toward hers. Their lips came together, joining in a slow kiss. He lifted her into his arms and carried her onto the mattress.

Gracie clutched at the comfort of his body against hers. She welcomed him into herself with hungry need. Though his own desire was great, he remained gentle and patient. Sleep came as they stayed wrapped in each other's arms.

Something woke Jin in the wee hours of the morning. He'd thought he'd felt a presence watching them while they slept. Jin ran his hand across Gracie's naked back. She was sleeping deeply against his chest, staying in contact with his warm body. His arms were still wrapped protectively around her.

Touching her hair softly, he thought about their time together. They were friends. Well, more than friends now. He enjoyed Gracie's company. She'd gone from being a complication to being a necessity in his life. He wasn't sure how or when that had happened. He just knew he needed her.

His mobile buzzed on the floor beside the mattress. He grabbed it quickly before it could wake her. It was an unknown number. Bryn. "I'm alive."

"One of these days I'm not going to be there to give a shit," Bryn said. "What's your status?"

Jin grinned and kissed the top of Gracie's head. "Gracie's with me. She's safe, but in no shape to travel."

"Care to elaborate, because I have an anxious audience."

Jin sobered a bit when he remembered Gracie's father. "She had a few sessions with the Druid. Tell our friend, she's safe with me and needs her rest."

"Our big friend is missing and he's left his tagalong behind." Jin heard a loud disagreement on the other end of the line when Bryn shared the information. "We'll meet in the morning at the Olympic Torch."

"Tell him I promise to keep her safe. I'm hanging up now."

"Thanks a lot, you little shit." Bryn's voice was cut off when Jin hung up.

Gracie stirred a bit, but he stroked her back and she quieted again. Frank was missing. That couldn't be good. Then a familiar scent, drifted across the covers. He sniffed and reached his fingers out to pick up a small object just out of the light of his phone. A cigar butt, still warm. Frank had come looking for his daughter. How the hell he'd found them, Jin couldn't guess.

Clearly, the only reason Jin didn't have a hole in his head right now was Gracie's sleeping form. The cigar butt was a clear message. Jin wasn't to forget their deal. He'd been prattling on in his thoughts like a schoolgirl about some kind of life with Gracie. He was being selfish again. Gracie was safer with her father than she could ever be with him. Jin would keep her safe until Frank came for her. Then he'd let her go. It was the right thing to do, but God it hurt.

Chapter Thirty-One

Gracie lay across Jin's chest listening to him breathe deeply in sleep. She carefully lifted up and leaned her head on her hand to watch his face. So much for her promise to herself to stay away from bad boys. She brushed a strand of stray hair out of his face. He'd come after her at great risk. Jin cared for her. and she was falling hard for him. But that didn't mean they should be together.

It was time to use her gift. The tingle of power gathered at her forehead within her third eye. Her visions were coming to her easier now. She'd accepted who she was, as all true Seers must.

Her third eye opened, and the bed fell away. She Saw two images, two directions in her mind's eye. Gracie shifted her Sight between them. Nothing like this had happened to her before. Normally, she saw one future and one reality. Now, two had formed.

She turned her focus to the one on the left. Jin held her hand tightly as they ran through the same forest she'd Seen when first laying eyes on him. Desperate fear was in this future. Someone was hunting them. They came to a cliff. Jin circled around, but they were out of places to run. A shot rang out. Dark fluid spread across Jin's chest. He dropped forward. Her screams of grief fell away.

Gracie turned to the other vision. They were lying on a picnic blanket in the middle of a park called "Coal Harbour." A fountain and grass stretched out to a bike path rolling beside the sea. Jin kissed her. They both looked down at the blanket between them. Jin put a finger into a bundle of blankets and gently lifted it out again. A tiny fist clutched at his finger. Happiness. It seemed that she would never feel it again.

A hand stroked her cheek. She came back to the present and opened her eyes. Jin was looking at her.

"What did you see? You were away for a long time."

Gracie couldn't tell him what she'd seen. She wasn't sure what her visions meant yet. And nobody reacted well to news of their own death. She'd learned the hard way to stay silent. "Oh, we were just having a picnic in a place called Coal Harbour."

"That's here in Vancouver." Jin moved his fingers to her hair. "What were we doing?"

Gracie grinned and leaned in for a long kiss. He rolled her on her back and nibbled along her neck. She hummed low and let her hands wander over the sculptured muscles of his body, smooth beneath her fingers. Her teeth found his earlobes. He shivered with a groan as she nipped.

Jin's cell phone started vibrating, then it started beeping. The insistent phone grew louder until it became an obnoxious alarm. He twisted around to grab the phone and looked at the display. Rubbing his eyes, he read the message.

"Time to go?" Gracie asked, rolling off the mattress.

"Unfortunately, yes." Jin told her. "Bryn is reminding me we're supposed to be meeting him at the Olympic Torch right now. And he suggests I bring you quickly before he comes looking for us."

He picked up her clothes from the floor where they'd thrown them. "I don't think our friends trust me with your safety, darling." Jin chuckled and tossed her the clothes. "Get dressed. Myles has a motorcycle out back."

She sniffed at the sweat-stained scrubs and crinkled her nose. Pulling them on reluctantly, she stumbled to a tiny bathroom at the rear of the cabin with no hot water or clean towels. Myles certainly was neglecting the place. She rifled through the sparse supplies and found some mouthwash.

Jin shut the door behind them as they went in search of the motorcycle Myles kept in a small shed. It was gassed up and ready to go. Gracie wrapped her arms tightly around Jin's body as they rode through the wooded neighborhood. In only minutes, the bike pulled onto the highway and headed toward Vancouver. Gracie leaned into Jin's back, feeling the warmth of him against the wind and smelling the musky scent of their deep sleep together. A big part of her wished they'd keep driving and never stop.

Soon, downtown Vancouver lined the south side of the harbor. Tall glass buildings reached high, competing with each other for the best view. Gracie breathed in the fresh sea air. It was beautiful here, and their ride was ending much too quickly.

After they ditched the bike, Jin guided her down the sidewalk toward the harbor where a white, curved building seemingly floated over the waters. It looked like a ship. They rounded the front of the building. He laughed when she gasped at the real cruise ship moored beside the docks.

"That is Canada Place. I'll take you there when everything is over. As for now, we have to meet Bryn and Myles at the Olympic Torch." Jin sniffed the air as they walked to the Vancouver Convention Centre. He led her down a cement walkway to a cluster of shops where they bought themselves Belgian chocolate mochas and breakfast sandwiches.

Gracie couldn't take her eyes off the harbor with its beautiful clean waters and busy bush plane traffic. Canada wasn't what she had expected at all. It had a wild beauty with a cosmopolitan feel. Jin took her up a set of stairs, and Gracie's jaw dropped. There, standing like a beacon to the world, was the torch from the 2010 Winter Olympics.

Jin pulled her close and kissed her. "It's good to see you happy, darling."

"Thanks for hurrying down to meet us," Bryn said beside them. He sounded angry, but his eyes smiled as he looked at Jin's arm around her waist. "You okay, Gracie?"

She stood away from Jin and lifted up on her toes to kiss Bryn's cheek. "I'm better. Thanks for coming after me."

"Anytime. Listen, we should go. I don't like being this close to Eleanor's safe house." Bryn motioned over his shoulder at a line of tall glass structures. The

Wainwrights hadn't allowed her outside the hotel. She had no idea such beauty was so close to her prison.

"There you are!" Myles rushed toward them and handed Gracie a bag of clothes. "I hope we got your size right."

"Thanks, Myles. I'll go change."

In the ladies room, she pulled on the denim Bermuda shorts and melon knit top. Comfortable sandals completed the outfit. Gracie checked out her new look in the restroom's half mirror. Her human glamour was like a comfortable pair of jeans, but a bit of her real form showed through as well. She was starting to like what she saw, but wondered if others—humans—could see her true form.

Walking carefully out of the ladies room, she hurried over to ask Jin if she had put on her glamour correctly. He, Bryn and Myles were in a deep conversation that was getting a little heated. They stopped talking abruptly when they noticed her.

"So, what's next?" she asked, stepping forward to take Jin's offered hand.

"Today is Midsummer's Eve. We need to come up with a plan to catch my would-be assassin while stopping an invasion. Let's talk on the way to Coal Harbour." He gave her a mischievous grin, knowing that she'd recognize the name. "We'll walk along the seawall. Gracie enjoys the harbor view."

They all walked beside the water, listening to Jin give an account of their escape from the hotel. The convention center was obscured by the walls and buildings behind them as they made a lazy turn. Gracie saw a large park a short distance ahead. Coal

Harbour's grounds overlooked the waters. She recognized the beautiful green lawn and the bright blooming flowers.

In the very center of the park was a fountain with children leaping through the jets that spurted up from the ground. Behind them was a food stand that had been built under a terrace on the street above. It was a beautiful place where she immediately felt at home.

They selected a table beside the fountain, and Myles went to grab them something to drink from the cafe. He zigzagged around several children racing to the fountains; their mothers sat together on the lawn, talking and laughing in the warm sun. The memory of her second vision gave Gracie new hope and determination to make it out of this mess. She and Jin were going to have that picnic here together even if it took every ounce of her power to banish the other future.

"It's amazing to see this place in the here and now," she said.

"Well, enjoy it while you can," Bryn told her. "We have to get you out of the city. I don't trust Eleanor to leave you in peace."

"I don't have a passport. She said she told the US Government about my powers. They were happy to be rid of me. Whatever that means." Gracie shrugged.

"The United States is neutral territory, darling," Jin explained. "Seelie Descendants can't cross their border in either direction without permission first— well legally, anyway."

Bryn patted her arm. "They don't want nasty battles on their property like the skirmish in Vegas.

Somebody is going to catch hell for that one." He smiled at Gracie. "Don't worry though. I'll take care of the passport problem."

A fake passport for a fake life? For the first time, Gracie had no set schedule or a plan for the future. Her new life was going to be very different from now on. The thought was exciting as well as frightening, but she believed she was prepared to embrace the adventure.

"So, what next?"

"My mother told me the Clan Council had sufficient cause to consider I was telling the truth about the dark elf's involvement in the Girard murders," Jin said. His expression showed he was relieved. "They called off the Griffin. The memo Vince gave us about the demon is another good start to prove my innocence, but to get Clan protection from this sorcerer and his pet, I'll have to tie the true culprit to the conspiracy. We need to draw them out into the open."

Myles set down the ale he'd bought for them all. "How do we do that?"

"We offer them a chance to kill me that they couldn't possibly pass up."

They sat silently around the table, watching Jin take a long drink from his glass. The fountains gurgled, splashing to the ground. Children shouted and laughed as they played. The sounds of happiness began to fade. Gracie frowned at the determination in his eyes. She couldn't let him go down this path.

"What about your idea of disappearing off the grid again? Remember?" Bryn eyed Jin over his ale.

"I have other considerations now." Jin squeezed Gracie's hand. "I want it ended."

"I see, well, we'll need a plan." Bryn pushed aside his glass. He didn't look pleased with Jin's crazy idea, either.

Jin looked at each of them in turn. "I've been thinking about that. What we need is an old-fashioned ambush. I'll take a walk in the woods while you and Myles cover me with rifles." He waved his hand across the water to the dense forests. "We have the perfect cover."

"A walk in the woods?" Gracie had a sick, sinking feeling in her heart. The bad vision was well on its way to coming true. "I mean. Who would believe you're out for a casual stroll? Wouldn't it be better to pretend to go sightseeing?"

"She makes a good point," Myles said. "Vancouver has a great many sights, but then again we don't want to put innocent people at risk either. What about Stanley Park?"

"Brilliant, Myles!" Jin slapped a hand on the table. "I could pop into the aquarium or see the rose gardens and then eventually lead them to Prospect Point. That's where we can lay the trap."

"Sounds like a plan. I would love to go sightseeing," Gracie agreed.

A frown came to Jin's normally calm face. He shook his head. Gracie rolled her eyes. Things had changed between them. He was getting sentimental about her, but they had no time for that now.

"What? A pre-cog would be handy to have while you're being stalked by a killer," she insisted.

"You can help best by staying in the hotel." He kissed her hand and laced their fingers together. "The Unseelie Court may come in force. I don't want you there when they break through the veil. It will be bloody, darling. I want you to stay someplace safe."

"Not likely, Jin. We started this thing together and we'll end it together."

"No!" Jin got out of his chair and stood to look at her. "We have friends who'll see that you remain safe."

"Yeah, about them," Myles said uncomfortably. "They've both gone missing without a word."

"Damn it!" Jin, completely out of character, swore loud enough to make a few mothers turn around. "Perhaps our large friend will answer my phone call. Excuse me."

Gracie turned to Jin's two allies. "Guys, you have to help me talk Jin into letting me come along."

"He's as stubborn as they come. He won't change his mind," Bryn told her.

Gracie grabbed Bryn's hand and squeezed. "You don't understand. Jin has to let me come along. I've Seen us on the run. I must be there to guide him, Bryn. Otherwise..."

He looked at her a long time and then nodded. A cloud of worry came into his eyes. Bryn loved Jin like a son—that was clear. He motioned with his head behind her. She turned to see Jin coming back. He didn't look happy.

"Looks like I'm tagging along after all." No way would she leave Jin to face his future alone, not when she could do something to change it.

Chapter Thirty-Two

Stanley Park was a thousand acres of Canadian splendor completely surrounded by the Pacific Ocean. A thin strip of land connected it to downtown Vancouver with its skyscrapers and bush planes. Inside the park, natural beauty abounded from the trellised awnings covering the rose gardens to the breathtaking views from Prospect Point. None of these could compare to the natural beauty sitting beside him in their horse-drawn carriage.

"We'll be reaching Prospect Point soon. There's a cafe by the overlook. I'm told it has a wonderful gift shop. You could wait for me." Jin put an arm around her shoulder.

Gracie gave him a long look. She shared a wide streak of stubbornness with her father. No argument Jin or Bryn had given Gracie could sway her from coming with him.

"That's nice, but I'll be joining you."

Gracie leaned her head on his shoulder. She played with the Canadian jade beaded bracelet he'd bought her by the totems. Her eyes had sparkled with pleasure when he'd given it to her as if those jade beads had been emeralds and diamonds. She was having a good time, and if she was happy, so was he. God knew she deserved a little happiness after what she'd been through. He just wished she'd listen to him and return to the safety of the city.

Her body suddenly stiffened. "Jin, two men are following us."

"I know. They've been following us since we left Coal Harbour. I hope our friends were able to lose their tail. Bryn and Myles should be setting up their positions right about now. Everything has to be in place before dusk, including us."

Prospect Point had a spectacular view of the ocean and the land across the bridge. He and Gracie waited beside the railings as the last busload of wandering tourists were herded back into their tour bus. The two left the overlook and went inside the log cabin-like cafe. Jin selected a section with a wonderful view of the bridge. Sitting next to the balcony railing, they sipped iced tea and finished a late luncheon.

Gracie fiddled with a piece of maple candy. She caught him staring. "You're having as much fun as I am," she said.

"I admit I am. I'm enjoying watching you enjoy yourself. One day I'll take you to Europe. There's so much to see. We'll travel all over..." His voice faded. He was talking foolish fantasy again. "Let's focus on today. That's the smart thing to do. Are you a fan of hiking?"

"I guess so. Dad took me to Bear Mountain a few times and we spent the day walking along the trails. Why?"

"It's time to walk off our meal. Last chance, Gracie. We could call a cab and get you to a safe location in a few minutes." He knew the offer wouldn't be accepted.

"Let's go."

They walked across the road to Prospect Trail. Gracie lifted the GPS. They looked at the little screen together. Their trail would lead them to a junction. Two other trails met beside the main park drive. One crossed the road and gave the hiker a quick walk to the cliffs. The other led deeper into the trees. Stanley Park might have been adjacent to a large city, but it encompassed forestland. Tall trees and carpets of thick ferns could easily hide assassins beside the trail.

Sunlight fell in spots through the dense boughs, casting patterns along the path. Jin noticed one of the delicate fern leaves bobbing about ten yards to their right. Gracie turned her head to look.

"Keep your eyes forward," he told her. "We don't want them to think they've been spotted."

They'd talked about her vision of the two of them being chased in a forest that she'd seen when they first set eyes on each other. Discussed was a watered-down version. She'd argued with him until he'd promised to let her use her gift to keep them safe. They both knew the dangers, but in her vision she'd had no landmarks to reference. They had no way to prepare. They only had her reflexes to rely on.

The sounds of birdsong and car motors stopped abruptly. Something wasn't right. It felt as if they were the only living beings left in the park. Gracie pulled Jin quickly to their left, into the safety of a hollowed-out log standing vertically against a hill. The bullet missed his head by inches. Damn! They hadn't reached the ambush points yet. Bryn couldn't offer cover fire. Their enemy's attack had come too soon.

"We need to reach Bryn," Jin said.

Running off the trail, they headed northeast through the trees. Bryn had given each of them a GPS and marked his position, so they could find him. Keeping their bodies low, they let the ferns help hide them. Bryn wasn't very far away. Jin almost felt as if the assassin who took a shot at them knew Bryn's location and wanted to kill them before Bryn could get a shot off. It wouldn't be the first time his enemies seemed to have foreknowledge.

"Chicago Bears rule," Gracie called to the stack of overturned tree trunks on the hill. She got no answer. Her foreboding had returned, she indicated with a nod to Jin. The two of them carefully crept up to the logs to look over the top. Bryn's pack was still there, but no Bryn. Jin crawled inside the blind with Gracie following. The rifle Bryn had so carefully cleaned that morning lay in the dirt.

Someone had found him out. Someone close to Jin or maybe Bryn. Eleanor Wainwright's words that she'd so pointedly thrown at her son echoed in his mind. She'd warned him that the culprit was the person with the most to benefit from his death. He crouched down to check the footprints. Not much of a struggle had taken place. That meant Bryn had been captured by surprise by someone he knew and trusted. Whoever it was must have Bryn now. That person had to know how close Bryn and Jin were. Bryn had better not be hurt. The villain would find no place to hide from Jin's fury then.

"Oh no. Myles! We have to warn him." Gracie adjusted the GPS again to find Myles' position. He was farther south on the other side of the trail located diagonally in the direction they'd come from earlier. Easing out of the abandoned blind, Jin led Gracie beside a tree trunk. The forest looked deserted.

Gracie's body went stiff as another vision hit her. She twisted out of the way and onto the ground just as a spear of water struck the tree trunk by her head. Bark flew from the tree, exposing a deep hole in the trunk's flesh.

"Bloody Qing! What is he doing here?" Jin hissed. He pulled Gracie behind another log and answered the question her eyes were asking him. "Qing is my brother. He's the heir to the Zhao Clan. If he's here that means my father is as well."

"Why the hell is he trying to kill me?" Gracie cried.

Jin growled in frustration as another spear of water struck close to them. He should have expected an appearance by the Zhao Clan the moment his mother had taken Gracie. Jin's father would naturally be worried what Gracie would mean to the balance of power among the Clans. Of course there was the typical element of competition between the Zhao and Wainwright families. Her existence was just another power play between his parents. Zhao Long had been in the number one seat for centuries. He wouldn't allow anything to disrupt his position. Gracie's death would take the uncertainty out of the game.

"I need to have a chat with my brother."

"Jin, I..." Gracie let her words fall away, and she nodded. Jin kissed her and then he was gone in a gust of wind. His body became the gentle breeze rustling the leaves and brushing against the ferns.

Lifting to the treetops, he began searching for any sign of his brother. Movement in the ferns below drew his attention. He darted between the tree boughs, coming closer. No one was there. Water rushed toward him. Jin fell back, missing the strike by a breath.

"Do you imagine I wouldn't know the presence of your body by now, Brother?" Qing stepped out of the trees. The fluid nature of his true form was translucent among the ferns and beams of sunlight.

"Listen, Qing, Gracie isn't the enemy. You have to let her go."

"Still meddling in Clan affairs, pariah?" Qing lifted his palm, power at the ready. "You have pushed our patience much too far. Others will see to the precog now. I have waited for this day. It's time to show Father who really should have been named the Hand of Justice."

Others? Jin burst away from Qing in a frenzied wind. Their confrontation would wait for another time. Gracie was alone and vulnerable. Her safety came first before another battle of sibling rivalry. Qing's spear grazed Jin across his back. The pain made him lose focus. His air elemental form fell away and he was cast into his elvin body. Blood mixed with water, soaking his shirt, and he fell on the trail hard. His GPS shattered into unusable pieces beside him.

Rolling off the dirt path, Jin scanned the landscape looking for movement.

Qing stormed out of the foliage in a wave of fists and kicks. He was on top of Jin with an unexpected burst of speed. His solid fists struck at Jin's face, cutting skin and bruising flesh. Shouts down the trail announced the arrival of Qing's men. They were on the hunt. Gracie didn't have a chance withstanding their power.

"I'm sorry, Brother. Playtime is over." Jin brought the full power of his air elemental form into one burst from the center of his chest. Qing's body propelled over the trail and slammed against a tree trunk. He tumbled to the ground and stayed there. Their rivalry wasn't over, of course; Qing would insist upon a rematch, and Jin would be only too happy to comply.

He found Gracie crouching beside a fallen log. She was a little shaken, but otherwise unharmed. For a pre-cog, evasion was as powerful a weapon as a gun. Gripping her hand, he took her on the run through the ferns. He abandoned their plan to find Myles; his cousin was safer out of sight. The Prospect Point parking lot was a long way off, but if they could just reach it, perhaps they could summon a cab.

A blast of powerful water jet struck close to Gracie's running legs. Damn! His brother was already back in the hunt. Qing struck again and again, each water spike getting closer to Gracie. Her capture had been his duty before their fight, and now Qing had something to prove.

They were sitting ducks on the open trail. Jin pulled Gracie into the forest. Her vision warned them to roll to the right, but she'd waited a little too long. Suddenly, a water spike caught her on the side of the leg. It gashed the skin at the lower thigh. Blood rolled down her calf and into her hiking shoes. Qing wasn't playing around. He wanted Gracie lame in order to slow them down.

"We have to lose Qing." Jin pressed at the gash in her leg. "I think we're being driven."

"Driven? To where?"

"I don't know. Can you walk?"

They raced forward, heading blindly through the woods. Then their vantage point cleared abruptly, and their feet struck asphalt. Jin looked up and down the road. He saw no vehicles. A road this wide could only be Stanley Park Drive. A blast of water struck the pavement beside his foot. They bolted across the road and back into the safety of the trees. Running blind, they had no idea where they were going. In their flight from Qing, Gracie had lost the GPS with the trails outlined on it. They were lost and hurrying at full speed.

Jin pulled Gracie to a stop right before she ran over a cliff. They looked down several hundred feet to the ocean beneath them. "I think we know where they wanted us to run," he said. "We can't go forward and we can't go back."

"They're coming." Gracie turned to face the forest. "I can't see who it is!"

Bryn stepped out of the trees. His head was bleeding. He had a murderous look of hatred on his face. Their situation must be worse than Jin suspected. Bryn wasn't prone to showing emotions around the Descendants. He considered it a matter of honor.

Myles stepped out of the trees behind him, pressing the barrel of his gun in Bryn's back. It took Jin a long moment to register what exactly he was seeing. He couldn't believe it. Yet, there was Myles with a rifle aimed at Bryn. His cousin's face was a mask of triumph, shame and resentment. He shoved Bryn toward Gracie and Jin with a brutality Jin hadn't suspected he could possess.

"You can't choose your fucking treacherous family, can you?" Bryn came to stand beside Jin. "This explains how they always knew we were coming. Viper knew about the wire. Shit. She knew about everything."

"Myles? It was you?" Gracie shook her head. She was trembling in Jin's arms. "Why couldn't I See what you were planning?"

"Because you're just like everyone else. You all look down upon me." Myles gritted his teeth and spat. "I'm a Seelie Descendant. Oh I'm not powerful like Jin or you, but my powers do have their uses. Don't you remember the headaches you kept getting in Vegas? Didn't it occur to you that you only got them when I was around?" He huffed when he directed his words back at Jin. "And, Cousin, don't you remember Mummy's headaches? I can suppress mental powers. Not enough to disable them, but to hide myself."

Jin regarded the man he'd grown up with and thought to be one of the few people he could trust.

This betrayal shook the foundations of his world. "Why, Cousin? Why would you betray me and want me dead?"

"Why?" Myles seemed genuinely surprised by Jin's confusion. "You left me with all the responsibility of running the business. When things started falling apart, I tried to tell you, but you were too busy with your latest crusade. I had to turn to other sources to borrow money."

"I would have given you the money, Cousin. Why didn't you ask?"

"Maybe I was tired of you carrying me, Jin. You always had money, women... Why not me? It was my turn, Jin, my turn to be you. My human friends in South America were happy to lend me anything I needed in exchange for importing special cargo into the United States and Canada."

"Drugs, you mean," Bryn said. "Myles, you stupid bastard. Those guys are rough business partners."

"You have no idea." Myles' face went pale. "I skimmed a little from their earnings. They caught on and demanded payment in full on my debt. They told me since I had stolen from them they wouldn't honor our agreement. I had to do something drastic, so I took out a rather large life insurance policy on Jin."

"Then you decided to hurry my demise along by putting the death mark out on me." Jin stared into Myles' eyes and watched him squirm. "You went to the Clans for help in getting rid of me. But they think you're a Normal. They wouldn't have talked to you directly. You had a partner, Myles. Who is it?"

A living nightmare slithered out of the trees to coil beside Myles. Viper had been horribly burned. Her head was disfigured, stuck between her human form and a snake's hooded skull. Her grotesque features were nauseating. Crazed topaz eyes, hungry for revenge, focused on Gracie in Jin's arms.

"Well, well, isn't this romantic?" She moved closer to them. Gracie buried her face in Jin's shirt. "Do I horrify you, dear little Titania? That will never do."

Viper lifted the two revolvers she carried. "Don't worry, Titania, you won't have to look upon me for very much longer. I'm going to take you apart one piece at a time while your lover watches."

"Leave her alone, Viper." Jin pulled Gracie behind him. "It's me you want."

"I think it's time you learned that not everything is about you, Jin." Viper laughed and bounced the barrel of her gun against her disfigured cheek. "Druid concocted this elaborate plan to bring down the Wainwright Clan. He used little Titania to start a war. Myles helped by driving the car that almost ran down Raul. He made sure to let us know your every move. All of Druid's careful planning, and he winds up in the hospital looking like dog meat."

Viper grinned more widely. "Druid isn't here now, though. I'm in charge, and I say Titania must pay. She's the one who broke my fang. She's the one who pushed me into the fire and caused me to freeze in mid-transformation! It's time for her to suffer as I've suffered."

Jin raced through their options in his mind. He could jump and strike Viper to distract her while Bryn pulled Gracie to safety, but Myles was there with his rifle trained on them. Viper wouldn't go down easily, either. In her current form, she was very strong.

Jin looked at Myles. He could jump over to Myles, break his treacherous neck and shoot Viper in the back. No, Viper had two guns on Bryn and Gracie. She was quick and deadly. Her trigger fingers wouldn't hesitate. He had only one option left. Trickery.

"What's the plan when I'm dead? Myles collects the insurance money and you split the reward. Everyone else lives happily ever after?"

"Don't be absurd. The insurance policy wasn't real." Viper smiled her snake smile. "Why should I pay reward money for a death no longer necessary?"

"What?" Myles cried and came to stand beside her. "I need that money, Viper. We had a deal."

Viper turned her angry snake eyes on him, her guns still trained on her captives. "You're insignificant and weak. Be glad that I'm letting you leave with your life."

Myles swung the rifle at her head, but she dodged him. Without a second of hesitation, Viper gave Myles two rounds right in his gut. The young man sank to his knees. His ruddy face was full of shock as he stared down at his own essential fluids gushing through his hands. Myles fell forward, his blood soaking into the ground.

"Time for you to join him," Viper said, turning her guns on the others. Jin braced himself to make a move, any move.

Thick black fog rolled down the trail, covering ferns and trees in its filth. Jin recognized its sulfur stench even before the Hellfire rushed up from the ground like a geyser. The demon had found him again.

"What's happening?" Gracie cried.

Viper laughed through her distorted mouth. Her eyes glowed in the Hellfire as her remaining fang dripped with venom. "Dinner time!"

Chapter Thirty-Three

"I smell the blood of the innocent!"

Gracie's ears burned with each vile syllable. The voice, hellish and wrong, wasn't meant for the light of day. Black claws scratched at the edges of the midnight fog. Scraping and tearing earth and air, the creature pulled its tar body from the depths of the fiery pit. Its tattered, leathery wings spread wide to block the filtered rays of sun.

"I believe you've met the Shadow Demon, Jin. Oh dear. It looks hungry enough for two dishes." Viper kept her weapon fixed upon them.

Gracie stood paralyzed before the monster born from every televangelical fire-and-brimstone sermon. Demons were real. Did that mean angels were real too? Gawd, they could sure use one about now.

"Hold, Demon." Beings, male and female, began to take shape in the black fog. Gray skin stretched taut over sharp bony cheeks. Five pairs of white orbs with ash pupils regarded their group from under long wisps of snowy hair. Each wore armor of dull black that looked worn and well used. They were heavily armed.

"Who are they?" Gracie asked in a whisper.

"Dark elves from the Unseelie Court. I recognize two of them. The one in the cloak is a sorcerer. The ugly one to his right is the bastard who tried to kill my father."

"Where is Druid?" The Unseelie Sorcerer glared across the distance at them. "We have done as he asked. The dragon is weakened and the Clans are in chaos. Why is he not here to complete our contract?"

Viper lowered her weapon. Ignoring Gracie and Jin for the new visitors, she turned to meet them. They followed her serpentine glide as she approached. The demon ignored her, keeping its unshakable attention focused on Jin. It would be ready for them to attempt escape.

"Druid is simply out of the picture. I'm the one you'll have to deal with from now on. If you want to rule the Human Realm again, you'll give me control of the Clans. All of them, not just the Wainwrights."

"Your ambition is as ugly as your appearance." The sorcerer's gaunt face tightened as a vicious smile spread across his elvin face. Large eyes examined Viper's disfigured form. They stopped at her misshapen head. He said something low to his companions. The Unseelie laughed, showing their sharpened teeth. Gracie couldn't feel sorry for Viper. She'd earned every bit of torment they could give her.

But Viper had some tricks left up her sleeve. "You're so superior, aren't you? Druid wasn't a complete fool. He put a safeguard on the portal. I can slam its magic closed, throwing your little group out of MY realm. You're here by my leave." She spat at the sorcerer's feet. "I won't grant your armies permission to enter this world until you've killed Jin. He's right there. I've captured him for you. Perhaps your demon can finally do its job now."

"Your lack of respect is vexing, Usurper." The sorcerer stood away from the others, raising his arms skyward. "Very well. I will grant your request. The pariah's innocent blood must flow before our contract is fulfilled and the veil opened. One body more won't matter much."

The Unseelie sorcerer flicked a hand, freeing his pet demon to make the strike. The shadowy body pounced forward as if it had been restrained for centuries. Its claws stabbed at Viper's exposed throat. They ripped her apart with brutal attacks until her body was no longer recognizable. The clawed hand lifted her broken shape to its mouth, devouring her flesh in one gulp.

Jin disappeared in a short burst of air. In an instant Gracie caught sight of him again beside the sorcerer. He pulled a combat knife from one of the Unseelie belts and severed the dark elf's ear then tossed the piece of flesh to the ground beside the demon's clawed feet. It turned to sniff at the morsel before greedily snatching it up.

The featureless face lifted toward its old master, and a malicious laugh chilled Gracie's heart to the core. Then it struck. Struggle as he might, the sorcerer couldn't escape those massive claws as he was dragged down into the Hellfire. His companions held their weapons toward the pit, helpless to save him.

"The demon's gone. So is it over then?" Gracie asked Bryn.

"No, Seer," a dark elf said, lifting his eyes away from the pit. "The blood of this innocent will still open the veil. Our contract remains in play." Their new leader called to his soldiers. "Take them! Midsummer's Eve is upon us."

"Hold, trespassers!" Bryn commanded.

His appearance began to change as he stepped away from Gracie. The tall man with aging features vanished. Pale hair fell in straight locks about his shoulders to frame a perfect and ageless face. Robes of deep forest green swept about his ankles. Ornate silver bracelets circled his arms. A circlet of moonlight rested lightly upon pale-blond hair. He looked like an elf lord from a fairytale book. She'd never seen anything more beautiful.

"No innocent blood will be spilled this night." Bryn pulled a long sword covered with runes upon its blade.

"You are so very noble, Lord Brynmor! One might wonder why you are here as well? I suspect your kind regret giving this land up as much as we do."

Air puffed beside her. Jin had returned. "The last thing we want is to be in the middle of a Sidhe battle. I got lucky with the sorcerer. These dark elves are battle hardened and ready."

"We can't leave Bryn to face them on his own."

Gawd, she wished she'd been born with a combat power like the others. She was helpless, standing there watching Bryn hold his ground as the dark elves came toward him. Their weapons were ready to taste blood.

"The humans will fall as our armies overrun them this night. We will revel in their blood as we take their cities."

"We can't let them get through, Jin! What about all those innocent people? They don't stand a chance against creatures like this."

"The sorcerer and his friends used a temporary portal with Druid's help. They can't stay long. In order to march their armies through the veil, they must use magic fueled by sacrificial blood. I've no intention of giving it to them to start a war," Jin told her.

Something brushed lightly on Gracie's cheek. A tiny figure about the size of a child's doll floated in the air at her shoulder—a woman, iridescent one moment and completely white the next.

"Fog fairy." Jin's eyes followed the little being as she fluttered around them. "She seems to like you. She recognizes her own."

"What do you mean?" Gracie extended her hand and the fairy rested on it.

"Fog fairies bring images of the past and the future to those they choose to help. They also open portals to Otherworld if asked by a member of the Seelie Court. Bryn is taking us to Otherworld."

A blanket of cool mist spread through the trees, coming to engulf them. Tingles covered Gracie's skin as her human glamour fell away. The neatly trimmed trails of Stanley Park were erased as nature took control again. Ancient trees circled about them. Rock rose up from the forest floor, towering into a mountain's rocky foothill.

Beings of light and forest stepped out of the trees. More Seelie elves like Bryn had come to join the fight. They were armed with swords and bows. One elf stood away from the others. Her hair hung down in blond white ribbons to the hip. A band of gold rested upon her head, precious stones hanging down from the crown. Robes of pure white shone from beneath a robe of gold, and runes sparkled like stars from her garments. In her hand swirled a brilliant spark of life. Magic.

"Now we're talking!" Gracie did a quick fist pump in support. There was just one problem. She and Jin were standing right in the middle of the battlefield. Light and Dark. Good and Evil. The intensity upon the combatants' faces spoke of an ancient feud. They would go after each other hot and heavy whether she and Jin were in the way or not.

Someone struck first from out of the mists and hit one of the dark elves. He didn't fall down; in fact, the blast didn't seem to affect him at all. The dark elf grinned hungrily. Then the peaceful foothills of Otherworld exploded in a volley of blasts and arrows.

Jin, now in his elfin form, threw Gracie over his shoulder and raced through the battling Sidhe. All she could see from her current vantage point was twisting backs and kicking legs. Jin stopped behind a rock outcrop and put her down. The sounds of battle echoed off the stone in deafening thunder. They were cornered with impenetrable wall behind them and battling Sidhe in front.

A body dropped behind them then. Gracie jumped with a squeal. Standing over the dead dark elf was a hovering nightmare in a wide-brim hat. His body seemed to float above the ground, suspended in the shroud he wore. His deadly gaze met hers for a moment and then he turned to Jin.

"Watch your back, kid," the deep voice warned Jin.

A short, hairy troll-like creature appeared from behind him. His smile widened across large teeth. "Hi, Gracie. Boy, she sure turned out pretty, didn't she, Frank?"

"Ape?" Gracie pushed around Jin. She looked at the shrouded messenger of death floating before her. "Dad?"

"Hello, Punkin."

There came a point at which a girl simply could be pushed too far. Gracie had reached that mile marker in her last session with Druid. Either she could accept the fact her dad was a nightmarish killer or she could lose it and spend the rest of her life in a padded cell sucking tapioca pudding through a straw. Option one had Jin in it and a dad who would cut through concrete to save his daughter.

The nightmare took a deep drag on his cigar and then rolled it in his fingers. "I guess you have a million questions," he said meekly.

"Yeah, I thought you were captured or dead or...or human." She gripped his big hand with her much smaller one. "Gawd, I'm glad to see you alive. I just don't know where to start. I guess you should tell me about you and Mom."

Jin cleared his throat. "I'll see if I can find an opening." He gave a nod to her dad. "Be ready when I return."

"I'll, uh, go stand guard." Ape hurried away.

"Your friend is a little reckless," Dad said with a grunt.

"Just like someone else I know."

"Before I met your mother, I was a whole lot worse." He swallowed hard and crumpled the cigar absently in his hand. She'd never seen her dad nervous before. Bracing herself for the truth, she gave him an encouraging smile.

"I was the type of Seelie Descendant the Clans would hire to fix problems. Hell, I guess I shouldn't try to sugarcoat it. I was an assassin. I'd been hired by someone from a rival Clan to kill your mother. It seems this other Clan had grown jealous that the Wainwrights had more than one pre-cog."

Her dad chuckled and shook his head. "She was waiting for me when I broke into her apartment. Jessica had my favorite dinner ready with a bottle of wine. She even had candles. One look at that sweet face, and I was hers. I became Jessica's handler, her protector."

He lifted Gracie's right wrist and looked at the tattoo there. "You are every bit as beautiful as your mother, maybe even prettier because you've got some of me in you." He smiled sadly. "Your mother was the sweetest, smartest and kindest person I'd ever met. Lord Wainwright, Eleanor's father, didn't approve of us being together. Jessica stood against the Wainwright Clan, refusing to end our relationship. It wasn't until we faked our deaths that we were finally free."

"I wish I could remember her." Gracie steadied herself. "Dad, what happened to Mom?"

"They killed her, Punkin." The hardness to his face told Gracie her father still hadn't gotten over the hurt. "She chose to give her own life to save you and me. Your mom put that mental block on your mind to keep you hidden. I promised her to keep you safe and out of the Clan life, no matter the cost."

"So you took me to San Diego?"

"I thought it would be a good place to raise a kid. Eventually I married Brenda, and we took her last name, Berry, so you'd have a mother. I never loved Brenda, and she knew it. There was nobody but Jessica for me." Dad turned to her and put his large hand over hers. "You understand why I didn't tell you about who we really were, don't you?"

Gracie's eyes filled with tears. "I should be furious with you for lying to me, but I can't be, Dad. I've seen firsthand the cruelty of the Clans. It was really brave of you to give up what you were, stop killing for money and turn into a model citizen. I'm proud of you, Dad."

"Well, that's not exactly true."

"Gawd, Dad, there's more?" Gracie folded her arms.

"Did you really think the business was so popular on its own, Punkin?" Her dad shook his head. "I took the occasional job and my clients paid me by buying office supplies."

A sharp gust of wind blew down from the rock. Panting hard, Jin landed beside her dad. His shirt had a few new gashes in it. He'd seen trouble, attested to by all the nasty scratches on his face.

"I hate to break this up, but it's time we thought about getting out of here."

"The kid's right," Ape called, rushing down from the rock face. "Look!"

Gracie understood now why everyone called her dad's friend "Ape." He swung up to the top of the rock formation. They climbed up to joined him. Dark elves were streaming out of holes opening up from the ground. The battle had heated up, and it was getting closer. Their small group was about to be overrun.

Chapter Thirty-Four

A sea of dark elves surged toward the Seelie defenders. Bryn stood at their center, knee deep in blood and gore. He was an unstoppable warrior, leading his men to mow through the oncoming horde. Jin slammed a fist down on the rock when he saw his friend stumble, but Bryn righted his stance and swung his blade upward to decapitate an unlucky dark elf. Bryn was a damn good warrior, but his energy wasn't infinite. He'd tire soon against such odds.

Jin could think of only one way to save Bryn and get Gracie back where she belonged. He'd give the dark elves something else to concentrate on. He'd give them the key to the veil.

He slid off the outcrop back into the safety of its rock body. Holding out his arms, he helped Gracie down. Frank and Ape jumped down to join them. Their faces displayed the same somber conclusion he had accepted. The Sidhe battle would soon overtake them.

"Get Gracie out of here, Frank."

"What are you saying?" Gracie grabbed his arm, pulling him around. "You can't stand against them alone."

"I can hold them off until you escape." He gently pried her hand away and headed around the outcrop.

Gracie sprinted in front of him, blocking his path. "Don't be stupid! After everything we've been through, you think I'd leave you behind? We're staying together."

Jin tried to push her away, but she held firm. "You'll only be in my way. I'm better off handling this alone," he growled.

"Right. Before we met you managed to get yourself kicked out of the Clans and accused of murder." Gracie hugged him and put a hand on his cheek. "You need me to keep you alive."

Gracie kissed him long and hard. When her lips left his, Jin hugged her close. Then he pinched a nerve on her neck and she collapsed against him, unconscious. He swept her up and held out her limp body to her father.

"Damn it, Frank. You need to take her away from here!"

"You'd give your life up for her?" Frank ran his finger across her cheek. "It looks like she doesn't want to go."

"Take her." Jin pushed Gracie's body into Frank's chest again, but Frank wasn't making a move to catch her. Moist eyes closed as Frank leaned down to kiss her forehead.

Frank stood away from Jin. "Gracie's every bit as stubborn as her mother. It's time for you to leave now, kid. She needs you."

Jin was stunned. "What about you?"

"You aren't a killer. I am. Now go before I beat your ass." Frank's brim grew wider, and the power in his eyes burned from beneath its shadow. "Don't let me down, kid."

Frank stormed out of their hiding place like a silent fog of death. He struck the dark elves at the rim of the battle. His shadowy body swirled around his unsuspecting enemy as he cleared a path for his daughter and the man she loved. Ape pushed Jin forward with a grunt. That was the last bit of encouragement he needed. He put Gracie over his shoulder and ran. Moving at his top speed, he headed recklessly through the trees.

"Stop, Pariah!" A dark elf came at him, swinging an axe at Jin's head. The elf's teeth, ragged and sharp, snapped inches away from the flesh on his arm. Then the elf's head fell away in pieces, cauterized by an unholy circle. Frank. He was Hell's own killing storm. Jin pushed his body faster. He wasn't about to be the man who disappointed Frank the Zed.

Trees and shrub whipped by as he ran. The sounds of battle grew distant, but would he be far enough away? He was running blind again, this time in a forbidden part of Otherworld. Bryn had brought them here; he must have planned an exit for them as well.

"You did it again!" Gracie slapped at his back. He lowered her to her feet, waiting as she rubbed her sore neck.

"Where are Dad and Ape?"

"They stayed behind to cover our escape."

"We have to go back!"

"No, darling. We need to find our way to the Human Realm." He took her hand and forced a lie he hoped he wouldn't regret. "Your father is one of the most powerful Descendants I've ever seen. He'll come out of this alive, I promise. Come on, we have to keep going."

The treetops above them burst into flame. Screams and angry shouts penetrated the forest. Shockwaves from expelled killing magic knocked them to the ground. The battle was close, but it wasn't the same battle they'd just left. The sounds of clashing swords and axes striking armor were absent this time.

"This sounds like a Clan war." Jin pulled Gracie to her feet. "We have to run hard. If they catch us..."

"I know. You don't have to say it."

Jin rubbed at his stinging eyes. Smoke and sulfur swirled around the tree trunks making seeing a clear direction impossible. He held Gracie's hand tightly, guiding her away from the sounds of battle. They had to get out of this forest while the Sidhe and the Descendants were focused on their fighting.

Pulsing magic from the misty borders of Otherworld summoned just ahead. They'd be back in the Human Realm soon, but where would the unpredictable borders take them? Stanley Park was over a thousand acres of thick forest surrounded by water. They were running blind.

"Jin, we have to turn back." Gracie pulled at his hand. "We're not leaving our friends here."

"I'm afraid you're wrong, Miss Berry."

Eleanor stepped out of the mist like a shade. A nasty-looking gash bloodied her torn pant leg while soot and earth dirtied her cheeks. But she was still the cold statue Jin had grown to resent. He twisted to a standing position, giving full attention to the predator who gave birth to him.

"Let us pass, Mother." He moved a little to block Gracie from her view. "I won't let you ruin Gracie's life."

"As I ruined yours?" Eleanor's smile was a bitter one. "Don't forget I gave you life, and it's within my right to take it again. You were just a political experiment designed by my father. Oh, I argued against keeping you. I'd already given him a grandchild and heir. He wouldn't listen, wouldn't allow me to rid my body of the thing growing inside of it. My father wanted a lever to control the great Zhao Long. He caged me like an animal until I gave birth to you."

Her words lashed out at him, causing old wounds to open and new ones to bleed. He'd gone through life fabricating lies about her coldness toward him. He was the unruly one, testing her limited patience. His mother was a Clan leader, after all. She was too busy to deal with a troubled son. He'd never imagined she'd been forced to carry him by a ruthless father.

"What kind of a mother would say something so awful to her son?" Gracie circled her hands around his arm, giving him some of her warmth.

"A truthful one, Miss Berry."

A great shadow descended into the trees, engulfing the light in its dark folds. Hot wind blasted the ground, stripping away branches and bark. Jin fell to the forest floor. He covered his face against debris wrought by the fierce hurricane.

Boom! Boom! Boom! Tree trunks fell about them with each mighty flap of wings. Shivering like a child, Jin grasped hard at needles and dirt until they ground under his fingernails. The forest groaned as great claws dug into the earth about them. Stone became rubble and wood burst into tinder under the tremendous weight. Then the forest shook when Zhao released a mighty growl. Zhao Long had revealed his true form to the world on only a handful of occasions. Legend spoke of those who'd witnessed the rarity as having gone mad with terror.

Gracie screamed. Jin twisted away from the dragon and crawled to her. He threw his arms about her quivering body. In a gesture fraught with madness, he looked over his shoulder at Zhao Long. His father's form began to change. The hard, black scales fell away. An enormous snout, covered in blood and gore, dwindled. Then the mighty dragon was gone. A middle-aged Asian man stood in the deep depression of the dragon's claw print. Hard eyes took their group in with a calculating glance. Jin shrank away from his father's gaze. How could he or anyone else believe Zhao Long would be taken out with a single strike?

But one among them seemed unaffected by the great dragon's power. Eleanor Wainwright let her glamour fall away. Torn clothes covering her legs and torso fluttered off in bits of tattered fabric. Her aging skin tightened into frigid white stone. The green eyes—matching Jin's own—rolled back into her head. Snowy marble orbs moved in unnatural jerking movements to finally rest upon Zhao.

She was an Athena. An enormous marble statue, cold and dispassionate. When she spoke, her voice vibrated across the ages. "Stand out of my way, Zhao. Miss Berry has been accepted as part of the Wainwright Clan. She will accompany me to London."

Jin's parents stared at each other across the ruined trail, the great dragon and the marble statue locked in a battle of wills. No Clan Council would keep the peace between his parents this time. Bitter resentment had fermented for years between them. The two titans and their quarry stood in the middle of nowhere with only Jin to keep the peace. His throat tightened as he tried to swallow. This was a task he'd never been able to manage.

Zhao lifted a single eyebrow toward the heavens. "You're always demanding something, Ellie."

"Perhaps your men should have listened to my demands before they attacked my Clan in Wainwright territory! You've risked open war trying to take my pre-cog."

"For the hundredth time, I refuse your offer, Eleanor. That means you have no claim on me. Right?" Gracie directed her question at Zhao.

Hope with a generous serving of indignation had been dished out to his father. Jin winced. She was betting her salvation on the mercy of unswayable justice. Zhao had seen too many lifetimes to waste concern on a creature whose life light would burn out far quicker than his own. Just as he hadn't wasted effort on a replaceable son.

"You have the freedom to choose which Clan you will make a gift of your power and your loyalty. Until you make that commitment, I cannot guarantee your safety."

His stern gaze shifted to Jin for a fleeting moment and then returned to regard Gracie. He was trying to pressure her into making a snap decision. Manipulative bastard! Zhao relied on intimidation to bully the Clans and his children into obeying his iron will. Jin had acquiesced many times before. Things were different now. He was a pariah with nothing to lose.

"And if she doesn't want to be part of a Clan? What then, Father?" he demanded.

His father turned hard eyes toward them. "I should think that was obvious. The balance must be maintained, Jin. She will be put down."

"Put down?" Gracie pushed to her feet. "I won't be put down like an animal!"

Jin kept his gaze focused on Zhao. Beneath the serene face and his human glamour waited the crafty old dragon. His father would kill Gracie. Jin had no doubt. As champion for balance of power among the Clans, Zhao had dispensed his version of justice many times, never showing any visible remorse. His father wasn't waiting for Gracie's decision. His sire was waiting to see what he, Jin, would do.

More games and intrigue. Jin couldn't remember a time his parents hadn't used him as a pawn in their power struggle. God, he was so tired of it. He'd made the decision to walk away from their world a year ago. Now he understood his father had considered the rebellion a childish tantrum. At this moment, both parents were watching him. His mother's folded arms and the impatient tilt of her head broadcasted that she, too, thought Jin would one day return to his senses. She was wrong. He was about to do the unthinkable.

"That's not going to happen." His voice was an explosion crashing through the strained silence. "I won't let it happen."

He threw off his elvin form and brought the full power of an air elemental about himself. A sudden gust of wind lifted Gracie off the forest floor. She screamed as Jin sent her flying back a few hundred feet. He ignored her shouting. Every ounce of focus and will he had must be reserved for Zhao. Challenging his father was suicide. The odds were against him, but sometimes miracles happened.

"You go against my word again?" A deafening roar shook the trees about them. Dust flew up in great plumes of brown, blasted by unseen wings. Fire flickered out of Zhao's nostrils, making his eyes glow in the flames.

"My patience with you has been exhausted, boy. You think you're in love with this girl now. Is that it? Don't be foolish. That affection will fade in time."

"You would know." His mother's spite turned on Zhao Long. "Between wives, Long? Tell me. Did you grow tired of the last one and roast her as you did the others? Or did she grow weary of you? Such a foolish old lizard."

"Enough of this! I'm so tired of your squabbles and intrigue. Our lives are at stake and all you can do is..." Jin shook his head. Trying to explain was a waste of valuable time. "Why can't you just leave me in peace?"

Eleanor lifted her chin to regard him as if she'd never seen him before. "Very well, my son. Your parents and the Clans will leave you alone in peace. I think your father and I can provide you with a modest fund to start you on your way. The charges against you have been dropped, and the death mark has failed. You may roam the Human Realm alone, unobstructed, if that is your heart's desire."

She was offering him the ultimate prize. His freedom. He could have his life back. The tension and frustration began to melt away. He'd be free of them at last. He would under no more death threats and wouldn't have to run. He could be happy for the first time since, well, ever.

"Wait. You said I could roam alone."

"The price of your freedom is Miss Berry. Hand her over to us, and you get what you want."

She'd almost convinced him no strings were attached to their offer. Eleanor Wainwright was a formidable politician who brokered multimillion-dollar deals and crushed governments. Gracie wasn't a person to her, simply an asset. If Jin took the offer and walked away, Gracie would lose the humanity she held so dear. He couldn't let that happen.

"No deal. Gracie doesn't want any part of your Clans either. I won't stand by and let her be taken against her will." He stared at the two political animals who were his parents. "You both claim to be dedicated to protecting your families. Well, you've seen what dangers are waiting to take advantage of this petty feud you've fostered for so long. We won't be a party to it."

"Stop playing the fool." Eleanor raised her hand. Three of her guard stepped out of the mist. "Go get the girl away from him."

She turned to Zhao. "I'm sure given the circumstances, Miss Berry will change her mind. Druid has grown a bit unruly lately. I need a new pre-cog. You may kill him if you wish."

"That's going to come as a big surprise to Druid," Jin muttered.

"I will give you this last chance, my son." Zhao's throat rumbled with a disappointed sigh. "Very well. You've chosen your path against me. I won't stop them to save you. Should they fail, I'll end your short life myself."

Jin took a battle-ready stance to face their attackers. Avoiding his father's eyes, Jin focused his attention on the three most dominant of Eleanor's security team. They came at Jin with powers on full. He was outnumbered and they all knew it.

Chapter Thirty-Five

Telekinetic energy surged toward Jin like an invisible tsunami. It brought debris and stone on its crest, knocking him backward. His elemental body cushioned the fall and lifted him up above the cloud of dust. A frosty wind shoved at him from behind, sending Jin to the ground head over heels. He rolled to his feet in solid form once again.

His mother's personal guard marched toward him, focusing on keeping Jin in place with their power. Their leader, a pretty mixture of elf and hearth fairy, thrust her hand toward him and twisted it sharply. She made a tight fist and yanked it back. Something inside Jin's body collapsed. He sunk to his knee, spitting up blood.

"Give us the pre-cog, Pariah. You aren't strong enough to stand against all of us."

Harsh white eyes were on him as he staggered back to a standing position. Swaying with the pain, he concentrated on her throat. His attack came with the piercing intensity of a fine jet of air. It struck her in the trachea, puncturing the cartilage. Blood seeped between her fingers as she desperately grabbed at her neck.

The two men following her into battle didn't waste effort on their fallen leader. They came at Jin from both sides. Their telekinetic power lifted him off his feet and hurled him against a tree trunk. He plummeted to the ground and landed hard.

"Jin!" Gracie knelt beside him.

"Help me up," he told her. She shook her head. "I won't let them take you. Please help me up."

Gracie supported him as he got to his feet. His body wavered between air and elf. They were coming with their full power, eager to let loose. Gracie bent down and lifted a fist-sized rock. She hurled it at the Clansman on the right. He caught the rock with his mental powers and gave her a snort. Then he positioned the rock, ready to throw it back at her.

"You don't want to do that, asshole!"

An orange ring of light sliced through the two remaining Wainwright Clansmen. They fell in gory pieces on the dirt. The massive black shadow that was Frank the Zed descended upon the scene. Zhao Long and Eleanor dove to the ground and rolled away from his impossibly fast strikes.

"Frank?" Zhao Long stopped in a crouch beside Jin's mother. The shock on his face was a rarity. There wasn't much on earth that could elicit emotion from Jin's unflappable father. Jin completely understood his reaction. Looking into Frank's angry face was like looking at death itself.

"Keep your punk ass in the dirt, Zhao. Don't forget our last tangle. I've only grown stronger with age." Frank stabbed a finger at Eleanor. "Don't do it, Ellie or I'll give you a scar to match your other ass cheek."

"It seems you've come back from the dead, Frank." Eleanor clutched at her throat. Jin had never before seen his mother terrified. The day was starting to look up. "Why now?"

Frank stuck his trademark cigar in his lips and puffed. "You're fucking around with my kin. I'm the only one here with the right to say what happens to Gracie." He leaned in close to Jin's startled parents. "By right of blood."

"Blood?" Eleanor looked over at Gracie. The marble face withdrew and her human glamour was back. "She's Jessica's daughter."

"What's she talking about? How do you know my mother?" Gracie left Jin's side and took her father's offered hand. Daughter stood close to father as they stared down at the others.

"They were friends, Punkin, best friends. Your mom trusted Eleanor with all her secrets, but Ellie here couldn't stand Jessica's happiness." The power behind Frank's eyes flared as he looked at Eleanor. "You betrayed us. You betrayed her to your father. Now she's dead."

Bitter tears escaped Jin's mother's eyes. She shook with sobs. "I was in love with Jessica. You took her from me! You're the one responsible for her death."

"Jessica loved you too, but as a sister. You could never have had the type of relationship with her that you wanted, Ellie. Jessica made her choice and it wasn't you." Frank smiled at Gracie. "She chose us."

"You're wrong! She was driven away by Jin." His mother thrust a finger at him. The hatred and bitterness on her face brought back to his memory all those years of her cold disdain. "She made it quite clear she didn't want me the day Jin was born. I begged her to stay with me, so we could raise him together. She refused. And when I tried to drown him in the bath, she stole him from me and gave my son to Zhao."

"Be silent, Ellie. You agreed to play your father's whore the night we made Jin." Zhao Long stood and brushed the dirt off his pants. He offered her no help as she struggled to her feet. "I was only too happy to help Jessica escape from a murderous shrew like you."

"All these years, you held me responsible for your unrequited love, Mother?" Jin shuffled forward to join Gracie and Frank. Her own ambition had led her first to Druid and then to his father's bed. She'd given everything to be Clan leader by her own design, yet she couldn't see she was her own worse nightmare.

"I can't forgive you for all the hell you've put me through over the years, but I can feel pity for you. Living away from the person you love is a special kind of hell. I know," he told her.

"You pity me?"

Her tears of grief stopped abruptly. Eleanor Wainwright lifted her chin and squared her shoulders. His mother regained her regal air of cold indifference. She was the Athena again, goddess of the Wainwright Clan.

"Blood or not, you have no right to claim anyone, Frank. You aren't a Clan leader or even part of a Clan," Eleanor said.

Frank whistled. Several Seelie Descendants materialized out of the forest. Jin recognized them. They were all from either the Vento or the Girard

Clans. Twenty strong, they made a half circle behind Frank. One of them had Qing's unconscious body over his shoulder. Frank nodded and the Vento Clansman dropped Qing at his father's feet.

"You've got to learn to watch your back, kid. Consider yourself lucky my boys were there to take this slippery character out for you."

"Your boys? I dare say the heir to the Vento Clan won't like hearing that," Eleanor huffed.

"I am the heir of the Vento Clan by the laws of combat. I killed Raul and sent his severed fingers to Vento Clan headquarters as proof." Frank grinned viciously when her face paled. "The Girard Clan volunteered to be absorbed under my leadership."

"You can't do that! Not without support from another Clan!" Eleanor paced forward to face him.

"I can and I have," Frank told her, leaning dangerously close. "Are you sure you want to push the issue after what the Wainwright Clan did to my wife?"

Jin stared at the tense group, waiting to see what his mother would do. They'd stumbled across an old secret and she'd exposed her vulnerable side. He was certain she already regretted it. His mother stood up taller and struggled to compose herself. Yet he heard the slightest sliver of emotion in her voice when she spoke. "I am not my father."

"She's as sour as her old man," Ape said. He swung down from the treetops to join them on the forest floor. Ape had a bandage around his arm, but otherwise looked unharmed. "Maybe you're right about Canada. It would be better to take Gracie to Columbia."

"What's he talking about, Dad?"

The moment had come. Jin regarded father and daughter. They fit together, their relationship formed from many years of bonding and affection. Frank had kept her safe since birth. The battle with his mother's personal guard had proven to Jin he would be a poor substitute for Frank the Zed. It was time to let Gracie go.

"The kid and I made a deal. I wouldn't kill him and he would let me take you back into hiding. Geezus, look how miserable he is." Her dad sighed and pulled Gracie in for a hug. "I tried to protect you and hoped you'd do better than your mother. She fell in love with a punk criminal too."

"Who turned out to be a good man and a great father." Gracie hugged him tight. "You like Jin, Dad, I can tell. He is a good man. I've Seen it."

"Wait just a moment, Frank." His mother waved an impatient hand at Gracie. "Titania may be your daughter, but she's of value to all the Clans."

"So am I, remember? You just can't keep your nose out of my business, can you, Ellie?" Frank raised a glowing finger again. "Druid hurt my Gracie. I'm within my right as a Clan leader and father to take it out of your ass." He paused, watching Eleanor struggle with her rage. "But I'll accept the punishment Gracie's handler gave to Druid."

"Handler? You mean Jin?" Zhao Long came between them quickly. "Frank, I've known you for many years. We were friends once. I must tell you that I don't have much faith in Jin's ability to keep Titania safe."

"Ouch," Gracie murmured. "Are your parents always so..."

"Supportive? Yes," he said with a bitter smile.

"I can choose my daughter's handler just fine on my own. Thanks for your input." Frank gave Jin a quick look and nodded. "Neither of you give Jin enough credit. I wouldn't have chosen him if I didn't think he could do the job."

"And what if he grows bored with Gracie and leaves?" Eleanor folded her arms stubbornly. "Both of you must use your heads. What if one of our enemies outside the Clans get to her? She needs protection."

"That's Jin's job. He's her handler until I say different. Understood?" Frank told them. "Now is not the time to discuss this. We have a pile of dead bodies to take care of before the mist clears."

"Wait, Frank. What about Bryn and the Sidhe battle?" Jin wrapped an arm around Gracie's shoulder when she came to put comforting arms about him.

"Let the Sidhe worry about their own backyard. Ape and I stayed long enough to see you escape and then we got the hell out of there."

Frank shook his head and slapped a hand on Jin's back. Considering the shape Jin was in after his battle with the Wainwrights, the tap almost knocked him to the ground.

"Don't worry about Bryn, kid. He was in the thick of things enjoying the hell out of himself. Another troop of Seelie came to join the fray after you left. Both sides aren't happy unless they get to fight each other at least once every century."

News of Bryn was a welcome relief. He'd stood in the breach to protect Jin, Gracie and the Human Realm. Bryn deserved every honor the Seelie Court would certainly bestow upon him. Then he needed to get his arse back home.

Jin and Gracie headed toward a fallen log away from their parents. His entire body ached. He needed to sit down. As far as he was concerned, this was his mother's territory and she could clean it up. The lack of support from his parents was nothing new, but Frank's belief in him was something he was proud of. He'd earned a trust not easily given. Frank was willing to surrender his precious daughter's life to the man who loved her.

"So, what do you think about your new job?"

"Handler?" He smiled back and held her close. "I think I'll like the position. Are there any perks?"

Gracie kissed him. "I'll show you later."

Several minutes went by, and their parents were still in deep conversation. Frank murmured something low and approached them. He waved a hand to one of his men. The Clansmen hurried over, gingerly carrying a hat box. He held it out at arm's length for Frank.

"What's in the box, Dad?"

"It's a gift for a friend in the hospital."

"That's sweet," she said and hugged him.

"The mists are rolling back. I can see the Human Realm and Stanley Park. Do you kids want a ride into town? Ape will take you."

"Thanks, Dad." Gracie kissed his cheek and started to follow Ape toward the edge of the mists.

Frank tapped Jin on the arm and lifted the lid when Gracie's back was turned to them. Dead eyes stared up, stuck in a permanent look of terror. Glen wouldn't be anyone's enthrall ever again. Frank snapped the lid closed. He pointed his deadly finger at Jin.

"See you at Christmas, kid."

Epilogue

The elevator doors opened onto a very clean and soothing hospital wing. Gracie saw the Descendant guards lining the hall and knew she was in the right spot. She lifted her chin and walked past the guards as though she owned the place. She expected someone to try and stop her, but they nodded their head and let her pass. Gracie had been ready to cause a scene if they didn't let her inside. She'd never get this chance again. Jin had gone with Bryn to run an errand in the city for a few hours. He'd flip if he knew she went to speak with Druid by herself.

Gracie took a deep breath before entering his room. She didn't like hospitals anyway, but the patient in this room made the place ten times creepier.

He was waiting for her. One eye was swollen shut, but the other blue eye took her in with a glance. Both arms and one of Druid's legs were in casts. His skin was badly bruised. Gracie felt no pity for him.

"You're late, Titania." His cracked lip grinned.

"I stopped for cupcakes. Don't show off."

Gracie sat down in the chair beside his bed. Bryn had come back to the Human Realm after being decorated as a hero and patriot by his queen. He was a bit beaten up, but would recover. Bryn had convinced her he deserved cupcakes, his favorite, to recover faster.

The two Descendant guards left the room. Druid must have left orders for her arrival. He'd prepared for his vision of her visit, but their interaction was going to be led by her this time.

"You're not worried that I might pull the plug or something?" Gracie leaned back and watched his face. The expression was a little less arrogant, but he still had that superior attitude about him. "I don't have much time, so let me get straight to the point. I had a vision with two different possible futures."

She saw a hungry twinkle in his eye. "It appears that my training helped you after all, my dear. You've unlocked another level of your power and discovered the real reason pre-cogs are so sought after." Druid groaned a little as he tried to sit up. Gracie didn't make a move to help him. If that meant she was holding a grudge, so be it.

"If a pre-cog feels an intense emotion for someone, love or hate, then when she sees two possible futures, she can choose which future they will have." He narrowed his eye to look at her more closely.

"You can control a person's future. You decide whether he has a good day or goes to his death. You seem to have inherited your mother's power. She saw two futures as well when the Wainwright Clan was chasing your parents. In one, her lover would die, and Jessica and you would be taken. In the second, Jessica would die, and you and your father would escape. She chose to give her own life to save you."

"Can you do it?" she asked the little man. Druid was a nasty teacher. He would be an even nastier enemy.

"No, the bonus gift that came with my pre-cog abilities was the ability to create illusions." He let a smile drift across his face again. "Of the two of us, you just became the more dangerous."

Gracie stood up and gripped her purse. "You remember that, Druid, the next time you think you can come after me. I have intense feelings of hatred for you."

"How like your unholy father you are." Druid turned his head, directing her attention to the hat box. She could only imagine what Dad had given him. He'd said he trusted Jin's punishment, but Dad was never one to let a slight go.

"I may be a pre-cog like my mother, Druid, but I'm my father's daughter, too. Don't ever think I won't do what I must to protect my future."

She left him to rot in his hospital bed. He was her past. The future was waiting for her at their new flat in Coal Harbour. The vision of flowers, wine and a fabulous dinner drifted across her third eye. Jin had gone all out for her. She smiled. Tonight was the beginning of their wonderful life together. Another vision tickled at the back of her neck. She silenced it. The rest of the future could wait until tomorrow.

THE END

Other Books
By This Author

The Mutant Casebook Series

Phantom Harvest (Book One)

Short Fiction

Lost Man's Parish

For more information about C. R. Richards, visit her website